MEGA PRINCESS™

kaboom!™

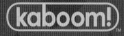

MEGA PRINCESS, August 2017. Published by KaBOOM!, a division of Boom Entertainment, Inc. Mega Princess is ™ & © 2017 Kelly Thompson, Adam Greene & Brianne Drouhard. Originally published in single magazine form as MEGA PRINCESS No. 1-5. All rights reserved. KaBOOM!™ and the KaBOOM! logo are trademarks of Boom Entertainment, Inc., registered in various countries and categories. All characters, events, and institutions depicted herein are fictional. Any similarity between any of the names, characters, persons, events, and/or institutions in this publication to actual names, characters, and persons, whether living or dead, events, and/or institutions is unintended and purely coincidental. KaBOOM! does not read or accept unsolicited submissions of ideas, stories, or artwork.

BOOM! Studios, 5670 Wilshire Boulevard, Suite 450, Los Angeles, CA 90036-5679.

Printed in China. First Printing.

ISBN: 978-1-68415-007-6, eISBN: 978-1-61398-678-3

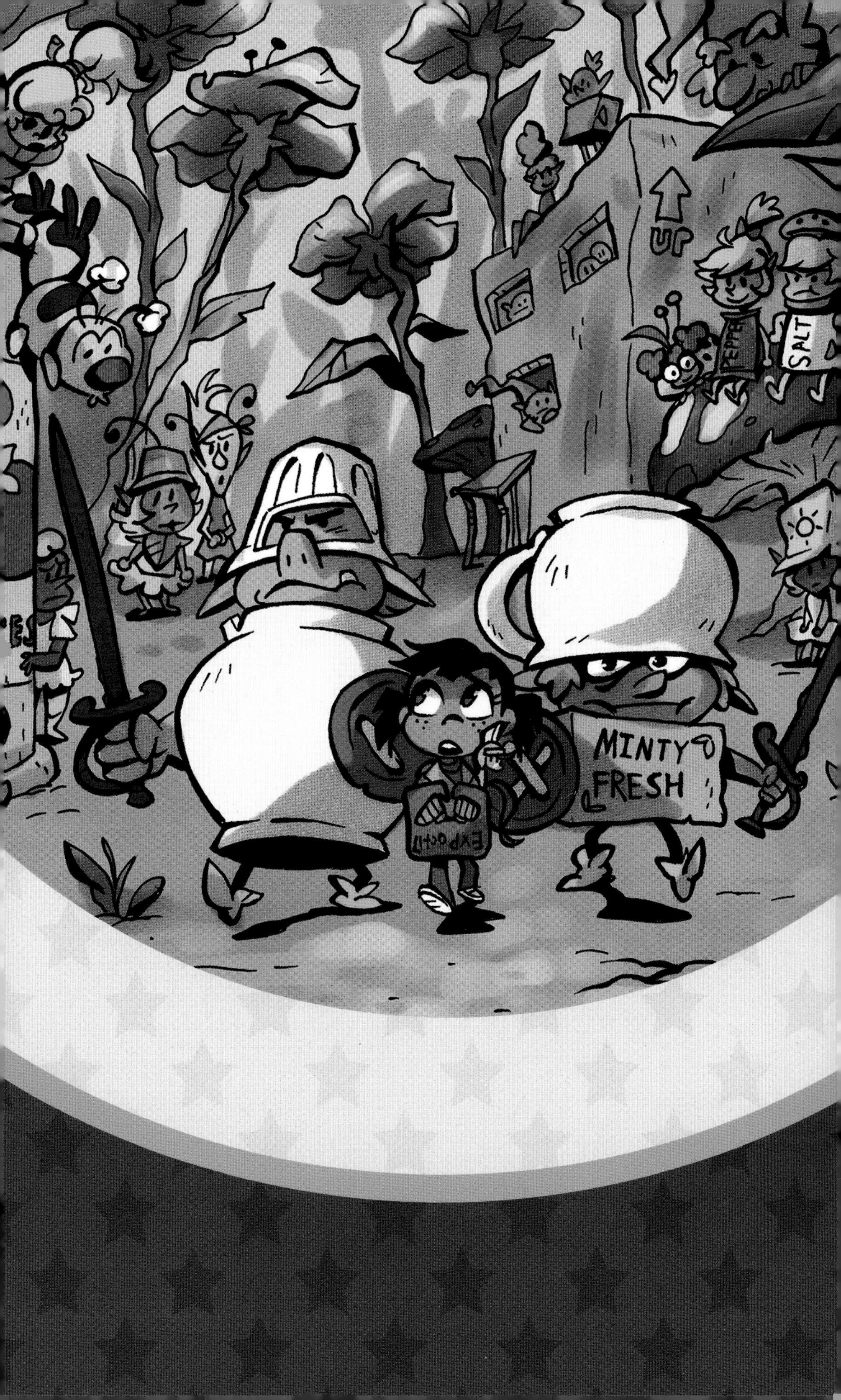
UP
PEPPER
SALT
MINTY
FRESH

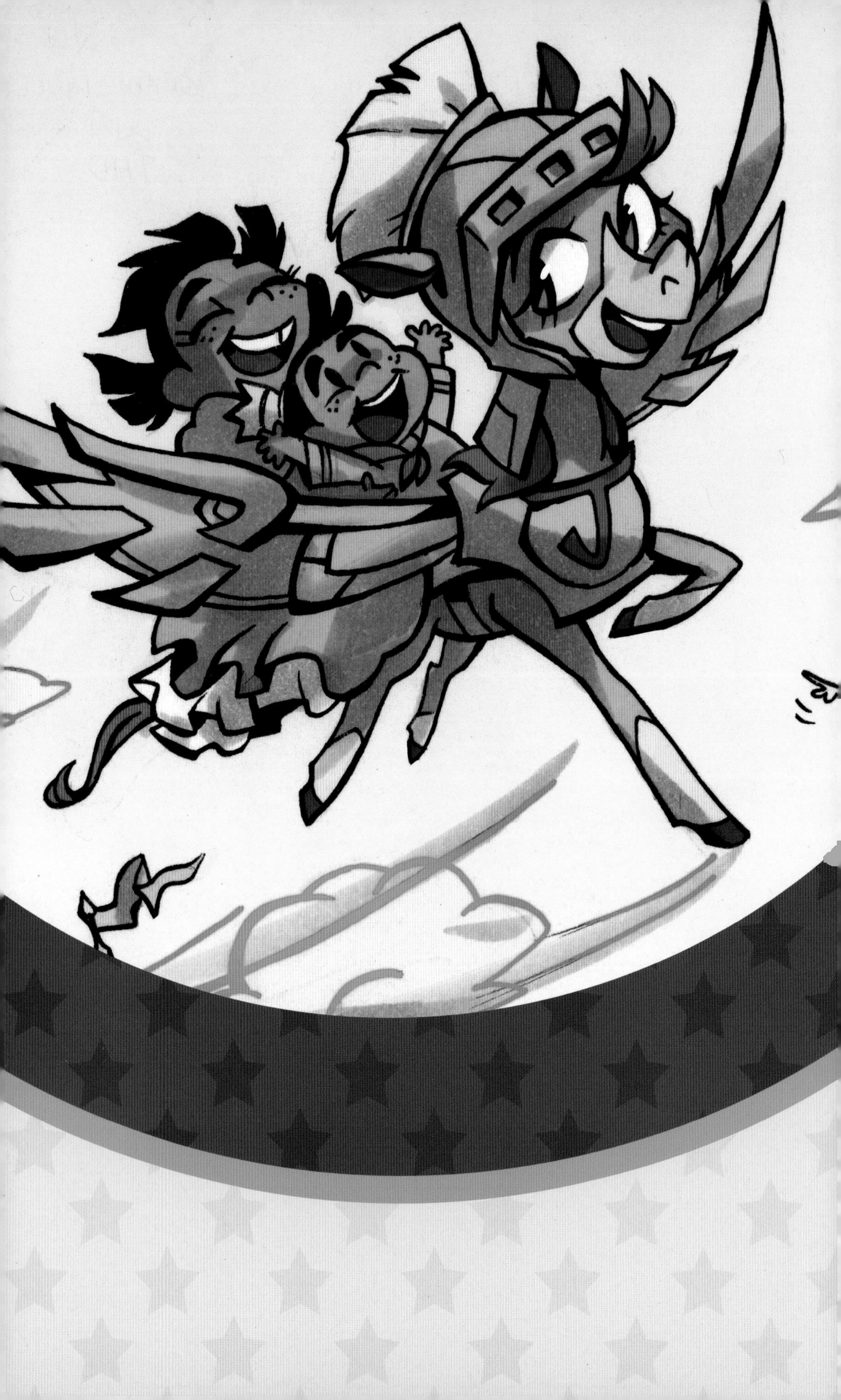

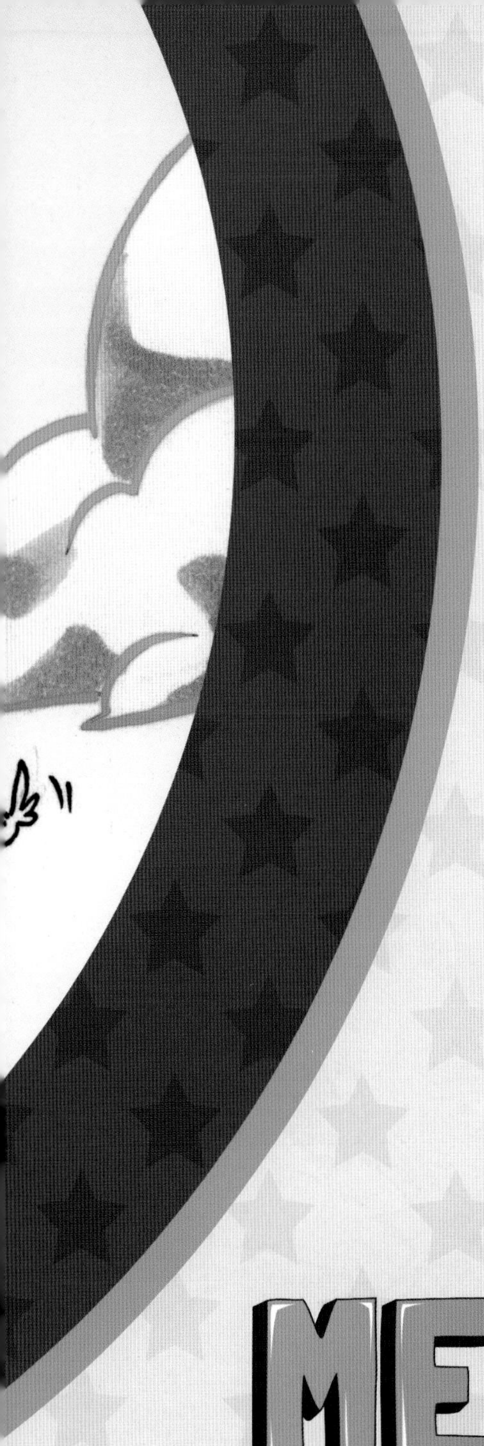

Written by
Kelly Thompson

Illustrated by
Brianne Drouhard

Colored by
M. Victoria Robado

Lettered by
Warren Montgomery

Cover by
Brianne Drouhard
With Colors by **M. Victoria Robado**

Designer
Michelle Ankley

Editors
Whitney Leopard & Sierra Hahn

MEGA PRINCESS™

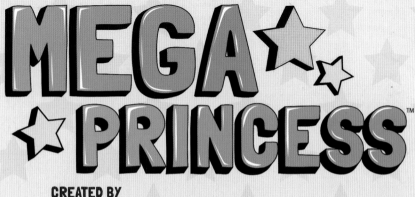

CREATED BY
KELLY THOMPSON, ADAM GREENE, and BRIANNE DROUHARD

Issue #1 Cover by
BRIANNE DROUHARD
With colors by M. VICTORIA ROBADO

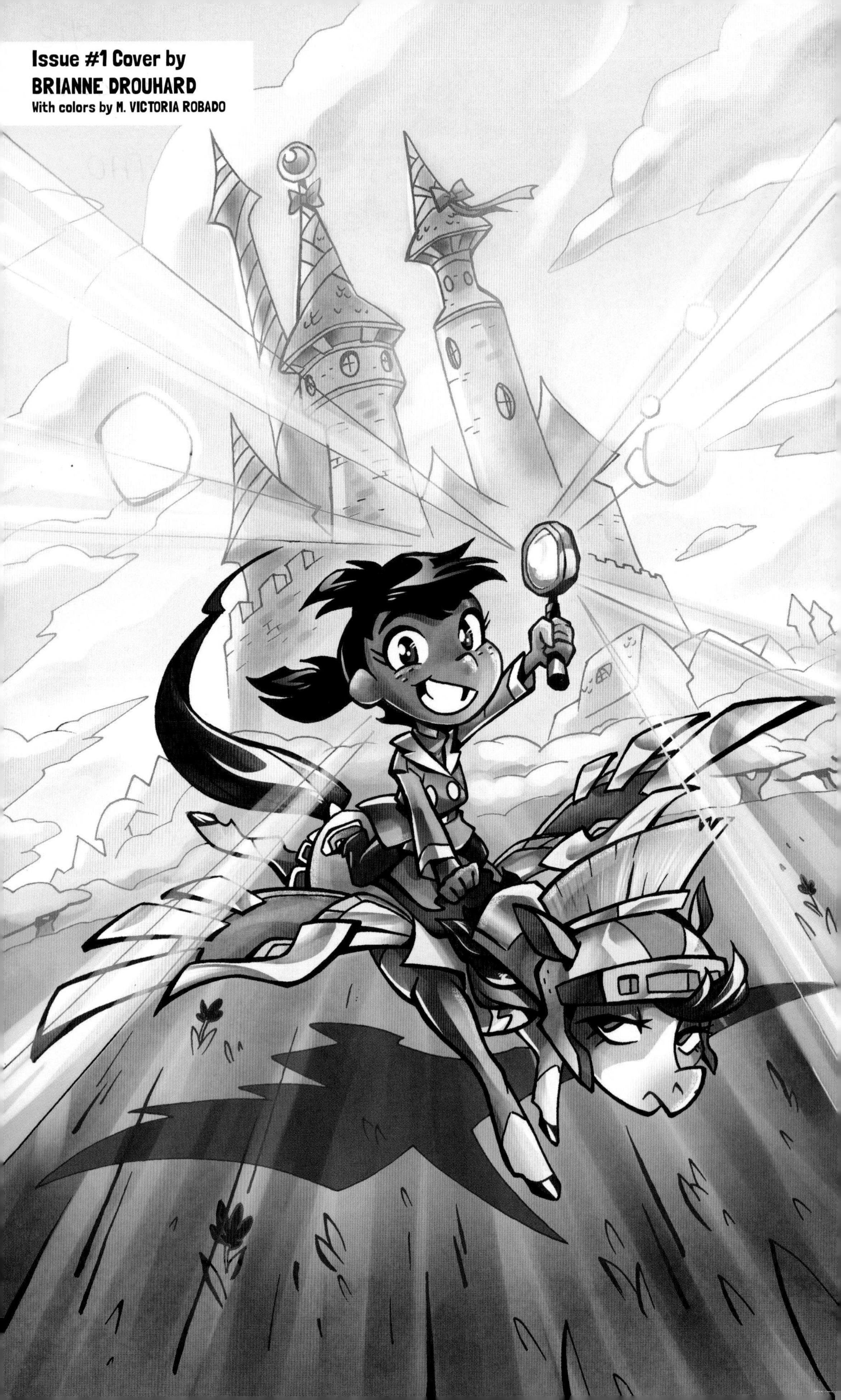

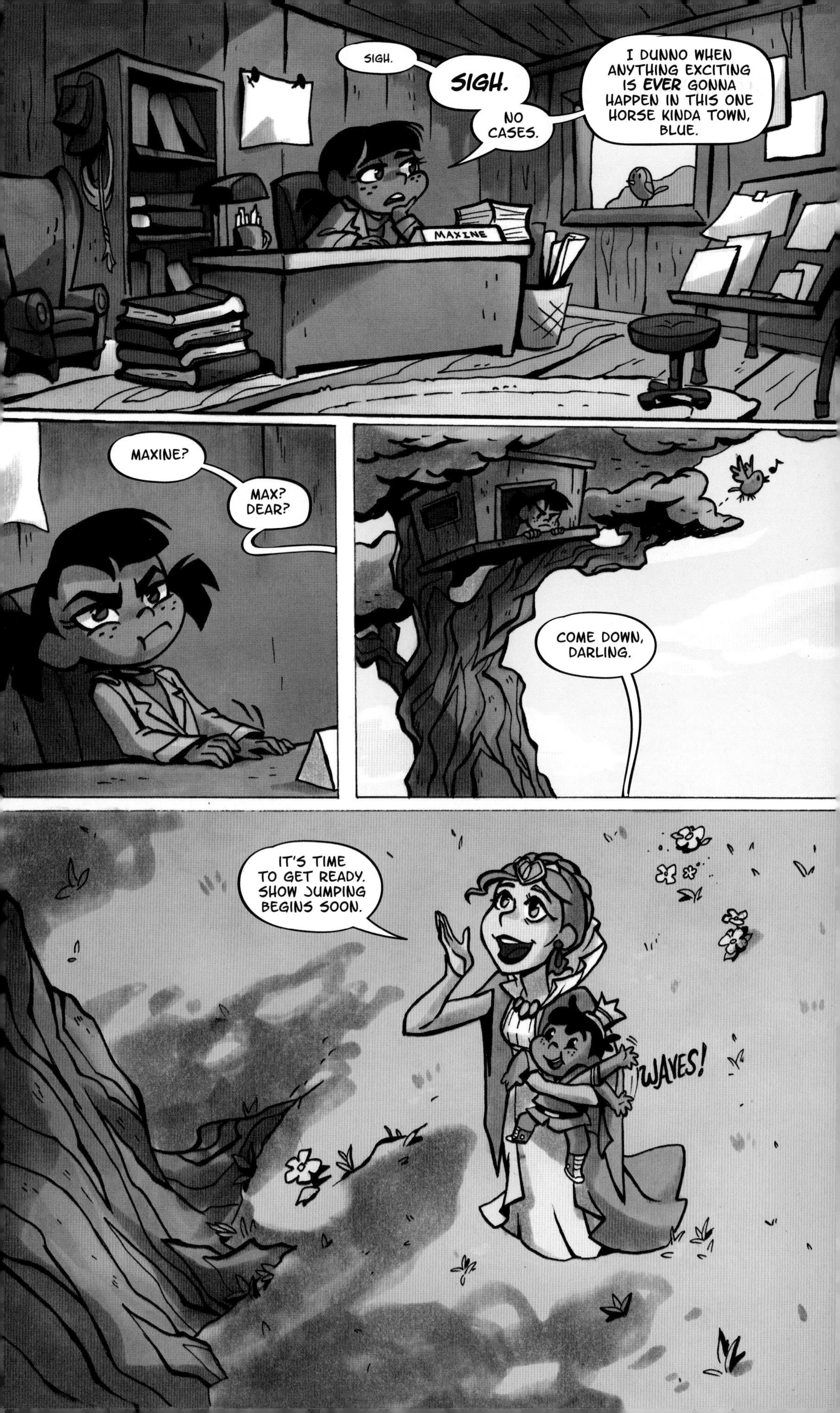
SIGH.
SIGH.
NO CASES.
I DUNNO WHEN ANYTHING EXCITING IS EVER GONNA HAPPEN IN THIS ONE HORSE KINDA TOWN, BLUE.
MAXINE
MAXINE?
MAX? DEAR?
COME DOWN, DARLING.
IT'S TIME TO GET READY. SHOW JUMPING BEGINS SOON.
WAVES!

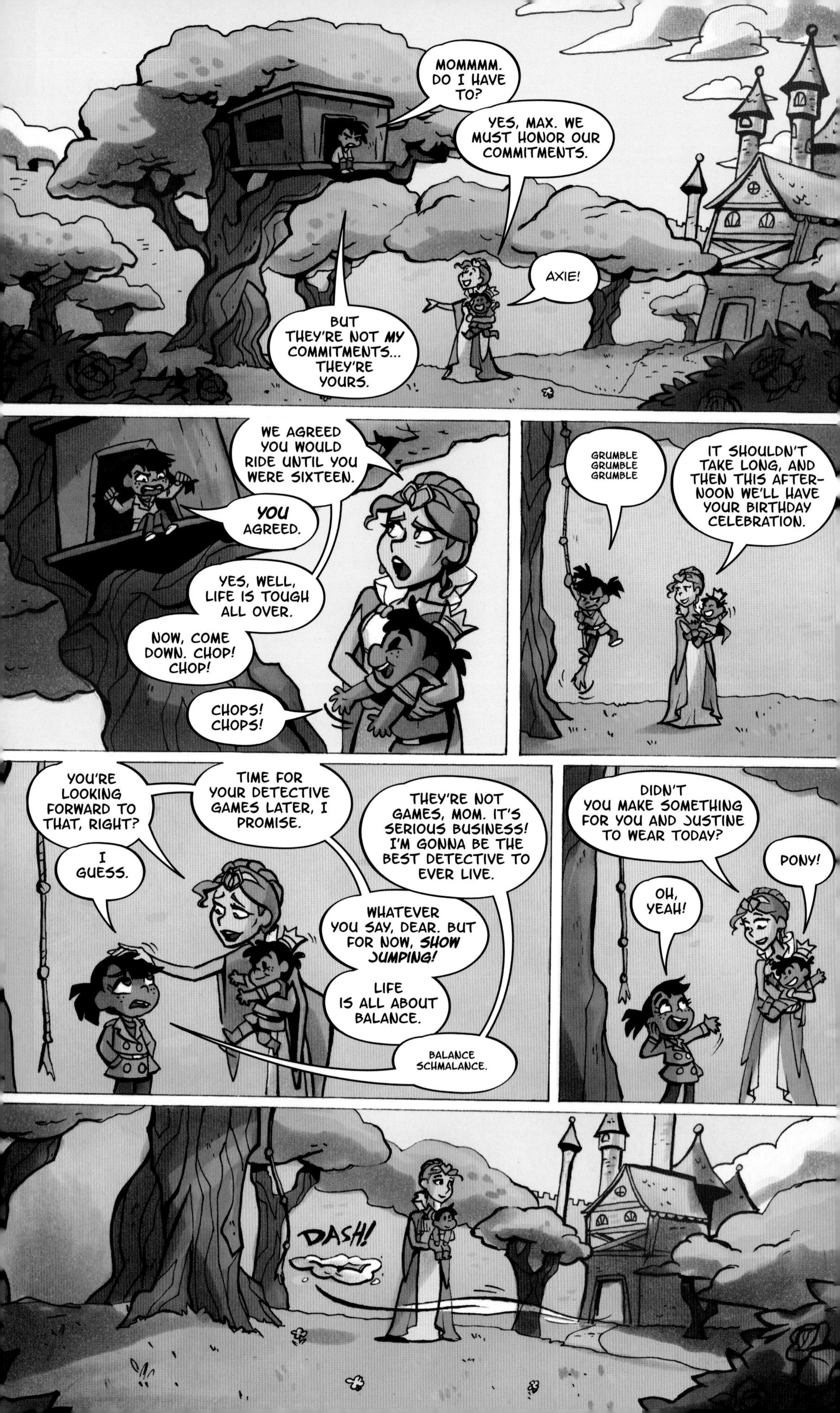
MOMMMM. DO I HAVE TO?
YES, MAX. WE MUST HONOR OUR COMMITMENTS.
BUT THEY'RE NOT MY COMMITMENTS... THEY'RE YOURS.
AXIE!
WE AGREED YOU WOULD RIDE UNTIL YOU WERE SIXTEEN.
YOU AGREED.
YES, WELL, LIFE IS TOUGH ALL OVER.
NOW, COME DOWN. CHOP! CHOP!
CHOPS! CHOPS!
GRUMBLE GRUMBLE GRUMBLE
IT SHOULDN'T TAKE LONG, AND THEN THIS AFTERNOON WE'LL HAVE YOUR BIRTHDAY CELEBRATION.
YOU'RE LOOKING FORWARD TO THAT, RIGHT?
I GUESS.
TIME FOR YOUR DETECTIVE GAMES LATER, I PROMISE.
THEY'RE NOT GAMES, MOM. IT'S SERIOUS BUSINESS! I'M GONNA BE THE BEST DETECTIVE TO EVER LIVE.
WHATEVER YOU SAY, DEAR. BUT FOR NOW, SHOW JUMPING!
LIFE IS ALL ABOUT BALANCE.
BALANCE SCHMALANCE.
DIDN'T YOU MAKE SOMETHING FOR YOU AND JUSTINE TO WEAR TODAY?
OH, YEAH!
PONY!
DASH!

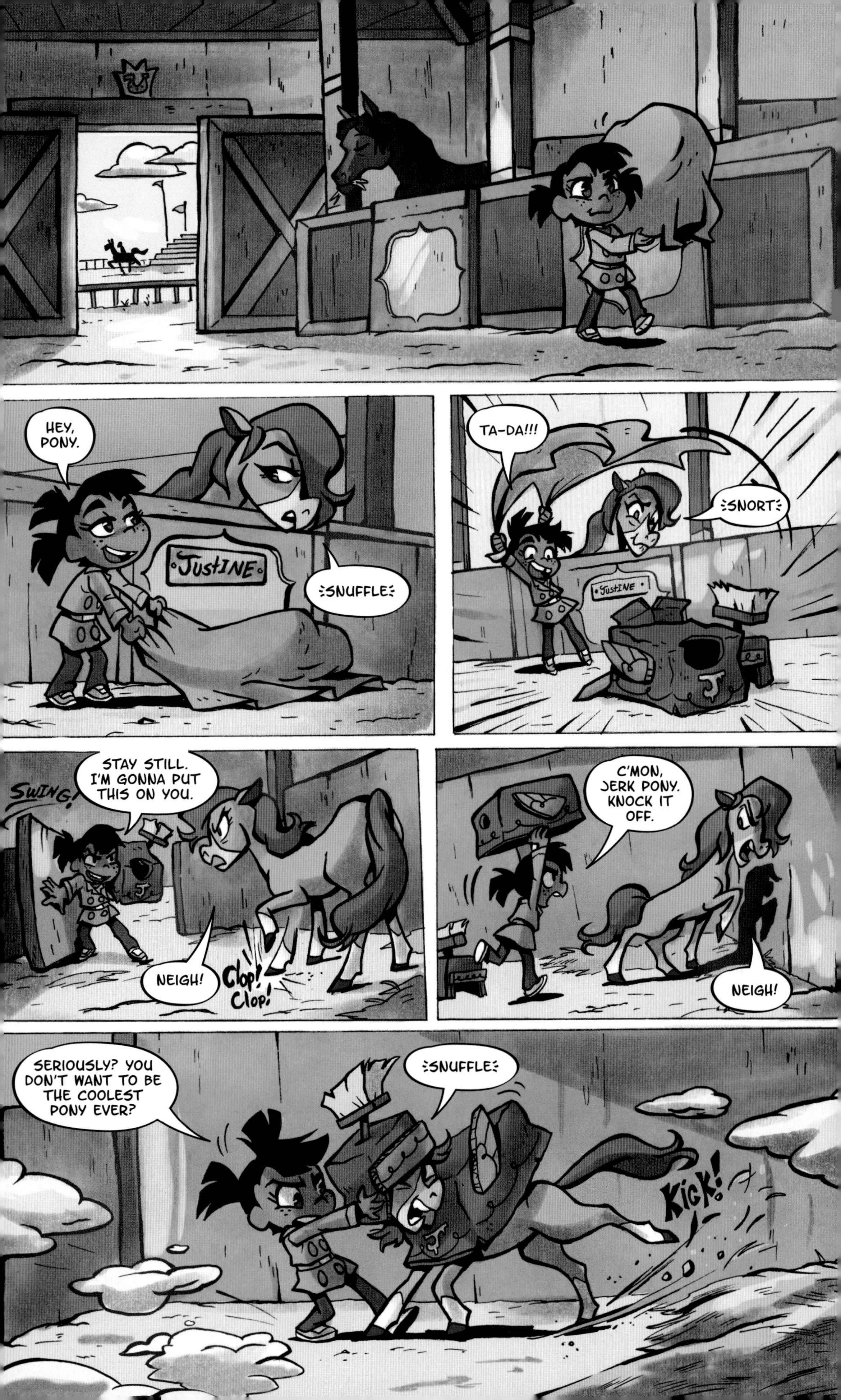

HEY, PONY.
JUSTINE
SNUFFLE
TA-DA!!!
SNORT
JUSTINE
SWING!
STAY STILL. I'M GONNA PUT THIS ON YOU.
NEIGH!
Clop! Clop!
C'MON, JERK PONY. KNOCK IT OFF.
NEIGH!
SERIOUSLY? YOU DON'T WANT TO BE THE COOLEST PONY EVER?
SNUFFLE
KICK!

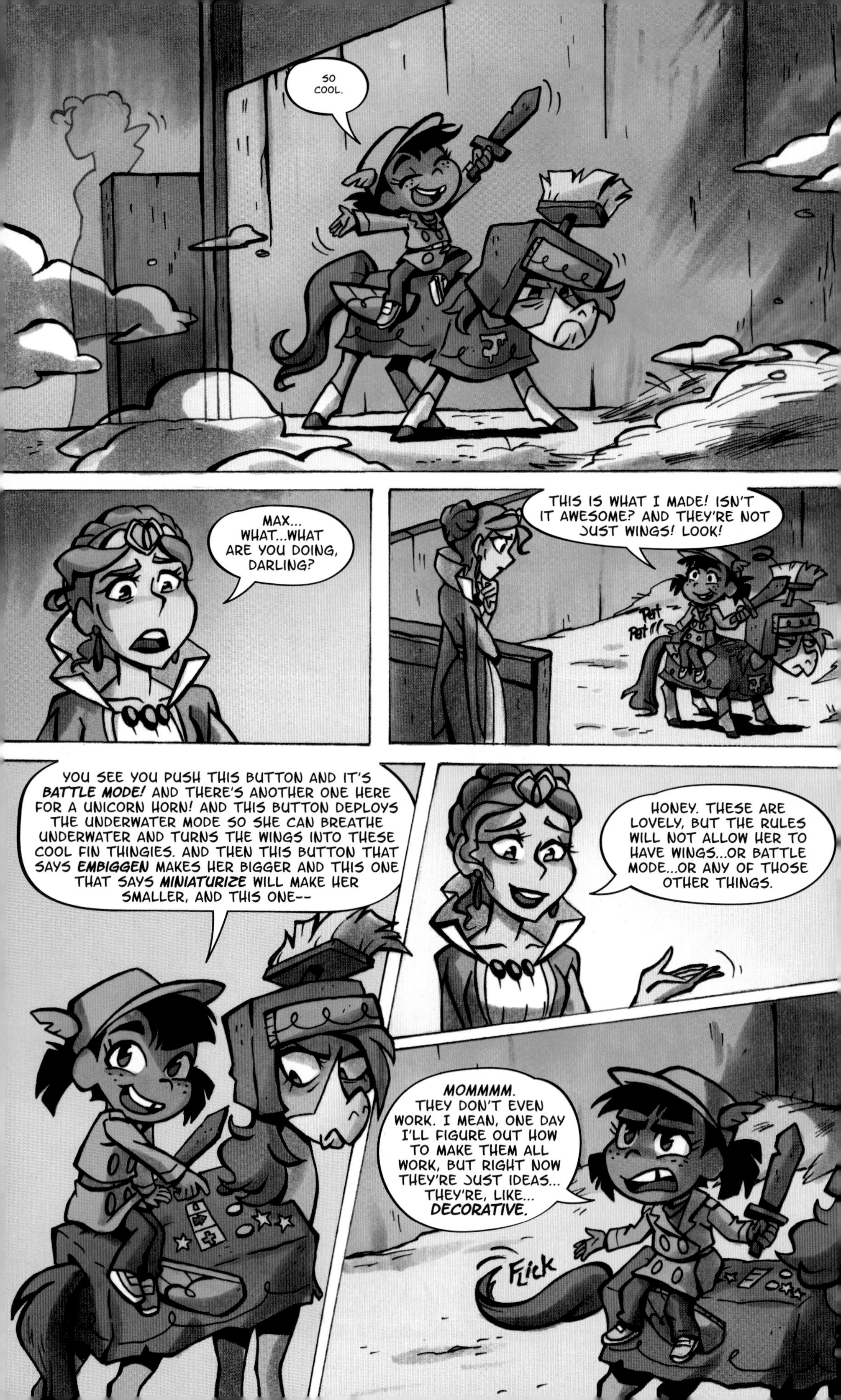
SO COOL.
MAX... WHAT...WHAT ARE YOU DOING, DARLING?
THIS IS WHAT I MADE! ISN'T IT AWESOME? AND THEY'RE NOT JUST WINGS! LOOK!
Pat Pat!!
YOU SEE YOU PUSH THIS BUTTON AND IT'S BATTLE MODE! AND THERE'S ANOTHER ONE HERE FOR A UNICORN HORN! AND THIS BUTTON DEPLOYS THE UNDERWATER MODE SO SHE CAN BREATHE UNDERWATER AND TURNS THE WINGS INTO THESE COOL FIN THINGIES. AND THEN THIS BUTTON THAT SAYS EMBIGGEN MAKES HER BIGGER AND THIS ONE THAT SAYS MINIATURIZE WILL MAKE HER SMALLER, AND THIS ONE--
HONEY. THESE ARE LOVELY, BUT THE RULES WILL NOT ALLOW HER TO HAVE WINGS...OR BATTLE MODE...OR ANY OF THOSE OTHER THINGS.
MOMMMM. THEY DON'T EVEN WORK. I MEAN, ONE DAY I'LL FIGURE OUT HOW TO MAKE THEM ALL WORK, BUT RIGHT NOW THEY'RE JUST IDEAS... THEY'RE, LIKE... DECORATIVE.
FLICK

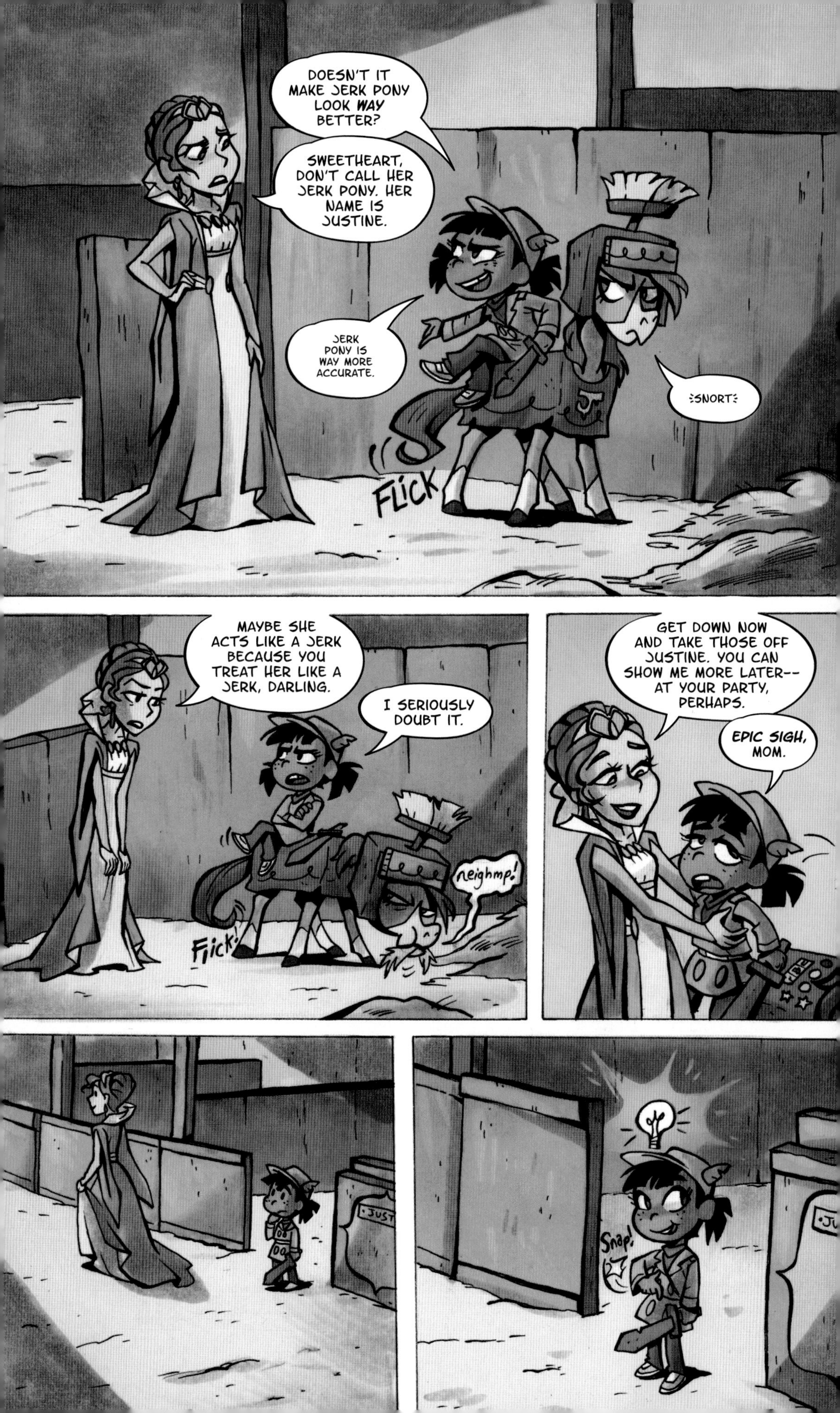
DOESN'T IT MAKE JERK PONY LOOK WAY BETTER?
SWEETHEART, DON'T CALL HER JERK PONY. HER NAME IS JUSTINE.
JERK PONY IS WAY MORE ACCURATE.
SNORT
FLICK
MAYBE SHE ACTS LIKE A JERK BECAUSE YOU TREAT HER LIKE A JERK, DARLING.
I SERIOUSLY DOUBT IT.
neighmp!
FLICK!
GET DOWN NOW AND TAKE THOSE OFF JUSTINE. YOU CAN SHOW ME MORE LATER--AT YOUR PARTY, PERHAPS.
EPIC SIGH, MOM.
JUST
Snap!
JU

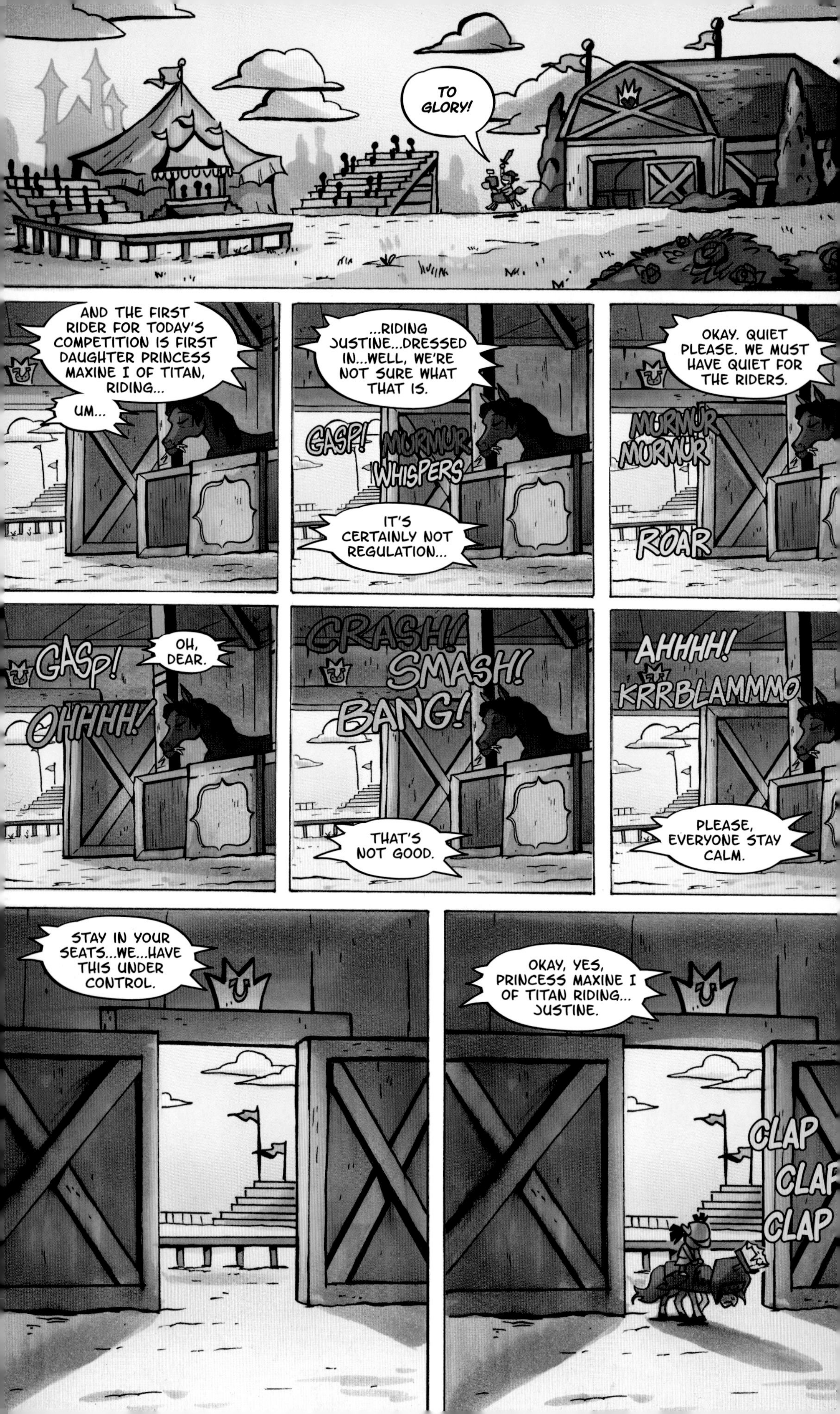
TO GLORY!
AND THE FIRST RIDER FOR TODAY'S COMPETITION IS FIRST DAUGHTER PRINCESS MAXINE I OF TITAN, RIDING...
UM...
...RIDING JUSTINE...DRESSED IN...WELL, WE'RE NOT SURE WHAT THAT IS.
GASP!
MURMUR
WHISPERS
IT'S CERTAINLY NOT REGULATION...
OKAY. QUIET PLEASE. WE MUST HAVE QUIET FOR THE RIDERS.
MURMUR
MURMUR
ROAR
GASp!
OH, DEAR.
OHHHH!
CRASH!
SMASH!
BANG!
THAT'S NOT GOOD.
AHHHH!
KRRBLAMMMO
PLEASE, EVERYONE STAY CALM.
STAY IN YOUR SEATS...WE...HAVE THIS UNDER CONTROL.
OKAY, YES, PRINCESS MAXINE I OF TITAN RIDING... JUSTINE.
CLAP
CLAP
CLAP

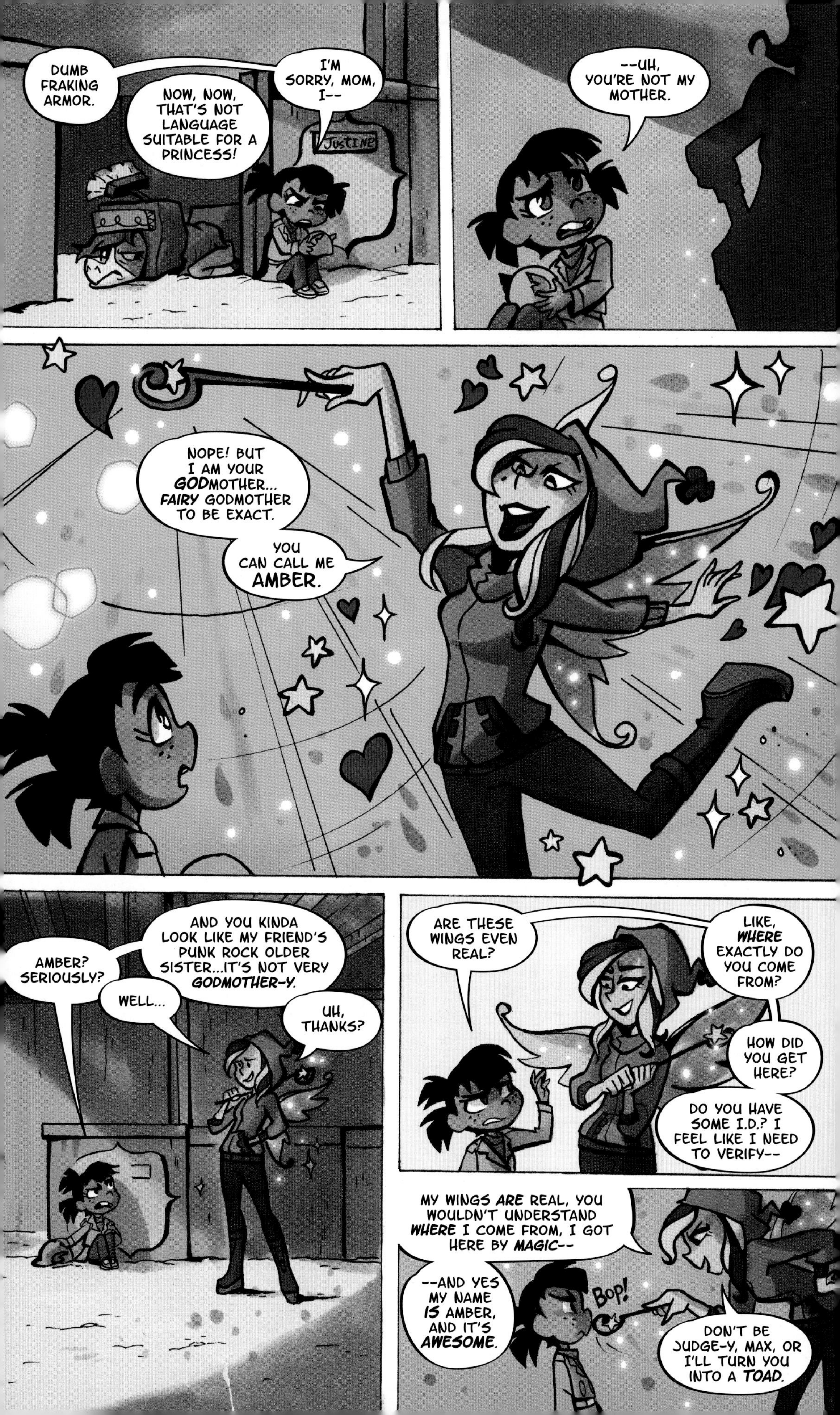
DUMB FRAKING ARMOR.
NOW, NOW, THAT'S NOT LANGUAGE SUITABLE FOR A PRINCESS!
I'M SORRY, MOM, I--
JUSTINE
--UH, YOU'RE NOT MY MOTHER.
NOPE! BUT I AM YOUR GODMOTHER... FAIRY GODMOTHER TO BE EXACT.
YOU CAN CALL ME AMBER.
AMBER? SERIOUSLY?
AND YOU KINDA LOOK LIKE MY FRIEND'S PUNK ROCK OLDER SISTER...IT'S NOT VERY GODMOTHER-Y.
WELL...
UH, THANKS?
ARE THESE WINGS EVEN REAL?
LIKE, WHERE EXACTLY DO YOU COME FROM?
HOW DID YOU GET HERE?
DO YOU HAVE SOME I.D.? I FEEL LIKE I NEED TO VERIFY--
MY WINGS ARE REAL, YOU WOULDN'T UNDERSTAND WHERE I COME FROM, I GOT HERE BY MAGIC--
--AND YES MY NAME IS AMBER, AND IT'S AWESOME.
BOP!
DON'T BE JUDGE-Y, MAX, OR I'LL TURN YOU INTO A TOAD.

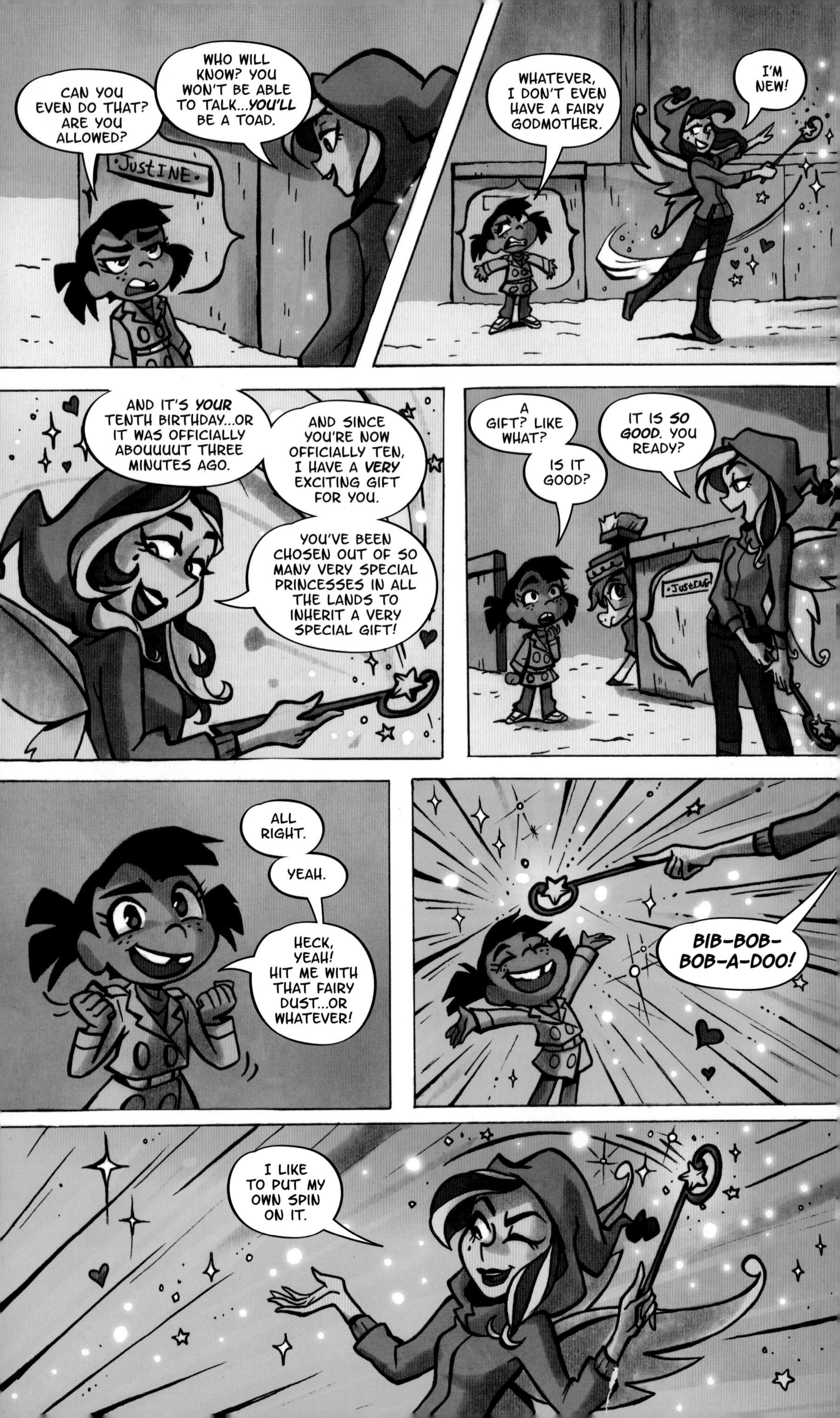
CAN YOU EVEN DO THAT? ARE YOU ALLOWED?
WHO WILL KNOW? YOU WON'T BE ABLE TO TALK...YOU'LL BE A TOAD.
JustINE
WHATEVER, I DON'T EVEN HAVE A FAIRY GODMOTHER.
I'M NEW!
AND IT'S YOUR TENTH BIRTHDAY...OR IT WAS OFFICIALLY ABOUUUUT THREE MINUTES AGO.
AND SINCE YOU'RE NOW OFFICIALLY TEN, I HAVE A VERY EXCITING GIFT FOR YOU.
YOU'VE BEEN CHOSEN OUT OF SO MANY VERY SPECIAL PRINCESSES IN ALL THE LANDS TO INHERIT A VERY SPECIAL GIFT!
A GIFT? LIKE WHAT?
IS IT GOOD?
IT IS SO GOOD. YOU READY?
ALL RIGHT.
YEAH.
HECK, YEAH! HIT ME WITH THAT FAIRY DUST...OR WHATEVER!
BIB-BOB-BOB-A-DOO!
I LIKE TO PUT MY OWN SPIN ON IT.

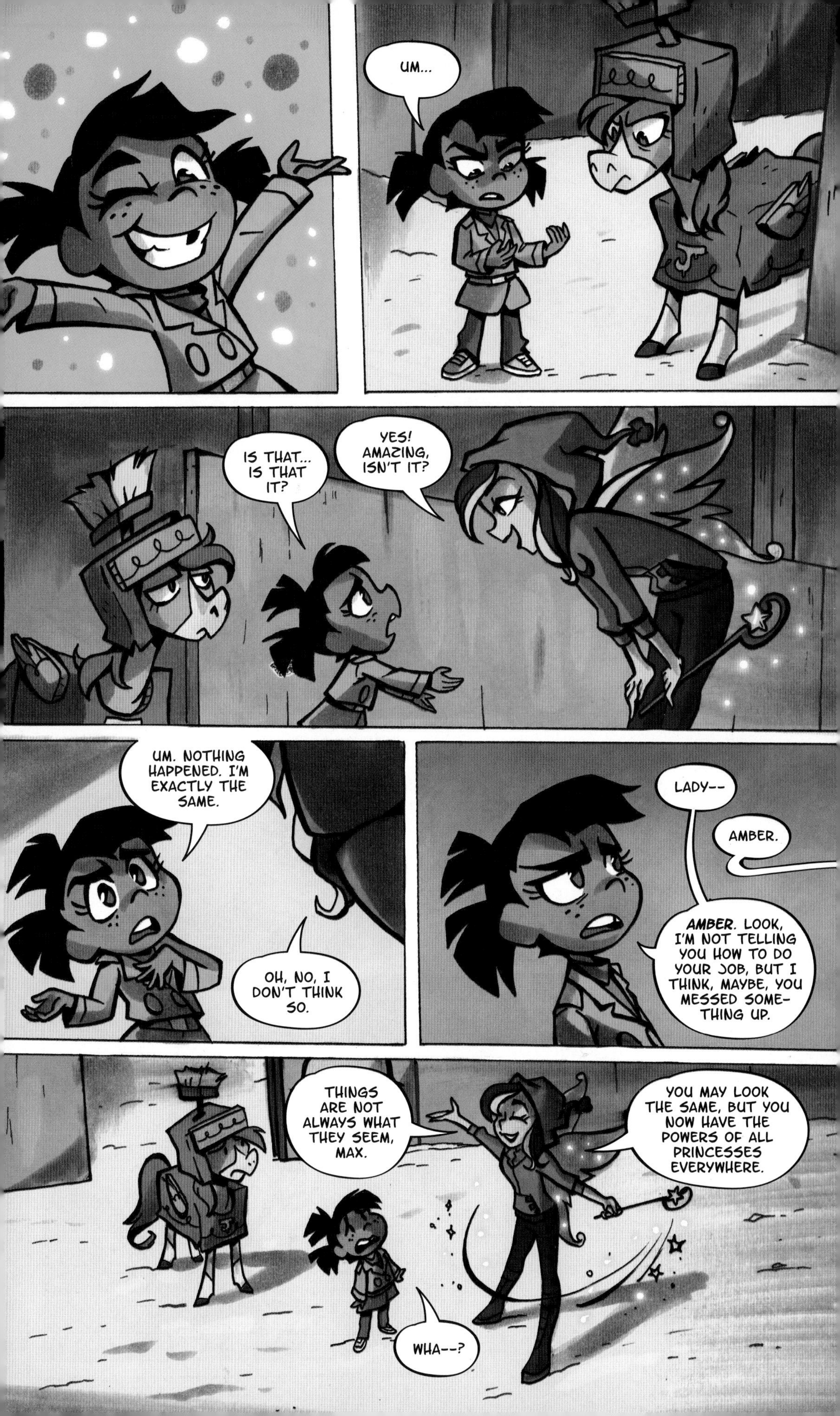
UM...
IS THAT... IS THAT IT?
YES! AMAZING, ISN'T IT?
UM. NOTHING HAPPENED. I'M EXACTLY THE SAME.
OH, NO, I DON'T THINK SO.
LADY--
AMBER.
AMBER. LOOK, I'M NOT TELLING YOU HOW TO DO YOUR JOB, BUT I THINK, MAYBE, YOU MESSED SOME-THING UP.
THINGS ARE NOT ALWAYS WHAT THEY SEEM, MAX.
YOU MAY LOOK THE SAME, BUT YOU NOW HAVE THE POWERS OF ALL PRINCESSES EVERYWHERE.
WHA--?

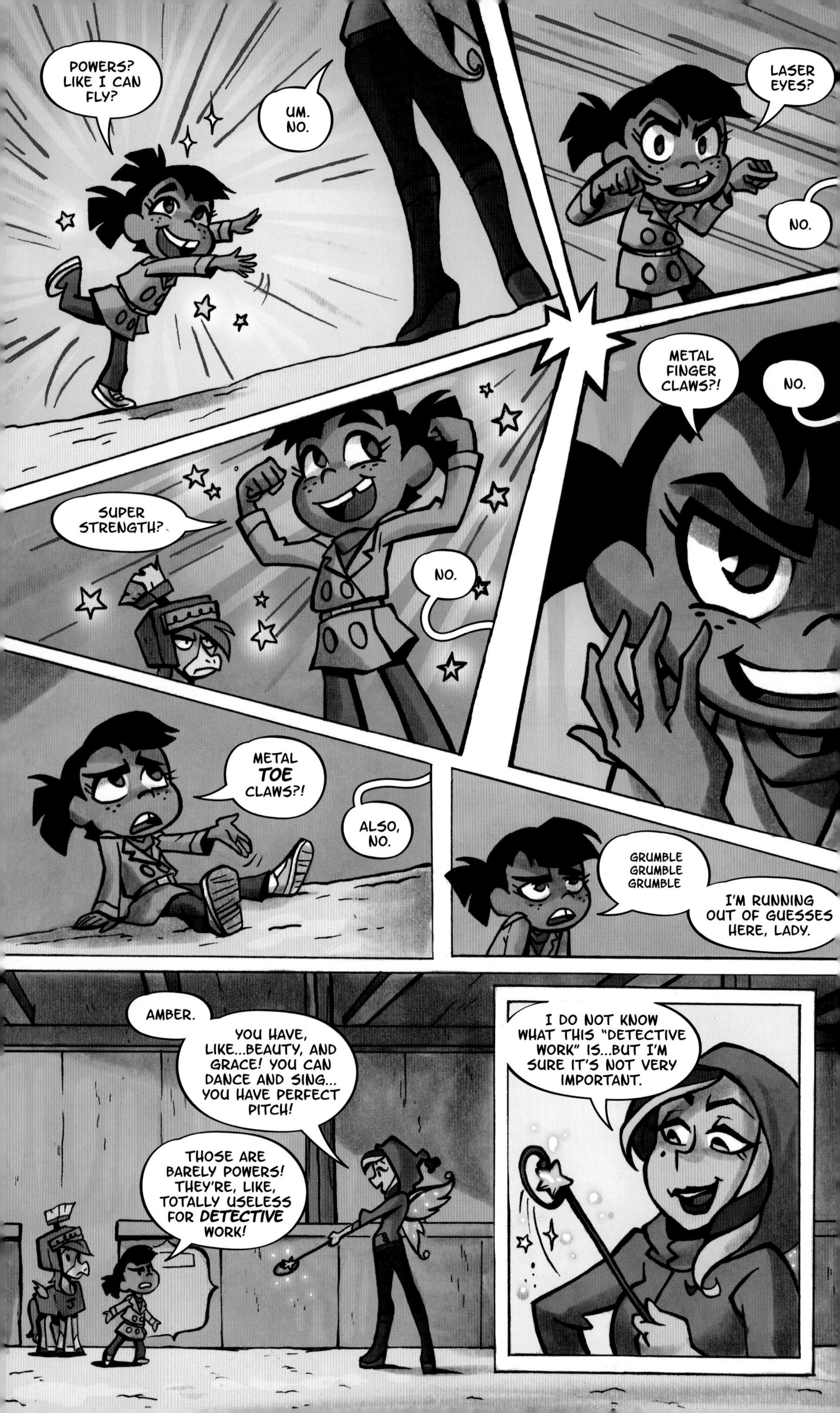
POWERS? LIKE I CAN FLY?
UM. NO.
LASER EYES?
NO.
SUPER STRENGTH?
NO.
METAL FINGER CLAWS?!
NO.
METAL **TOE** CLAWS?!
ALSO, NO.
GRUMBLE GRUMBLE GRUMBLE
I'M RUNNING OUT OF GUESSES HERE, LADY.
AMBER.
YOU HAVE, LIKE...BEAUTY, AND GRACE! YOU CAN DANCE AND SING... YOU HAVE PERFECT PITCH!
THOSE ARE BARELY POWERS! THEY'RE, LIKE, TOTALLY USELESS FOR *DETECTIVE* WORK!
I DO NOT KNOW WHAT THIS "DETECTIVE WORK" IS...BUT I'M SURE IT'S NOT VERY IMPORTANT.

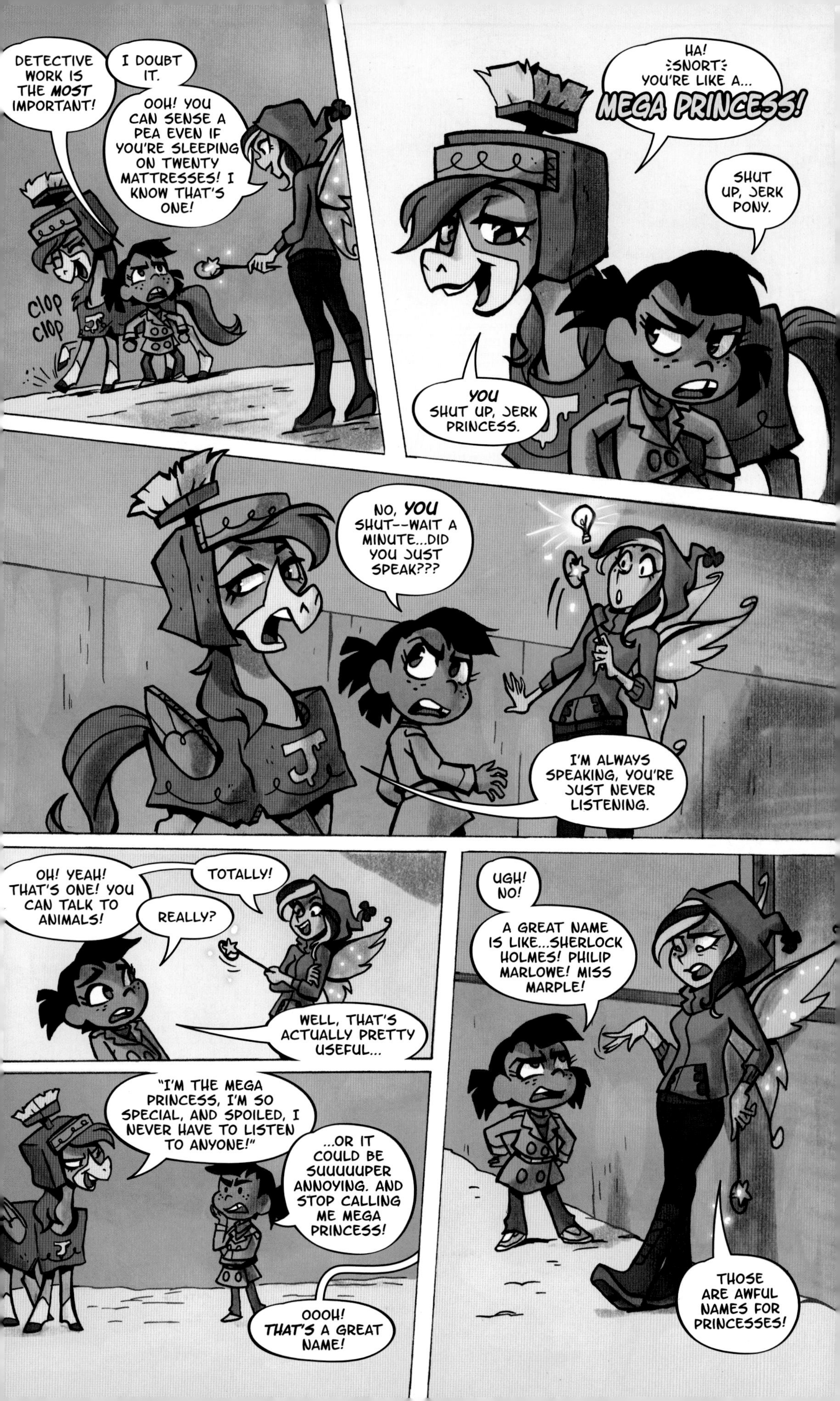
DETECTIVE WORK IS THE *MOST* IMPORTANT!
I DOUBT IT.
OOH! YOU CAN SENSE A PEA EVEN IF YOU'RE SLEEPING ON TWENTY MATTRESSES! I KNOW THAT'S ONE!
CLOP CLOP
HA! *SNORT* YOU'RE LIKE A... MEGA PRINCESS!
SHUT UP, JERK PONY.
YOU SHUT UP, JERK PRINCESS.
NO, *YOU* SHUT--WAIT A MINUTE...DID YOU JUST SPEAK???
I'M ALWAYS SPEAKING, YOU'RE JUST NEVER LISTENING.
OH! YEAH! THAT'S ONE! YOU CAN TALK TO ANIMALS!
TOTALLY!
REALLY?
WELL, THAT'S ACTUALLY PRETTY USEFUL...
"I'M THE MEGA PRINCESS, I'M SO SPECIAL, AND SPOILED, I NEVER HAVE TO LISTEN TO ANYONE!"
...OR IT COULD BE SUUUUUPER ANNOYING. AND STOP CALLING ME MEGA PRINCESS!
OOOH! *THAT'S* A GREAT NAME!
UGH! NO!
A GREAT NAME IS LIKE...SHERLOCK HOLMES! PHILIP MARLOWE! MISS MARPLE!
THOSE ARE AWFUL NAMES FOR PRINCESSES!

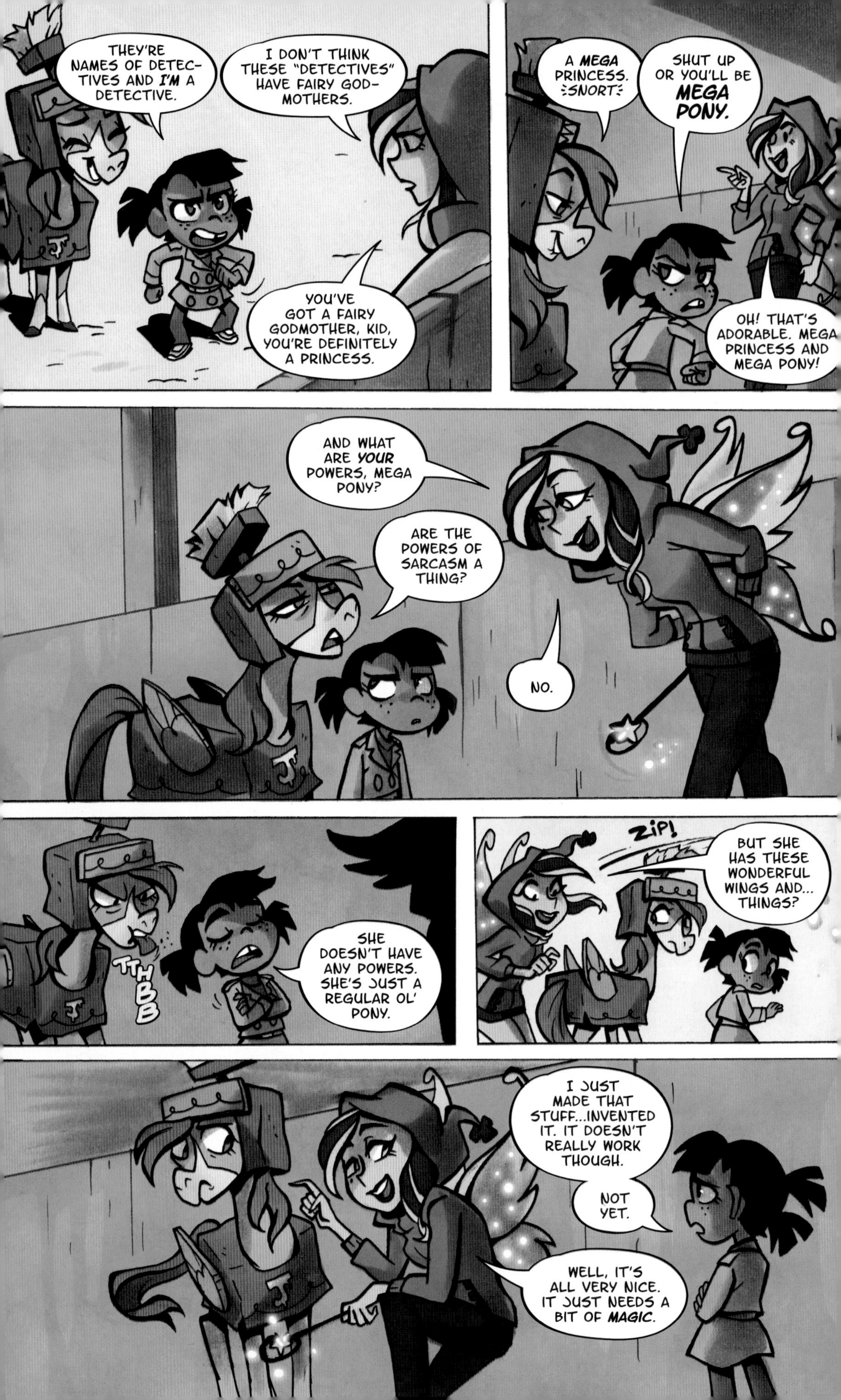
THEY'RE NAMES OF DETECTIVES AND I'M A DETECTIVE.
I DON'T THINK THESE "DETECTIVES" HAVE FAIRY GODMOTHERS.
YOU'VE GOT A FAIRY GODMOTHER, KID, YOU'RE DEFINITELY A PRINCESS.
A MEGA PRINCESS. SNORT
SHUT UP OR YOU'LL BE MEGA PONY.
OH! THAT'S ADORABLE. MEGA PRINCESS AND MEGA PONY!
AND WHAT ARE YOUR POWERS, MEGA PONY?
ARE THE POWERS OF SARCASM A THING?
NO.
TTHBB
SHE DOESN'T HAVE ANY POWERS. SHE'S JUST A REGULAR OL' PONY.
ZIP!
BUT SHE HAS THESE WONDERFUL WINGS AND... THINGS?
I JUST MADE THAT STUFF...INVENTED IT. IT DOESN'T REALLY WORK THOUGH.
NOT YET.
WELL, IT'S ALL VERY NICE. IT JUST NEEDS A BIT OF MAGIC.

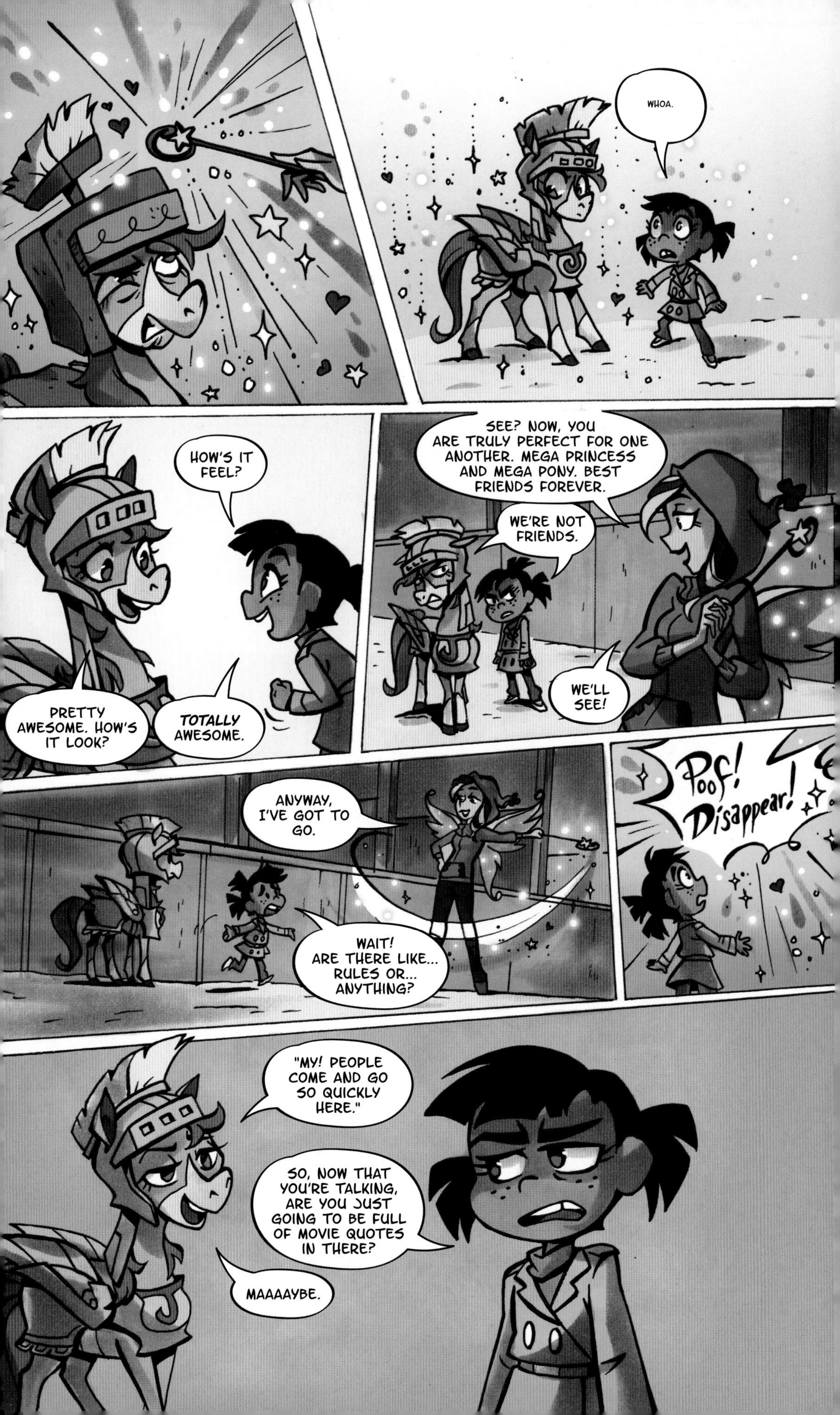
WHOA.
HOW'S IT FEEL?
PRETTY AWESOME. HOW'S IT LOOK?
TOTALLY AWESOME.
SEE? NOW, YOU ARE TRULY PERFECT FOR ONE ANOTHER. MEGA PRINCESS AND MEGA PONY. BEST FRIENDS FOREVER.
WE'RE NOT FRIENDS.
WE'LL SEE!
ANYWAY, I'VE GOT TO GO.
WAIT! ARE THERE LIKE... RULES OR... ANYTHING?
Poof! Disappear!
"MY! PEOPLE COME AND GO SO QUICKLY HERE."
SO, NOW THAT YOU'RE TALKING, ARE YOU JUST GOING TO BE FULL OF MOVIE QUOTES IN THERE?
MAAAAYBE.

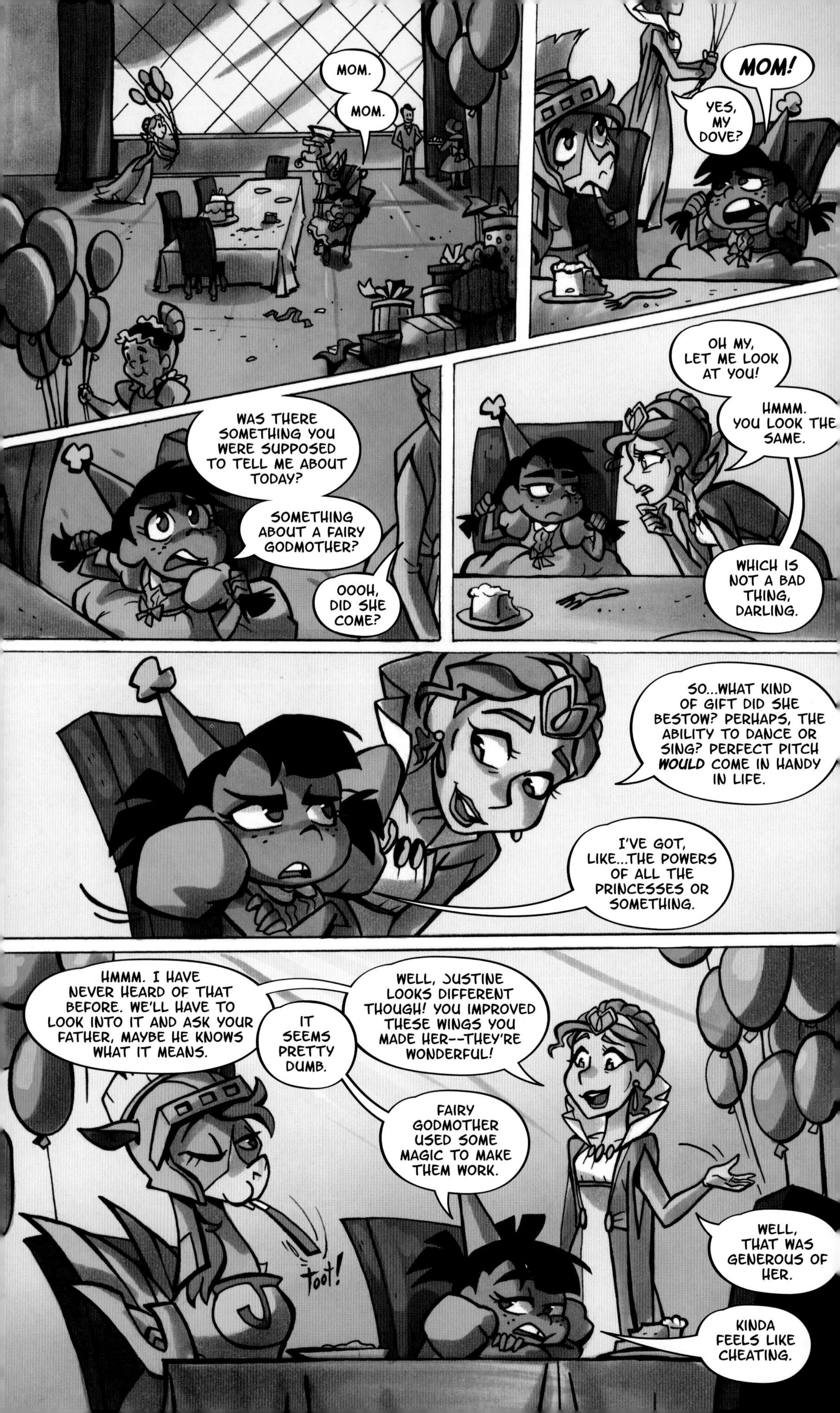
MOM.
MOM.
MOM!
YES, MY DOVE?
WAS THERE SOMETHING YOU WERE SUPPOSED TO TELL ME ABOUT TODAY?
SOMETHING ABOUT A FAIRY GODMOTHER?
OOOH, DID SHE COME?
OH MY, LET ME LOOK AT YOU!
HMMM. YOU LOOK THE SAME.
WHICH IS NOT A BAD THING, DARLING.
SO...WHAT KIND OF GIFT DID SHE BESTOW? PERHAPS, THE ABILITY TO DANCE OR SING? PERFECT PITCH WOULD COME IN HANDY IN LIFE.
I'VE GOT, LIKE...THE POWERS OF ALL THE PRINCESSES OR SOMETHING.
HMMM. I HAVE NEVER HEARD OF THAT BEFORE. WE'LL HAVE TO LOOK INTO IT AND ASK YOUR FATHER, MAYBE HE KNOWS WHAT IT MEANS.
IT SEEMS PRETTY DUMB.
WELL, JUSTINE LOOKS DIFFERENT THOUGH! YOU IMPROVED THESE WINGS YOU MADE HER--THEY'RE WONDERFUL!
FAIRY GODMOTHER USED SOME MAGIC TO MAKE THEM WORK.
toot!
WELL, THAT WAS GENEROUS OF HER.
KINDA FEELS LIKE CHEATING.

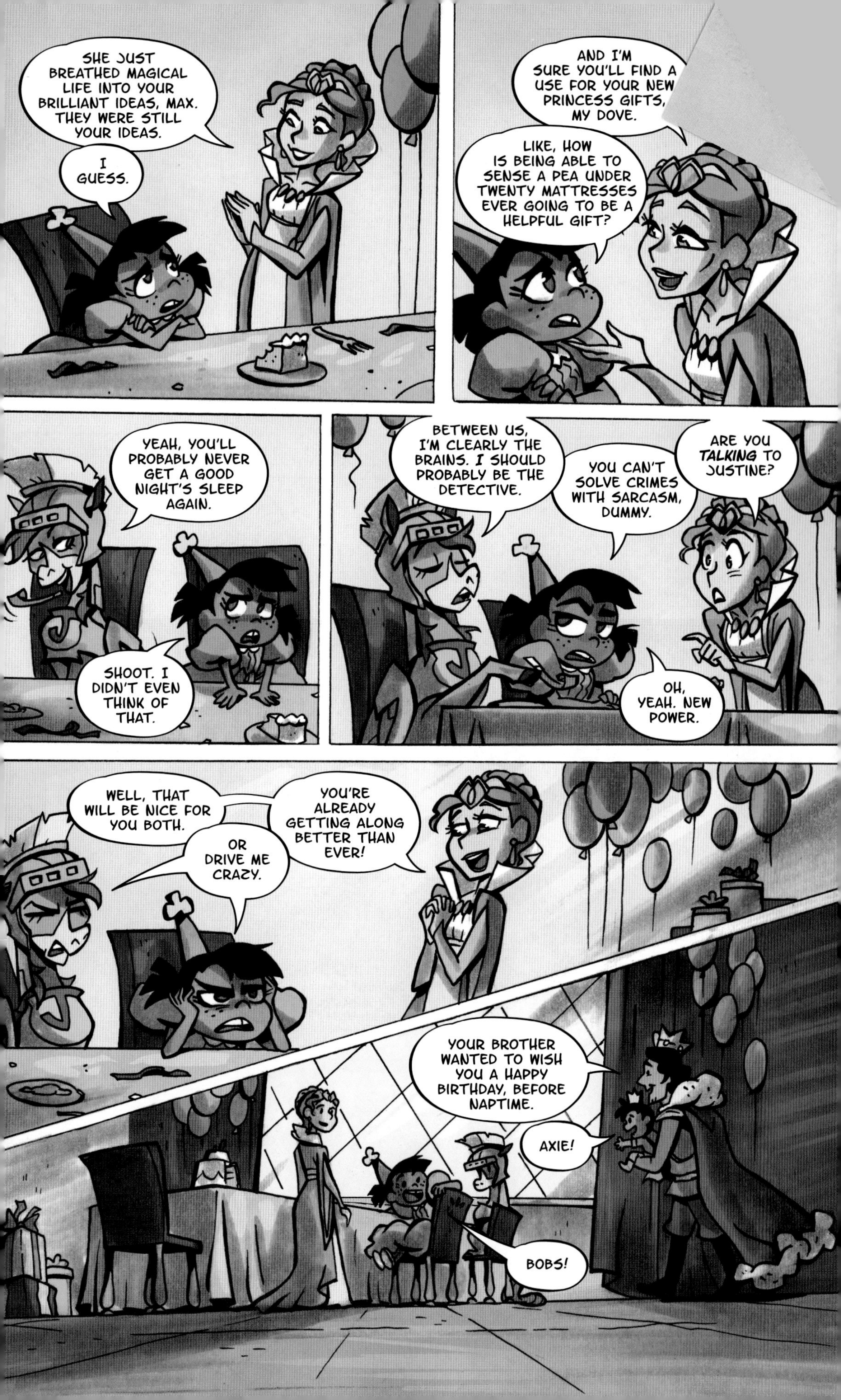
SHE JUST BREATHED MAGICAL LIFE INTO YOUR BRILLIANT IDEAS, MAX. THEY WERE STILL YOUR IDEAS.
I GUESS.
AND I'M SURE YOU'LL FIND A USE FOR YOUR NEW PRINCESS GIFTS, MY DOVE.
LIKE, HOW IS BEING ABLE TO SENSE A PEA UNDER TWENTY MATTRESSES EVER GOING TO BE A HELPFUL GIFT?
YEAH, YOU'LL PROBABLY NEVER GET A GOOD NIGHT'S SLEEP AGAIN.
SHOOT. I DIDN'T EVEN THINK OF THAT.
BETWEEN US, I'M CLEARLY THE BRAINS. I SHOULD PROBABLY BE THE DETECTIVE.
YOU CAN'T SOLVE CRIMES WITH SARCASM, DUMMY.
ARE YOU TALKING TO JUSTINE?
OH, YEAH. NEW POWER.
WELL, THAT WILL BE NICE FOR YOU BOTH.
YOU'RE ALREADY GETTING ALONG BETTER THAN EVER!
OR DRIVE ME CRAZY.
YOUR BROTHER WANTED TO WISH YOU A HAPPY BIRTHDAY, BEFORE NAPTIME.
AXIE!
BOBS!

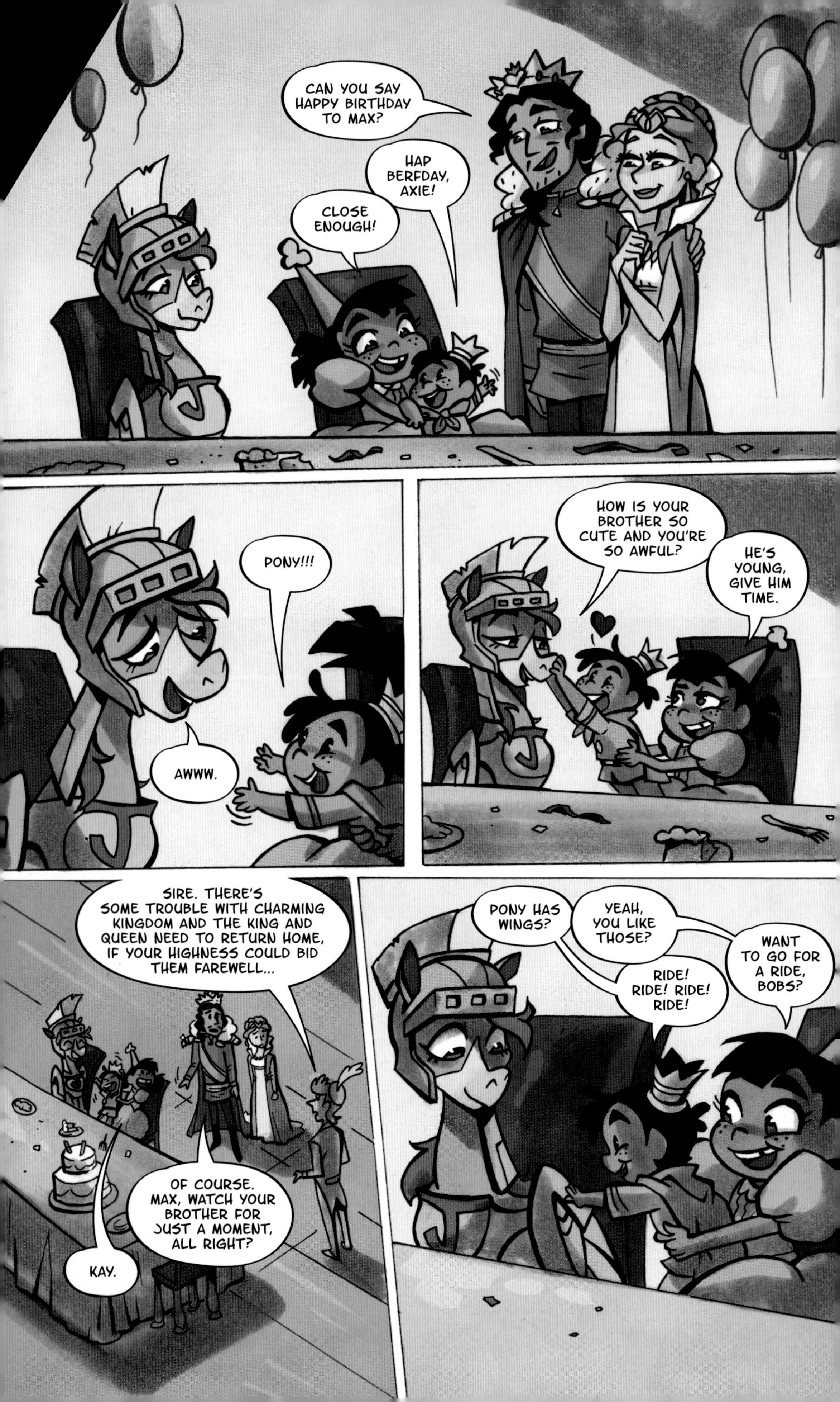
CAN YOU SAY HAPPY BIRTHDAY TO MAX?
HAP BERFDAY, AXIE!
CLOSE ENOUGH!
PONY!!!
AWWW.
HOW IS YOUR BROTHER SO CUTE AND YOU'RE SO AWFUL?
HE'S YOUNG, GIVE HIM TIME.
SIRE. THERE'S SOME TROUBLE WITH CHARMING KINGDOM AND THE KING AND QUEEN NEED TO RETURN HOME, IF YOUR HIGHNESS COULD BID THEM FAREWELL...
OF COURSE. MAX, WATCH YOUR BROTHER FOR JUST A MOMENT, ALL RIGHT?
KAY.
PONY HAS WINGS?
YEAH, YOU LIKE THOSE?
RIDE! RIDE! RIDE! RIDE!
WANT TO GO FOR A RIDE, BOBS?

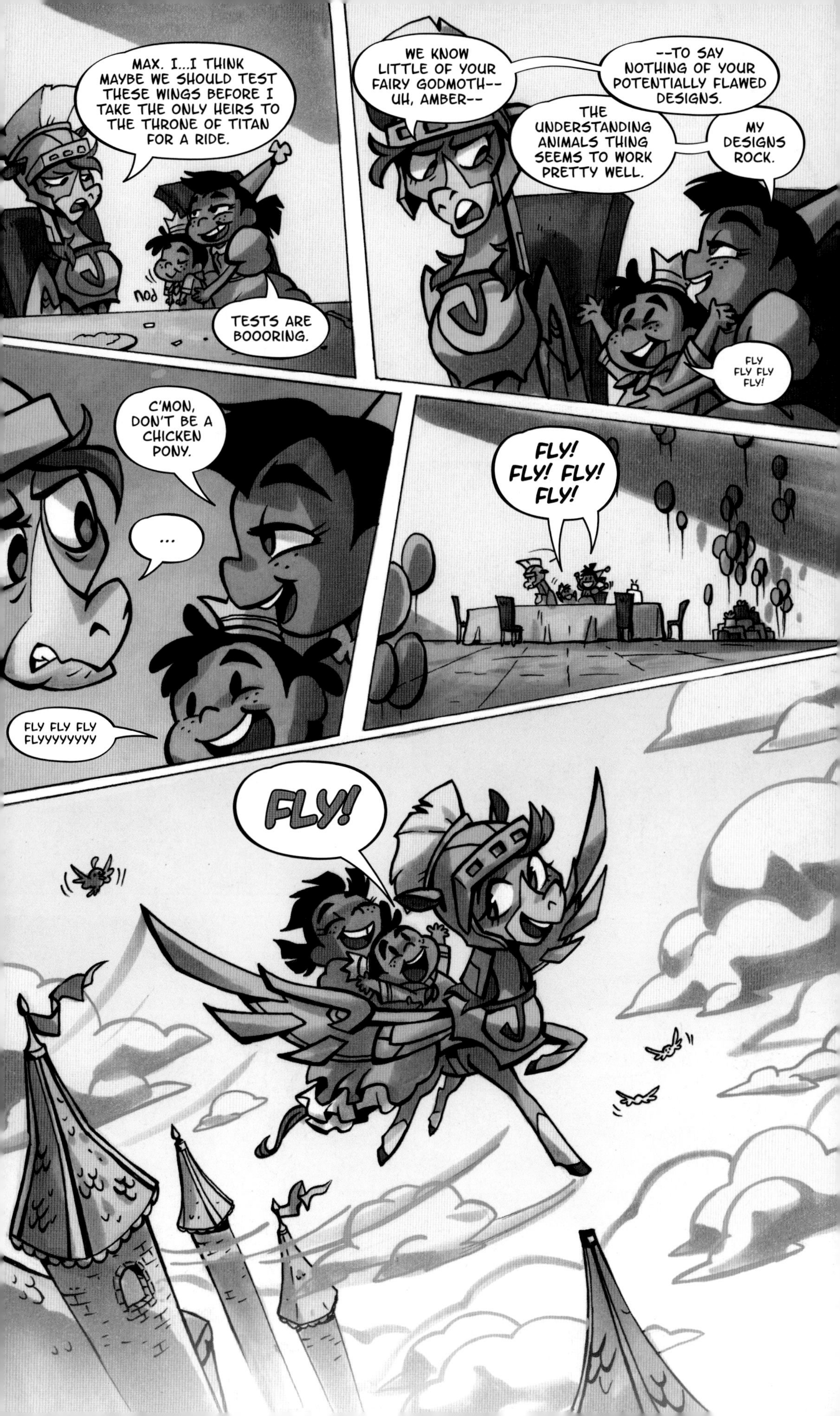
MAX. I...I THINK MAYBE WE SHOULD TEST THESE WINGS BEFORE I TAKE THE ONLY HEIRS TO THE THRONE OF TITAN FOR A RIDE.
nod
TESTS ARE BOOORING.
WE KNOW LITTLE OF YOUR FAIRY GODMOTH-- UH, AMBER--
--TO SAY NOTHING OF YOUR POTENTIALLY FLAWED DESIGNS.
THE UNDERSTANDING ANIMALS THING SEEMS TO WORK PRETTY WELL.
MY DESIGNS ROCK.
FLY FLY FLY FLY!
C'MON, DON'T BE A CHICKEN PONY.
...
FLY FLY FLY FLYYYYYYYY
FLY! FLY! FLY! FLY!
FLY!

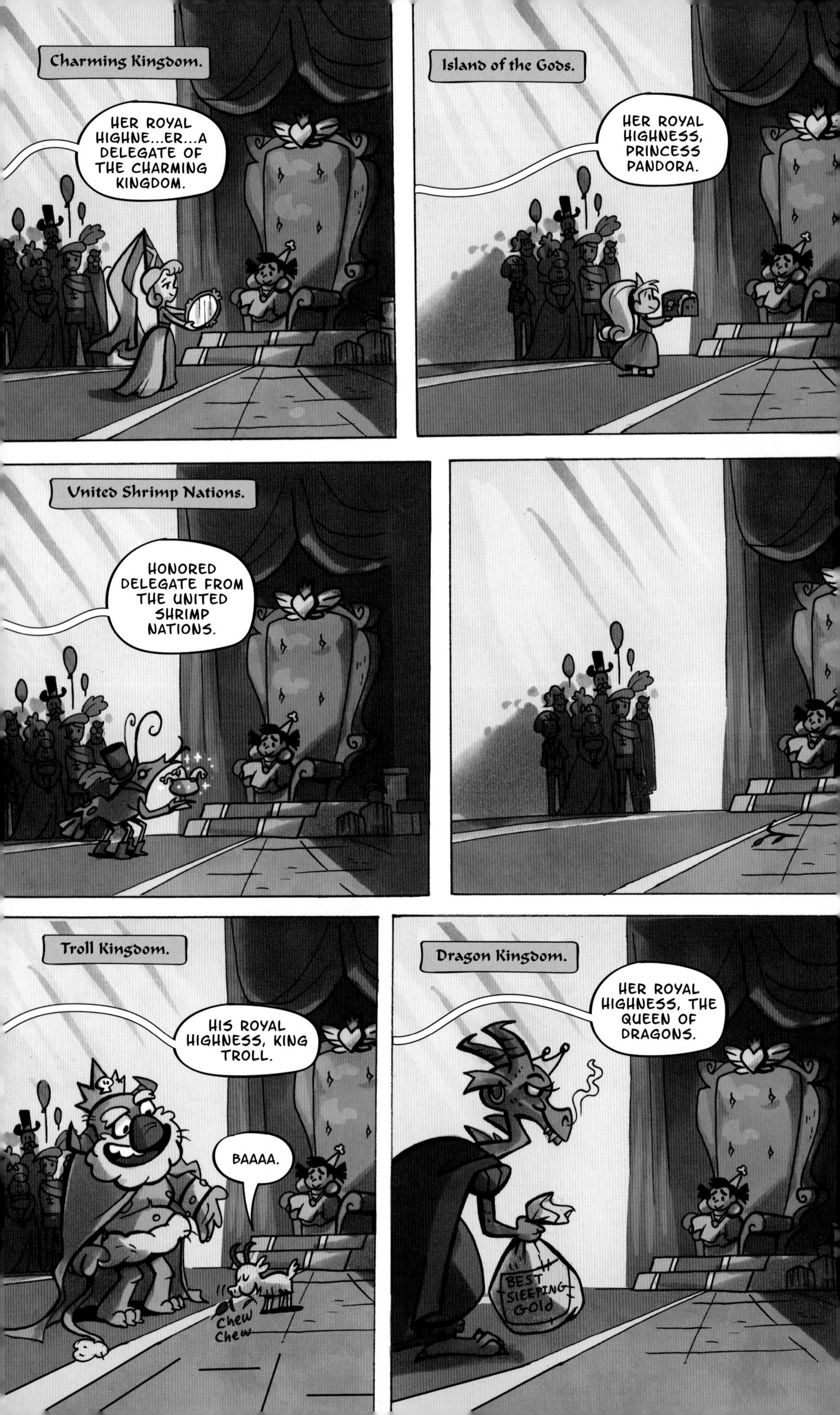
Charming Kingdom.
HER ROYAL HIGHNE...ER...A DELEGATE OF THE CHARMING KINGDOM.
Island of the Gods.
HER ROYAL HIGHNESS, PRINCESS PANDORA.
United Shrimp Nations.
HONORED DELEGATE FROM THE UNITED SHRIMP NATIONS.
Troll Kingdom.
HIS ROYAL HIGHNESS, KING TROLL.
BAAAA.
Chew Chew
Dragon Kingdom.
HER ROYAL HIGHNESS, THE QUEEN OF DRAGONS.
BEST SLEEPING Gold

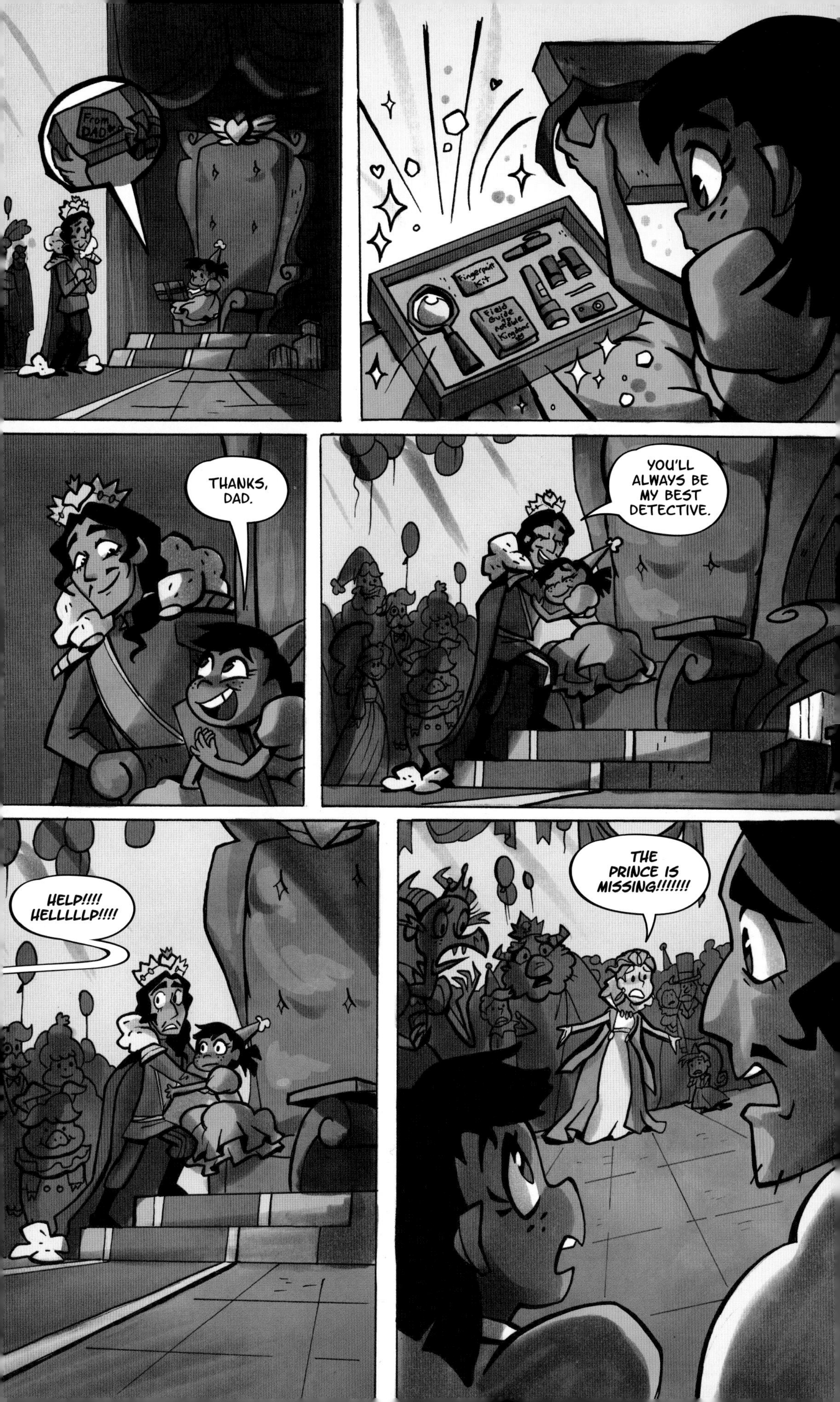
From DAD
Fingerprint Kit
Field Guide to Notable Kingdoms
THANKS, DAD.
YOU'LL ALWAYS BE MY BEST DETECTIVE.
HELP!!!! HELLLLLLP!!!!
THE PRINCE IS MISSING!!!!!!!

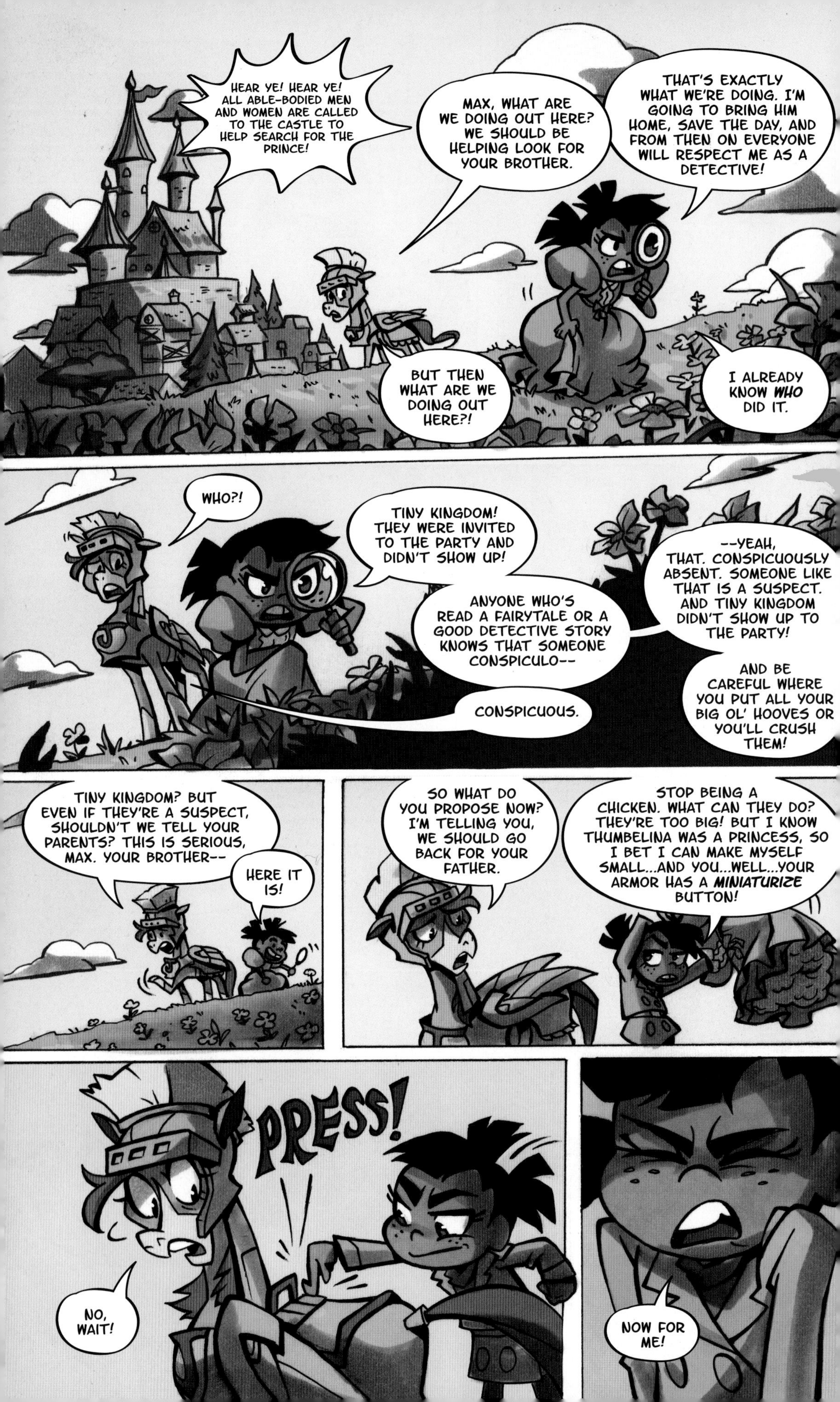
HEAR YE! HEAR YE! ALL ABLE-BODIED MEN AND WOMEN ARE CALLED TO THE CASTLE TO HELP SEARCH FOR THE PRINCE!
MAX, WHAT ARE WE DOING OUT HERE? WE SHOULD BE HELPING LOOK FOR YOUR BROTHER.
THAT'S EXACTLY WHAT WE'RE DOING. I'M GOING TO BRING HIM HOME, SAVE THE DAY, AND FROM THEN ON EVERYONE WILL RESPECT ME AS A DETECTIVE!
BUT THEN WHAT ARE WE DOING OUT HERE?!
I ALREADY KNOW *WHO* DID IT.
WHO?!
TINY KINGDOM! THEY WERE INVITED TO THE PARTY AND DIDN'T SHOW UP!
ANYONE WHO'S READ A FAIRYTALE OR A GOOD DETECTIVE STORY KNOWS THAT SOMEONE CONSPICULO--
CONSPICUOUS.
--YEAH, THAT. CONSPICUOUSLY ABSENT. SOMEONE LIKE THAT IS A SUSPECT. AND TINY KINGDOM DIDN'T SHOW UP TO THE PARTY!
AND BE CAREFUL WHERE YOU PUT ALL YOUR BIG OL' HOOVES OR YOU'LL CRUSH THEM!
TINY KINGDOM? BUT EVEN IF THEY'RE A SUSPECT, SHOULDN'T WE TELL YOUR PARENTS? THIS IS SERIOUS, MAX. YOUR BROTHER--
HERE IT IS!
SO WHAT DO YOU PROPOSE NOW? I'M TELLING YOU, WE SHOULD GO BACK FOR YOUR FATHER.
STOP BEING A CHICKEN. WHAT CAN THEY DO? THEY'RE TOO BIG! BUT I KNOW THUMBELINA WAS A PRINCESS, SO I BET I CAN MAKE MYSELF SMALL...AND YOU...WELL...YOUR ARMOR HAS A *MINIATURIZE* BUTTON!
PRESS!
NO, WAIT!
NOW FOR ME!

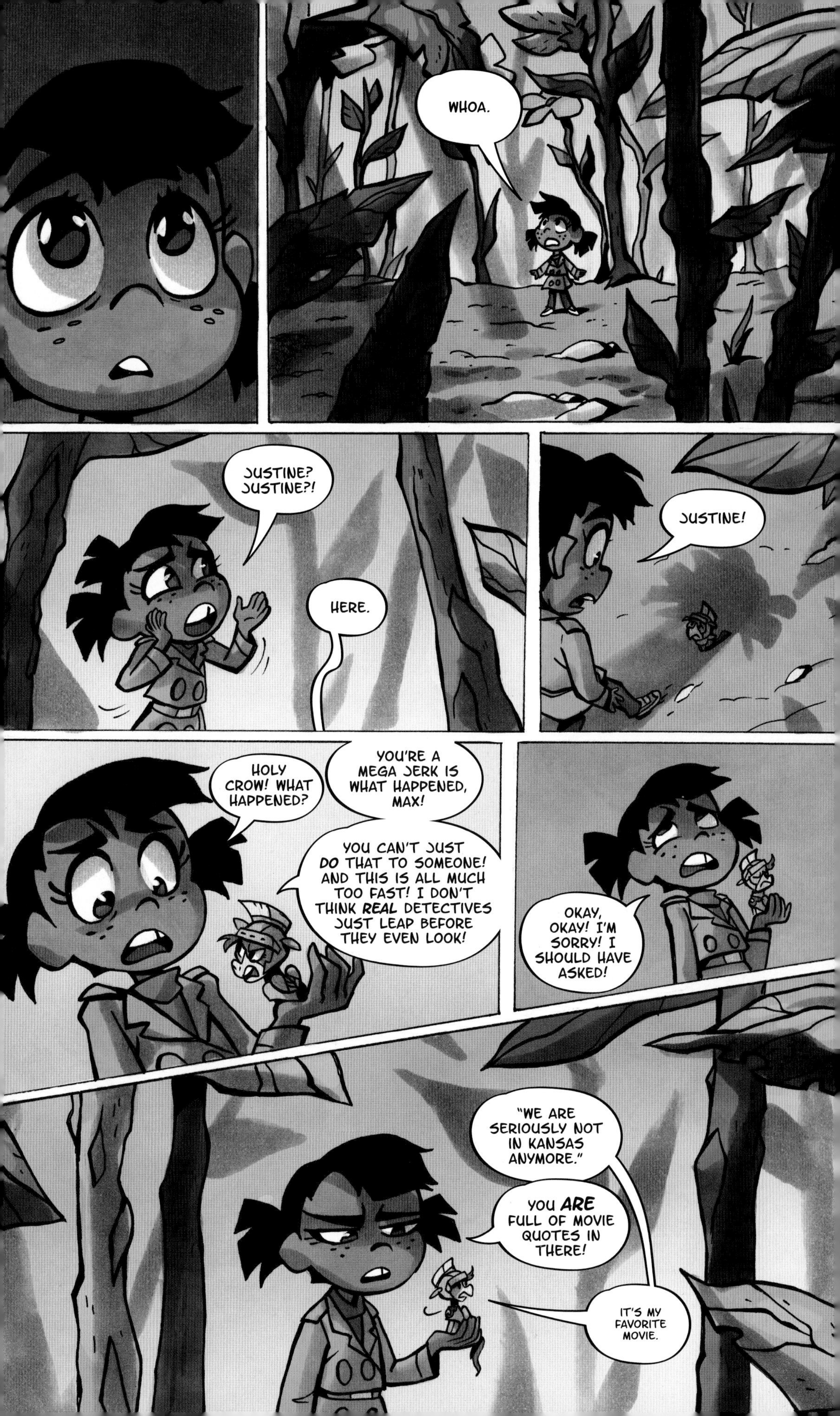
WHOA.
JUSTINE? JUSTINE?!
HERE.
JUSTINE!
HOLY CROW! WHAT HAPPENED?
YOU'RE A MEGA JERK IS WHAT HAPPENED, MAX!
YOU CAN'T JUST DO THAT TO SOMEONE! AND THIS IS ALL MUCH TOO FAST! I DON'T THINK REAL DETECTIVES JUST LEAP BEFORE THEY EVEN LOOK!
OKAY, OKAY! I'M SORRY! I SHOULD HAVE ASKED!
"WE ARE SERIOUSLY NOT IN KANSAS ANYMORE."
YOU ARE FULL OF MOVIE QUOTES IN THERE!
IT'S MY FAVORITE MOVIE.

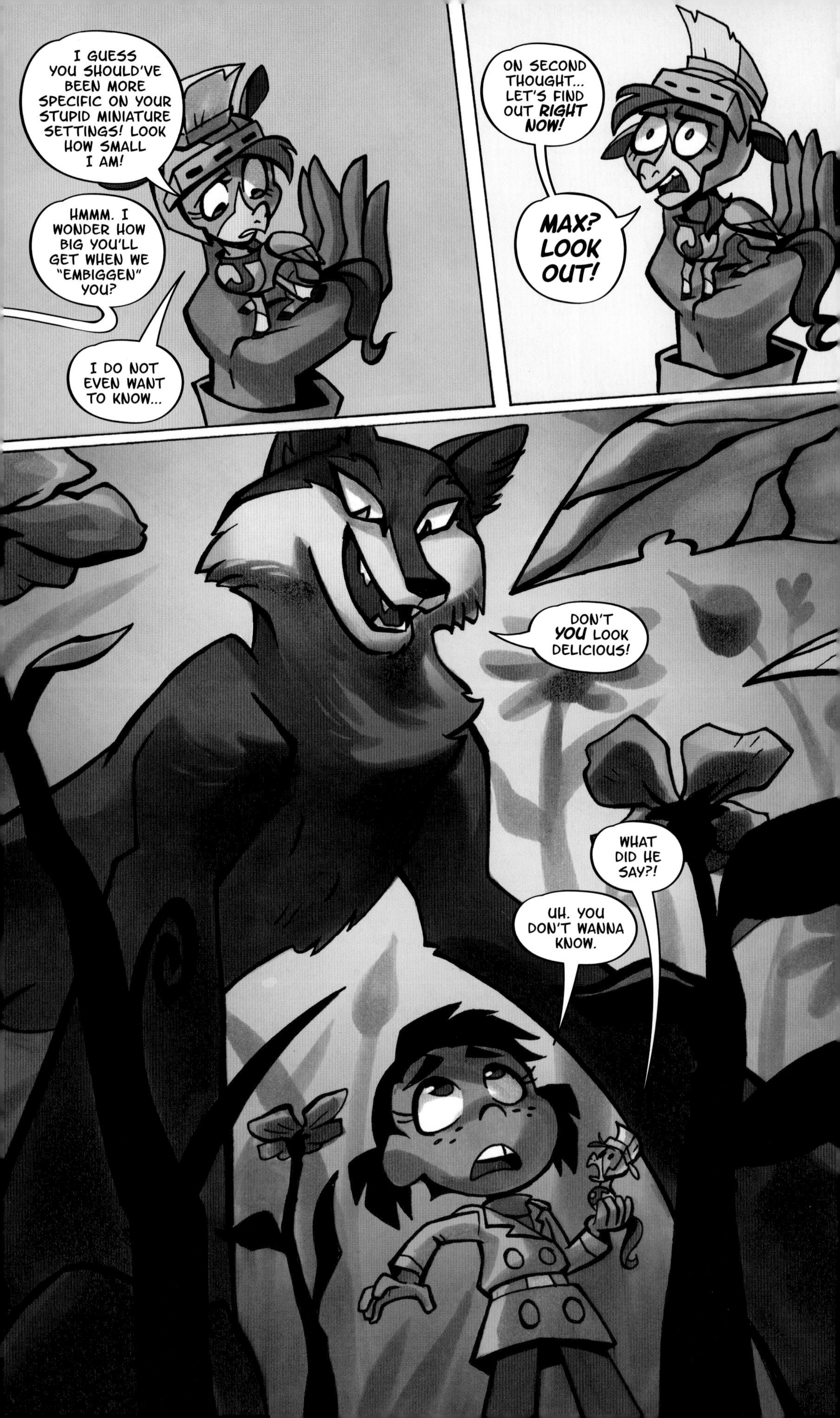
I GUESS YOU SHOULD'VE BEEN MORE SPECIFIC ON YOUR STUPID MINIATURE SETTINGS! LOOK HOW SMALL I AM!
HMMM. I WONDER HOW BIG YOU'LL GET WHEN WE "EMBIGGEN" YOU?
I DO NOT EVEN WANT TO KNOW...
ON SECOND THOUGHT... LET'S FIND OUT RIGHT NOW!
MAX? LOOK OUT!
DON'T YOU LOOK DELICIOUS!
WHAT DID HE SAY?!
UH. YOU DON'T WANNA KNOW.

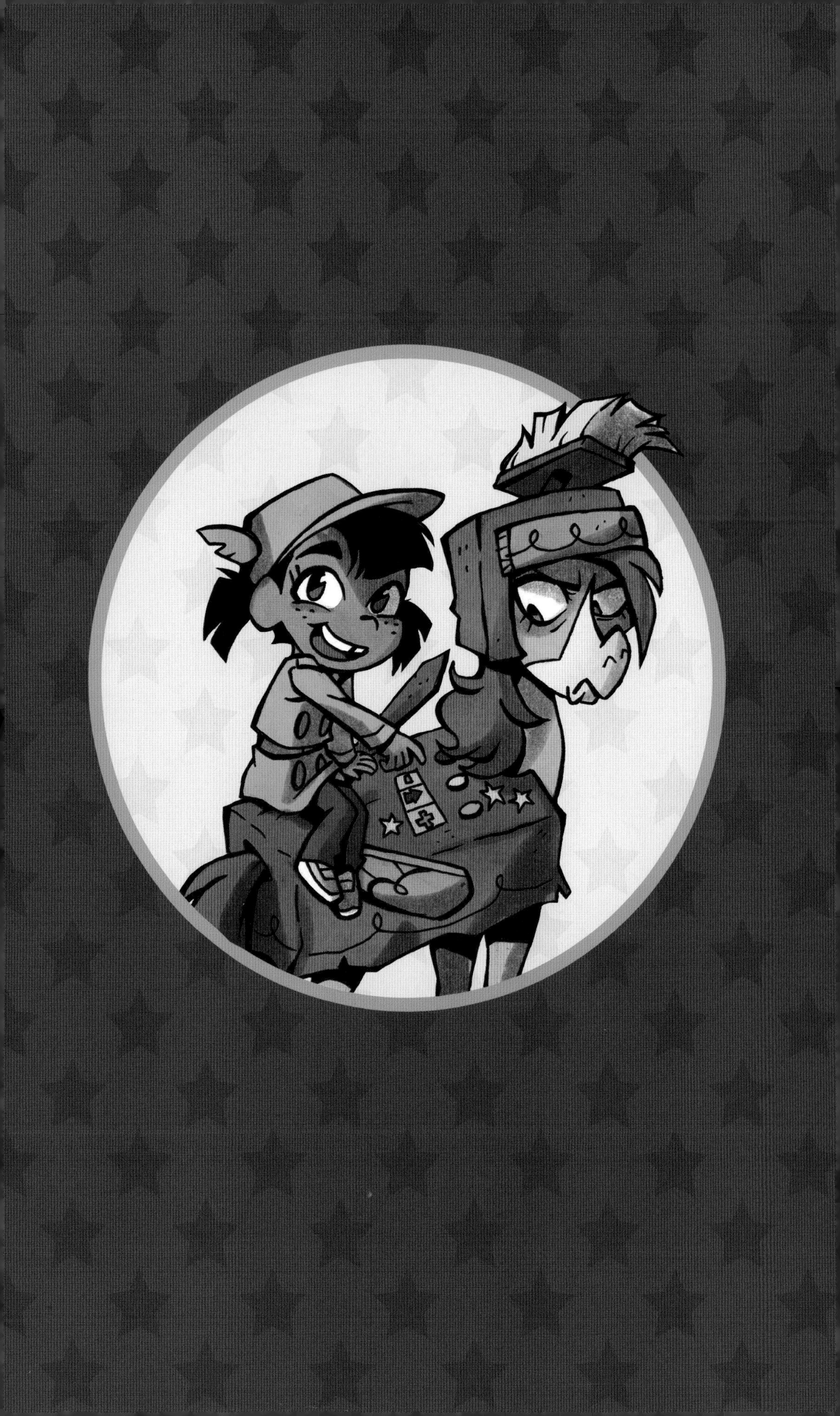

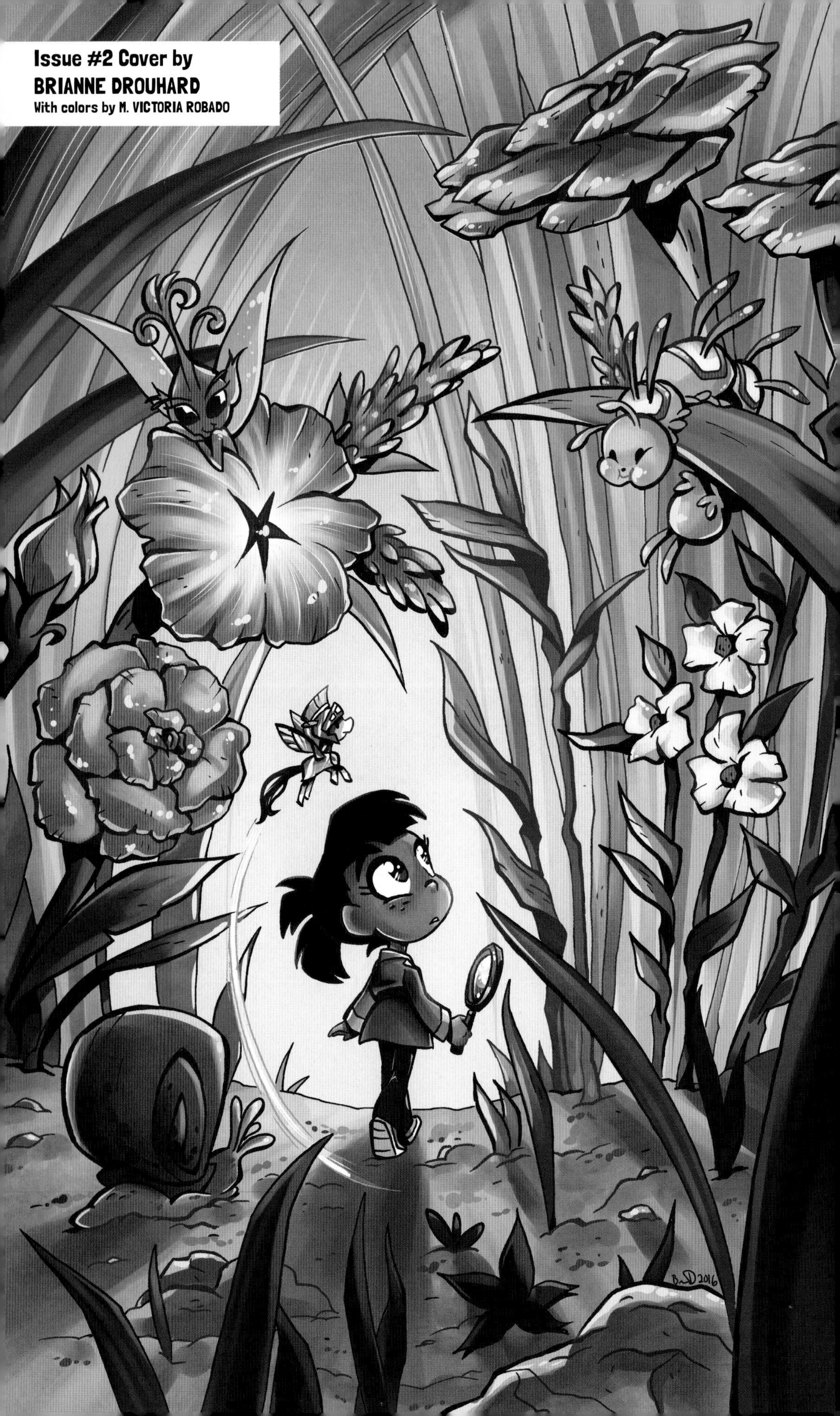

Issue #2 Cover by
BRIANNE DROUHARD
With colors by M. VICTORIA ROBADO

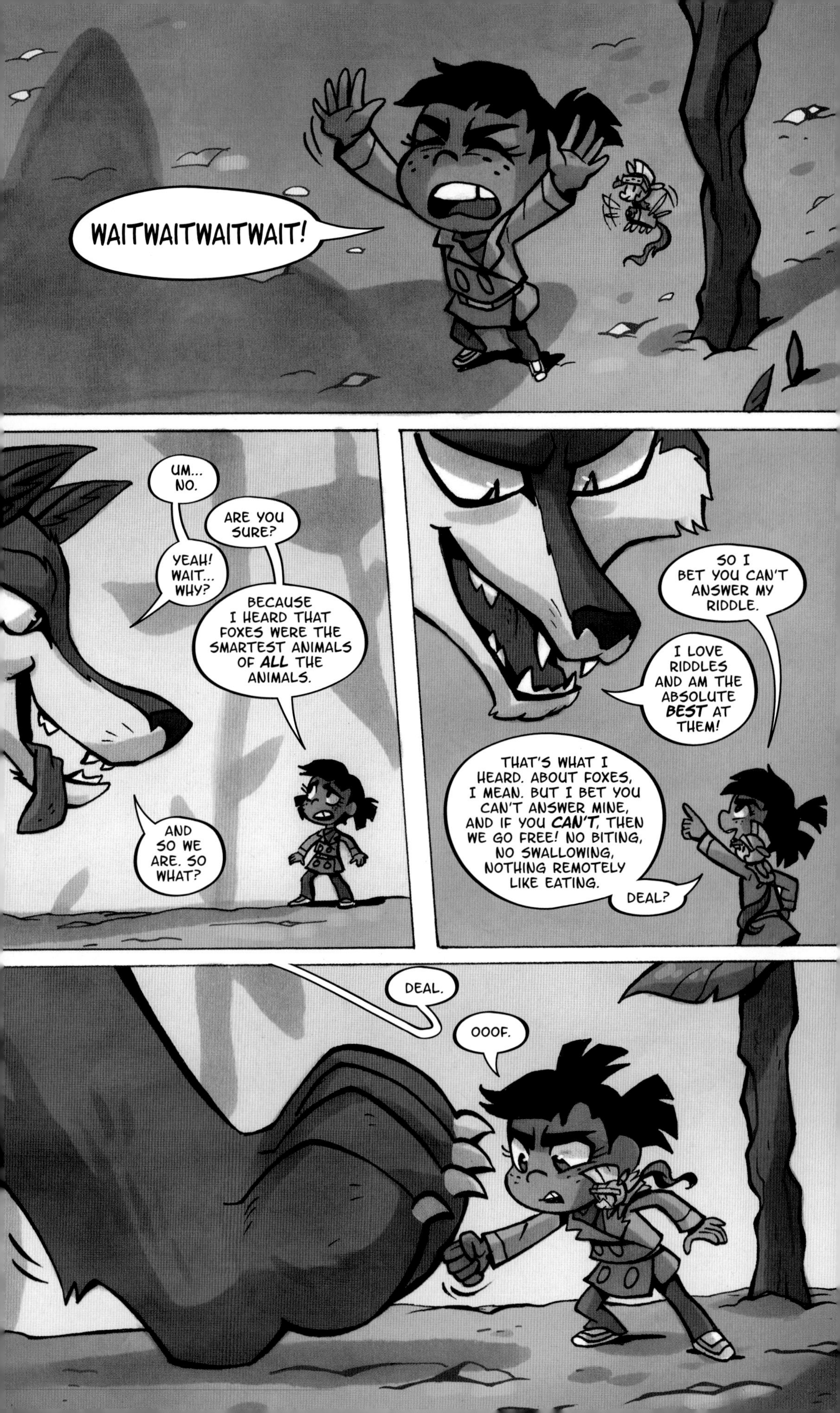
WAITWAITWAITWAIT!
UM... NO.
ARE YOU SURE?
YEAH! WAIT... WHY?
BECAUSE I HEARD THAT FOXES WERE THE SMARTEST ANIMALS OF ALL THE ANIMALS.
AND SO WE ARE. SO WHAT?
SO I BET YOU CAN'T ANSWER MY RIDDLE.
I LOVE RIDDLES AND AM THE ABSOLUTE BEST AT THEM!
THAT'S WHAT I HEARD. ABOUT FOXES, I MEAN. BUT I BET YOU CAN'T ANSWER MINE, AND IF YOU CAN'T, THEN WE GO FREE! NO BITING, NO SWALLOWING, NOTHING REMOTELY LIKE EATING.
DEAL?
DEAL.
OOOF.

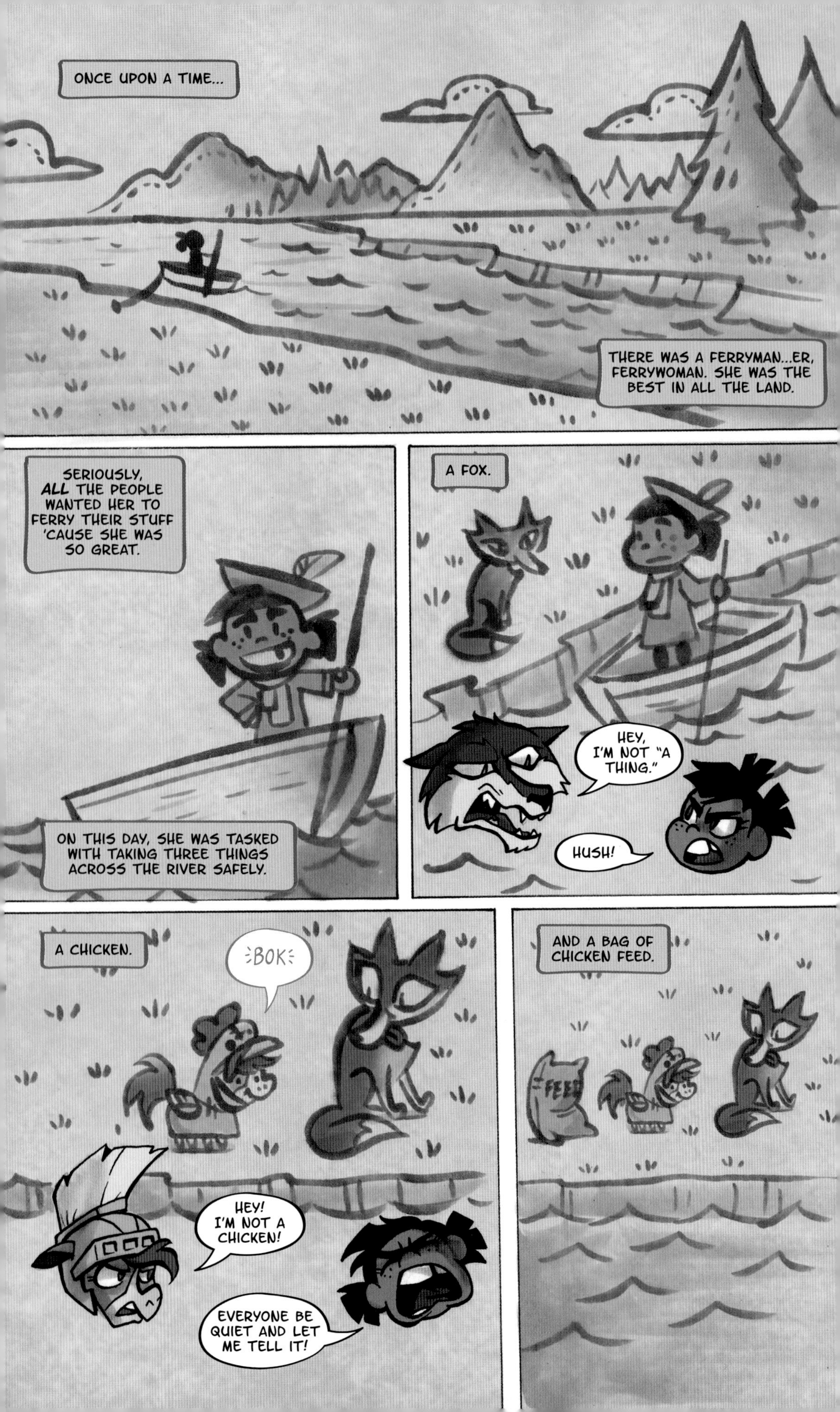
ONCE UPON A TIME...
THERE WAS A FERRYMAN...ER, FERRYWOMAN. SHE WAS THE BEST IN ALL THE LAND.
SERIOUSLY, ALL THE PEOPLE WANTED HER TO FERRY THEIR STUFF 'CAUSE SHE WAS SO GREAT.
ON THIS DAY, SHE WAS TASKED WITH TAKING THREE THINGS ACROSS THE RIVER SAFELY.
A FOX.
HEY, I'M NOT "A THING."
HUSH!
A CHICKEN.
BOK
HEY! I'M NOT A CHICKEN!
EVERYONE BE QUIET AND LET ME TELL IT!
AND A BAG OF CHICKEN FEED.
FEED

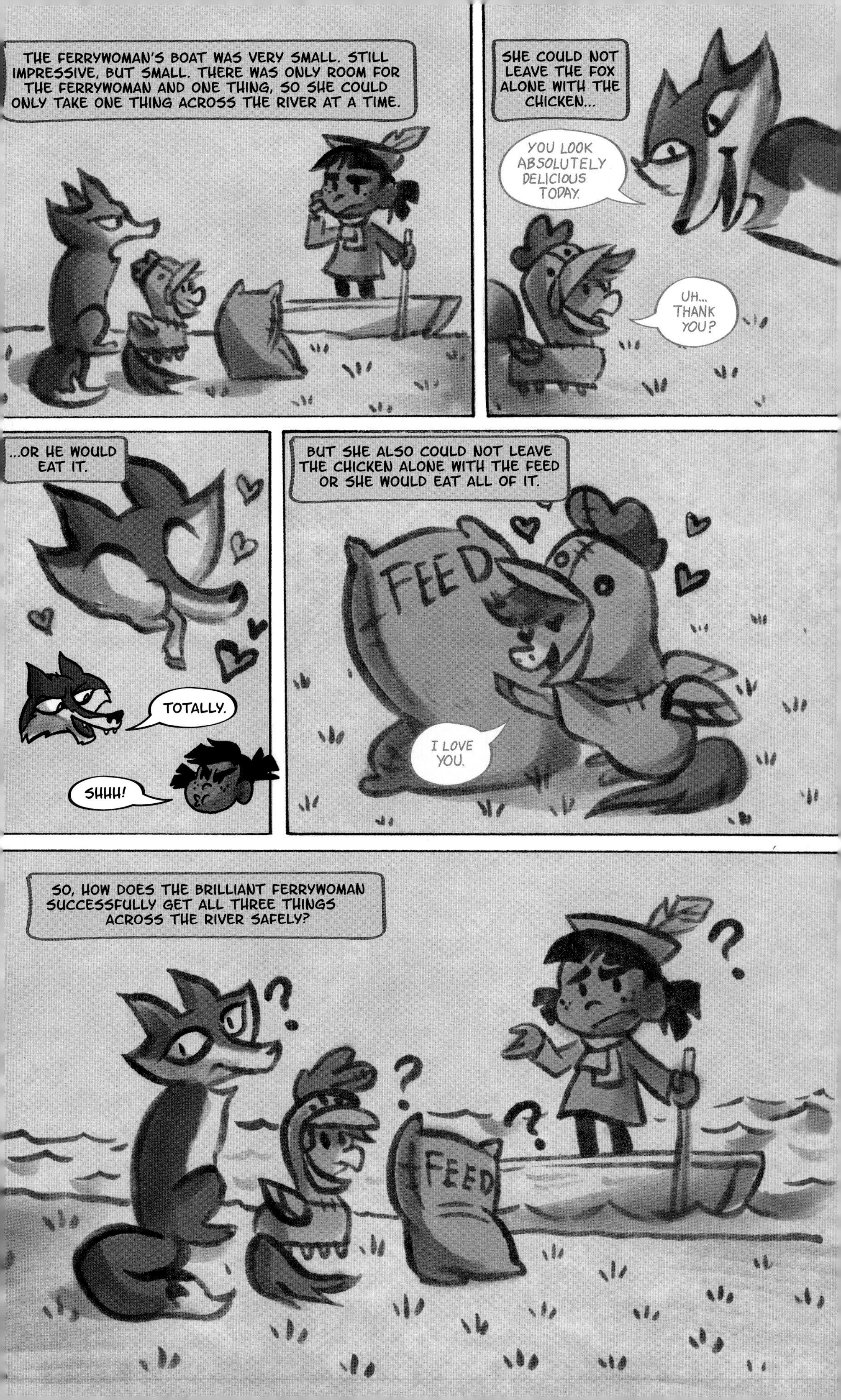
THE FERRYWOMAN'S BOAT WAS VERY SMALL. STILL IMPRESSIVE, BUT SMALL. THERE WAS ONLY ROOM FOR THE FERRYWOMAN AND ONE THING, SO SHE COULD ONLY TAKE ONE THING ACROSS THE RIVER AT A TIME.
SHE COULD NOT LEAVE THE FOX ALONE WITH THE CHICKEN...
YOU LOOK ABSOLUTELY DELICIOUS TODAY.
UH... THANK YOU?
...OR HE WOULD EAT IT.
TOTALLY.
SHHH!
BUT SHE ALSO COULD NOT LEAVE THE CHICKEN ALONE WITH THE FEED OR SHE WOULD EAT ALL OF IT.
FEED
I LOVE YOU.
SO, HOW DOES THE BRILLIANT FERRYWOMAN SUCCESSFULLY GET ALL THREE THINGS ACROSS THE RIVER SAFELY?
FEED

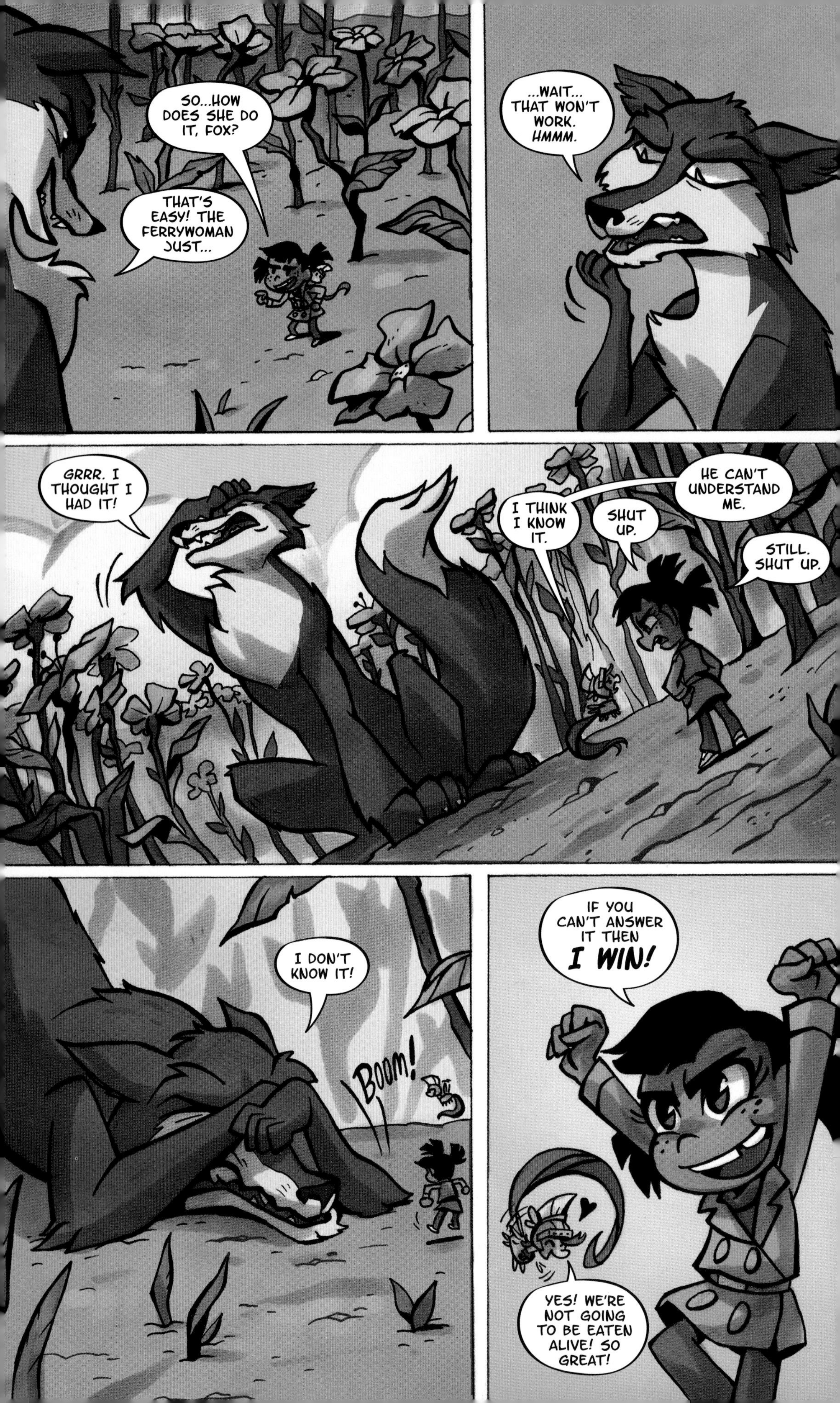
SO...HOW DOES SHE DO IT, FOX?
THAT'S EASY! THE FERRYWOMAN JUST...
...WAIT... THAT WON'T WORK. HMMM.
GRRR. I THOUGHT I HAD IT!
I THINK I KNOW IT.
SHUT UP.
HE CAN'T UNDERSTAND ME.
STILL. SHUT UP.
I DON'T KNOW IT!
BOOM!
IF YOU CAN'T ANSWER IT THEN I WIN!
YES! WE'RE NOT GOING TO BE EATEN ALIVE! SO GREAT!

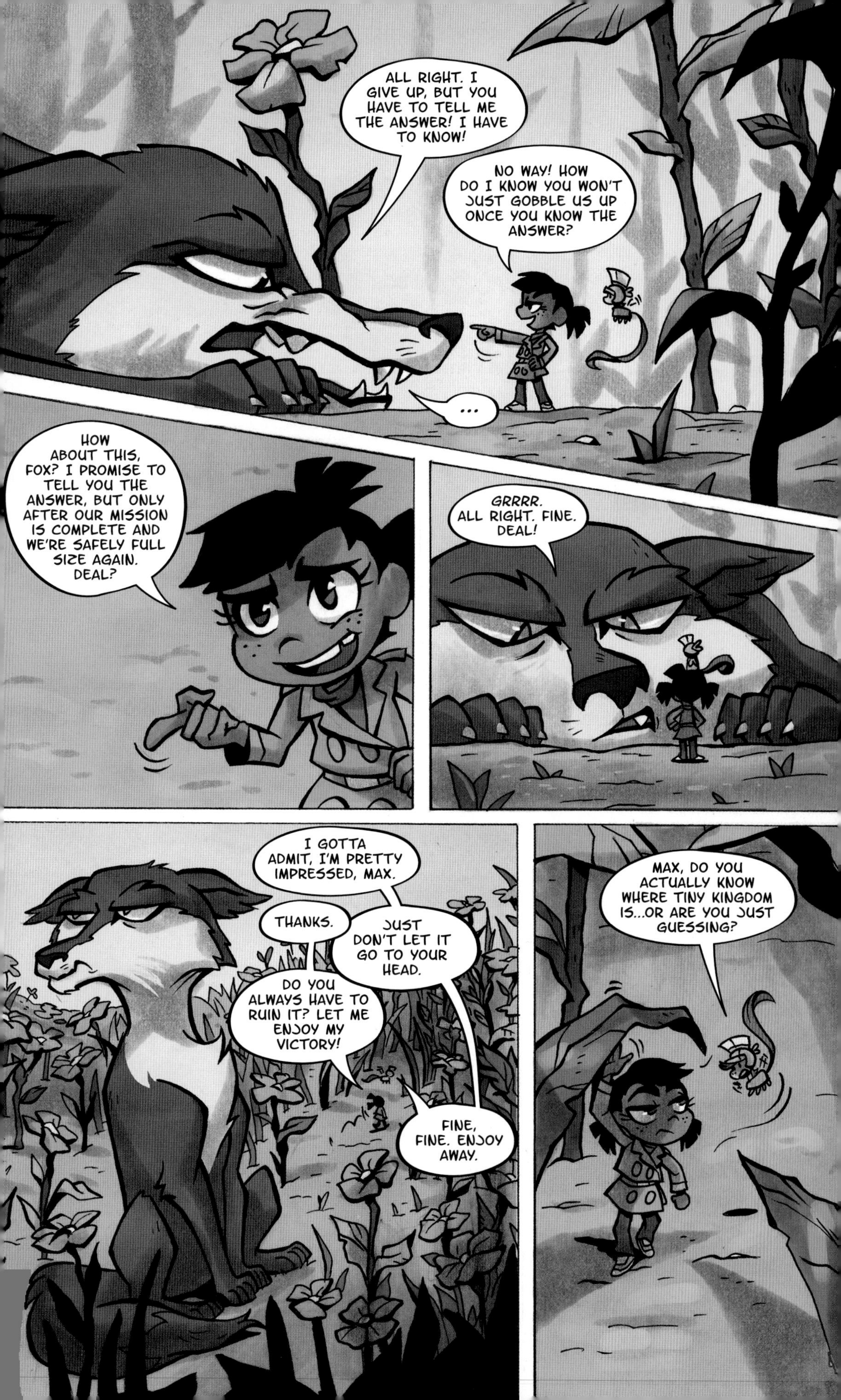

ALL RIGHT. I GIVE UP, BUT YOU HAVE TO TELL ME THE ANSWER! I HAVE TO KNOW!
NO WAY! HOW DO I KNOW YOU WON'T JUST GOBBLE US UP ONCE YOU KNOW THE ANSWER?
...
HOW ABOUT THIS, FOX? I PROMISE TO TELL YOU THE ANSWER, BUT ONLY AFTER OUR MISSION IS COMPLETE AND WE'RE SAFELY FULL SIZE AGAIN. DEAL?
GRRRR. ALL RIGHT. FINE. DEAL!
I GOTTA ADMIT, I'M PRETTY IMPRESSED, MAX.
THANKS.
JUST DON'T LET IT GO TO YOUR HEAD.
DO YOU ALWAYS HAVE TO RUIN IT? LET ME ENJOY MY VICTORY!
FINE, FINE. ENJOY AWAY.
MAX, DO YOU ACTUALLY KNOW WHERE TINY KINGDOM IS...OR ARE YOU JUST GUESSING?

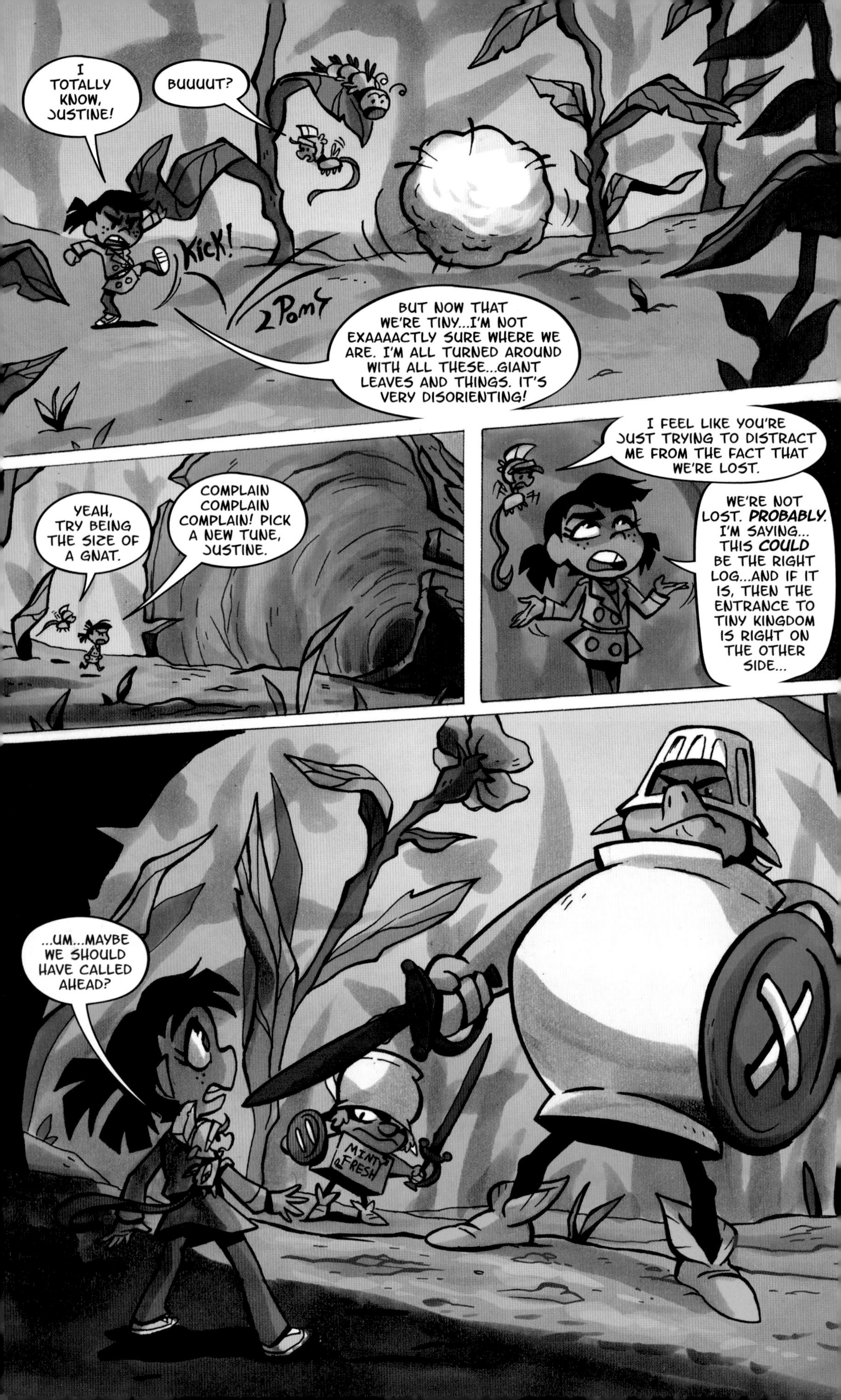
I TOTALLY KNOW, JUSTINE!
BUUUUT?
KICK!
BUT NOW THAT WE'RE TINY...I'M NOT EXAAAACTLY SURE WHERE WE ARE. I'M ALL TURNED AROUND WITH ALL THESE...GIANT LEAVES AND THINGS. IT'S VERY DISORIENTING!
YEAH, TRY BEING THE SIZE OF A GNAT.
COMPLAIN COMPLAIN COMPLAIN! PICK A NEW TUNE, JUSTINE.
I FEEL LIKE YOU'RE JUST TRYING TO DISTRACT ME FROM THE FACT THAT WE'RE LOST.
WE'RE NOT LOST. **PROBABLY.** I'M SAYING... THIS **COULD** BE THE RIGHT LOG...AND IF IT IS, THEN THE ENTRANCE TO TINY KINGDOM IS RIGHT ON THE OTHER SIDE...
...UM...MAYBE WE SHOULD HAVE CALLED AHEAD?
MINTY FRESH

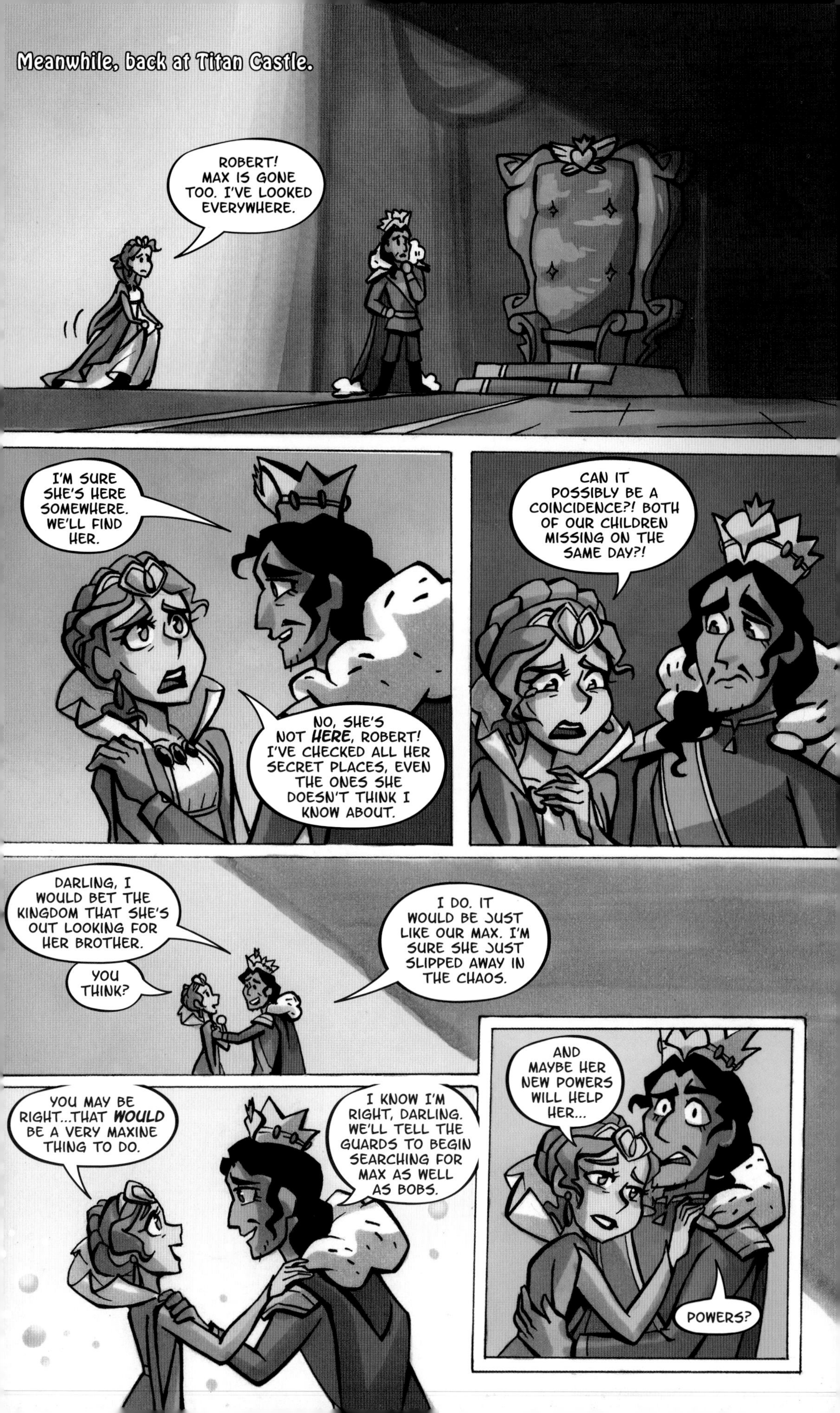
Meanwhile, back at Titan Castle.
ROBERT! MAX IS GONE TOO. I'VE LOOKED EVERYWHERE.
I'M SURE SHE'S HERE SOMEWHERE. WE'LL FIND HER.
NO, SHE'S NOT HERE, ROBERT! I'VE CHECKED ALL HER SECRET PLACES, EVEN THE ONES SHE DOESN'T THINK I KNOW ABOUT.
CAN IT POSSIBLY BE A COINCIDENCE?! BOTH OF OUR CHILDREN MISSING ON THE SAME DAY?!
DARLING, I WOULD BET THE KINGDOM THAT SHE'S OUT LOOKING FOR HER BROTHER.
YOU THINK?
I DO. IT WOULD BE JUST LIKE OUR MAX. I'M SURE SHE JUST SLIPPED AWAY IN THE CHAOS.
YOU MAY BE RIGHT...THAT WOULD BE A VERY MAXINE THING TO DO.
I KNOW I'M RIGHT, DARLING. WE'LL TELL THE GUARDS TO BEGIN SEARCHING FOR MAX AS WELL AS BOBS.
AND MAYBE HER NEW POWERS WILL HELP HER...
POWERS?

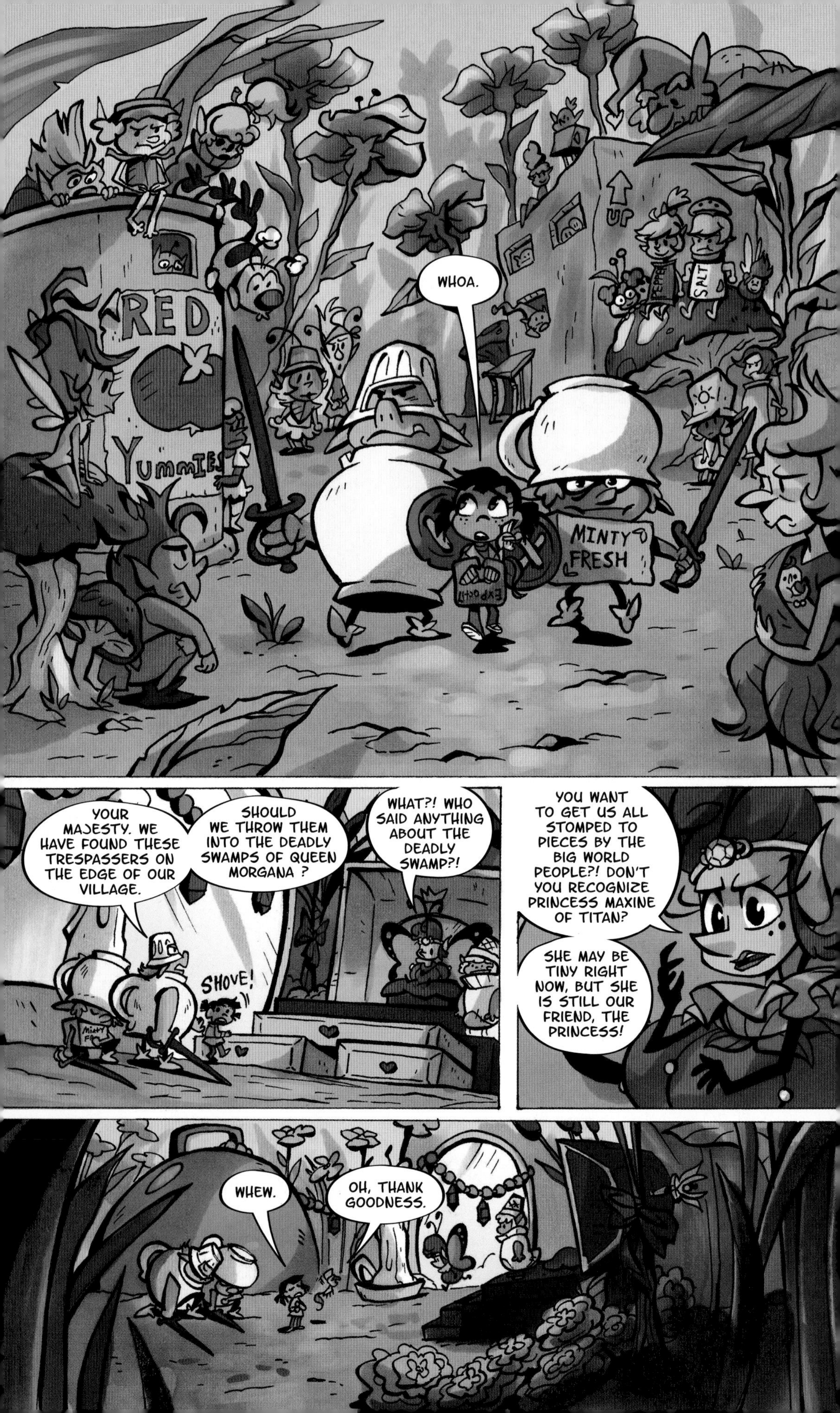
RED
Yummies
UP
PEPPER
SALT
WHOA.
MINTY FRESH
EMPORIUM
YOUR MAJESTY. WE HAVE FOUND THESE TRESPASSERS ON THE EDGE OF OUR VILLAGE.
SHOULD WE THROW THEM INTO THE DEADLY SWAMPS OF QUEEN MORGANA ?
WHAT?! WHO SAID ANYTHING ABOUT THE DEADLY SWAMP?!
SHOVE!
YOU WANT TO GET US ALL STOMPED TO PIECES BY THE BIG WORLD PEOPLE?! DON'T YOU RECOGNIZE PRINCESS MAXINE OF TITAN?
SHE MAY BE TINY RIGHT NOW, BUT SHE IS STILL OUR FRIEND, THE PRINCESS!
WHEW.
OH, THANK GOODNESS.

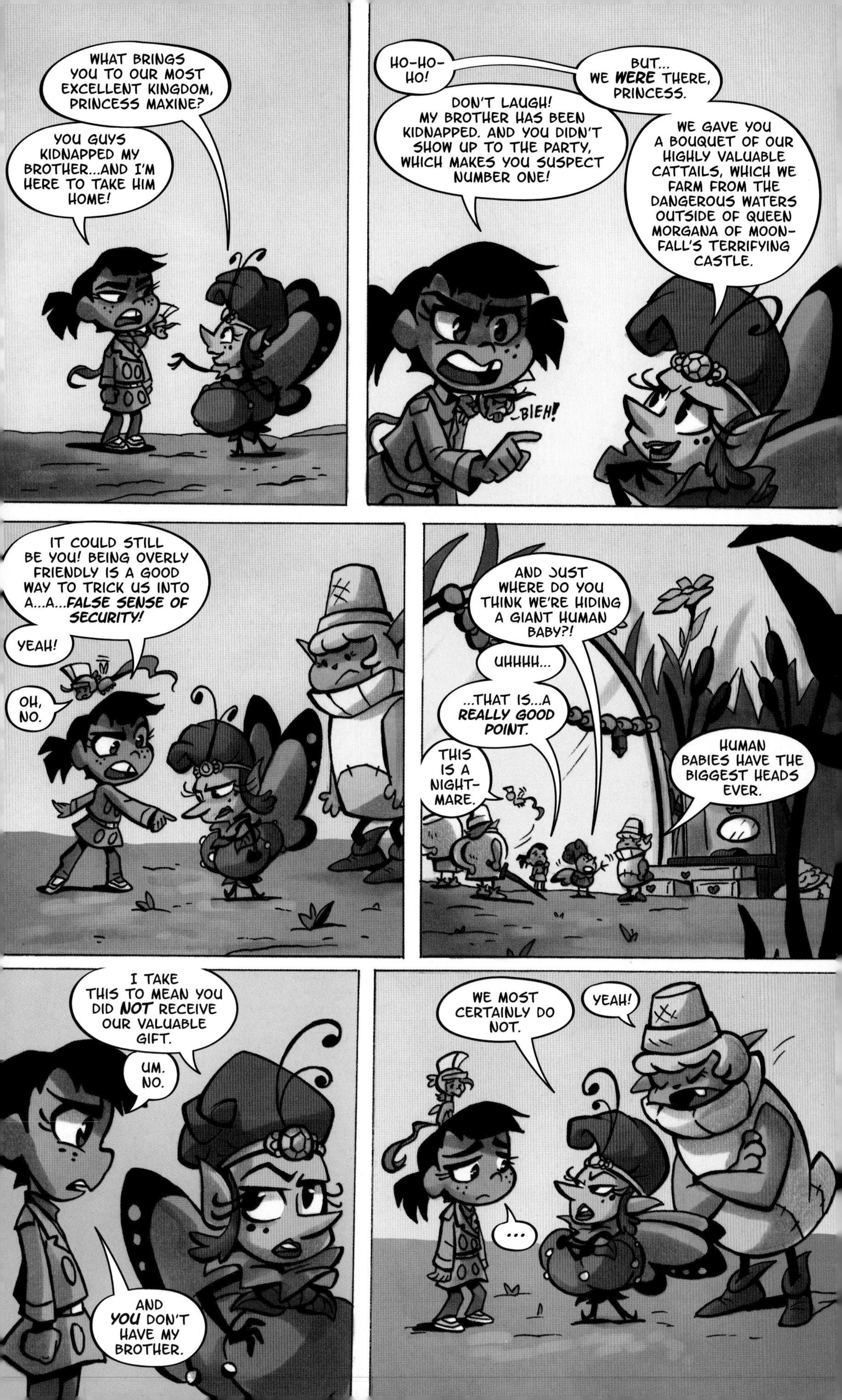
WHAT BRINGS YOU TO OUR MOST EXCELLENT KINGDOM, PRINCESS MAXINE?
YOU GUYS KIDNAPPED MY BROTHER...AND I'M HERE TO TAKE HIM HOME!
HO-HO-HO!
BUT... WE WERE THERE, PRINCESS.
DON'T LAUGH! MY BROTHER HAS BEEN KIDNAPPED. AND YOU DIDN'T SHOW UP TO THE PARTY, WHICH MAKES YOU SUSPECT NUMBER ONE!
WE GAVE YOU A BOUQUET OF OUR HIGHLY VALUABLE CATTAILS, WHICH WE FARM FROM THE DANGEROUS WATERS OUTSIDE OF QUEEN MORGANA OF MOON-FALL'S TERRIFYING CASTLE.
BIEH!
IT COULD STILL BE YOU! BEING OVERLY FRIENDLY IS A GOOD WAY TO TRICK US INTO A...A...FALSE SENSE OF SECURITY!
YEAH!
OH, NO.
AND JUST WHERE DO YOU THINK WE'RE HIDING A GIANT HUMAN BABY?!
UHHHH...
...THAT IS...A REALLY GOOD POINT.
THIS IS A NIGHT-MARE.
HUMAN BABIES HAVE THE BIGGEST HEADS EVER.
I TAKE THIS TO MEAN YOU DID NOT RECEIVE OUR VALUABLE GIFT.
UM. NO.
AND YOU DON'T HAVE MY BROTHER.
WE MOST CERTAINLY DO NOT.
YEAH!
...

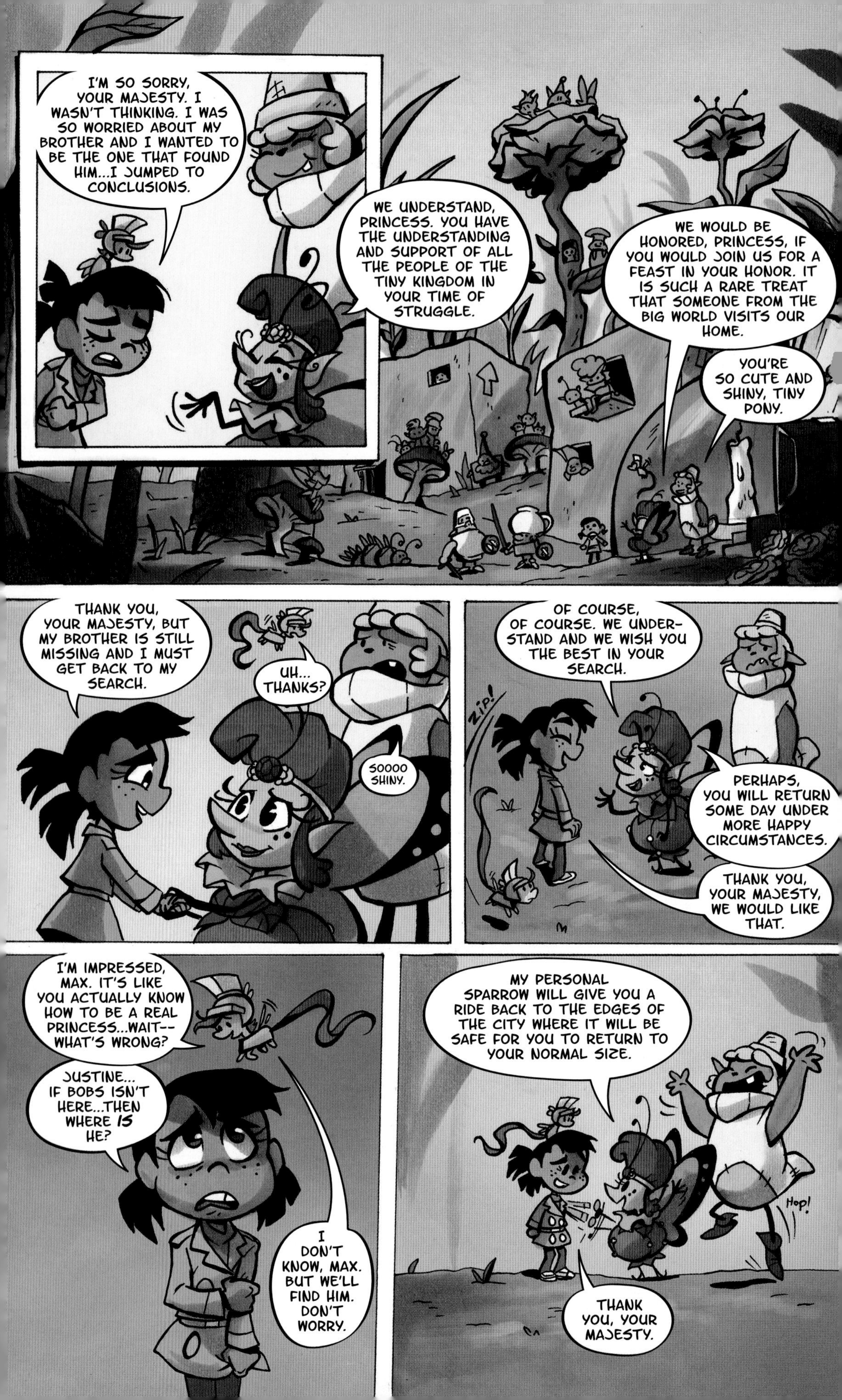
I'M SO SORRY, YOUR MAJESTY. I WASN'T THINKING. I WAS SO WORRIED ABOUT MY BROTHER AND I WANTED TO BE THE ONE THAT FOUND HIM...I JUMPED TO CONCLUSIONS.
WE UNDERSTAND, PRINCESS. YOU HAVE THE UNDERSTANDING AND SUPPORT OF ALL THE PEOPLE OF THE TINY KINGDOM IN YOUR TIME OF STRUGGLE.
WE WOULD BE HONORED, PRINCESS, IF YOU WOULD JOIN US FOR A FEAST IN YOUR HONOR. IT IS SUCH A RARE TREAT THAT SOMEONE FROM THE BIG WORLD VISITS OUR HOME.
YOU'RE SO CUTE AND SHINY, TINY PONY.
THANK YOU, YOUR MAJESTY, BUT MY BROTHER IS STILL MISSING AND I MUST GET BACK TO MY SEARCH.
UH... THANKS?
SOOOO SHINY.
OF COURSE, OF COURSE. WE UNDERSTAND AND WE WISH YOU THE BEST IN YOUR SEARCH.
ZIP!
PERHAPS, YOU WILL RETURN SOME DAY UNDER MORE HAPPY CIRCUMSTANCES.
THANK YOU, YOUR MAJESTY, WE WOULD LIKE THAT.
I'M IMPRESSED, MAX. IT'S LIKE YOU ACTUALLY KNOW HOW TO BE A REAL PRINCESS...WAIT--WHAT'S WRONG?
JUSTINE... IF BOBS ISN'T HERE...THEN WHERE *IS* HE?
I DON'T KNOW, MAX. BUT WE'LL FIND HIM. DON'T WORRY.
MY PERSONAL SPARROW WILL GIVE YOU A RIDE BACK TO THE EDGES OF THE CITY WHERE IT WILL BE SAFE FOR YOU TO RETURN TO YOUR NORMAL SIZE.
Hop!
THANK YOU, YOUR MAJESTY.

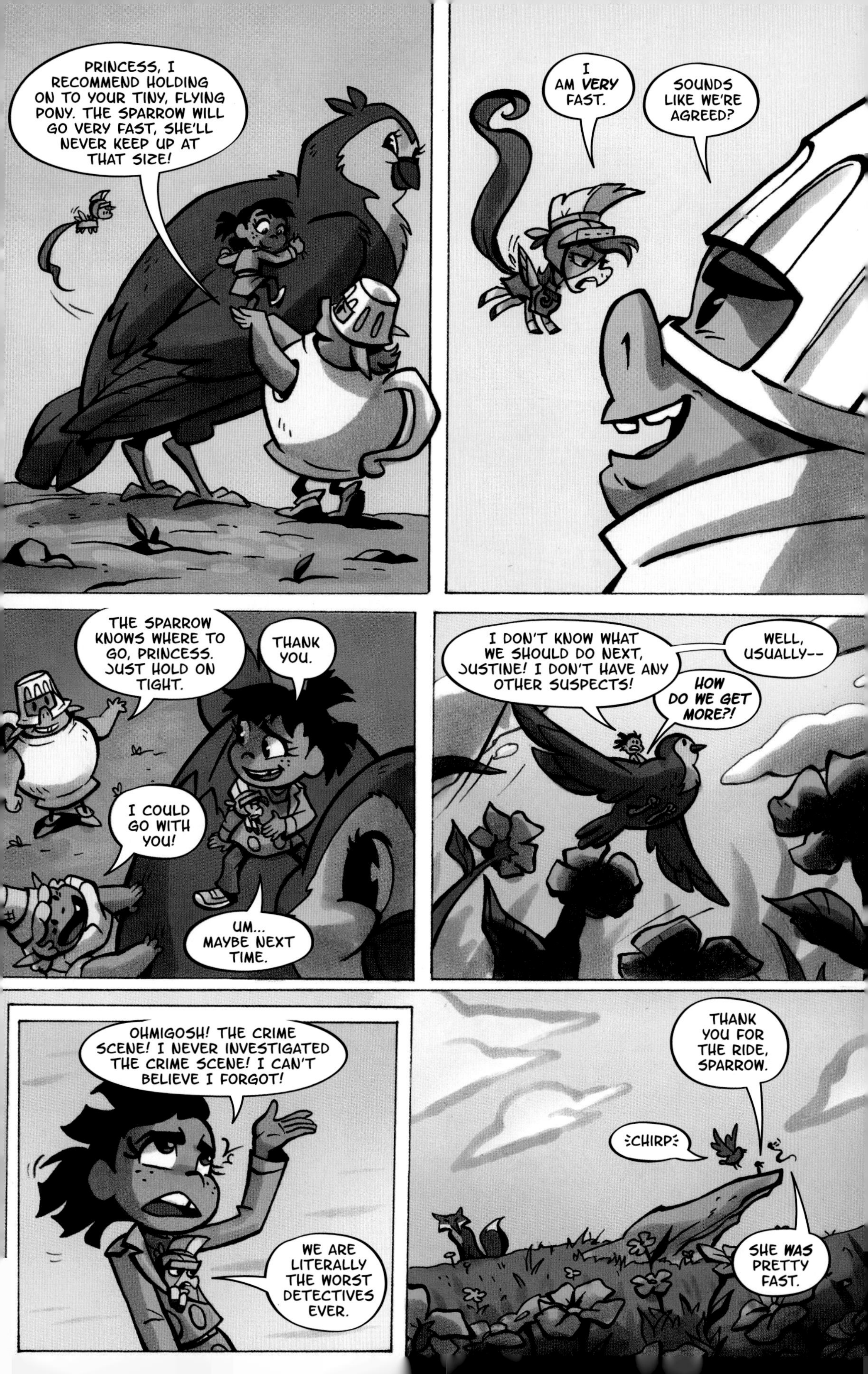
PRINCESS, I RECOMMEND HOLDING ON TO YOUR TINY, FLYING PONY. THE SPARROW WILL GO VERY FAST, SHE'LL NEVER KEEP UP AT THAT SIZE!
I AM **VERY** FAST.
SOUNDS LIKE WE'RE AGREED?
THE SPARROW KNOWS WHERE TO GO, PRINCESS. JUST HOLD ON TIGHT.
THANK YOU.
I COULD GO WITH YOU!
UM... MAYBE NEXT TIME.
I DON'T KNOW WHAT WE SHOULD DO NEXT, JUSTINE! I DON'T HAVE ANY OTHER SUSPECTS!
WELL, USUALLY--
HOW DO WE GET MORE?!
OHMIGOSH! THE CRIME SCENE! I NEVER INVESTIGATED THE CRIME SCENE! I CAN'T BELIEVE I FORGOT!
WE ARE LITERALLY THE WORST DETECTIVES EVER.
THANK YOU FOR THE RIDE, SPARROW.
CHIRP
SHE **WAS** PRETTY FAST.

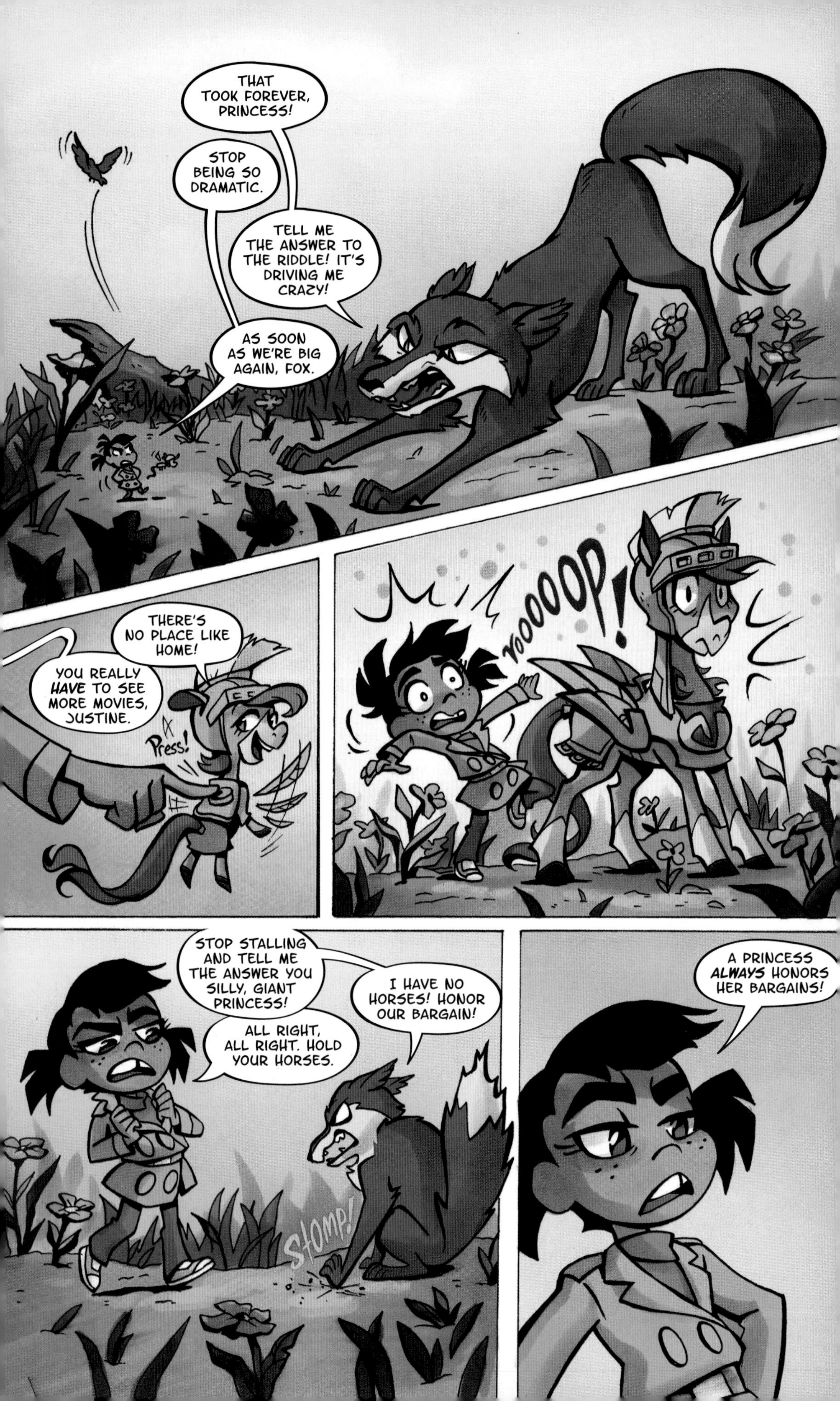
THAT TOOK FOREVER, PRINCESS!
STOP BEING SO DRAMATIC.
TELL ME THE ANSWER TO THE RIDDLE! IT'S DRIVING ME CRAZY!
AS SOON AS WE'RE BIG AGAIN, FOX.
THERE'S NO PLACE LIKE HOME!
YOU REALLY HAVE TO SEE MORE MOVIES, JUSTINE.
Press!
WOOOOOP!
STOP STALLING AND TELL ME THE ANSWER YOU SILLY, GIANT PRINCESS!
ALL RIGHT, ALL RIGHT. HOLD YOUR HORSES.
I HAVE NO HORSES! HONOR OUR BARGAIN!
STOMP!
A PRINCESS ALWAYS HONORS HER BARGAINS!

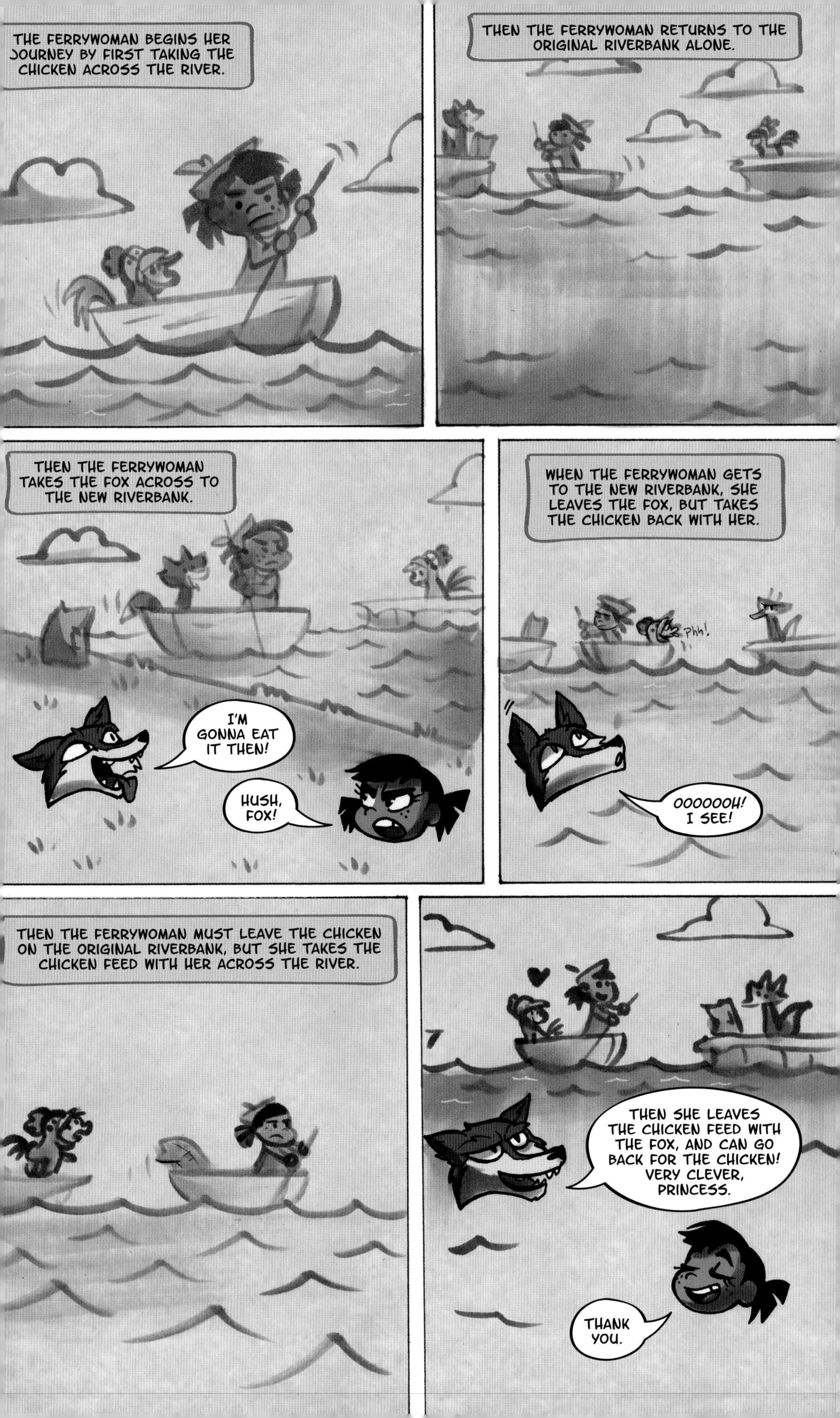
THE FERRYWOMAN BEGINS HER JOURNEY BY FIRST TAKING THE CHICKEN ACROSS THE RIVER.
THEN THE FERRYWOMAN RETURNS TO THE ORIGINAL RIVERBANK ALONE.
THEN THE FERRYWOMAN TAKES THE FOX ACROSS TO THE NEW RIVERBANK.
I'M GONNA EAT IT THEN!
HUSH, FOX!
WHEN THE FERRYWOMAN GETS TO THE NEW RIVERBANK, SHE LEAVES THE FOX, BUT TAKES THE CHICKEN BACK WITH HER.
Phh!
OOOOOOH! I SEE!
THEN THE FERRYWOMAN MUST LEAVE THE CHICKEN ON THE ORIGINAL RIVERBANK, BUT SHE TAKES THE CHICKEN FEED WITH HER ACROSS THE RIVER.
THEN SHE LEAVES THE CHICKEN FEED WITH THE FOX, AND CAN GO BACK FOR THE CHICKEN! VERY CLEVER, PRINCESS.
THANK YOU.

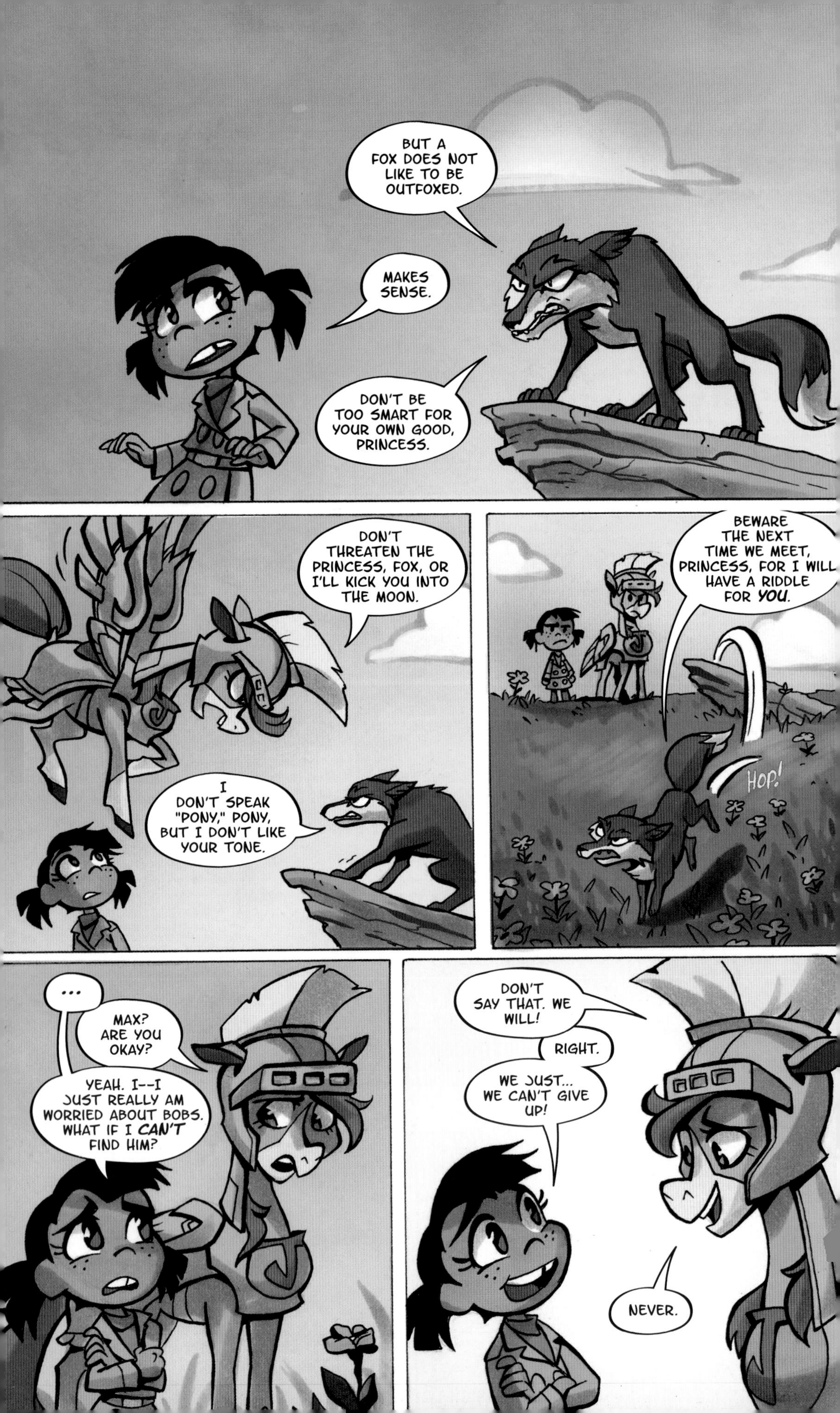
BUT A FOX DOES NOT LIKE TO BE OUTFOXED.
MAKES SENSE.
DON'T BE TOO SMART FOR YOUR OWN GOOD, PRINCESS.
DON'T THREATEN THE PRINCESS, FOX, OR I'LL KICK YOU INTO THE MOON.
I DON'T SPEAK "PONY," PONY, BUT I DON'T LIKE YOUR TONE.
BEWARE THE NEXT TIME WE MEET, PRINCESS, FOR I WILL HAVE A RIDDLE FOR *YOU*.
HOP!
...
MAX? ARE YOU OKAY?
YEAH. I--I JUST REALLY AM WORRIED ABOUT BOBS. WHAT IF I *CAN'T* FIND HIM?
DON'T SAY THAT. WE WILL!
RIGHT.
WE JUST... WE CAN'T GIVE UP!
NEVER.

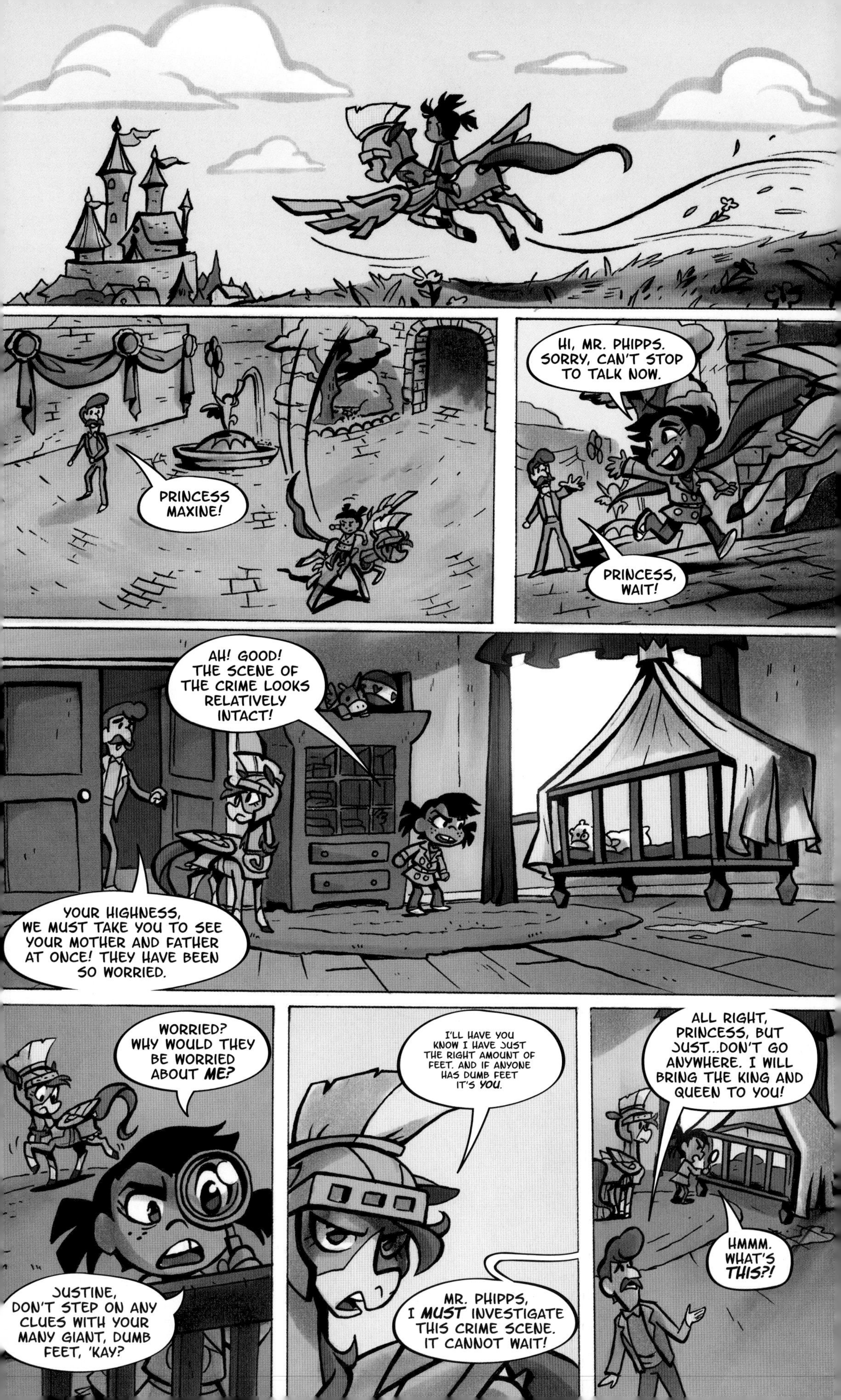
PRINCESS MAXINE!
HI, MR. PHIPPS. SORRY, CAN'T STOP TO TALK NOW.
PRINCESS, WAIT!
AH! GOOD! THE SCENE OF THE CRIME LOOKS RELATIVELY INTACT!
YOUR HIGHNESS, WE MUST TAKE YOU TO SEE YOUR MOTHER AND FATHER AT ONCE! THEY HAVE BEEN SO WORRIED.
WORRIED? WHY WOULD THEY BE WORRIED ABOUT ME?
JUSTINE, DON'T STEP ON ANY CLUES WITH YOUR MANY GIANT, DUMB FEET, 'KAY?
I'LL HAVE YOU KNOW I HAVE JUST THE RIGHT AMOUNT OF FEET. AND IF ANYONE HAS DUMB FEET IT'S YOU.
MR. PHIPPS, I MUST INVESTIGATE THIS CRIME SCENE. IT CANNOT WAIT!
ALL RIGHT, PRINCESS, BUT JUST...DON'T GO ANYWHERE. I WILL BRING THE KING AND QUEEN TO YOU!
HMMM. WHAT'S THIS?!

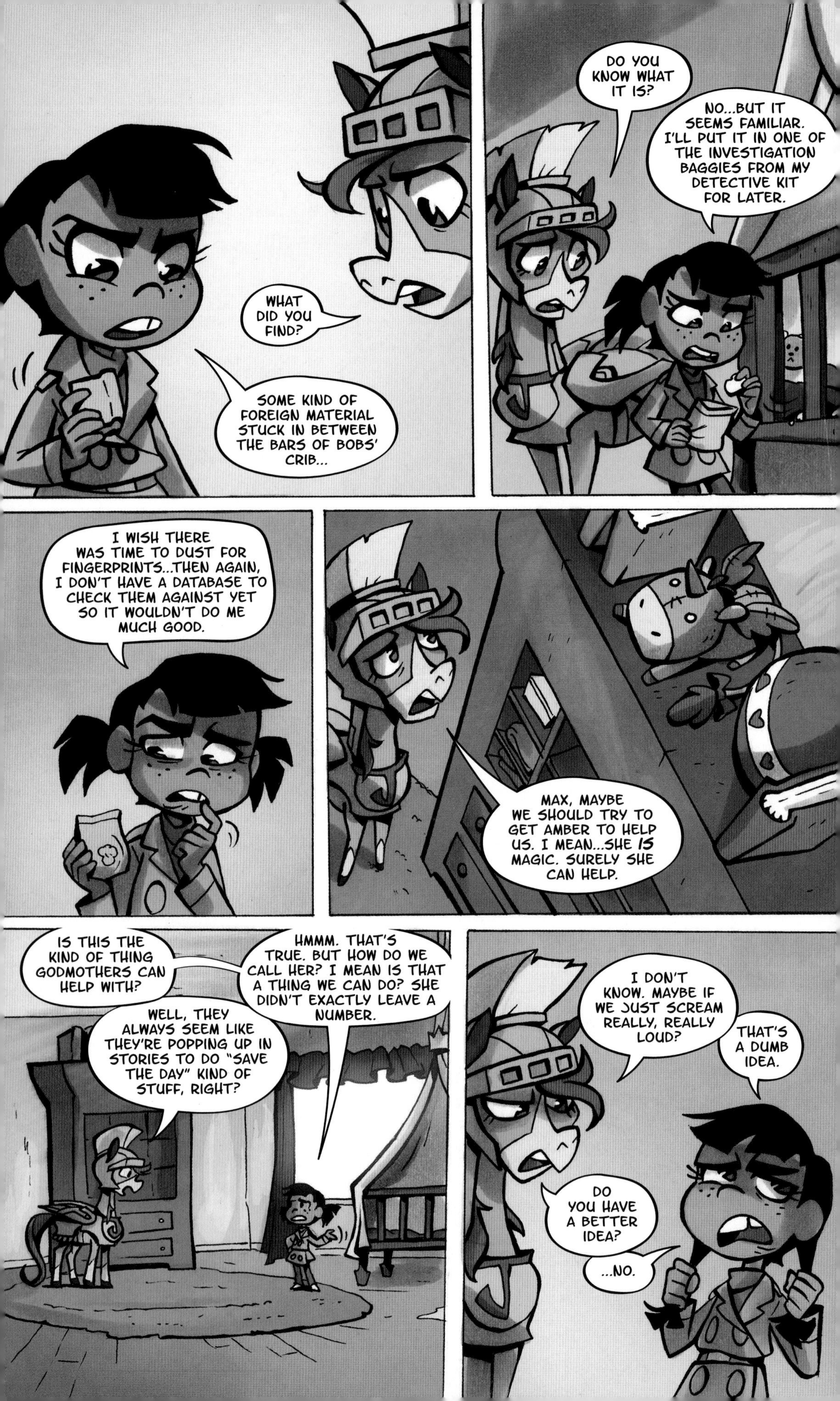
WHAT DID YOU FIND?
SOME KIND OF FOREIGN MATERIAL STUCK IN BETWEEN THE BARS OF BOBS' CRIB...
DO YOU KNOW WHAT IT IS?
NO...BUT IT SEEMS FAMILIAR. I'LL PUT IT IN ONE OF THE INVESTIGATION BAGGIES FROM MY DETECTIVE KIT FOR LATER.
I WISH THERE WAS TIME TO DUST FOR FINGERPRINTS...THEN AGAIN, I DON'T HAVE A DATABASE TO CHECK THEM AGAINST YET SO IT WOULDN'T DO ME MUCH GOOD.
MAX, MAYBE WE SHOULD TRY TO GET AMBER TO HELP US. I MEAN...SHE IS MAGIC. SURELY SHE CAN HELP.
IS THIS THE KIND OF THING GODMOTHERS CAN HELP WITH?
WELL, THEY ALWAYS SEEM LIKE THEY'RE POPPING UP IN STORIES TO DO "SAVE THE DAY" KIND OF STUFF, RIGHT?
HMMM. THAT'S TRUE. BUT HOW DO WE CALL HER? I MEAN IS THAT A THING WE CAN DO? SHE DIDN'T EXACTLY LEAVE A NUMBER.
I DON'T KNOW. MAYBE IF WE JUST SCREAM REALLY, REALLY LOUD?
THAT'S A DUMB IDEA.
DO YOU HAVE A BETTER IDEA?
...NO.

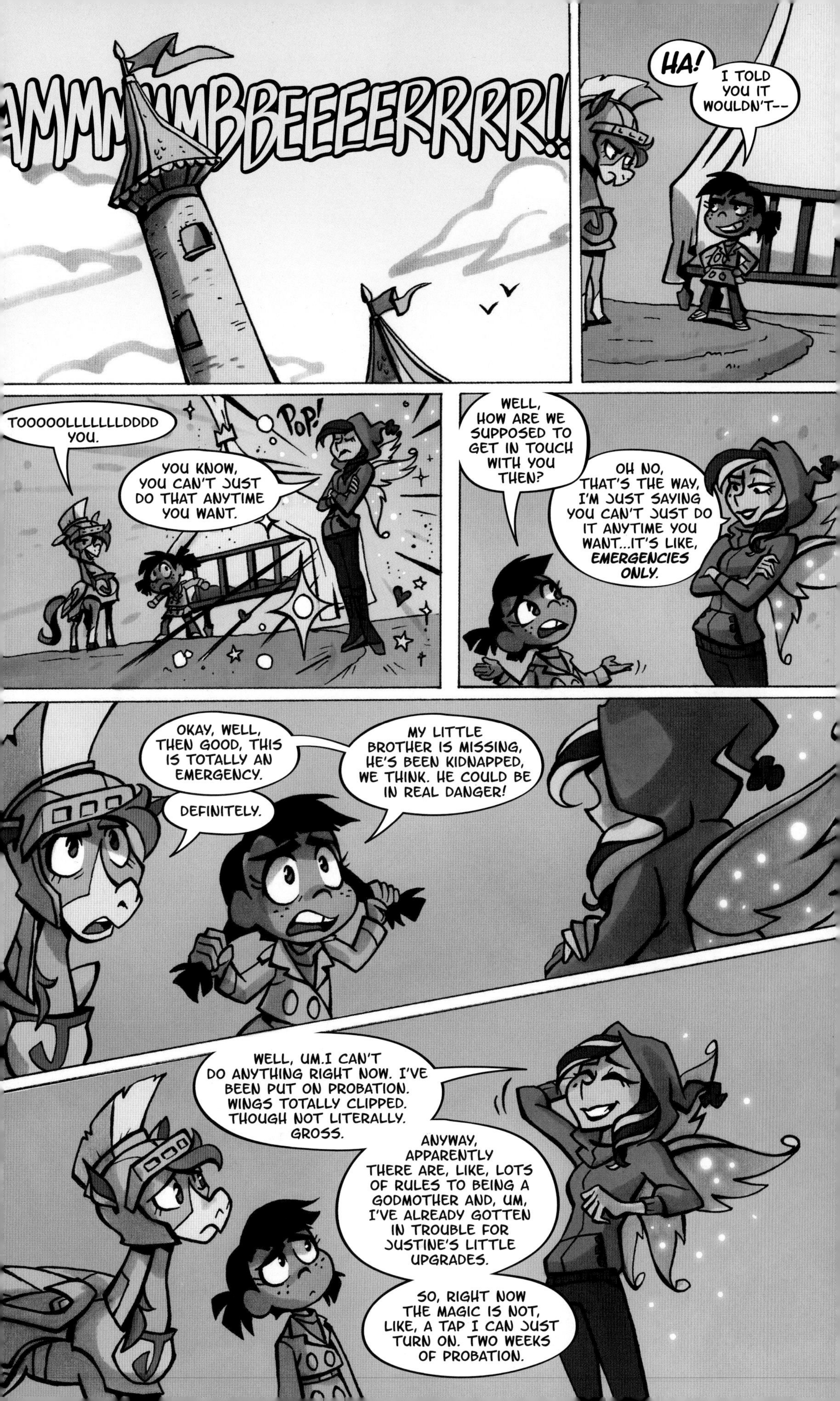
AMMMMMBBEEEEERRRRR!!
HA!
I TOLD YOU IT WOULDN'T--
TOOOOOLLLLLLLDDDD YOU.
POP!
YOU KNOW, YOU CAN'T JUST DO THAT ANYTIME YOU WANT.
WELL, HOW ARE WE SUPPOSED TO GET IN TOUCH WITH YOU THEN?
OH NO, THAT'S THE WAY, I'M JUST SAYING YOU CAN'T JUST DO IT ANYTIME YOU WANT...IT'S LIKE, EMERGENCIES ONLY.
OKAY, WELL, THEN GOOD, THIS IS TOTALLY AN EMERGENCY.
MY LITTLE BROTHER IS MISSING, HE'S BEEN KIDNAPPED, WE THINK. HE COULD BE IN REAL DANGER!
DEFINITELY.
WELL, UM.I CAN'T DO ANYTHING RIGHT NOW. I'VE BEEN PUT ON PROBATION. WINGS TOTALLY CLIPPED. THOUGH NOT LITERALLY. GROSS.
ANYWAY, APPARENTLY THERE ARE, LIKE, LOTS OF RULES TO BEING A GODMOTHER AND, UM, I'VE ALREADY GOTTEN IN TROUBLE FOR JUSTINE'S LITTLE UPGRADES.
SO, RIGHT NOW THE MAGIC IS NOT, LIKE, A TAP I CAN JUST TURN ON. TWO WEEKS OF PROBATION.

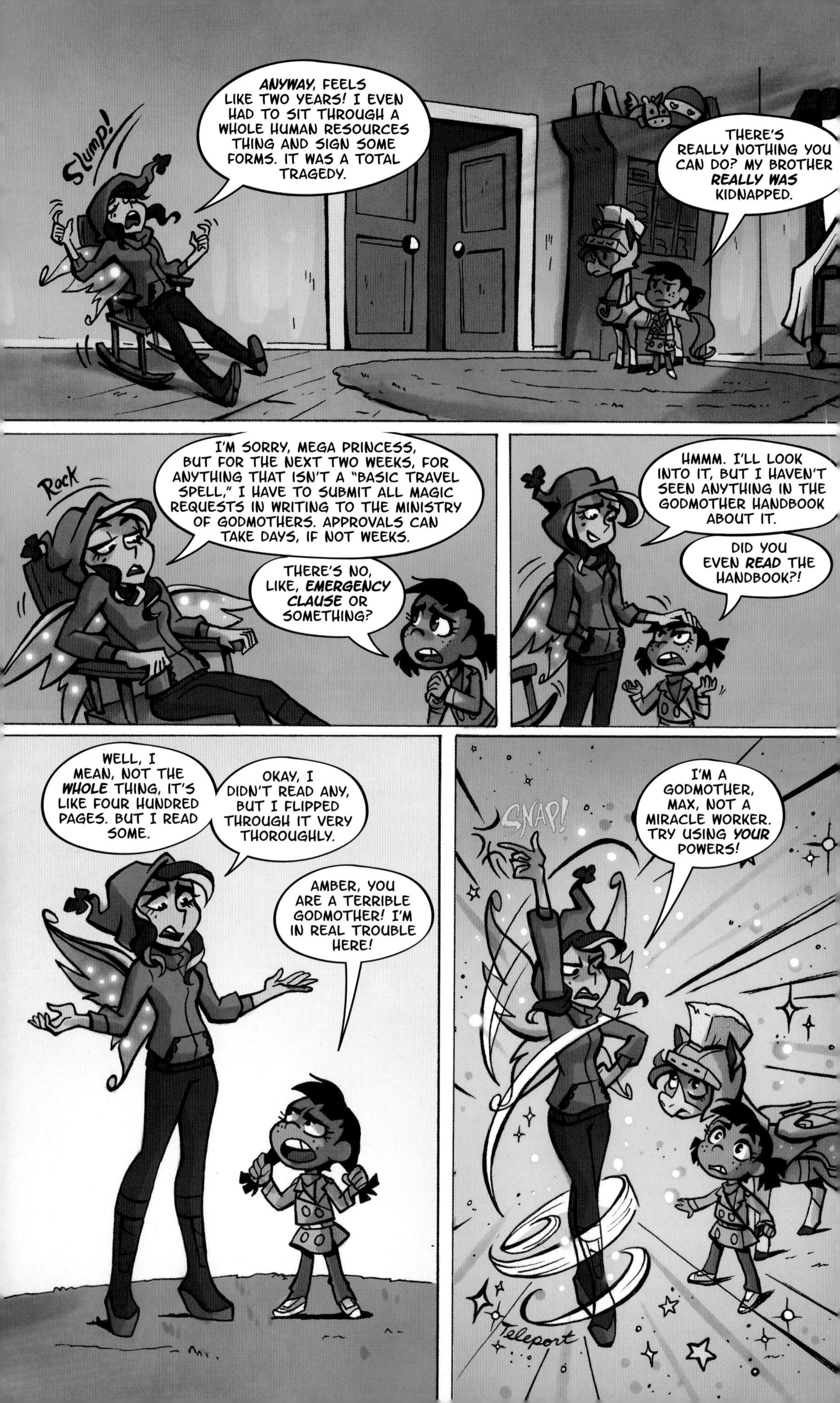
SLUMP!
ANYWAY, FEELS LIKE TWO YEARS! I EVEN HAD TO SIT THROUGH A WHOLE HUMAN RESOURCES THING AND SIGN SOME FORMS. IT WAS A TOTAL TRAGEDY.
THERE'S REALLY NOTHING YOU CAN DO? MY BROTHER REALLY WAS KIDNAPPED.
ROCK
I'M SORRY, MEGA PRINCESS, BUT FOR THE NEXT TWO WEEKS, FOR ANYTHING THAT ISN'T A "BASIC TRAVEL SPELL," I HAVE TO SUBMIT ALL MAGIC REQUESTS IN WRITING TO THE MINISTRY OF GODMOTHERS. APPROVALS CAN TAKE DAYS, IF NOT WEEKS.
THERE'S NO, LIKE, EMERGENCY CLAUSE OR SOMETHING?
HMMM. I'LL LOOK INTO IT, BUT I HAVEN'T SEEN ANYTHING IN THE GODMOTHER HANDBOOK ABOUT IT.
DID YOU EVEN READ THE HANDBOOK?!
WELL, I MEAN, NOT THE WHOLE THING, IT'S LIKE FOUR HUNDRED PAGES. BUT I READ SOME.
OKAY, I DIDN'T READ ANY, BUT I FLIPPED THROUGH IT VERY THOROUGHLY.
AMBER, YOU ARE A TERRIBLE GODMOTHER! I'M IN REAL TROUBLE HERE!
SNAP!
I'M A GODMOTHER, MAX, NOT A MIRACLE WORKER. TRY USING YOUR POWERS!
TELEPORT

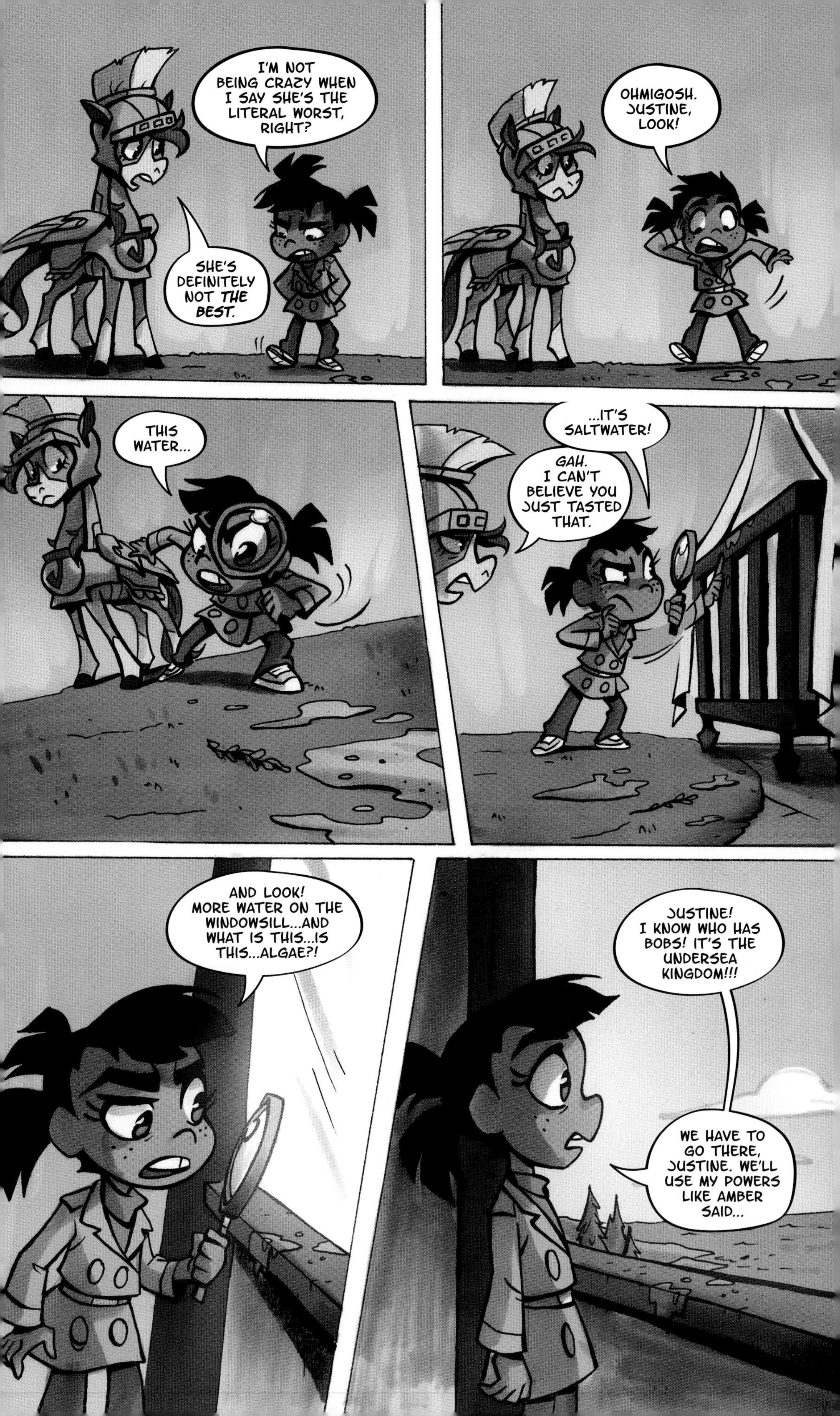
I'M NOT BEING CRAZY WHEN I SAY SHE'S THE LITERAL WORST, RIGHT?
SHE'S DEFINITELY NOT THE BEST.
OHMIGOSH. JUSTINE, LOOK!
THIS WATER...
...IT'S SALTWATER!
GAH. I CAN'T BELIEVE YOU JUST TASTED THAT.
AND LOOK! MORE WATER ON THE WINDOWSILL...AND WHAT IS THIS...IS THIS...ALGAE?!
JUSTINE! I KNOW WHO HAS BOBS! IT'S THE UNDERSEA KINGDOM!!!
WE HAVE TO GO THERE, JUSTINE. WE'LL USE MY POWERS LIKE AMBER SAID...

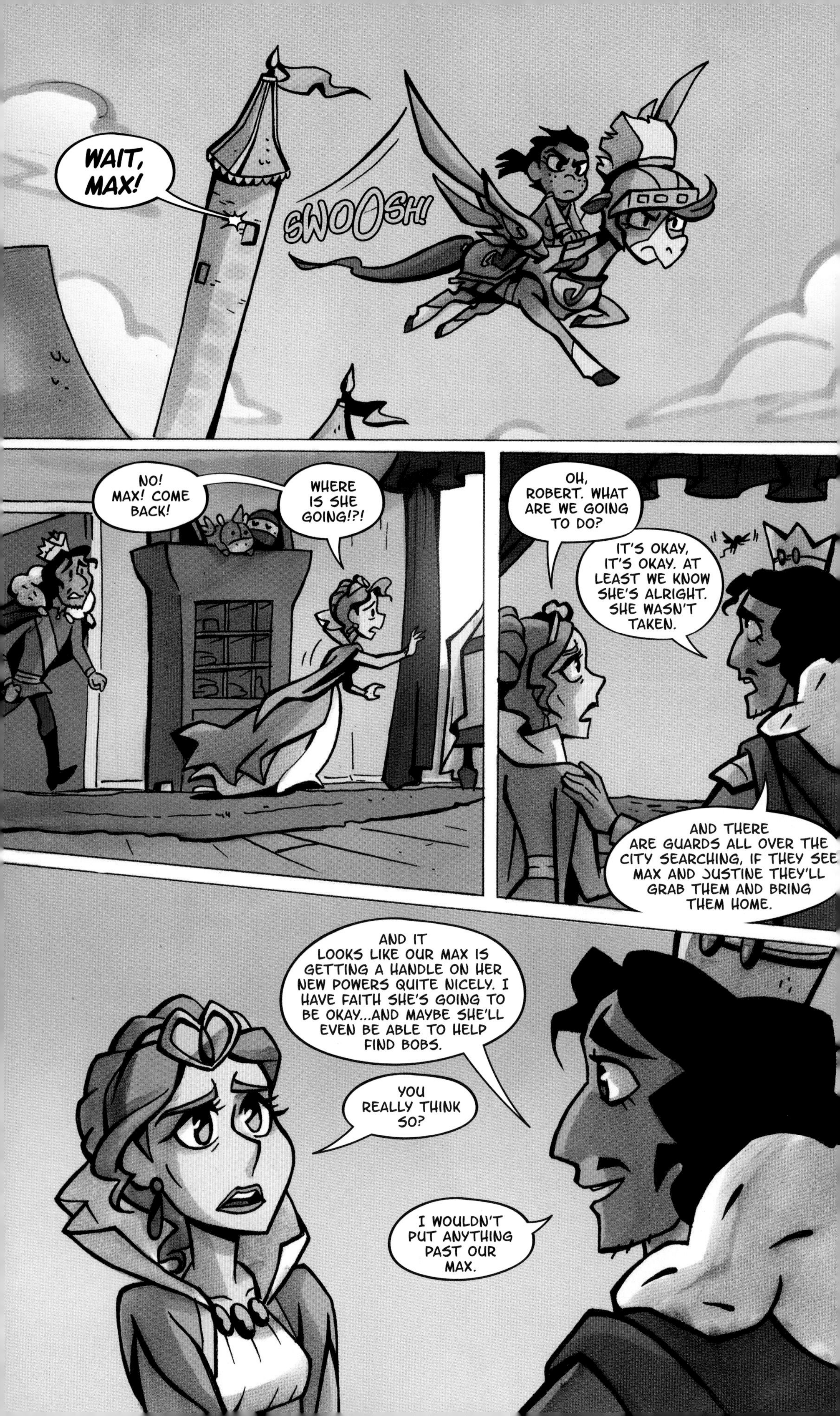
WAIT, MAX!
SWOOSH!
NO! MAX! COME BACK!
WHERE IS SHE GOING!?!
OH, ROBERT. WHAT ARE WE GOING TO DO?
IT'S OKAY, IT'S OKAY. AT LEAST WE KNOW SHE'S ALRIGHT. SHE WASN'T TAKEN.
AND THERE ARE GUARDS ALL OVER THE CITY SEARCHING, IF THEY SEE MAX AND JUSTINE THEY'LL GRAB THEM AND BRING THEM HOME.
AND IT LOOKS LIKE OUR MAX IS GETTING A HANDLE ON HER NEW POWERS QUITE NICELY. I HAVE FAITH SHE'S GOING TO BE OKAY...AND MAYBE SHE'LL EVEN BE ABLE TO HELP FIND BOBS.
YOU REALLY THINK SO?
I WOULDN'T PUT ANYTHING PAST OUR MAX.

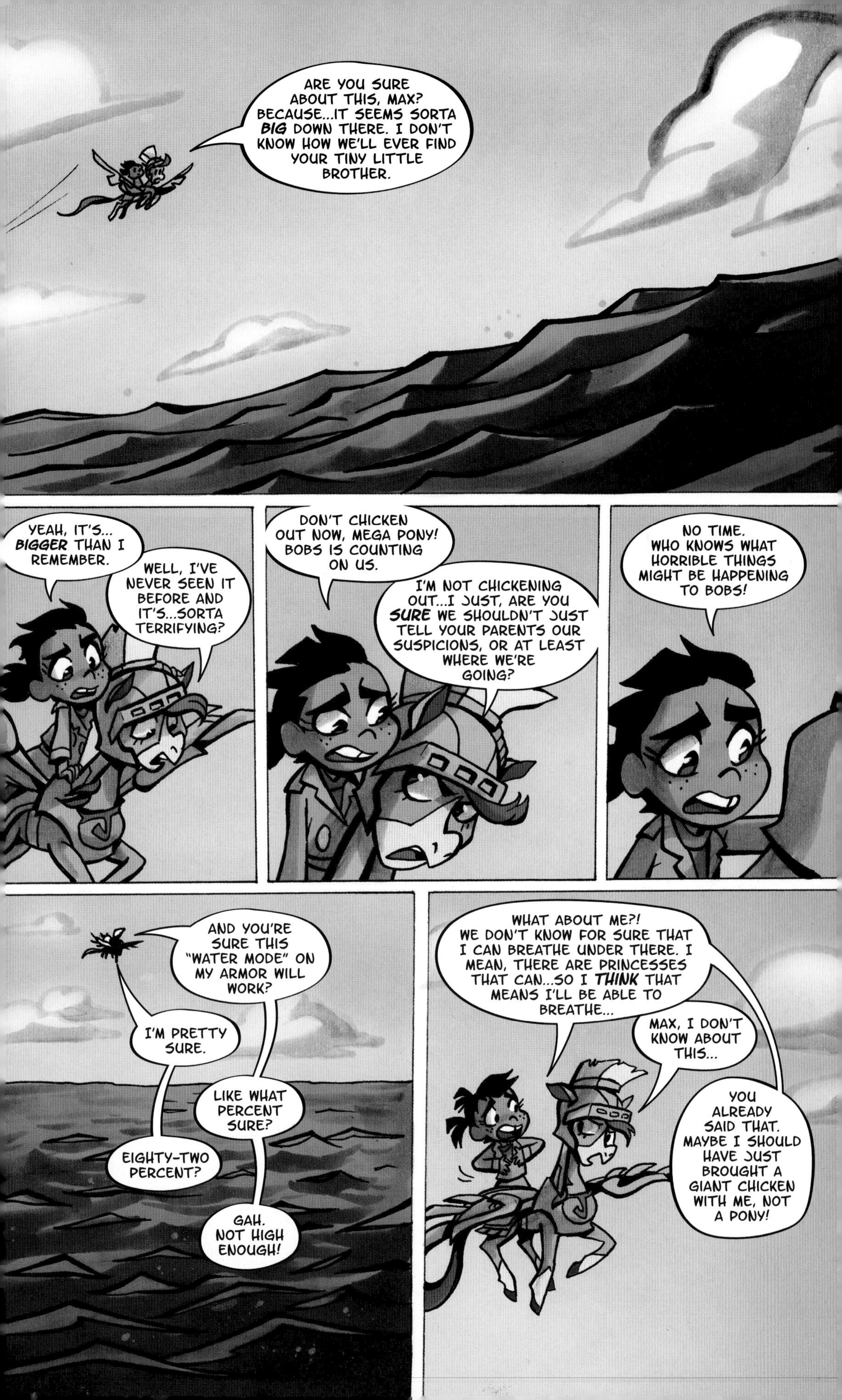
ARE YOU SURE ABOUT THIS, MAX? BECAUSE...IT SEEMS SORTA BIG DOWN THERE. I DON'T KNOW HOW WE'LL EVER FIND YOUR TINY LITTLE BROTHER.
YEAH, IT'S... BIGGER THAN I REMEMBER.
WELL, I'VE NEVER SEEN IT BEFORE AND IT'S...SORTA TERRIFYING?
DON'T CHICKEN OUT NOW, MEGA PONY! BOBS IS COUNTING ON US.
I'M NOT CHICKENING OUT...I JUST, ARE YOU SURE WE SHOULDN'T JUST TELL YOUR PARENTS OUR SUSPICIONS, OR AT LEAST WHERE WE'RE GOING?
NO TIME. WHO KNOWS WHAT HORRIBLE THINGS MIGHT BE HAPPENING TO BOBS!
AND YOU'RE SURE THIS "WATER MODE" ON MY ARMOR WILL WORK?
I'M PRETTY SURE.
LIKE WHAT PERCENT SURE?
EIGHTY-TWO PERCENT?
GAH. NOT HIGH ENOUGH!
WHAT ABOUT ME?! WE DON'T KNOW FOR SURE THAT I CAN BREATHE UNDER THERE. I MEAN, THERE ARE PRINCESSES THAT CAN...SO I THINK THAT MEANS I'LL BE ABLE TO BREATHE...
MAX, I DON'T KNOW ABOUT THIS...
YOU ALREADY SAID THAT. MAYBE I SHOULD HAVE JUST BROUGHT A GIANT CHICKEN WITH ME, NOT A PONY!

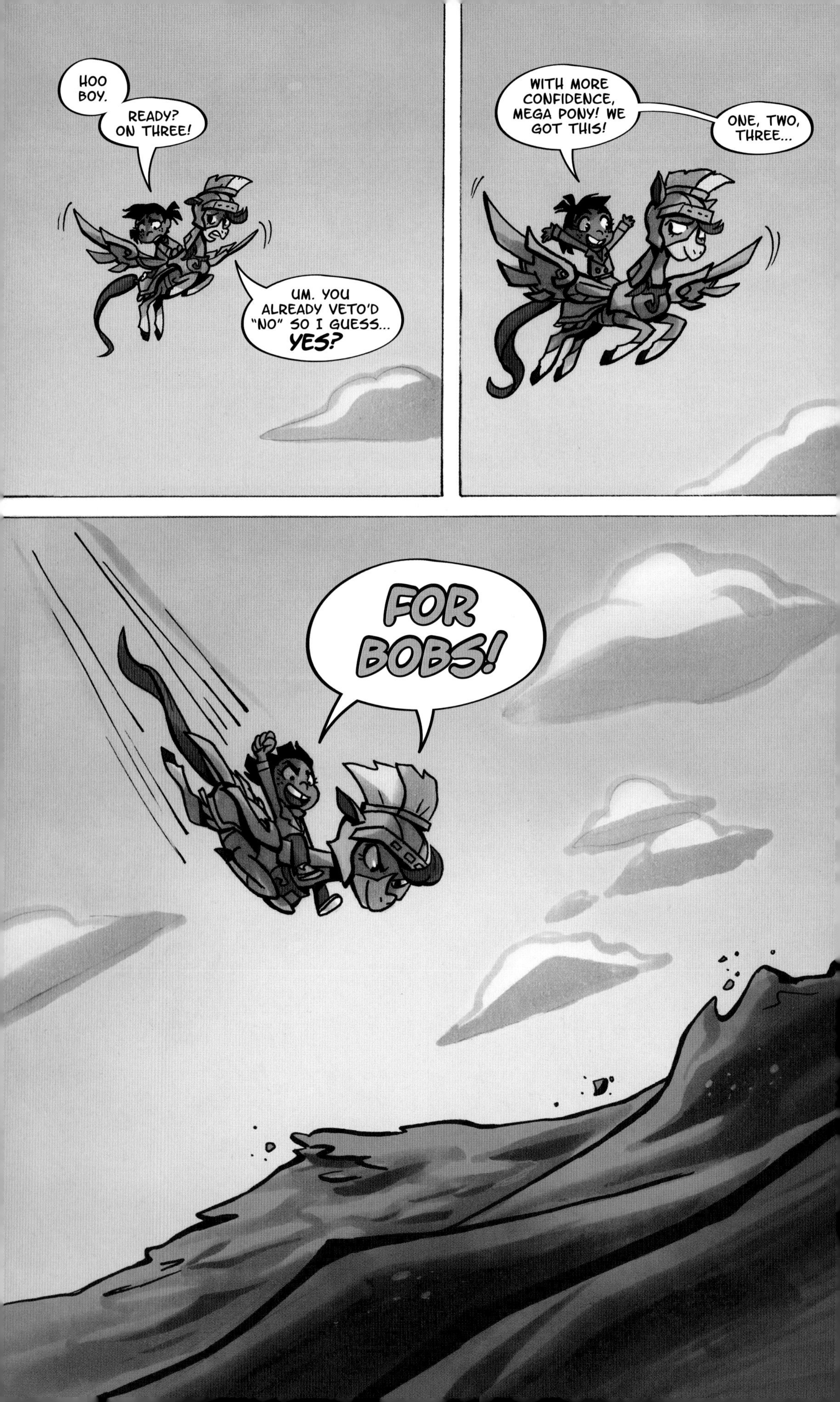
HOO BOY.
READY? ON THREE!
UM. YOU ALREADY VETO'D "NO" SO I GUESS... YES?
WITH MORE CONFIDENCE, MEGA PONY! WE GOT THIS!
ONE, TWO, THREE...
FOR BOBS!

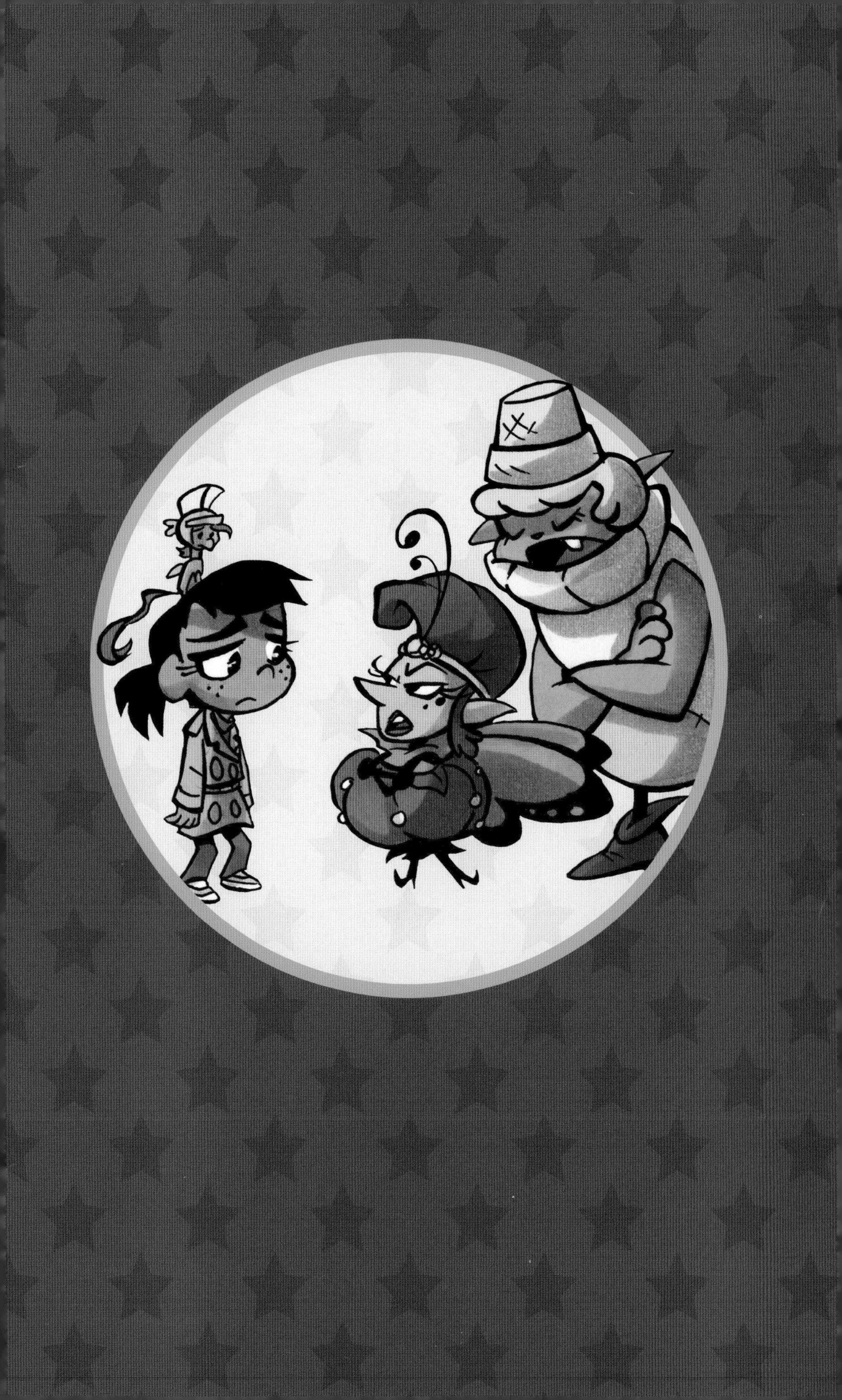

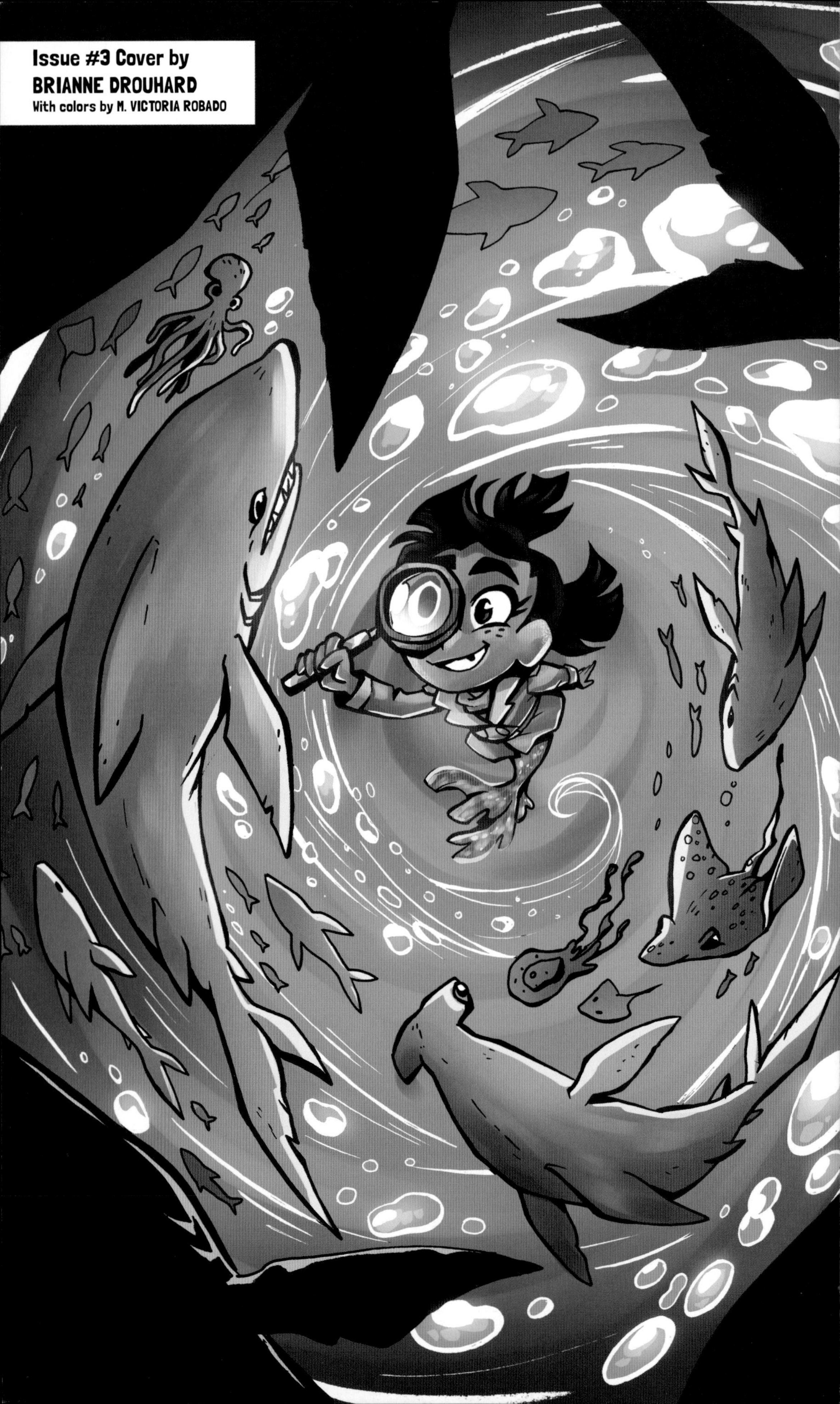

Issue #3 Cover by
BRIANNE DROUHARD
With colors by M. VICTORIA ROBADO

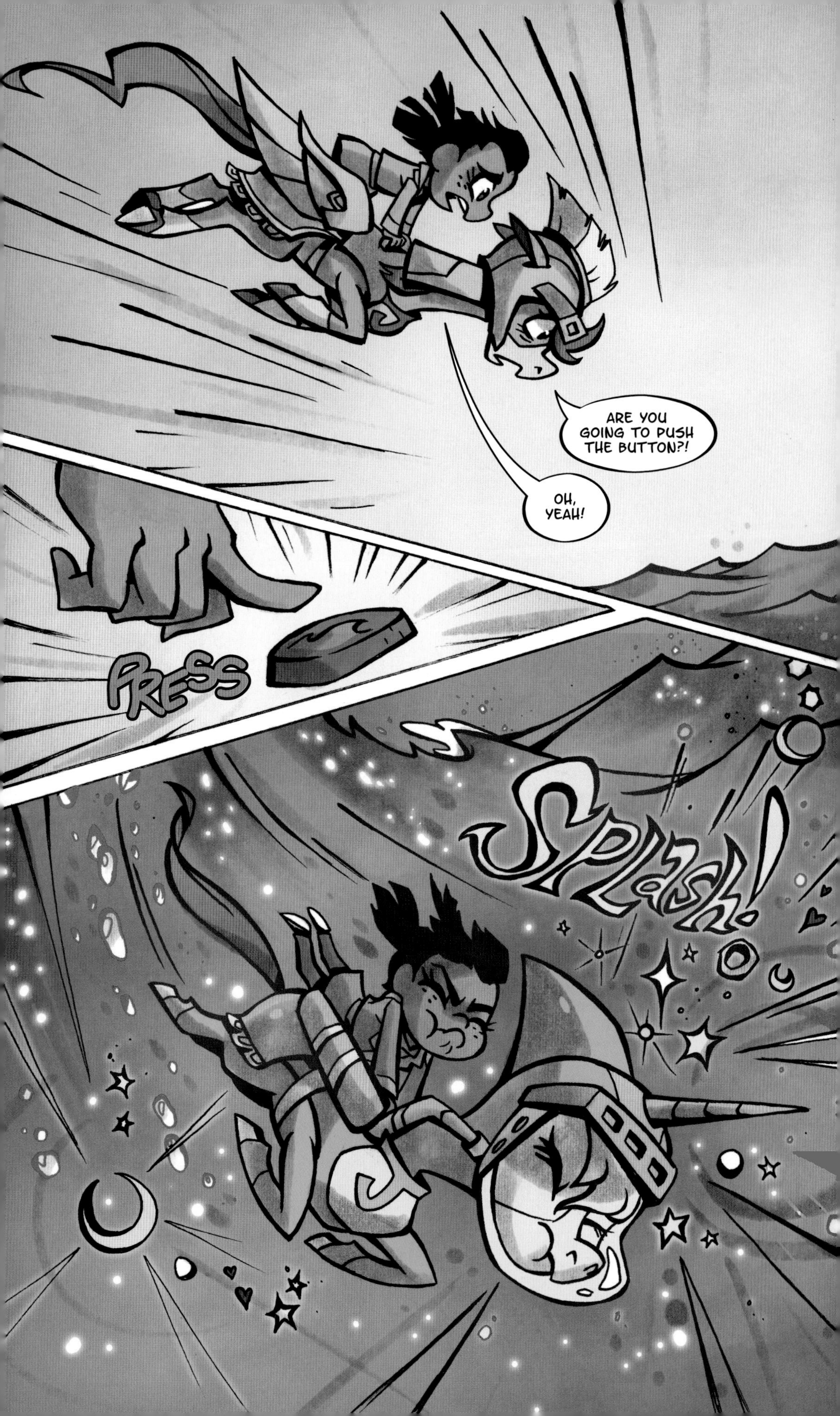
ARE YOU GOING TO PUSH THE BUTTON?!
OH, YEAH!
PRESS
SPLASH!

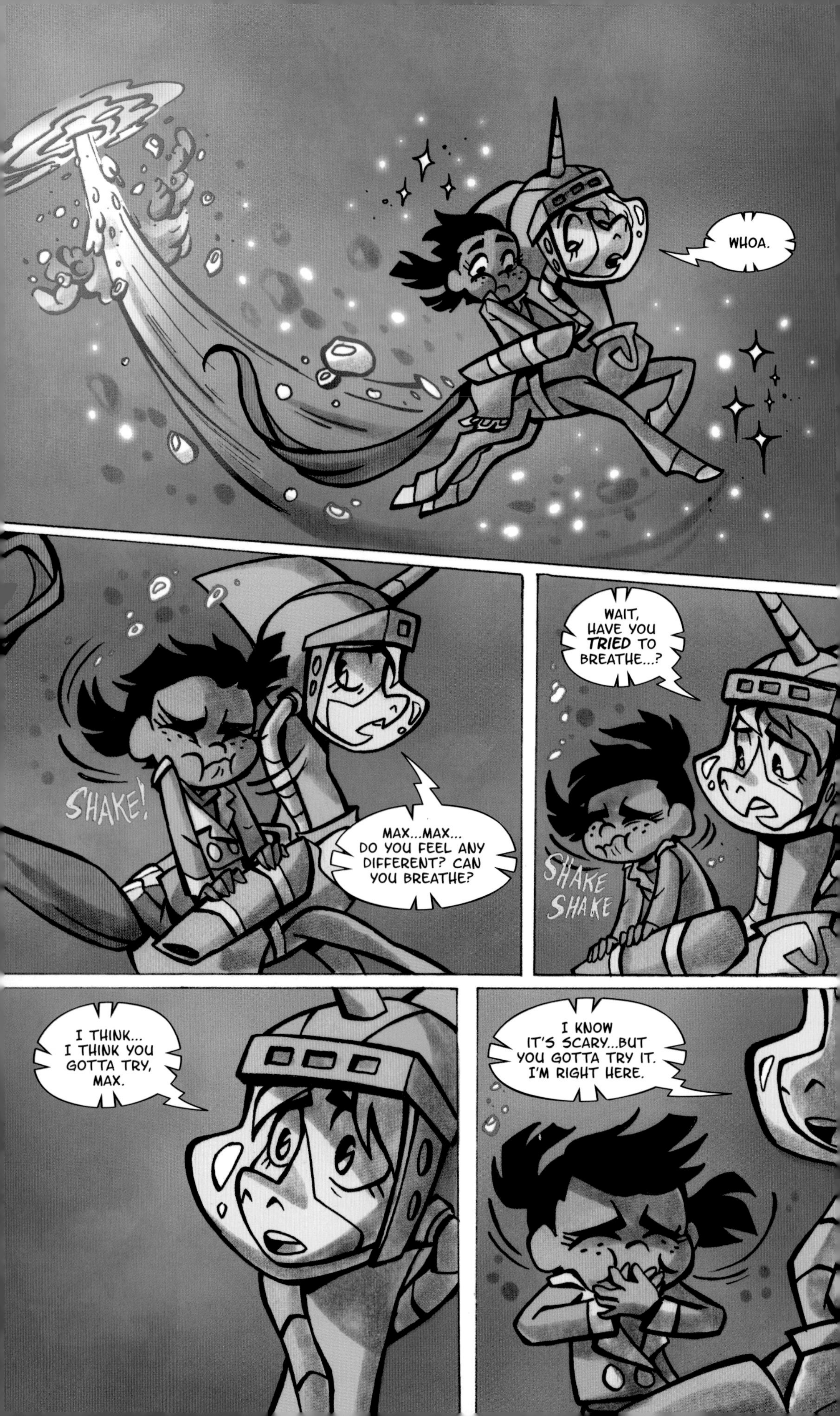
WHOA.
SHAKE!
MAX...MAX... DO YOU FEEL ANY DIFFERENT? CAN YOU BREATHE?
WAIT, HAVE YOU *TRIED* TO BREATHE...?
SHAKE SHAKE
I THINK... I THINK YOU GOTTA TRY, MAX.
I KNOW IT'S SCARY...BUT YOU GOTTA TRY IT. I'M RIGHT HERE.

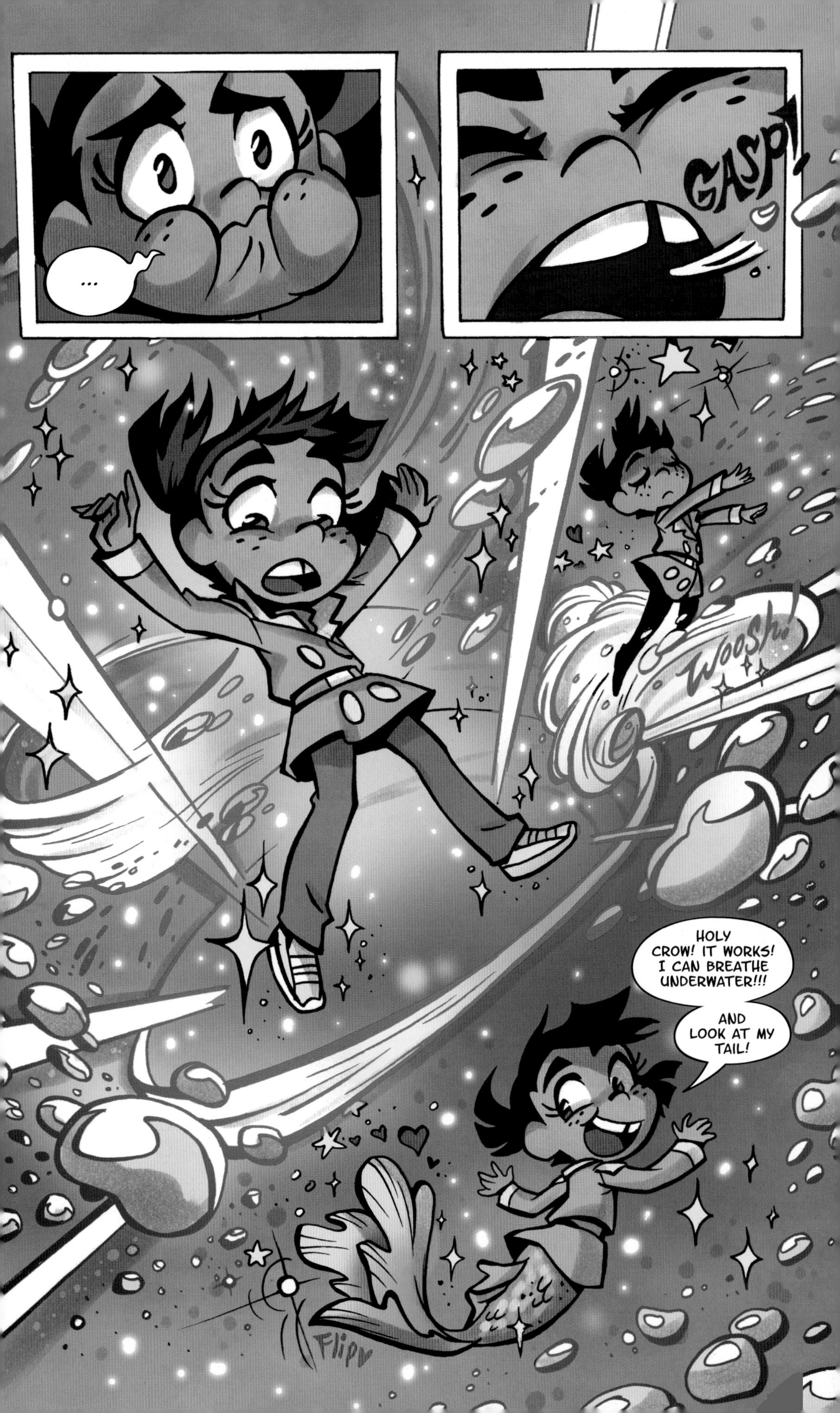
...
GASP!
WOOSH!
HOLY CROW! IT WORKS! I CAN BREATHE UNDERWATER!!!
AND LOOK AT MY TAIL!
FLIP

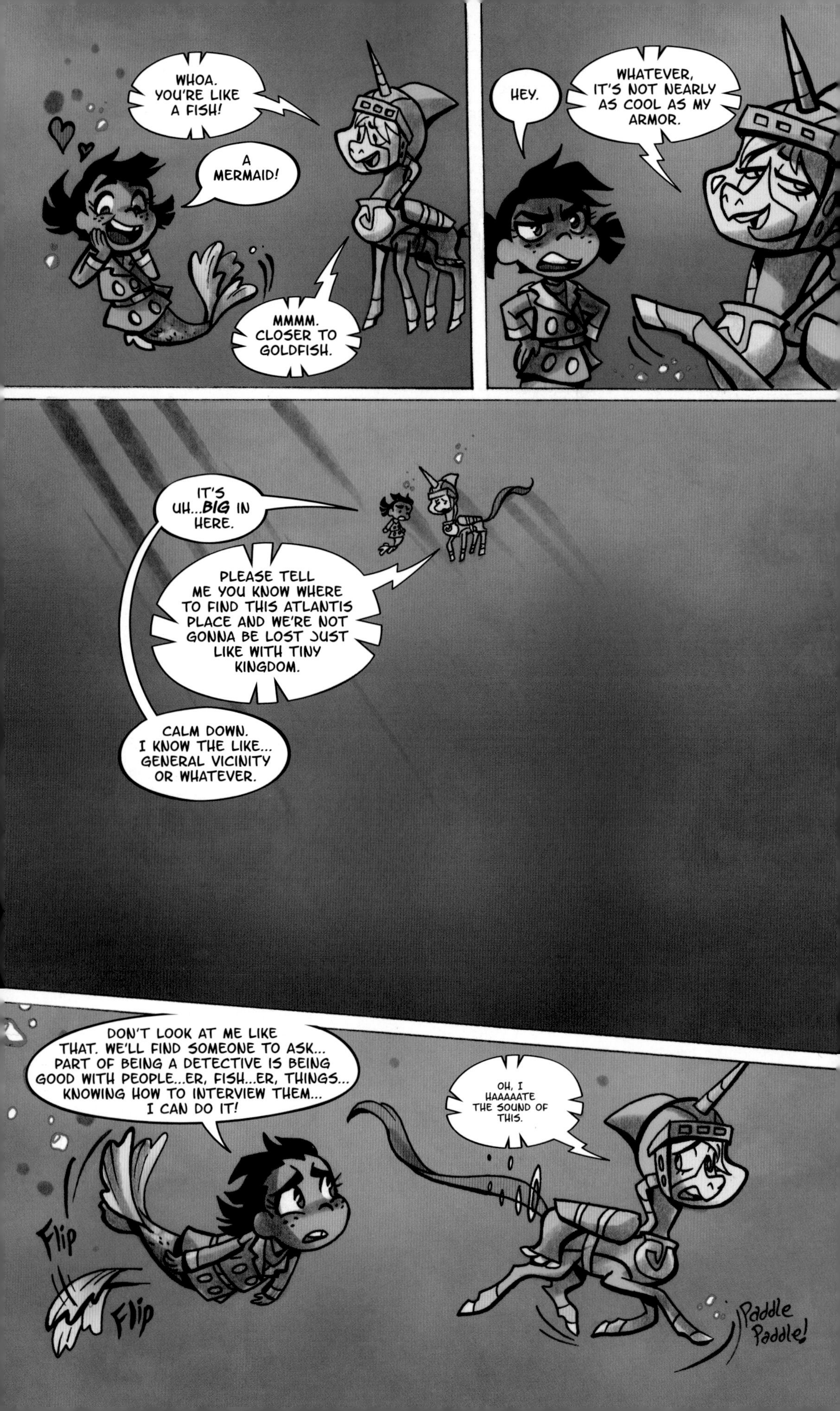
WHOA. YOU'RE LIKE A FISH!
A MERMAID!
MMMM. CLOSER TO GOLDFISH.
HEY.
WHATEVER, IT'S NOT NEARLY AS COOL AS MY ARMOR.
IT'S UH...BIG IN HERE.
PLEASE TELL ME YOU KNOW WHERE TO FIND THIS ATLANTIS PLACE AND WE'RE NOT GONNA BE LOST JUST LIKE WITH TINY KINGDOM.
CALM DOWN. I KNOW THE LIKE... GENERAL VICINITY OR WHATEVER.
DON'T LOOK AT ME LIKE THAT. WE'LL FIND SOMEONE TO ASK... PART OF BEING A DETECTIVE IS BEING GOOD WITH PEOPLE...ER, FISH...ER, THINGS... KNOWING HOW TO INTERVIEW THEM... I CAN DO IT!
OH, I HAAAAATE THE SOUND OF THIS.
Flip
Flip
Paddle Paddle!

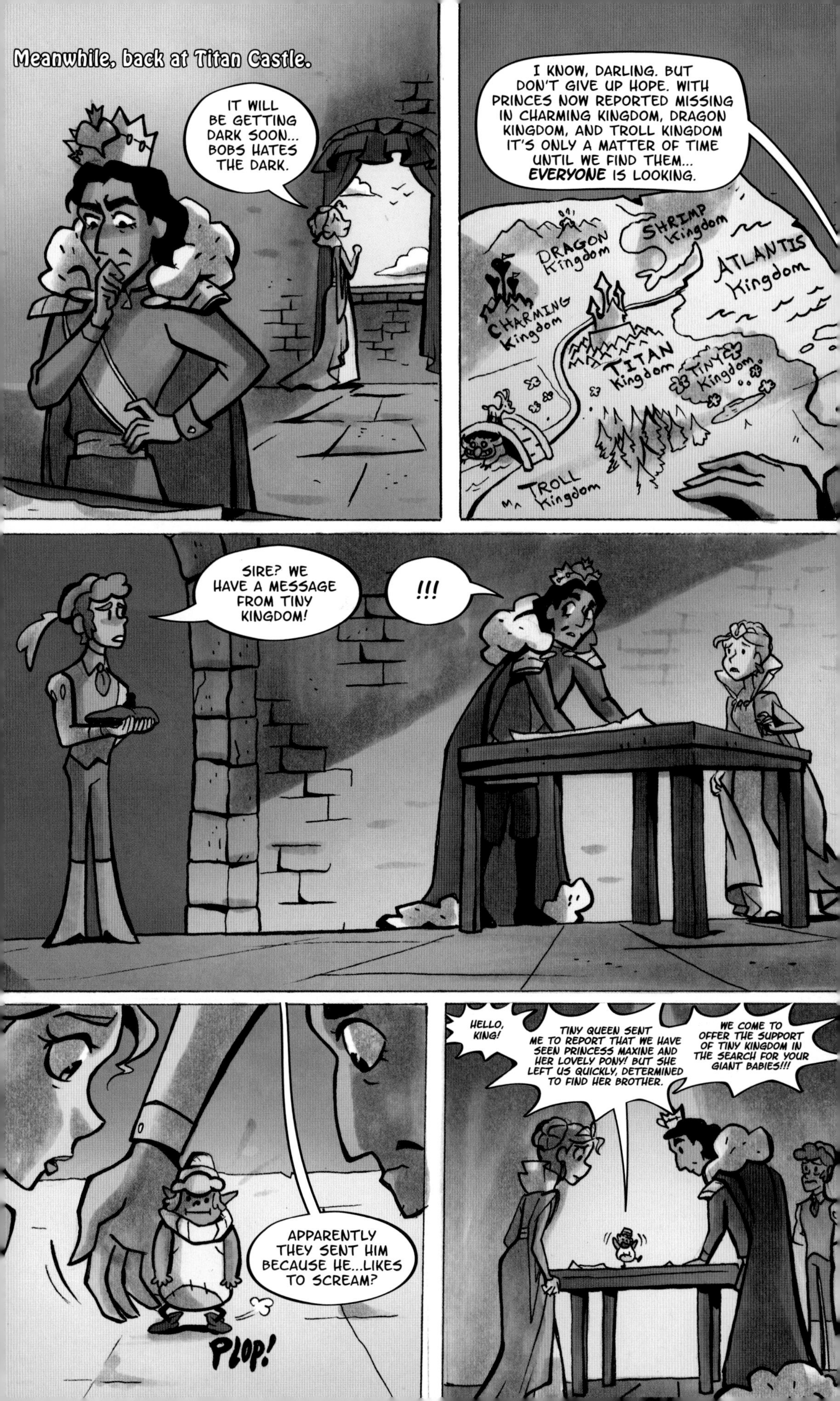

Meanwhile, back at Titan Castle.
IT WILL BE GETTING DARK SOON... BOBS HATES THE DARK.
I KNOW, DARLING. BUT DON'T GIVE UP HOPE. WITH PRINCES NOW REPORTED MISSING IN CHARMING KINGDOM, DRAGON KINGDOM, AND TROLL KINGDOM IT'S ONLY A MATTER OF TIME UNTIL WE FIND THEM... EVERYONE IS LOOKING.
DRAGON Kingdom
SHRIMP Kingdom
ATLANTIS Kingdom
CHARMING Kingdom
TITAN Kingdom
TINY Kingdom
TROLL Kingdom
SIRE? WE HAVE A MESSAGE FROM TINY KINGDOM!
!!!
APPARENTLY THEY SENT HIM BECAUSE HE...LIKES TO SCREAM?
PLOP!
HELLO, KING!
TINY QUEEN SENT ME TO REPORT THAT WE HAVE SEEN PRINCESS MAXINE AND HER LOVELY PONY! BUT SHE LEFT US QUICKLY, DETERMINED TO FIND HER BROTHER.
WE COME TO OFFER THE SUPPORT OF TINY KINGDOM IN THE SEARCH FOR YOUR GIANT BABIES!!!

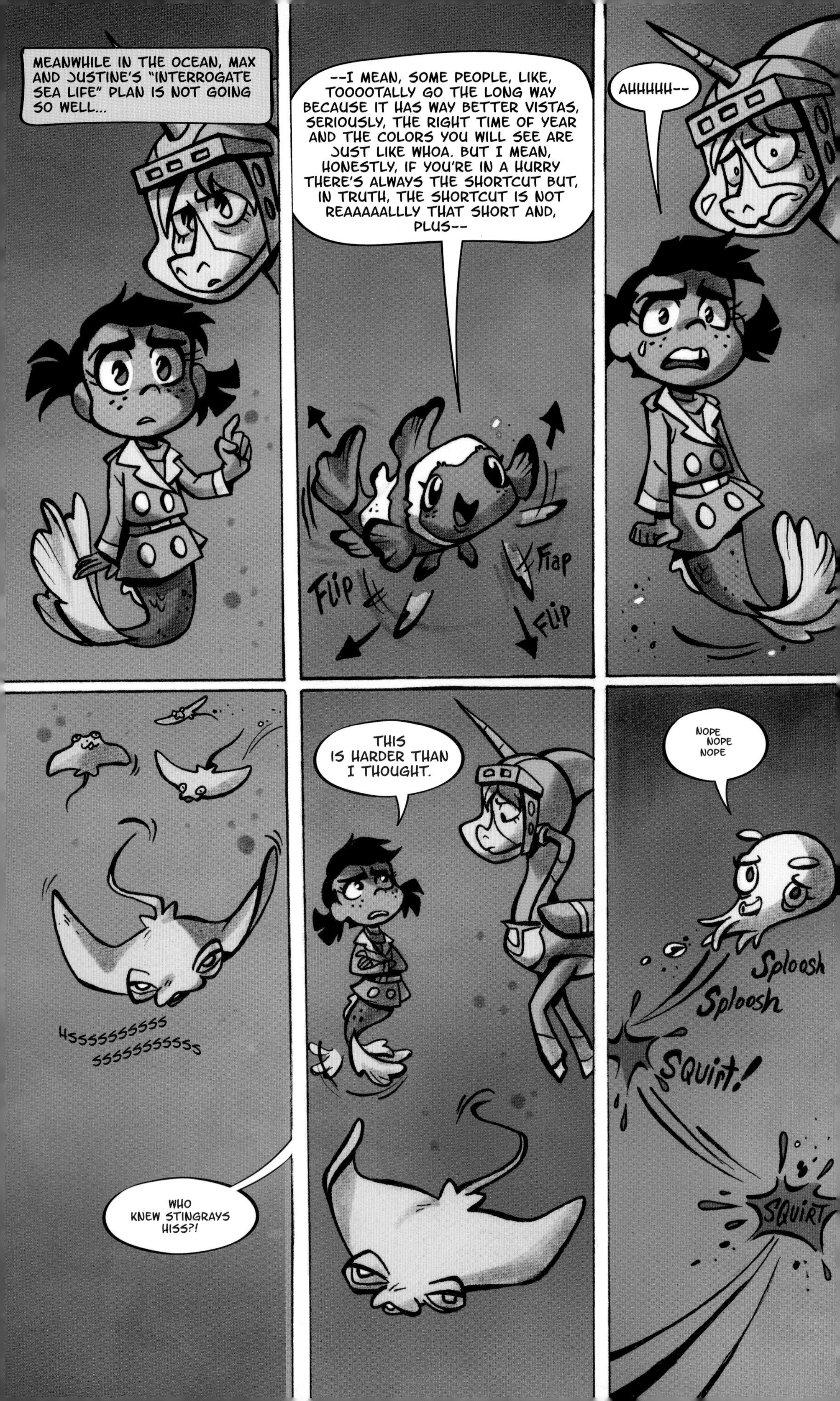
MEANWHILE IN THE OCEAN, MAX AND JUSTINE'S "INTERROGATE SEA LIFE" PLAN IS NOT GOING SO WELL...
--I MEAN, SOME PEOPLE, LIKE, TOOOOTALLY GO THE LONG WAY BECAUSE IT HAS WAY BETTER VISTAS, SERIOUSLY, THE RIGHT TIME OF YEAR AND THE COLORS YOU WILL SEE ARE JUST LIKE WHOA. BUT I MEAN, HONESTLY, IF YOU'RE IN A HURRY THERE'S ALWAYS THE SHORTCUT BUT, IN TRUTH, THE SHORTCUT IS NOT REAAAAALLLY THAT SHORT AND, PLUS--
FLIP
FLAP
FLIP
AHHHHH--
HSSSSSSSSSS
SSSSSSSSSSS
WHO KNEW STINGRAYS HISS?!
THIS IS HARDER THAN I THOUGHT.
NOPE
NOPE
NOPE
Sploosh
Sploosh
SQUIRT!
SQUIRT

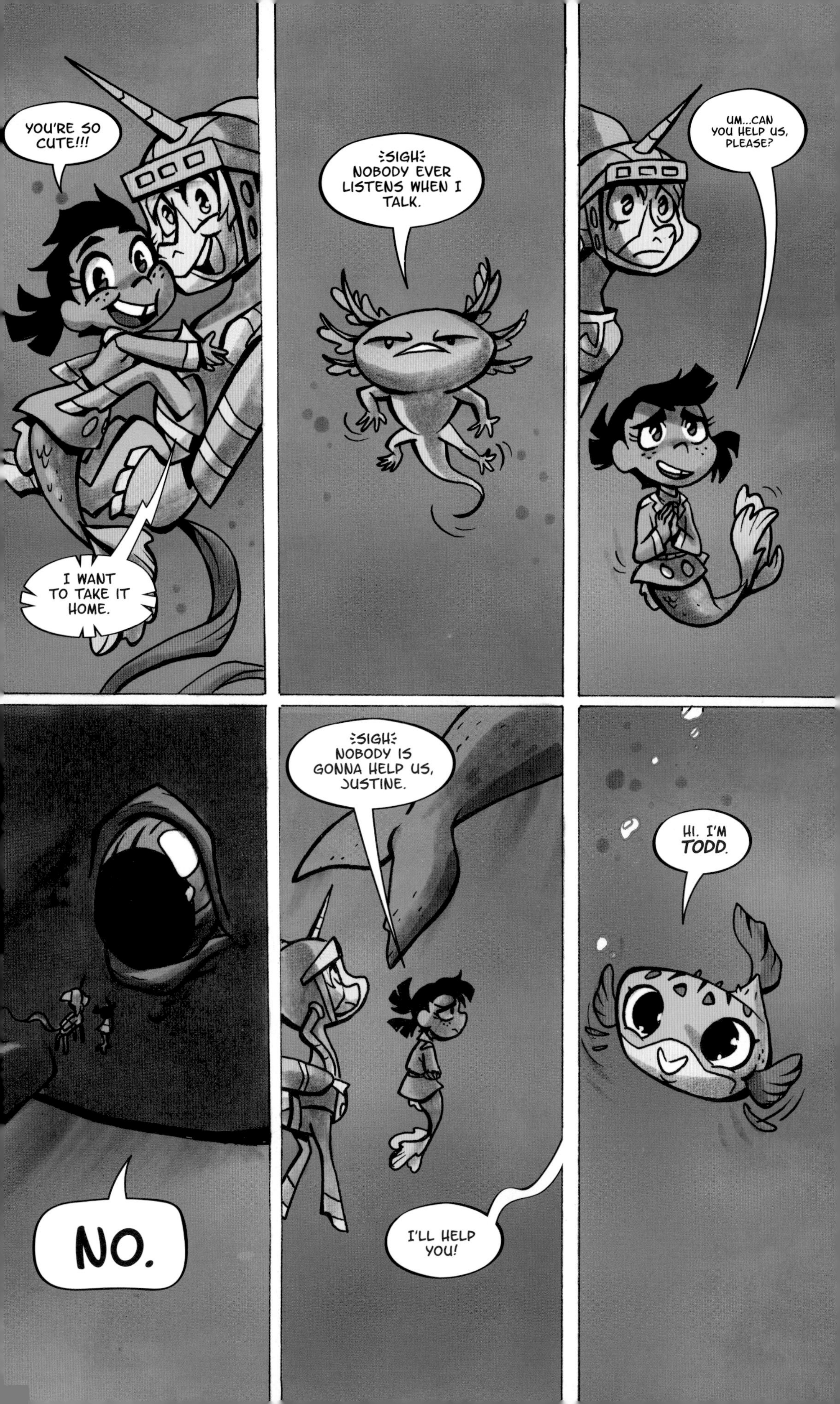

YOU'RE SO CUTE!!!
I WANT TO TAKE IT HOME.
SIGH NOBODY EVER LISTENS WHEN I TALK.
UM...CAN YOU HELP US, PLEASE?
NO.
SIGH NOBODY IS GONNA HELP US, JUSTINE.
I'LL HELP YOU!
HI. I'M TODD.

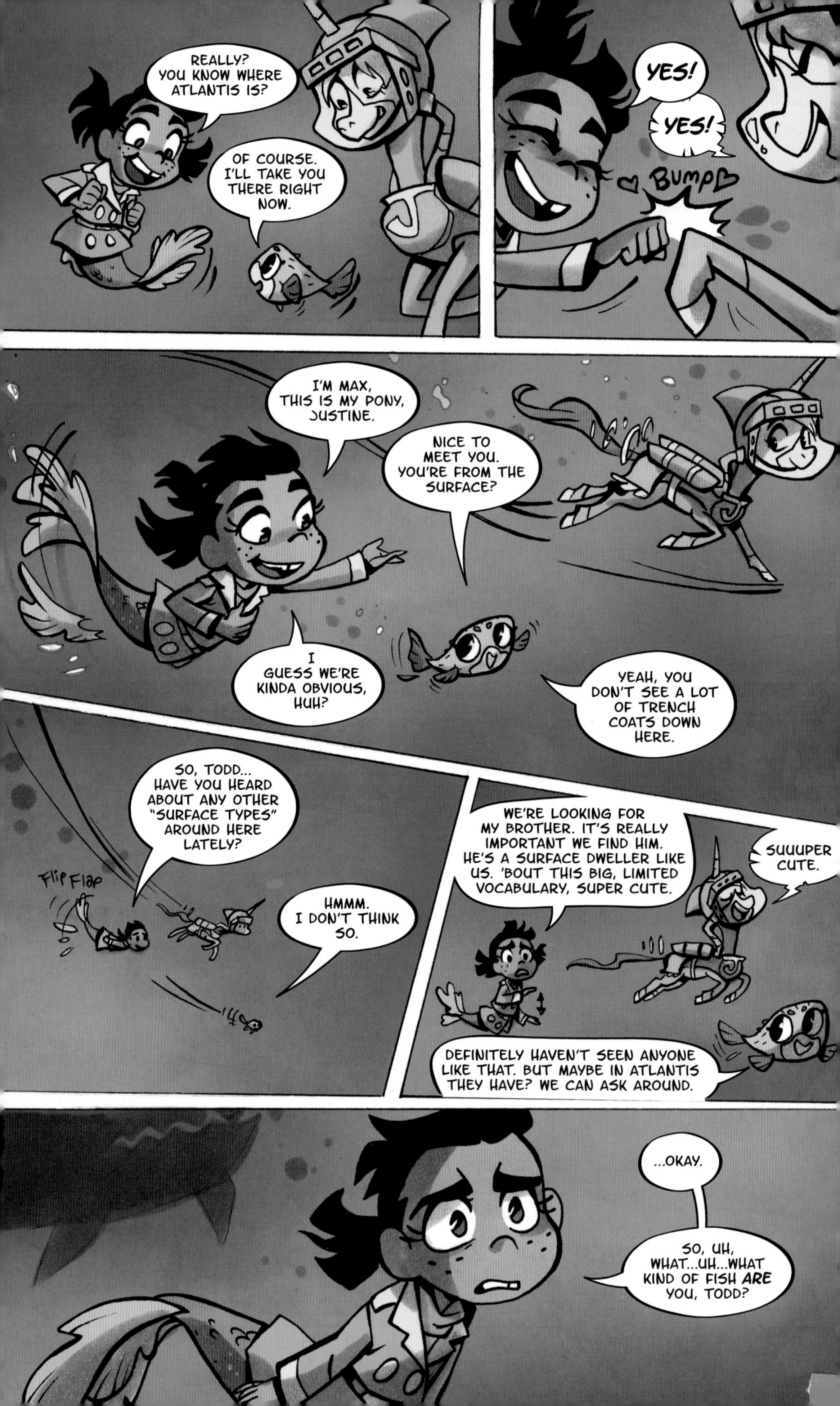
REALLY? YOU KNOW WHERE ATLANTIS IS?
OF COURSE. I'LL TAKE YOU THERE RIGHT NOW.
YES!
YES!
BUMP
I'M MAX, THIS IS MY PONY, JUSTINE.
NICE TO MEET YOU. YOU'RE FROM THE SURFACE?
I GUESS WE'RE KINDA OBVIOUS, HUH?
YEAH, YOU DON'T SEE A LOT OF TRENCH COATS DOWN HERE.
SO, TODD... HAVE YOU HEARD ABOUT ANY OTHER "SURFACE TYPES" AROUND HERE LATELY?
FLIP FLAP
HMMM. I DON'T THINK SO.
WE'RE LOOKING FOR MY BROTHER. IT'S REALLY IMPORTANT WE FIND HIM. HE'S A SURFACE DWELLER LIKE US. 'BOUT THIS BIG, LIMITED VOCABULARY, SUPER CUTE.
SUUUPER CUTE.
DEFINITELY HAVEN'T SEEN ANYONE LIKE THAT. BUT MAYBE IN ATLANTIS THEY HAVE? WE CAN ASK AROUND.
...OKAY.
SO, UH, WHAT...UH...WHAT KIND OF FISH ARE YOU, TODD?

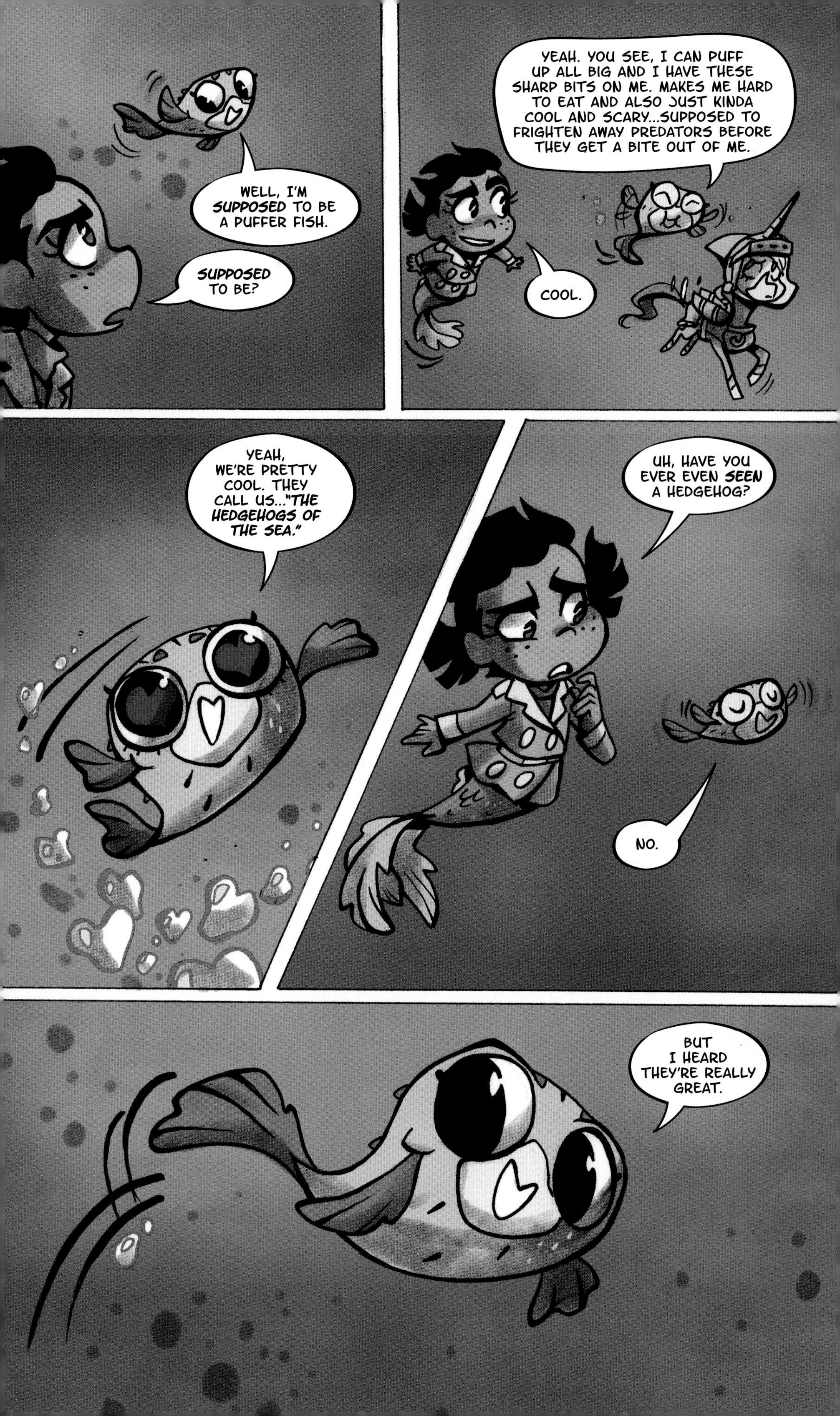
WELL, I'M SUPPOSED TO BE A PUFFER FISH.
SUPPOSED TO BE?
YEAH. YOU SEE, I CAN PUFF UP ALL BIG AND I HAVE THESE SHARP BITS ON ME. MAKES ME HARD TO EAT AND ALSO JUST KINDA COOL AND SCARY...SUPPOSED TO FRIGHTEN AWAY PREDATORS BEFORE THEY GET A BITE OUT OF ME.
COOL.
YEAH, WE'RE PRETTY COOL. THEY CALL US..."THE HEDGEHOGS OF THE SEA."
UH, HAVE YOU EVER EVEN SEEN A HEDGEHOG?
NO.
BUT I HEARD THEY'RE REALLY GREAT.

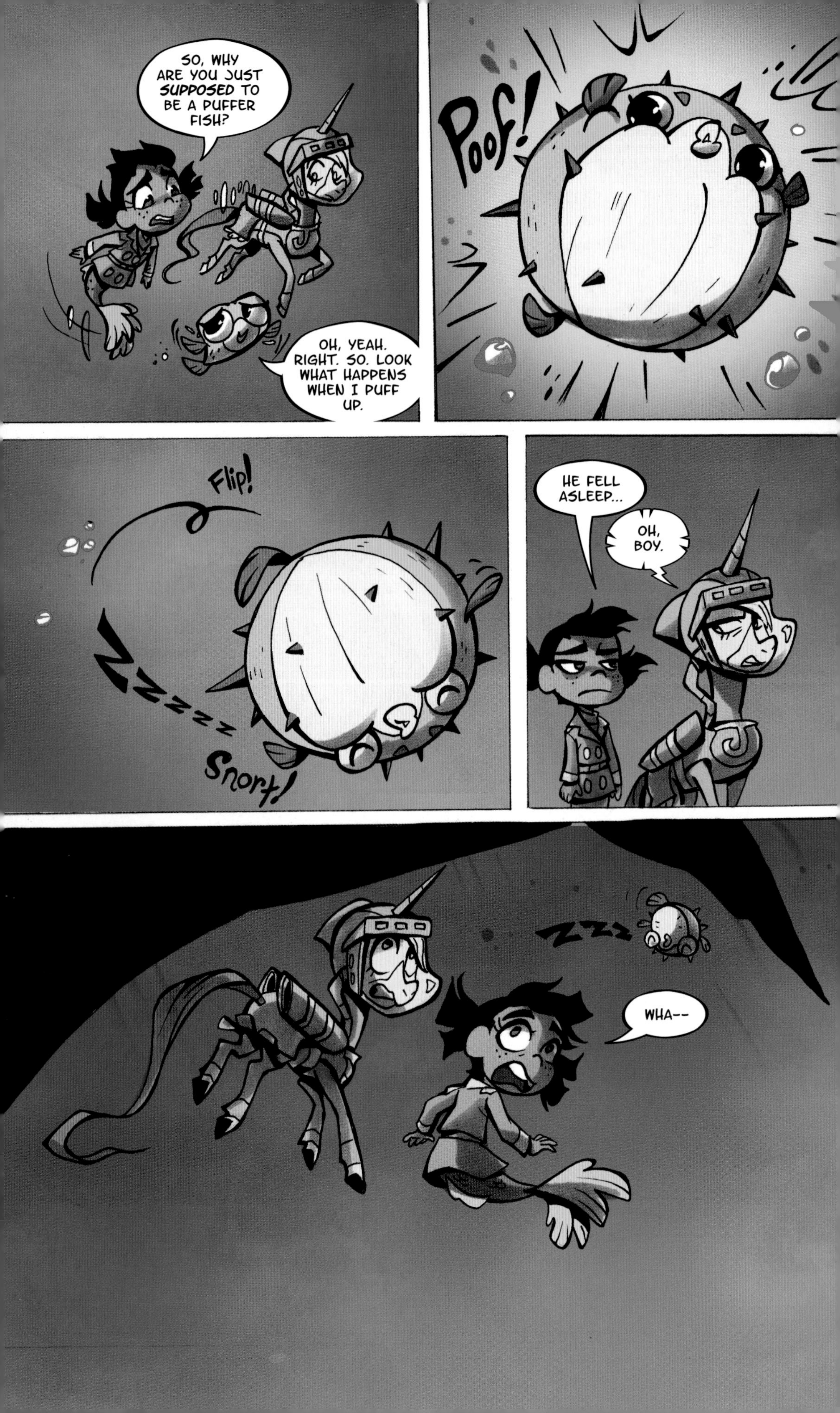
SO, WHY ARE YOU JUST SUPPOSED TO BE A PUFFER FISH?
OH, YEAH. RIGHT. SO. LOOK WHAT HAPPENS WHEN I PUFF UP.
Poof!
Flip!
ZZZZZZ
Snort!
HE FELL ASLEEP...
OH, BOY.
ZZZ
WHA--

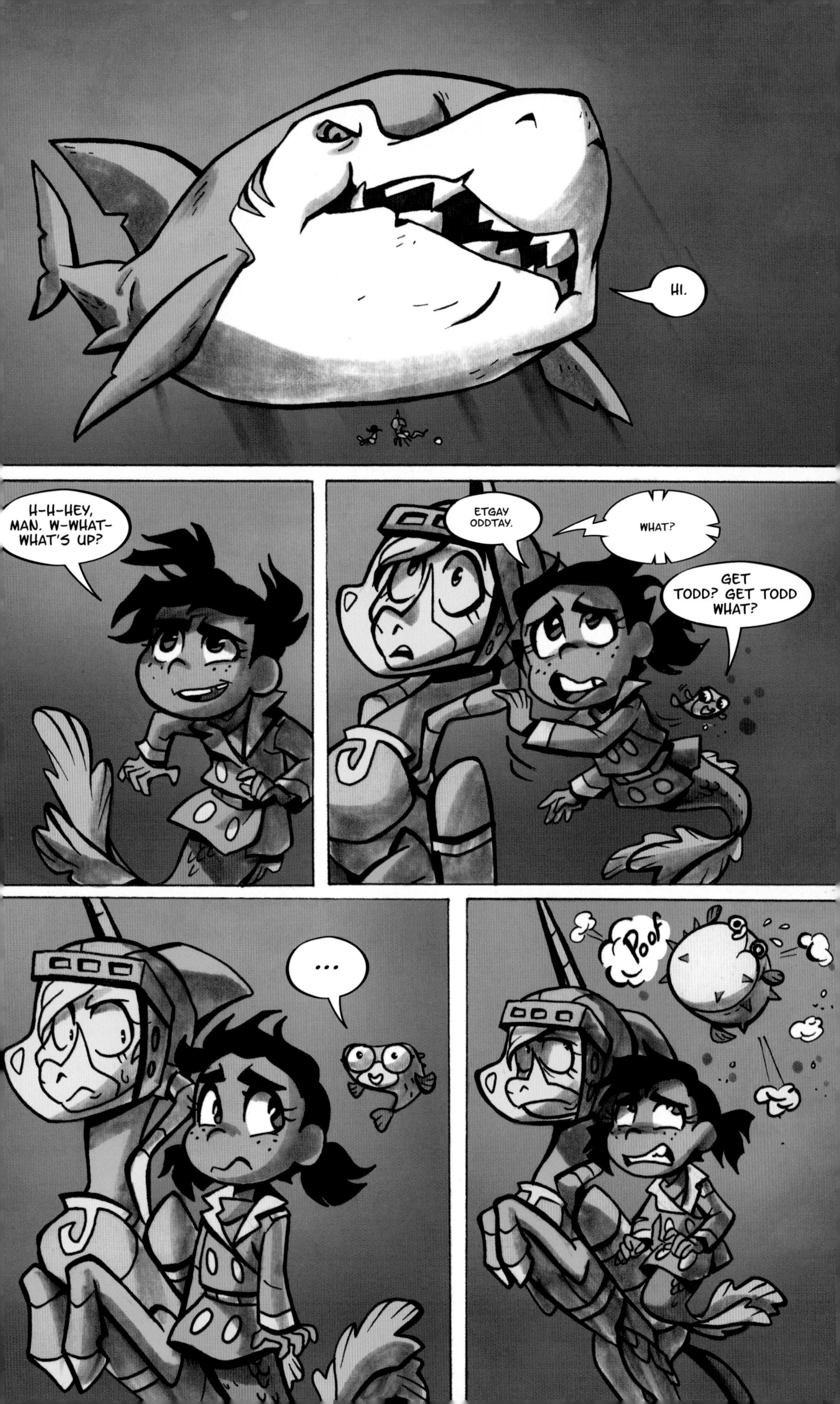
HI.
H-H-HEY, MAN. W-WHAT-WHAT'S UP?
ETGAY ODDTAY.
WHAT?
GET TODD? GET TODD WHAT?
...
Poof

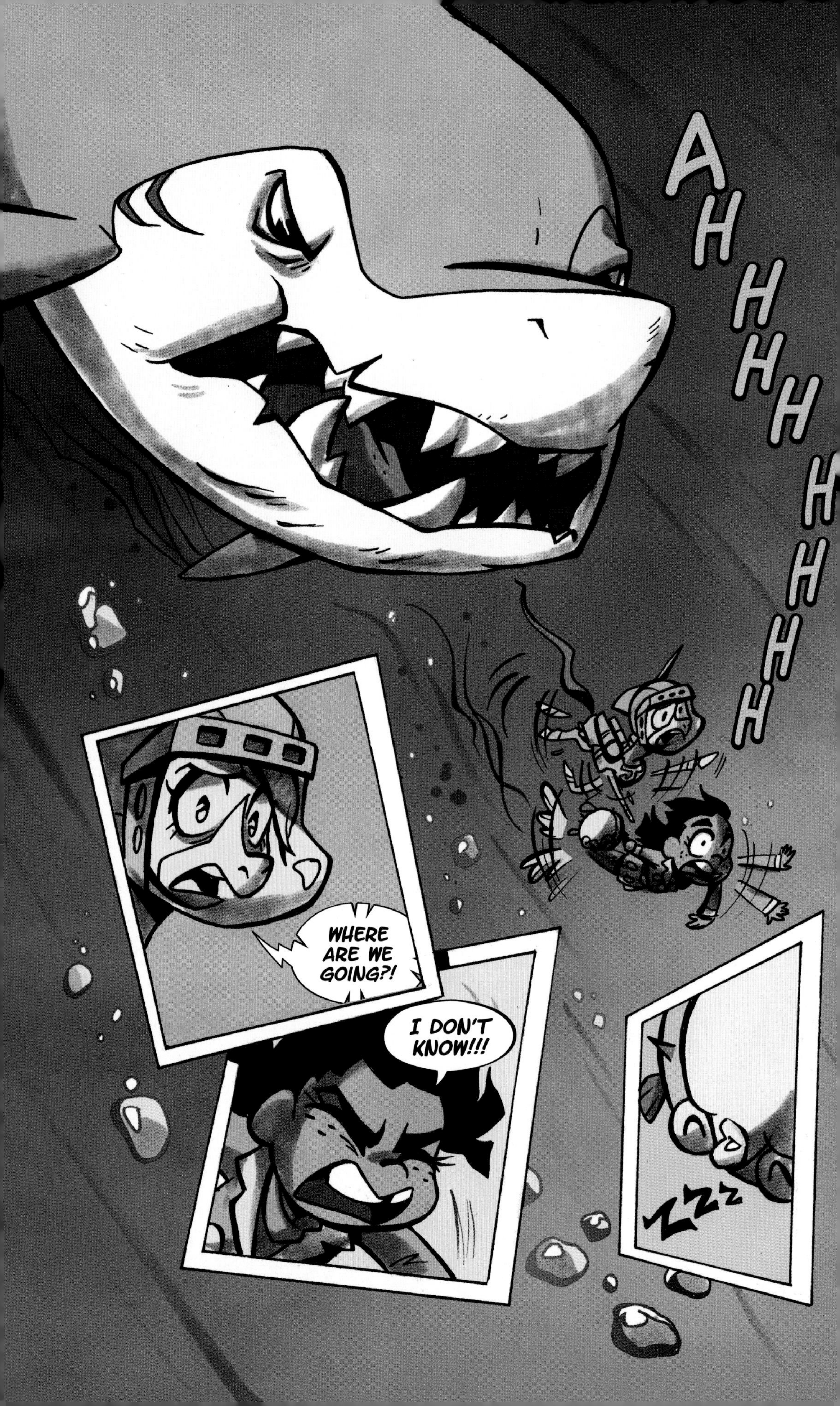
AHHHHHHHHHH
WHERE ARE WE GOING?!
I DON'T KNOW!!!
ZZZ

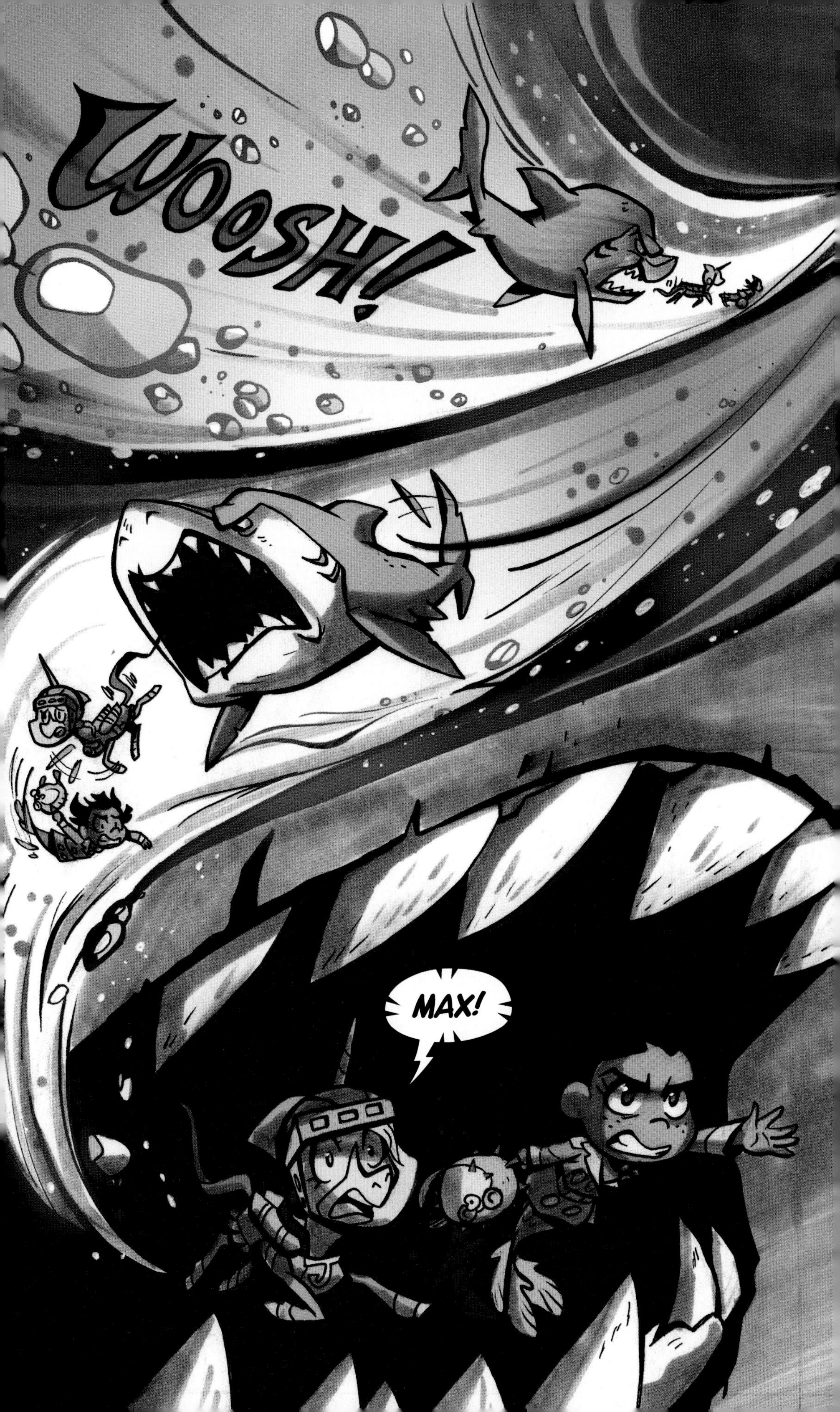
WOOSH!
MAX!

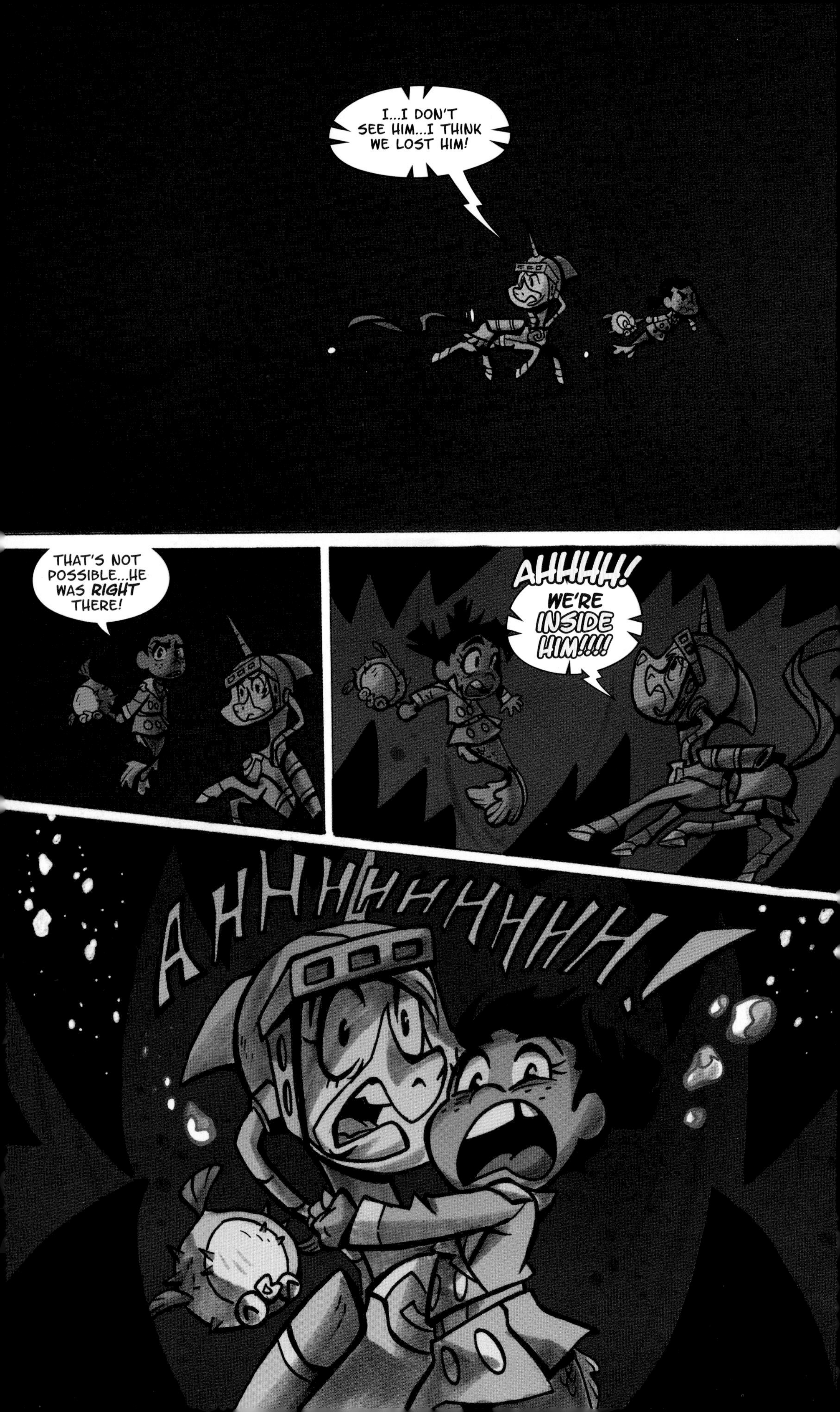
I...I DON'T SEE HIM...I THINK WE LOST HIM!
THAT'S NOT POSSIBLE...HE WAS **RIGHT** THERE!
AHHHH! WE'RE INSIDE HIM!!!!
AHHHHHHHHHHHH!

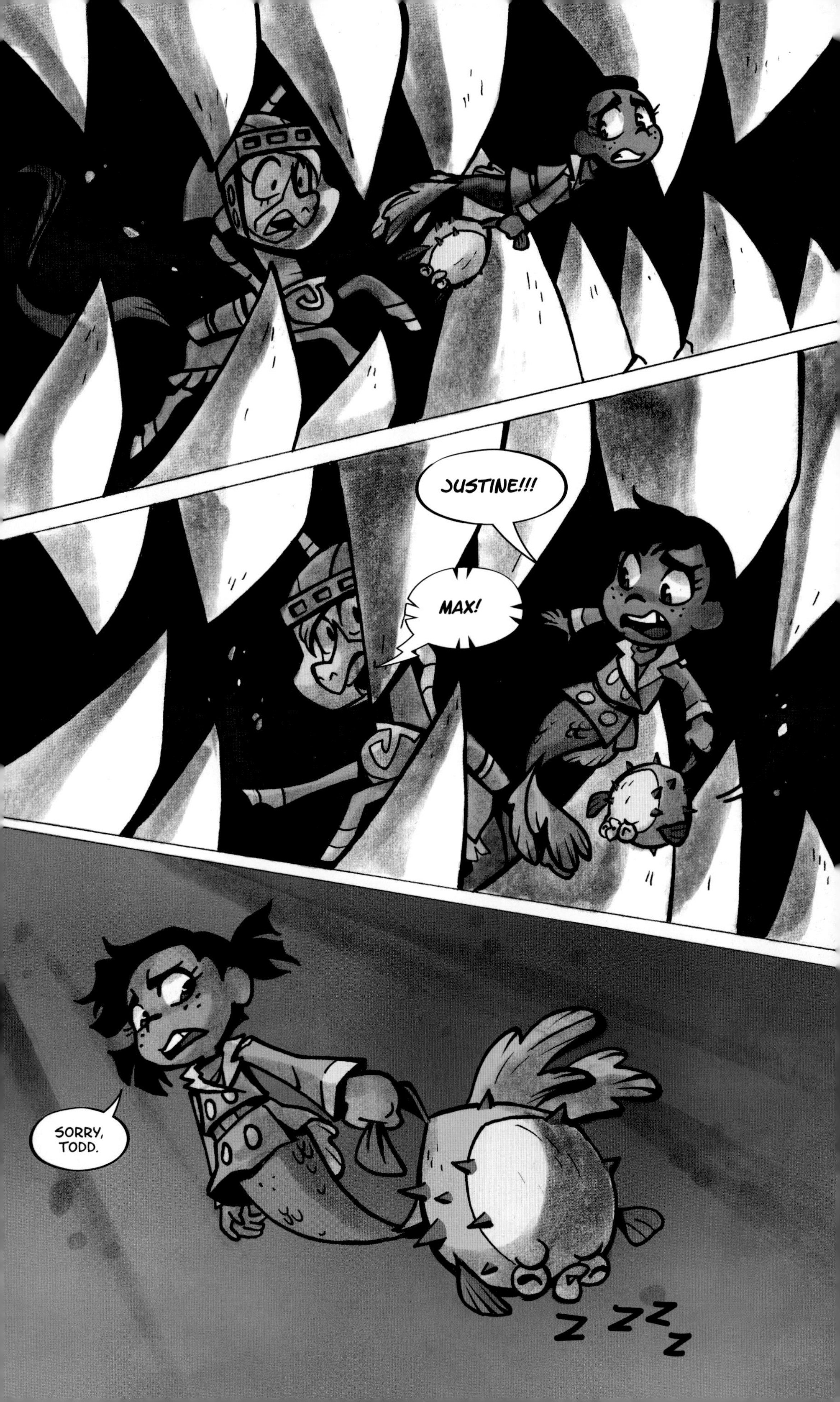
JUSTINE!!!
MAX!
SORRY, TODD.
ZZZZ

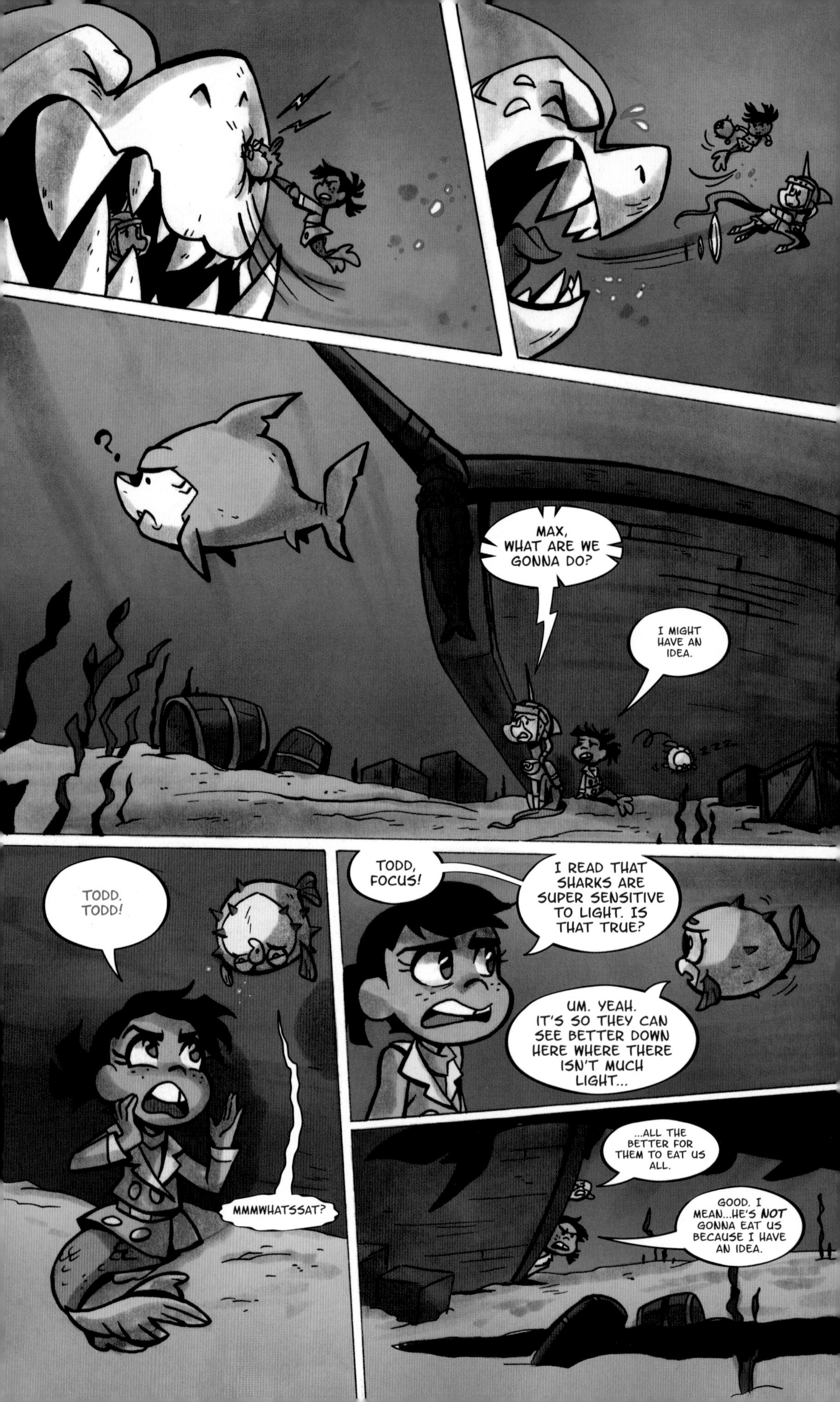
?
MAX, WHAT ARE WE GONNA DO?
I MIGHT HAVE AN IDEA.
Z Z Z
TODD. TODD!
MMMWHATSSAT?
TODD, FOCUS!
I READ THAT SHARKS ARE SUPER SENSITIVE TO LIGHT. IS THAT TRUE?
UM. YEAH. IT'S SO THEY CAN SEE BETTER DOWN HERE WHERE THERE ISN'T MUCH LIGHT...
...ALL THE BETTER FOR THEM TO EAT US ALL.
GOOD. I MEAN...HE'S NOT GONNA EAT US BECAUSE I HAVE AN IDEA.

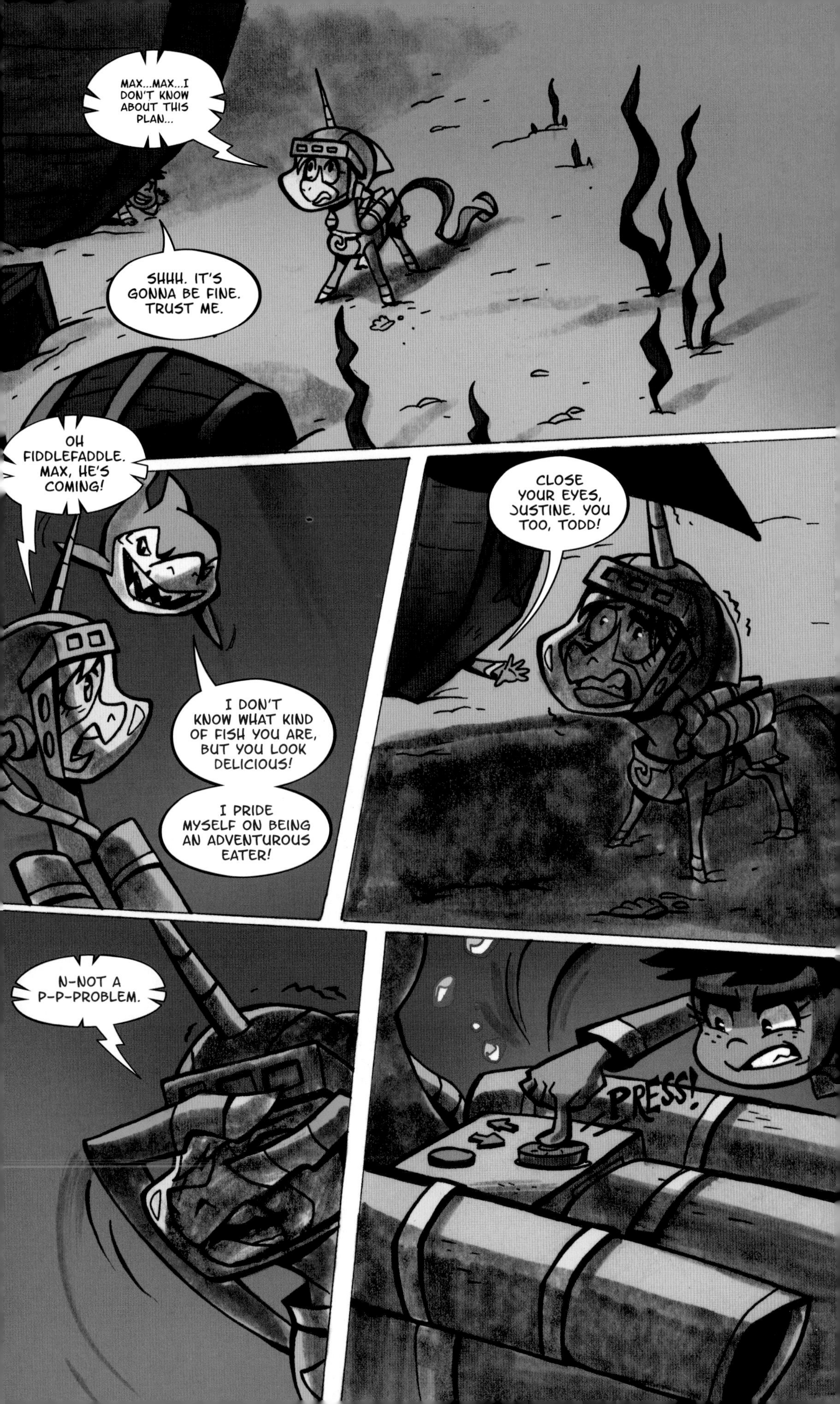
MAX...MAX...I DON'T KNOW ABOUT THIS PLAN...
SHHH. IT'S GONNA BE FINE. TRUST ME.
OH FIDDLEFADDLE. MAX, HE'S COMING!
I DON'T KNOW WHAT KIND OF FISH YOU ARE, BUT YOU LOOK DELICIOUS!
I PRIDE MYSELF ON BEING AN ADVENTUROUS EATER!
CLOSE YOUR EYES, JUSTINE. YOU TOO, TODD!
N-NOT A P-P-PROBLEM.
PRESS!

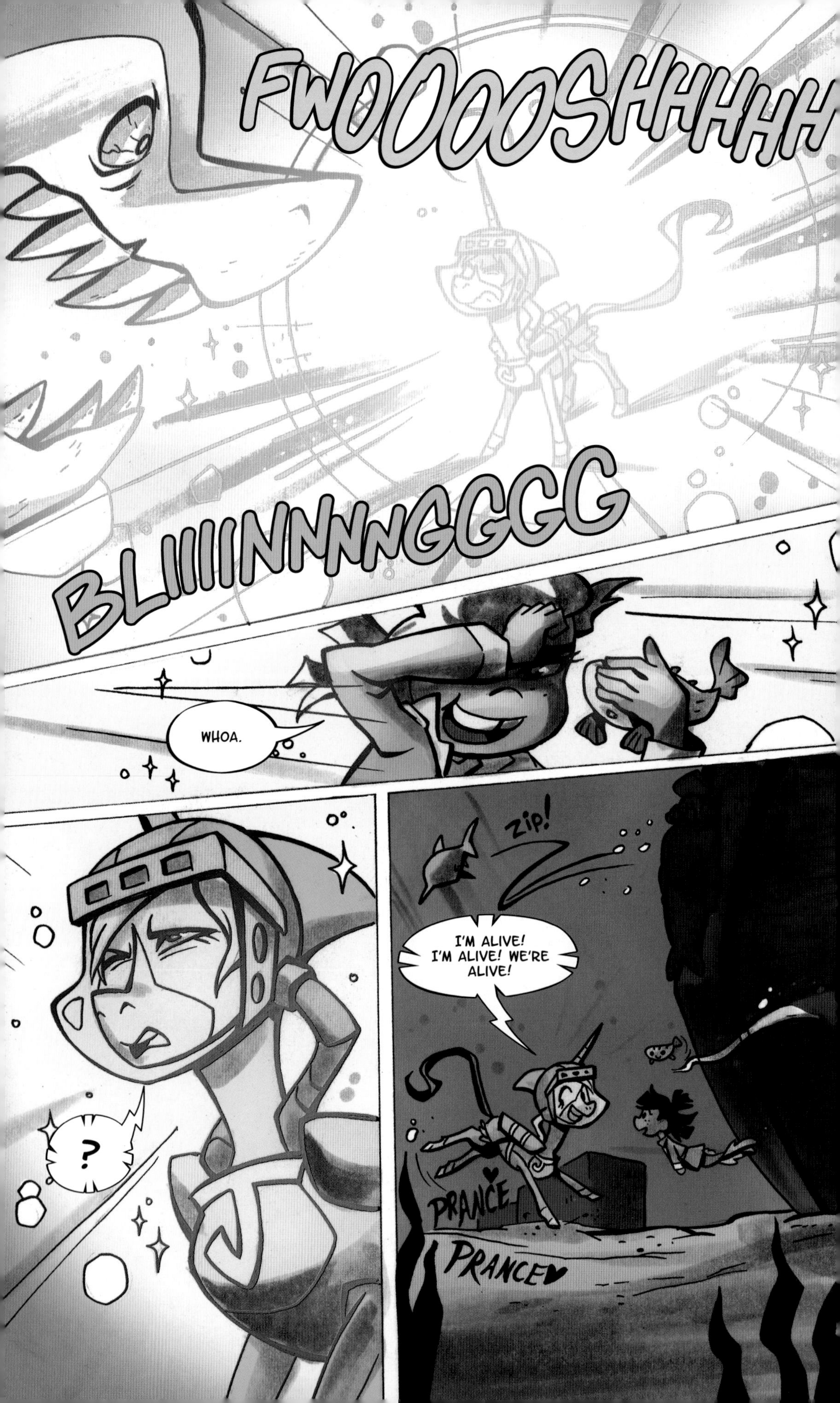

FWOOOOOSHHHHH
BLIIIINNNNGGGG
WHOA.
?
ZIP!
I'M ALIVE! I'M ALIVE! WE'RE ALIVE!
PRANCE
PRANCE

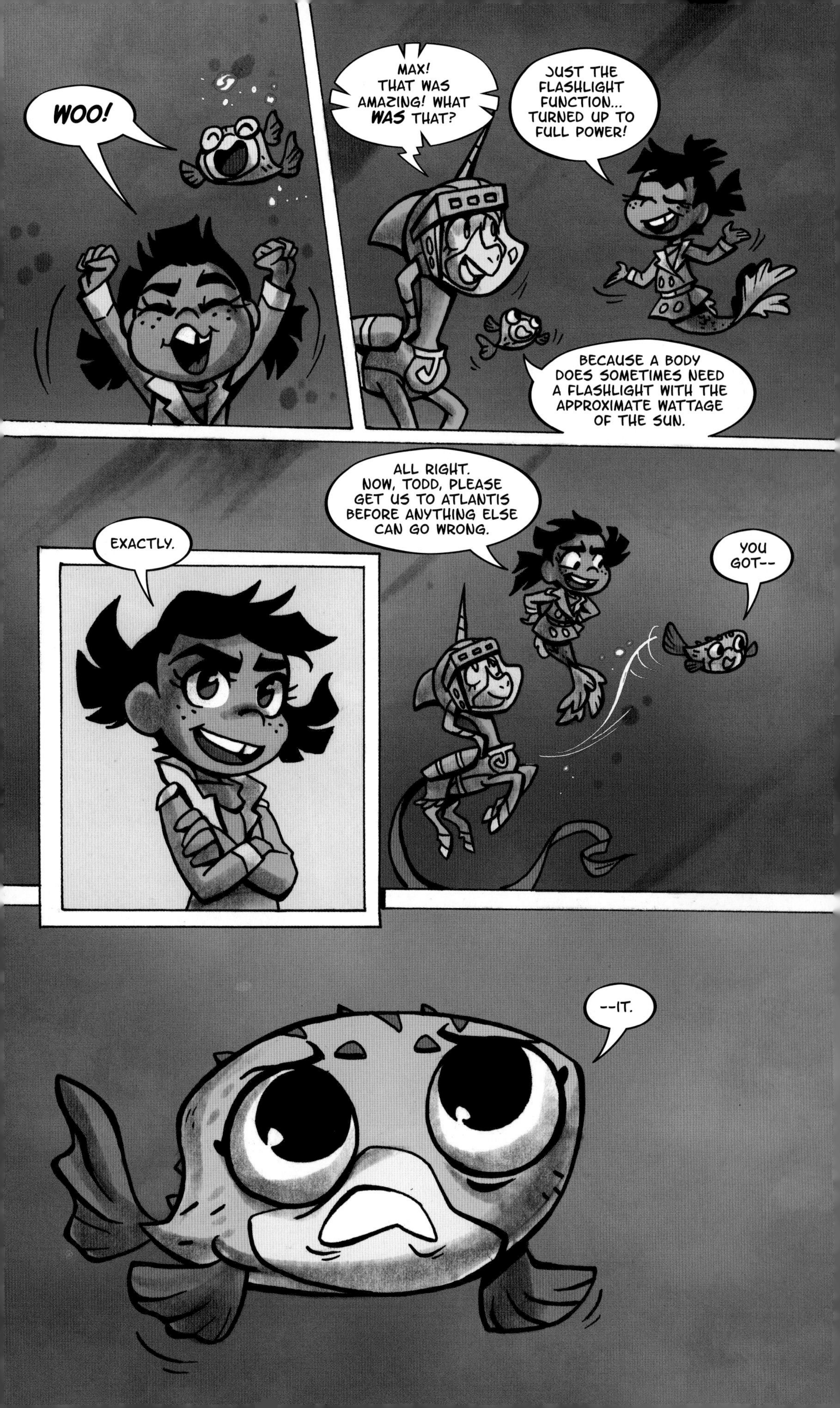
WOO!
MAX! THAT WAS AMAZING! WHAT WAS THAT?
JUST THE FLASHLIGHT FUNCTION... TURNED UP TO FULL POWER!
BECAUSE A BODY DOES SOMETIMES NEED A FLASHLIGHT WITH THE APPROXIMATE WATTAGE OF THE SUN.
ALL RIGHT. NOW, TODD, PLEASE GET US TO ATLANTIS BEFORE ANYTHING ELSE CAN GO WRONG.
EXACTLY.
YOU GOT--
--IT.

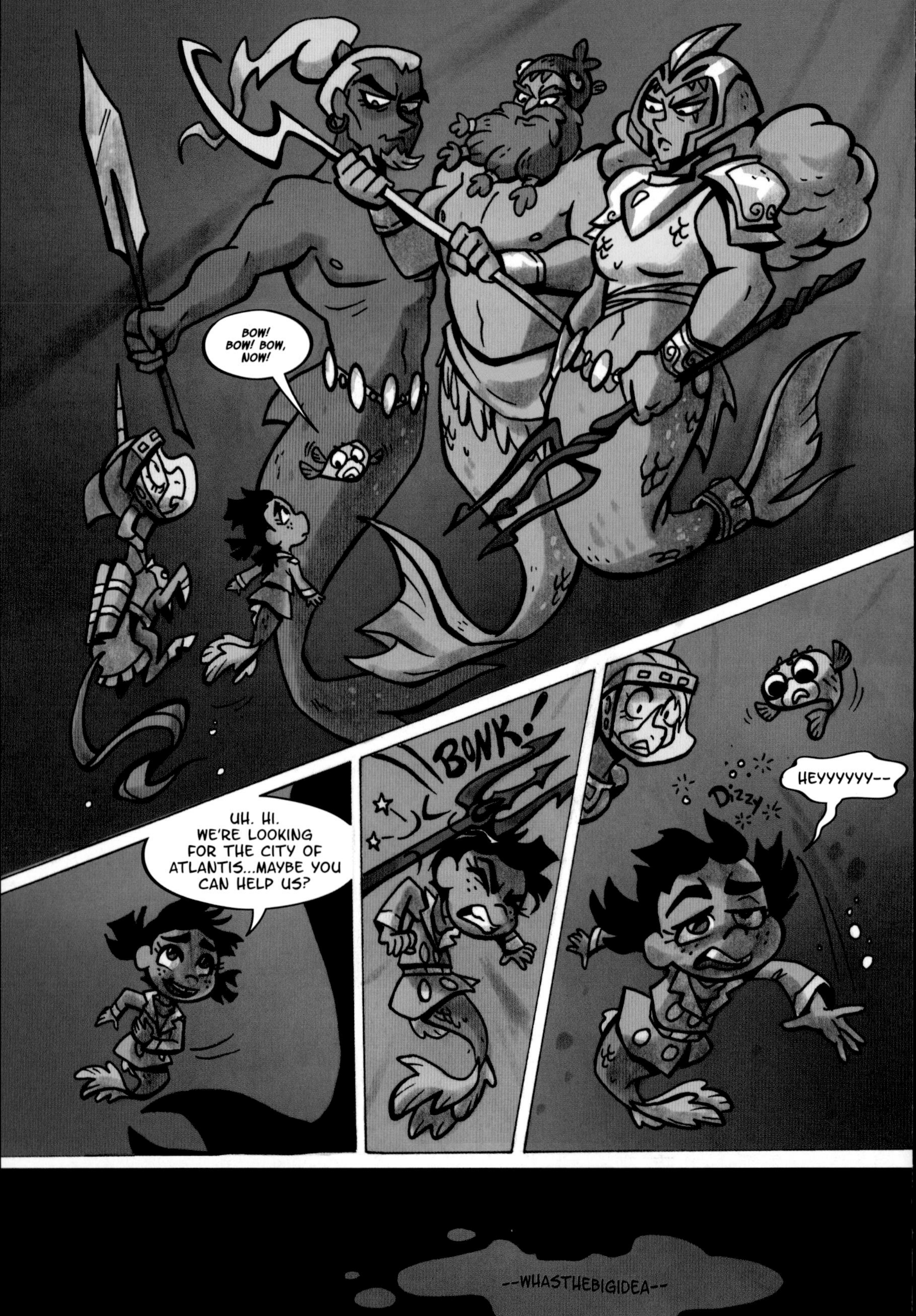
BOW! BOW! BOW, NOW!
UH. HI. WE'RE LOOKING FOR THE CITY OF ATLANTIS...MAYBE YOU CAN HELP US?
BONK!
DIZZY
HEYYYYYY--
--WHASTHEBIGIDEA--

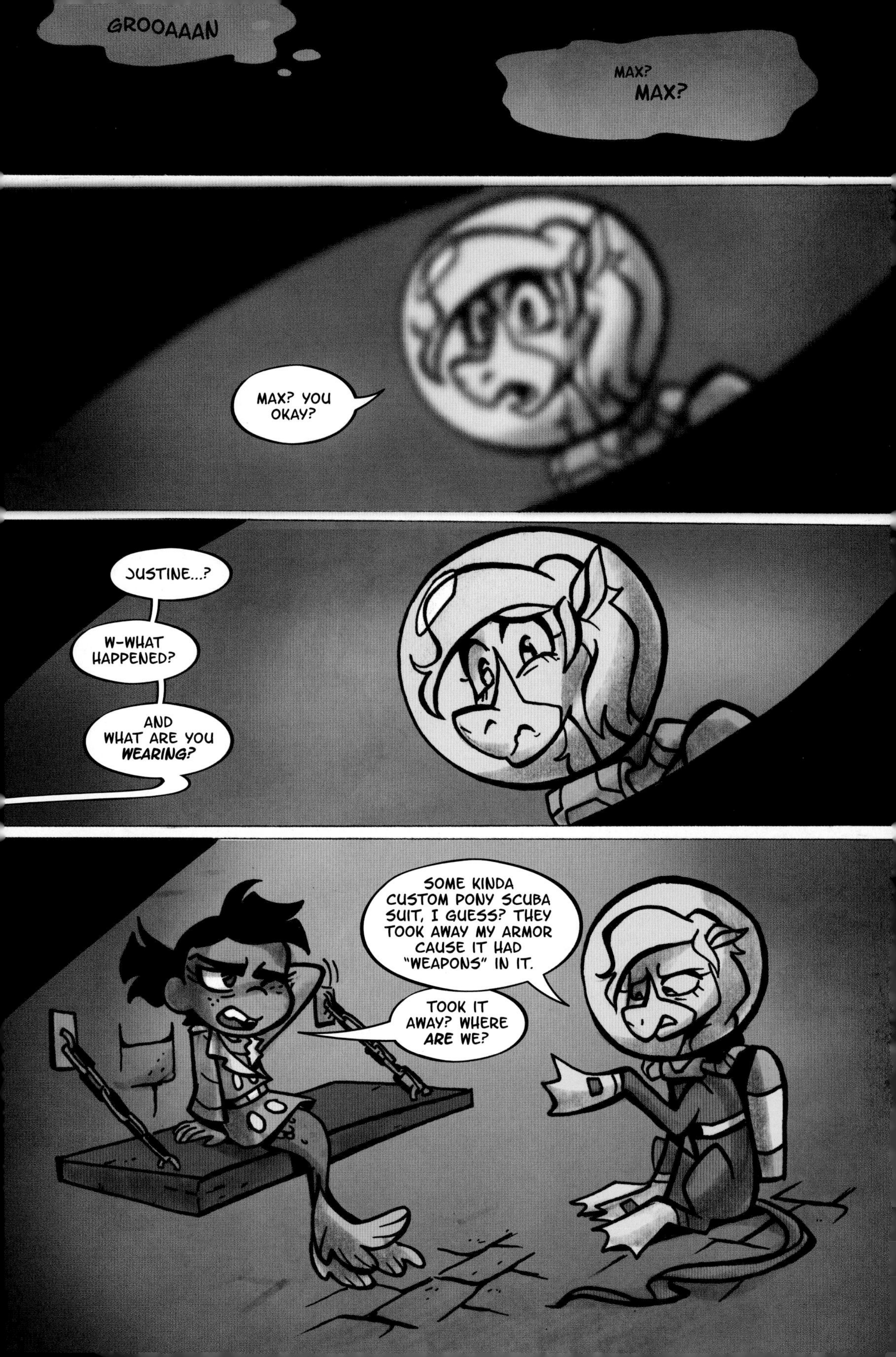
GROOAAAN
MAX? MAX?
MAX? YOU OKAY?
JUSTINE...?
W-WHAT HAPPENED?
AND WHAT ARE YOU *WEARING?*
SOME KINDA CUSTOM PONY SCUBA SUIT, I GUESS? THEY TOOK AWAY MY ARMOR CAUSE IT HAD "WEAPONS" IN IT.
TOOK IT AWAY? WHERE *ARE* WE?

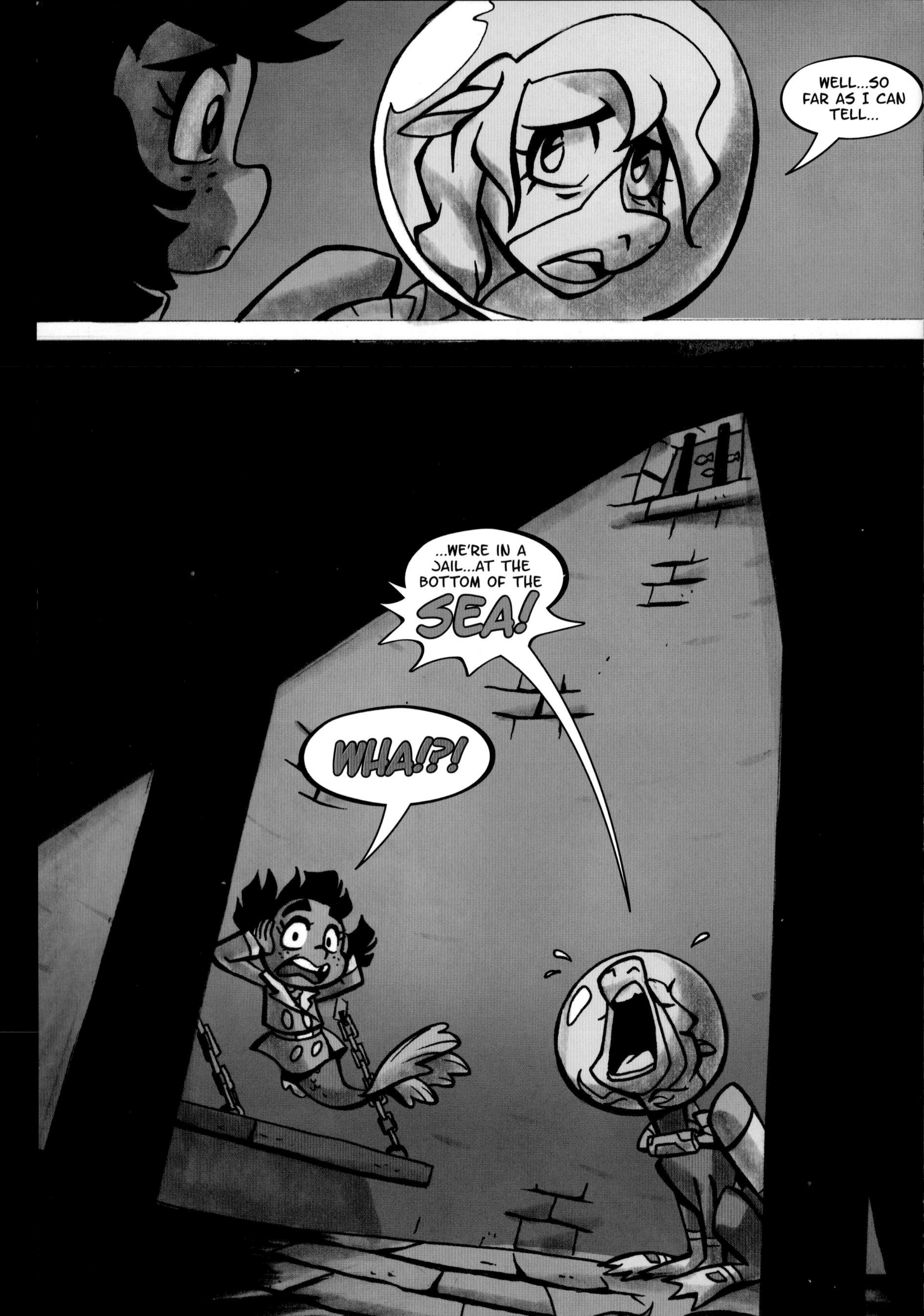
WELL...SO FAR AS I CAN TELL...
...WE'RE IN A JAIL...AT THE BOTTOM OF THE SEA!
WHA!?!

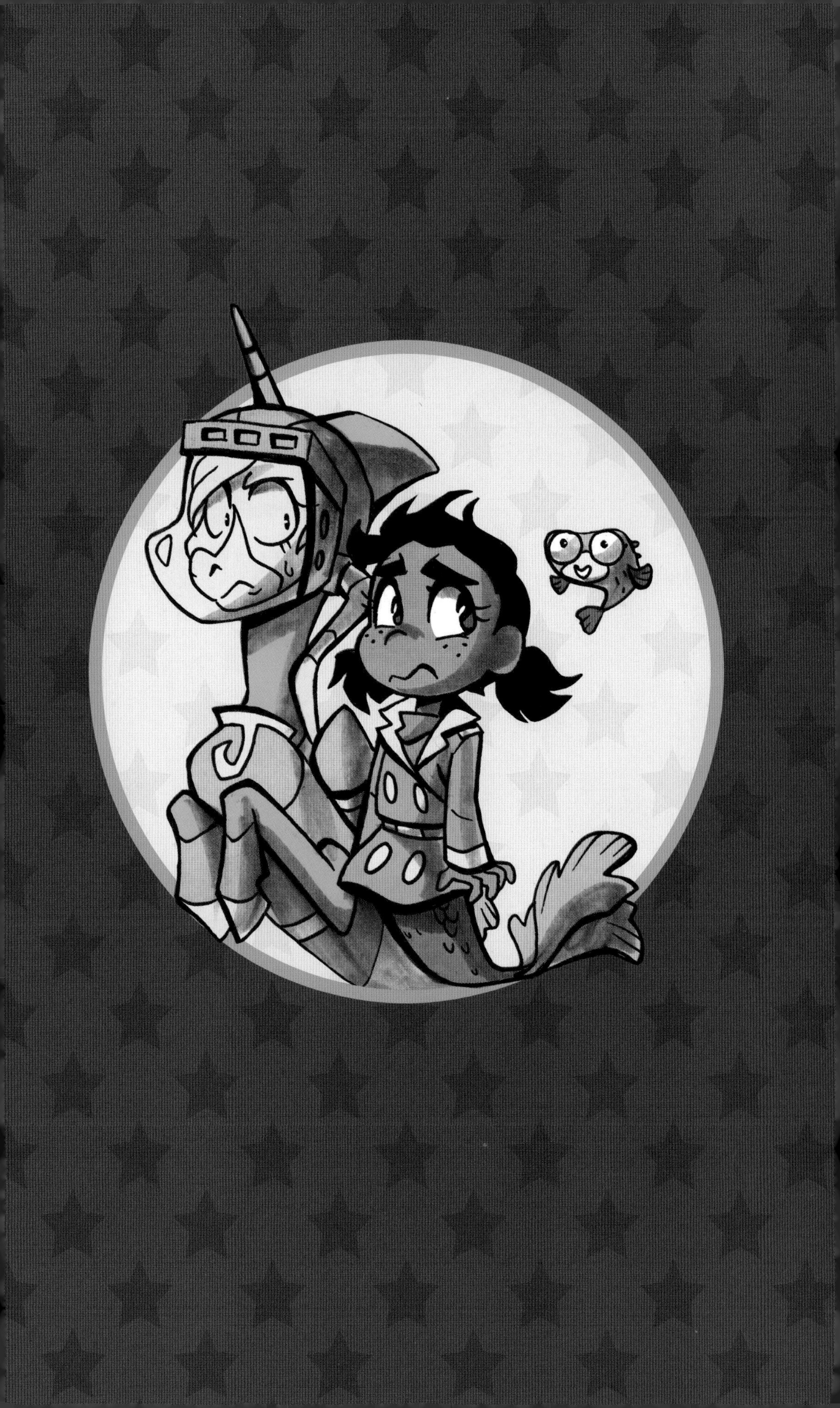

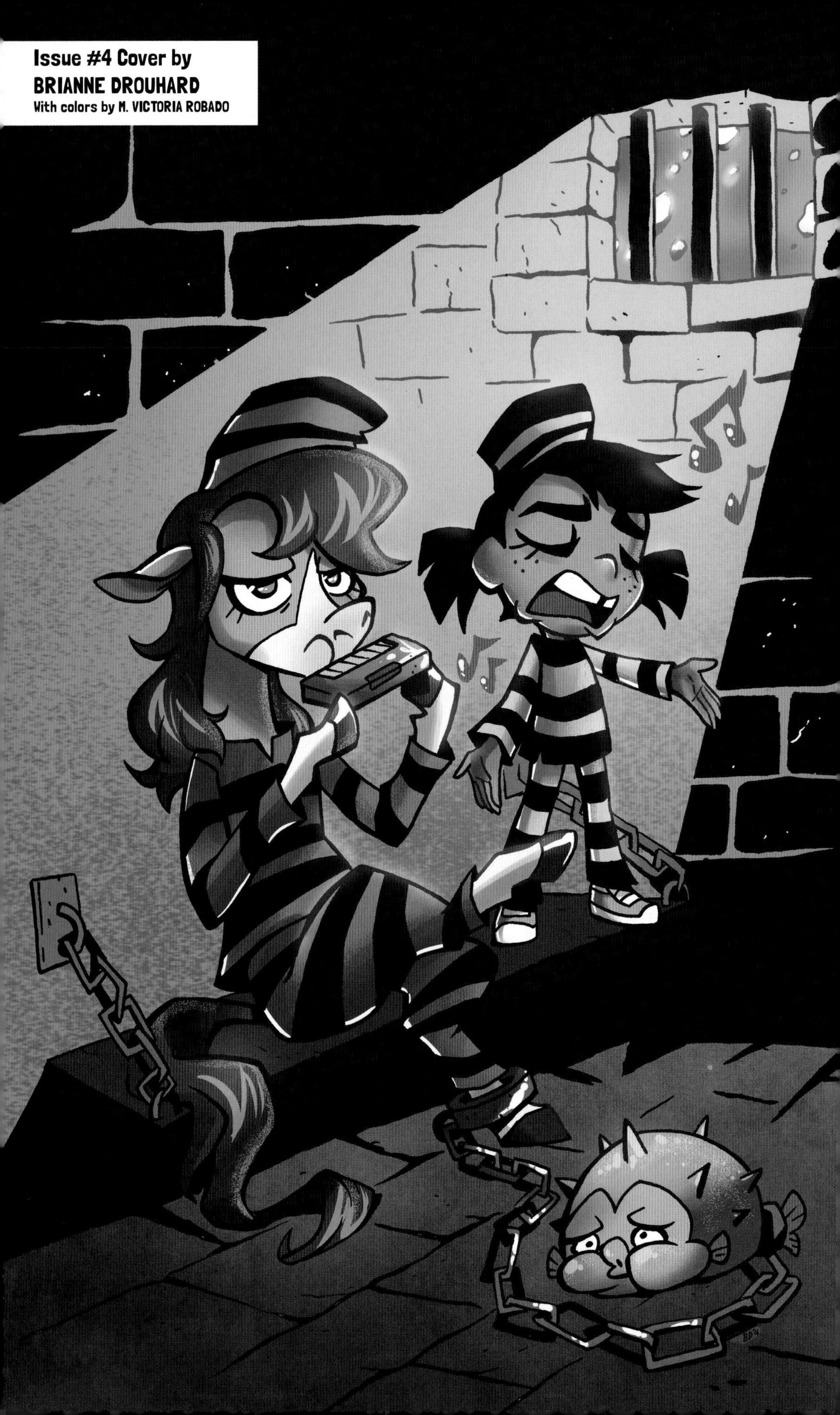

Issue #4 Cover by
BRIANNE DROUHARD
With colors by M. VICTORIA ROBADO

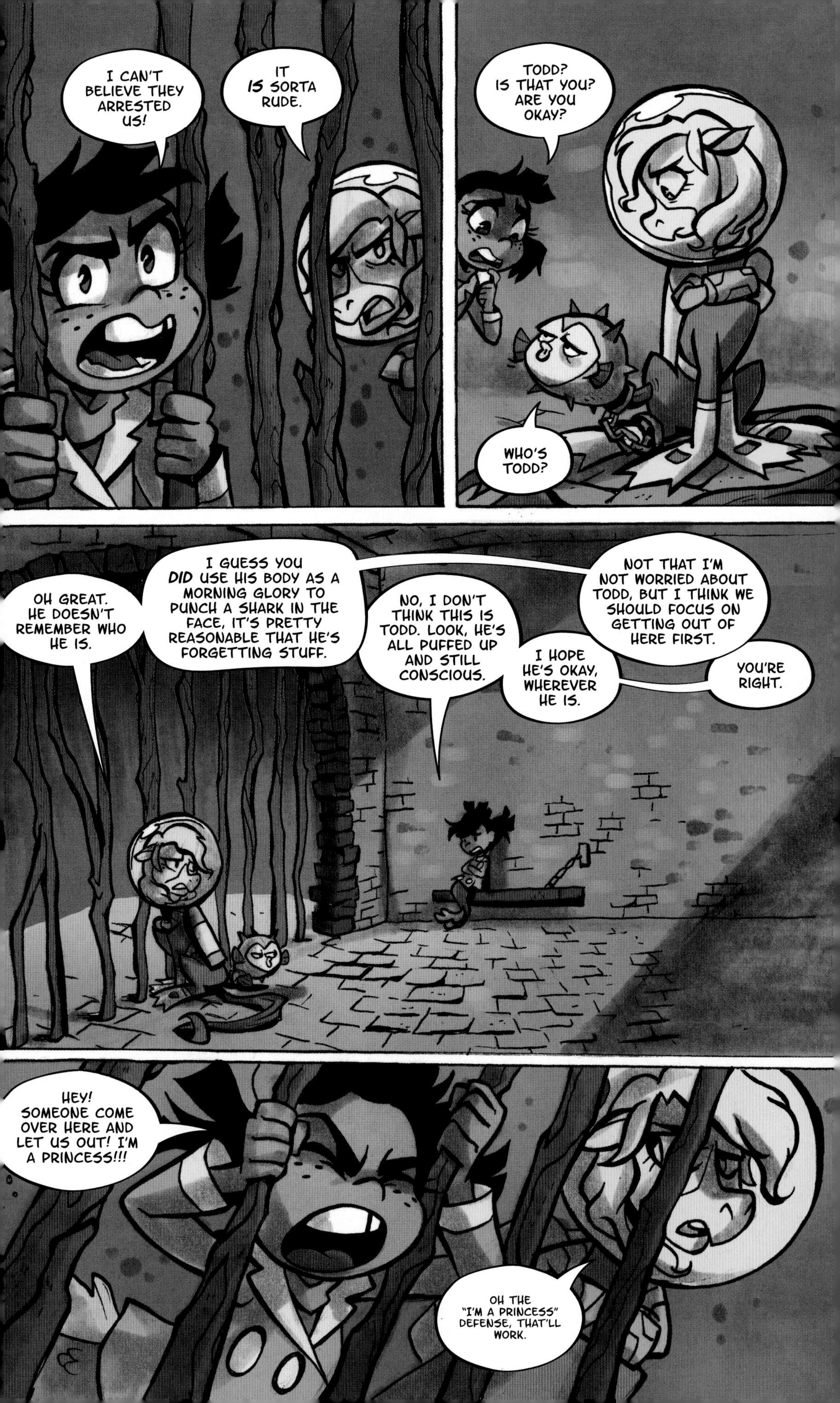
I CAN'T BELIEVE THEY ARRESTED US!
IT *IS* SORTA RUDE.
TODD? IS THAT YOU? ARE YOU OKAY?
WHO'S TODD?
OH GREAT. HE DOESN'T REMEMBER WHO HE IS.
I GUESS YOU *DID* USE HIS BODY AS A MORNING GLORY TO PUNCH A SHARK IN THE FACE, IT'S PRETTY REASONABLE THAT HE'S FORGETTING STUFF.
NO, I DON'T THINK THIS IS TODD. LOOK, HE'S ALL PUFFED UP AND STILL CONSCIOUS.
NOT THAT I'M NOT WORRIED ABOUT TODD, BUT I THINK WE SHOULD FOCUS ON GETTING OUT OF HERE FIRST.
I HOPE HE'S OKAY, WHEREVER HE IS.
YOU'RE RIGHT.
HEY! SOMEONE COME OVER HERE AND LET US OUT! I'M A PRINCESS!!!
OH THE "I'M A PRINCESS" DEFENSE, THAT'LL WORK.

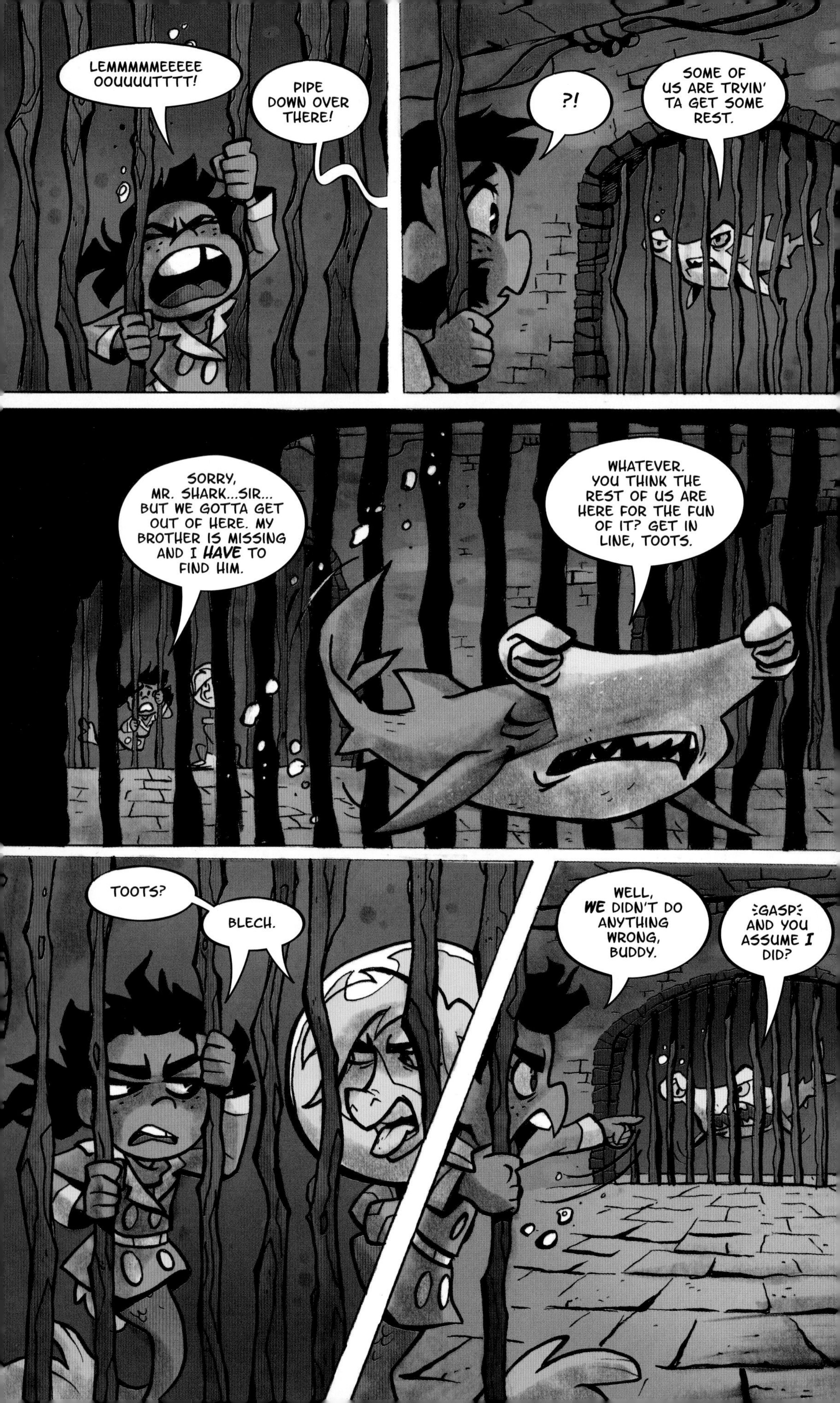
LEMMMMMEEEEE OOUUUUTTTT!
PIPE DOWN OVER THERE!
?!
SOME OF US ARE TRYIN' TA GET SOME REST.
SORRY, MR. SHARK...SIR... BUT WE GOTTA GET OUT OF HERE. MY BROTHER IS MISSING AND I HAVE TO FIND HIM.
WHATEVER. YOU THINK THE REST OF US ARE HERE FOR THE FUN OF IT? GET IN LINE, TOOTS.
TOOTS?
BLECH.
WELL, WE DIDN'T DO ANYTHING WRONG, BUDDY.
GASP AND YOU ASSUME I DID?

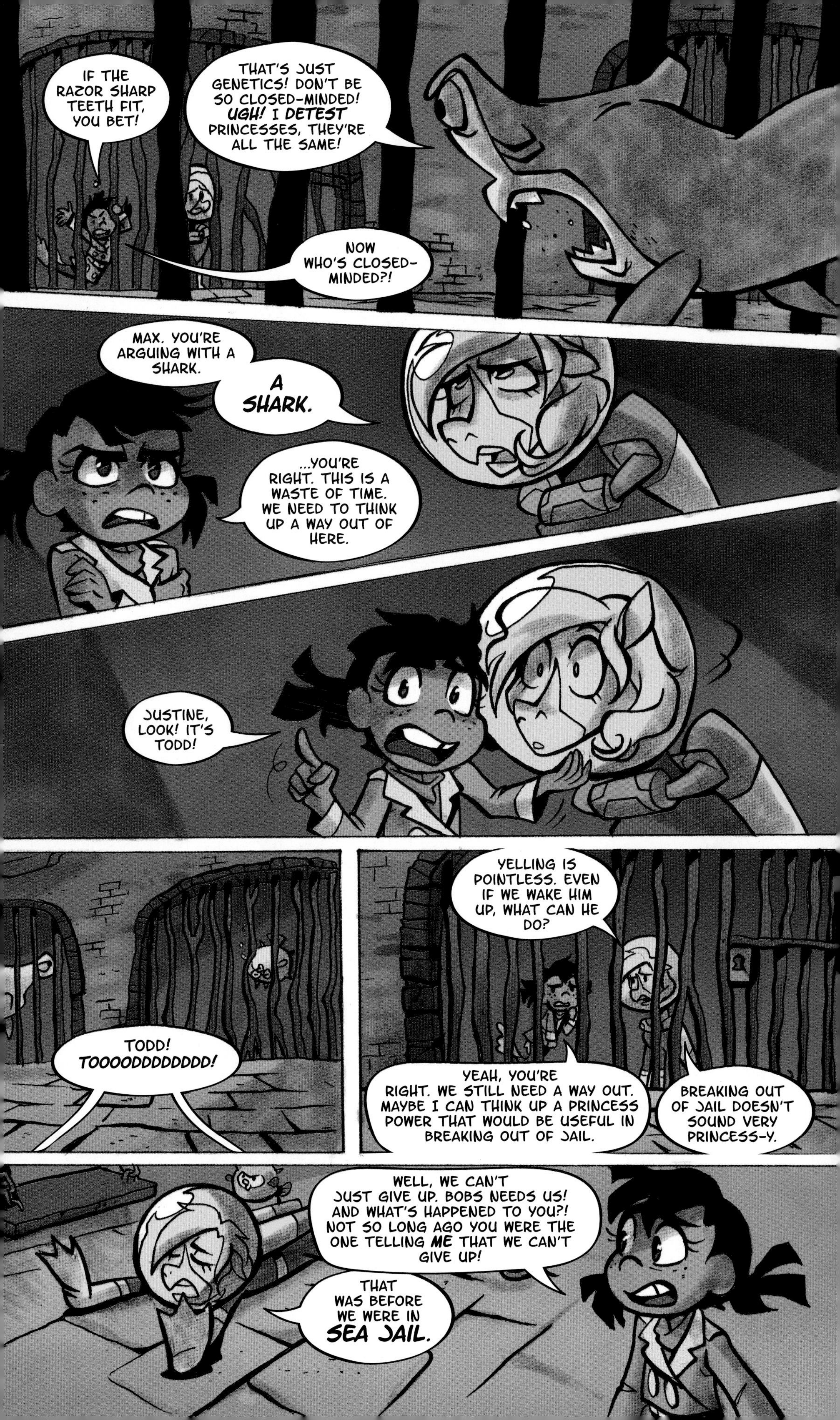
IF THE RAZOR SHARP TEETH FIT, YOU BET!
THAT'S JUST GENETICS! DON'T BE SO CLOSED-MINDED! UGH! I DETEST PRINCESSES, THEY'RE ALL THE SAME!
NOW WHO'S CLOSED-MINDED?!
MAX. YOU'RE ARGUING WITH A SHARK.
A SHARK.
...YOU'RE RIGHT. THIS IS A WASTE OF TIME. WE NEED TO THINK UP A WAY OUT OF HERE.
JUSTINE, LOOK! IT'S TODD!
TODD! TOOOODDDDDDDD!
YELLING IS POINTLESS. EVEN IF WE WAKE HIM UP, WHAT CAN HE DO?
YEAH, YOU'RE RIGHT. WE STILL NEED A WAY OUT. MAYBE I CAN THINK UP A PRINCESS POWER THAT WOULD BE USEFUL IN BREAKING OUT OF JAIL.
BREAKING OUT OF JAIL DOESN'T SOUND VERY PRINCESS-Y.
WELL, WE CAN'T JUST GIVE UP. BOBS NEEDS US! AND WHAT'S HAPPENED TO YOU?! NOT SO LONG AGO YOU WERE THE ONE TELLING ME THAT WE CAN'T GIVE UP!
THAT WAS BEFORE WE WERE IN SEA JAIL.

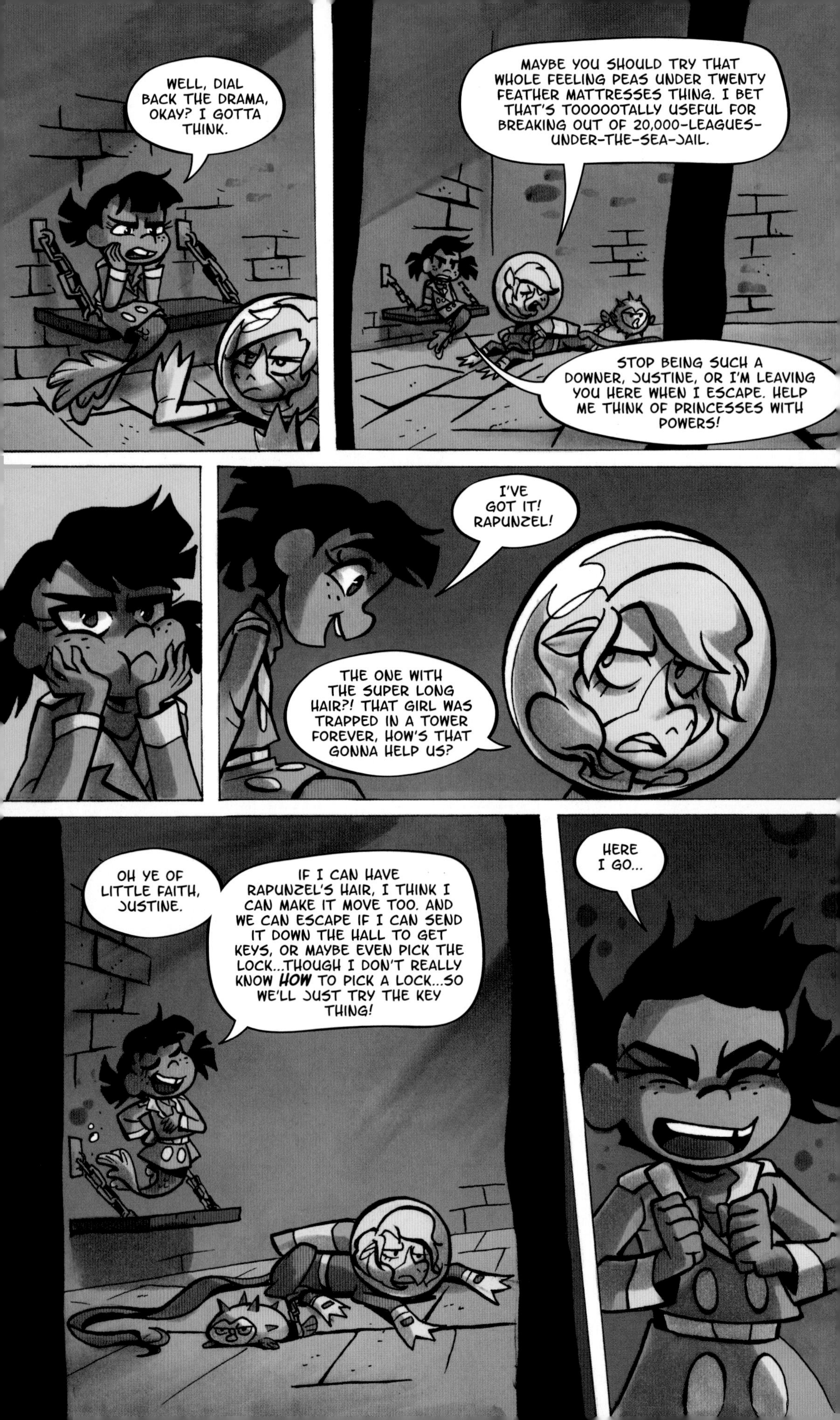
WELL, DIAL BACK THE DRAMA, OKAY? I GOTTA THINK.
MAYBE YOU SHOULD TRY THAT WHOLE FEELING PEAS UNDER TWENTY FEATHER MATTRESSES THING. I BET THAT'S TOOOOOTALLY USEFUL FOR BREAKING OUT OF 20,000-LEAGUES-UNDER-THE-SEA-JAIL.
STOP BEING SUCH A DOWNER, JUSTINE, OR I'M LEAVING YOU HERE WHEN I ESCAPE. HELP ME THINK OF PRINCESSES WITH POWERS!
I'VE GOT IT! RAPUNZEL!
THE ONE WITH THE SUPER LONG HAIR?! THAT GIRL WAS TRAPPED IN A TOWER FOREVER, HOW'S THAT GONNA HELP US?
OH YE OF LITTLE FAITH, JUSTINE.
IF I CAN HAVE RAPUNZEL'S HAIR, I THINK I CAN MAKE IT MOVE TOO. AND WE CAN ESCAPE IF I CAN SEND IT DOWN THE HALL TO GET KEYS, OR MAYBE EVEN PICK THE LOCK...THOUGH I DON'T REALLY KNOW *HOW* TO PICK A LOCK...SO WE'LL JUST TRY THE KEY THING!
HERE I GO...

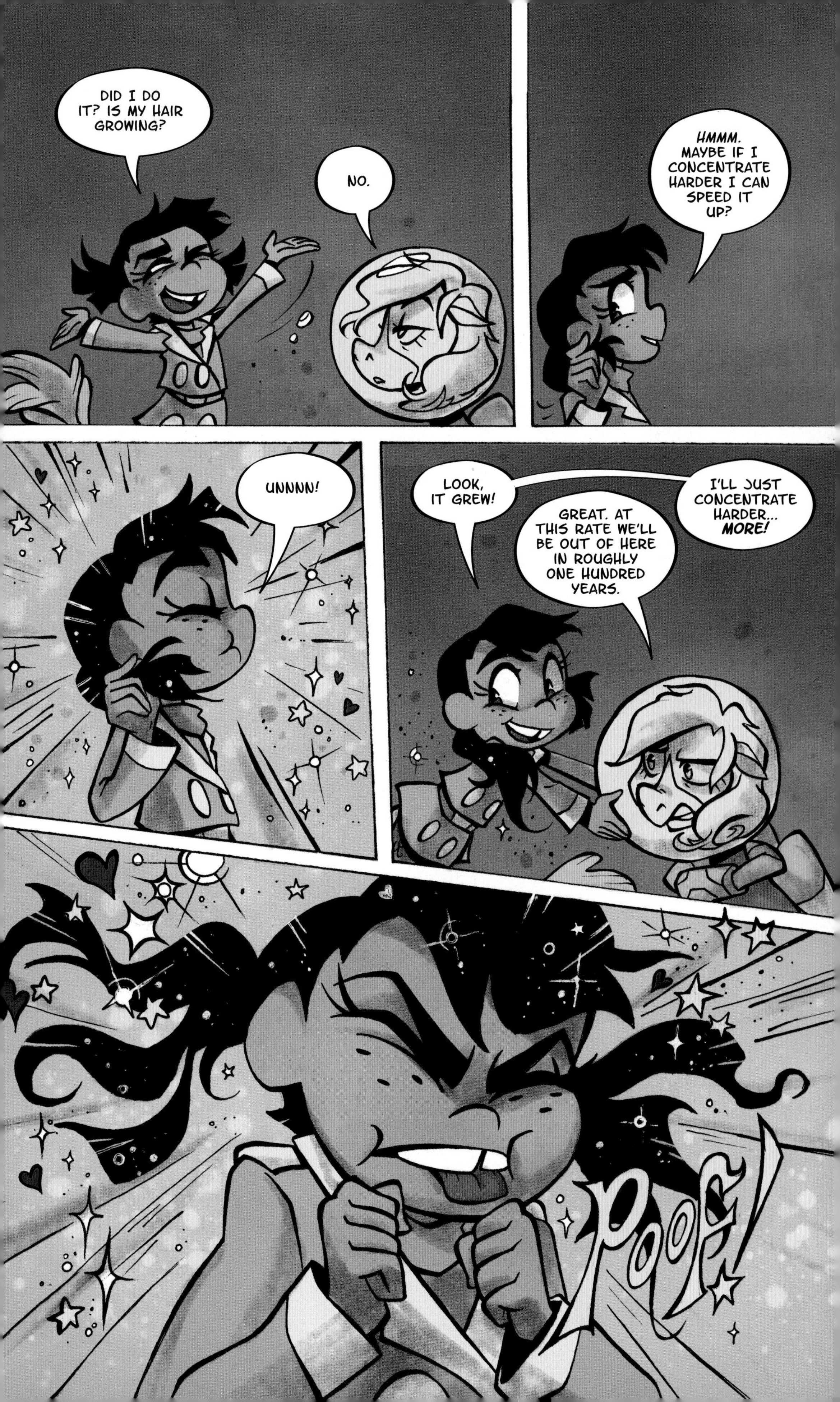
DID I DO IT? IS MY HAIR GROWING?
NO.
HMMM. MAYBE IF I CONCENTRATE HARDER I CAN SPEED IT UP?
UNNNN!
LOOK, IT GREW!
I'LL JUST CONCENTRATE HARDER... MORE!
GREAT. AT THIS RATE WE'LL BE OUT OF HERE IN ROUGHLY ONE HUNDRED YEARS.
POOF!

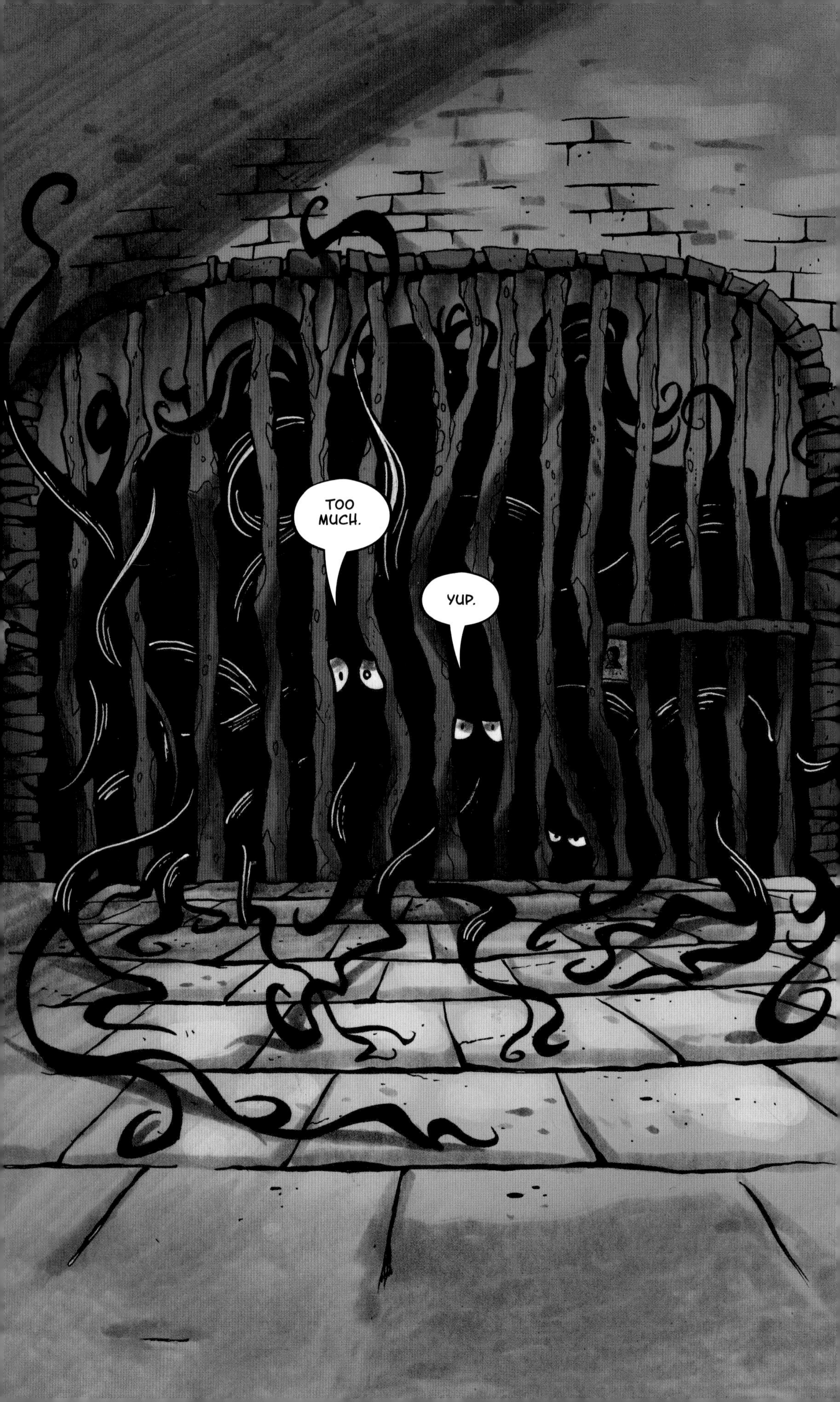
TOO MUCH.
YUP.

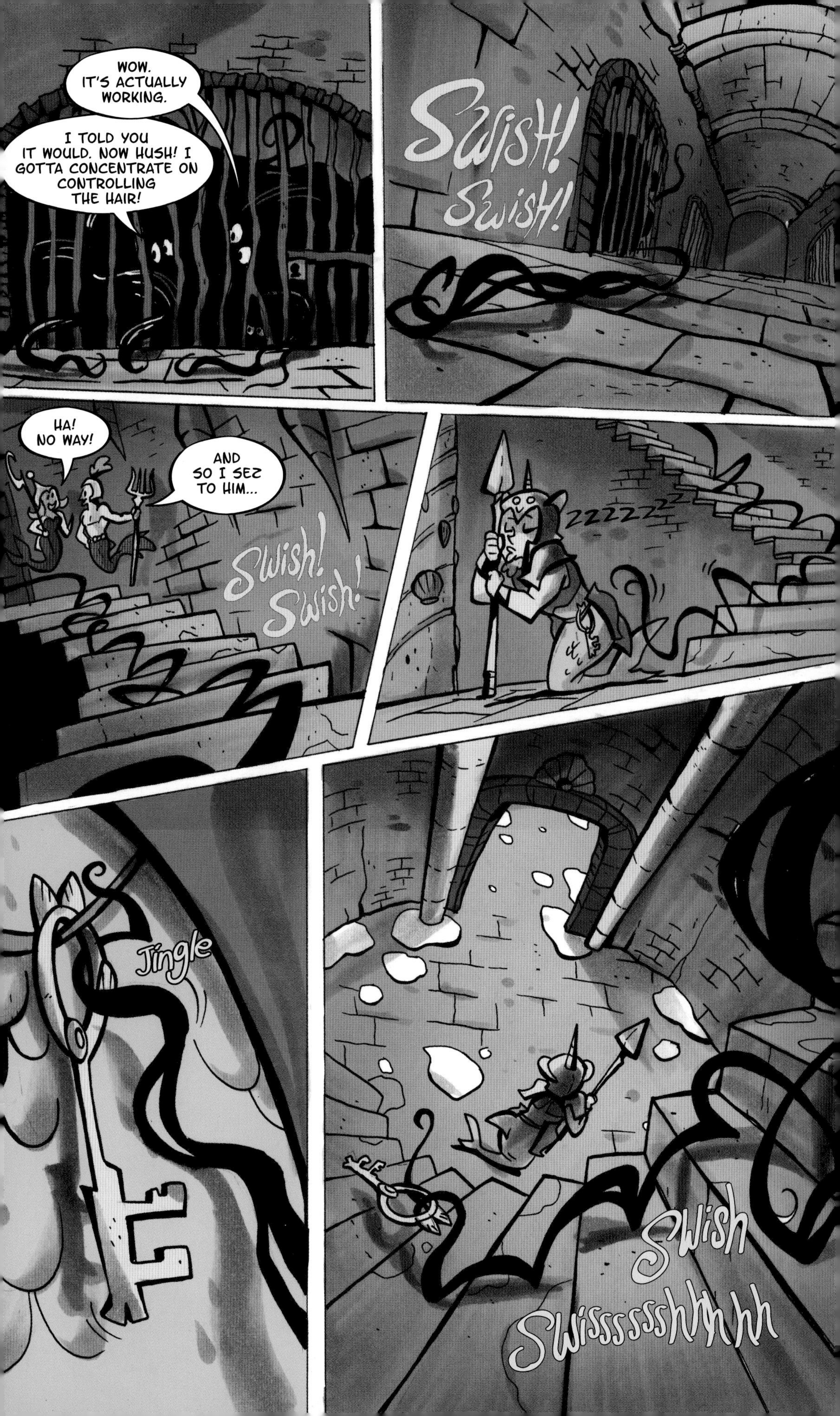
WOW. IT'S ACTUALLY WORKING.
I TOLD YOU IT WOULD. NOW HUSH! I GOTTA CONCENTRATE ON CONTROLLING THE HAIR!
SWISH! SWISH!
HA! NO WAY!
AND SO I SEZ TO HIM...
SWISH! SWISH!
ZZZZZZ
JINGLE
SWISH
SWISSSSSHHHHH

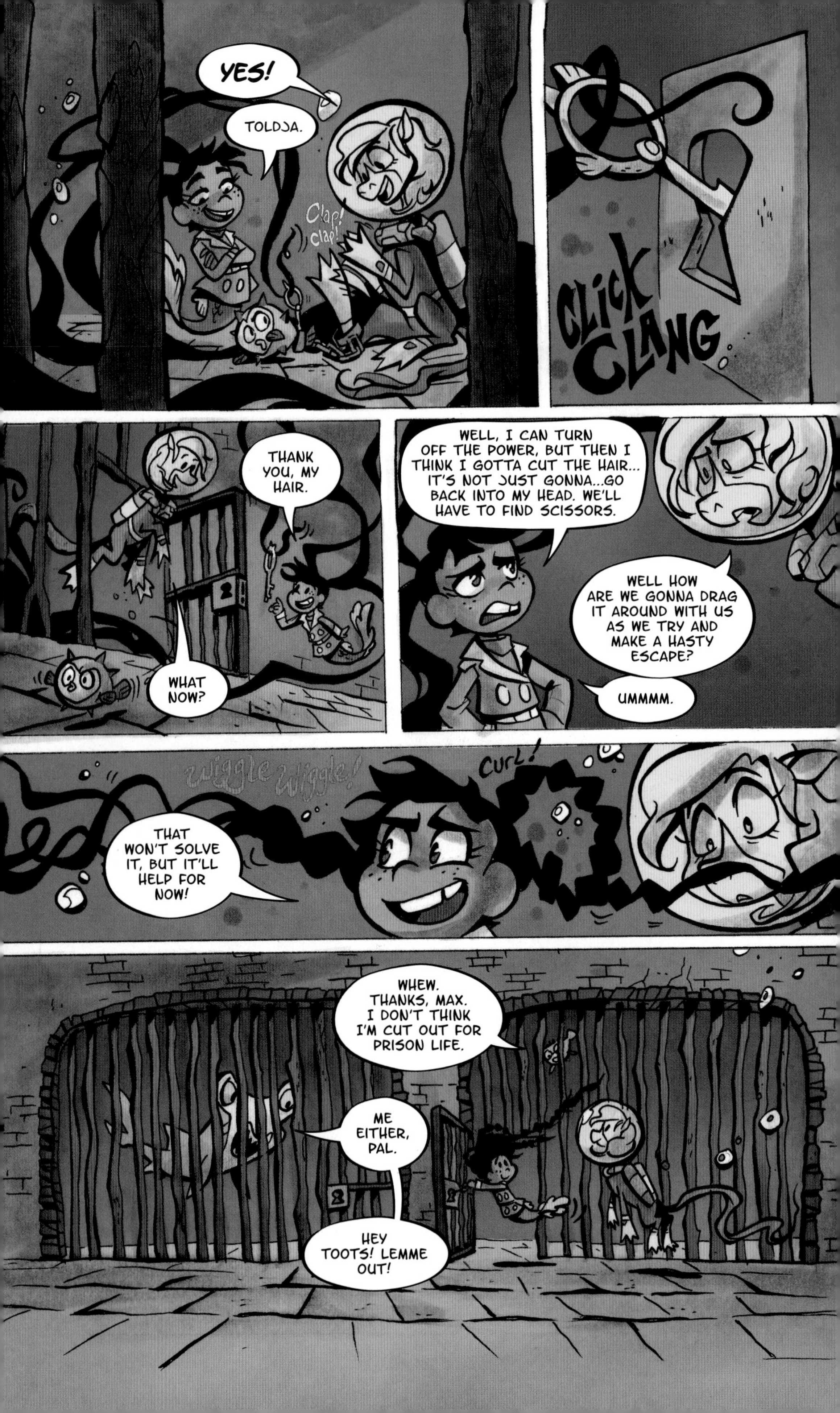
YES!
TOLDJA.
Clap! clap!
CLICK
CLANG
THANK YOU, MY HAIR.
WHAT NOW?
WELL, I CAN TURN OFF THE POWER, BUT THEN I THINK I GOTTA CUT THE HAIR... IT'S NOT JUST GONNA...GO BACK INTO MY HEAD. WE'LL HAVE TO FIND SCISSORS.
WELL HOW ARE WE GONNA DRAG IT AROUND WITH US AS WE TRY AND MAKE A HASTY ESCAPE?
UMMMM.
wiggle wiggle!
CURL!
THAT WON'T SOLVE IT, BUT IT'LL HELP FOR NOW!
WHEW. THANKS, MAX. I DON'T THINK I'M CUT OUT FOR PRISON LIFE.
ME EITHER, PAL.
HEY TOOTS! LEMME OUT!

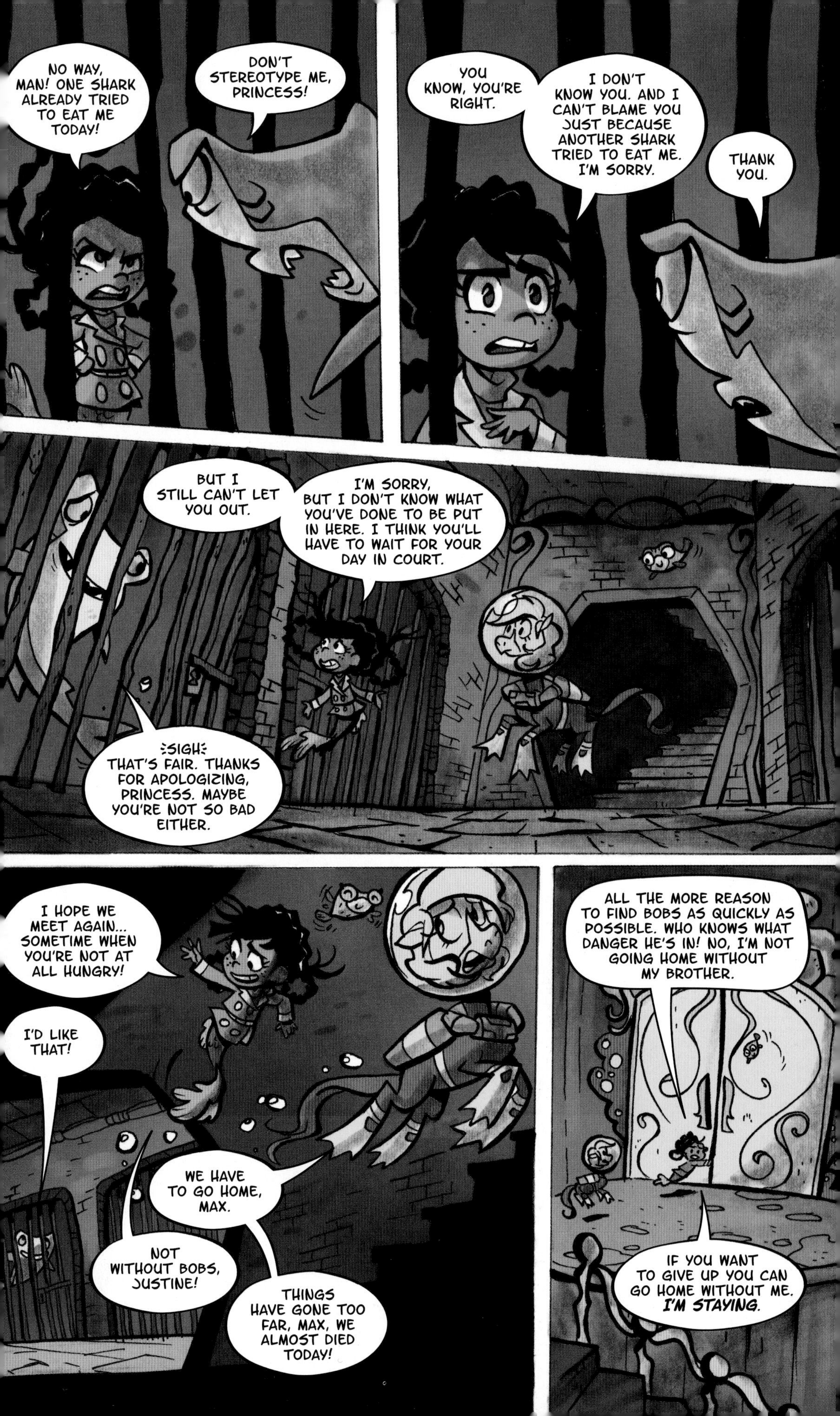
NO WAY, MAN! ONE SHARK ALREADY TRIED TO EAT ME TODAY!
DON'T STEREOTYPE ME, PRINCESS!
YOU KNOW, YOU'RE RIGHT.
I DON'T KNOW YOU. AND I CAN'T BLAME YOU JUST BECAUSE ANOTHER SHARK TRIED TO EAT ME. I'M SORRY.
THANK YOU.
BUT I STILL CAN'T LET YOU OUT.
I'M SORRY, BUT I DON'T KNOW WHAT YOU'VE DONE TO BE PUT IN HERE. I THINK YOU'LL HAVE TO WAIT FOR YOUR DAY IN COURT.
SIGH
THAT'S FAIR. THANKS FOR APOLOGIZING, PRINCESS. MAYBE YOU'RE NOT SO BAD EITHER.
I HOPE WE MEET AGAIN... SOMETIME WHEN YOU'RE NOT AT ALL HUNGRY!
I'D LIKE THAT!
WE HAVE TO GO HOME, MAX.
NOT WITHOUT BOBS, JUSTINE!
THINGS HAVE GONE TOO FAR, MAX, WE ALMOST DIED TODAY!
ALL THE MORE REASON TO FIND BOBS AS QUICKLY AS POSSIBLE. WHO KNOWS WHAT DANGER HE'S IN! NO, I'M NOT GOING HOME WITHOUT MY BROTHER.
IF YOU WANT TO GIVE UP YOU CAN GO HOME WITHOUT ME. *I'M STAYING.*

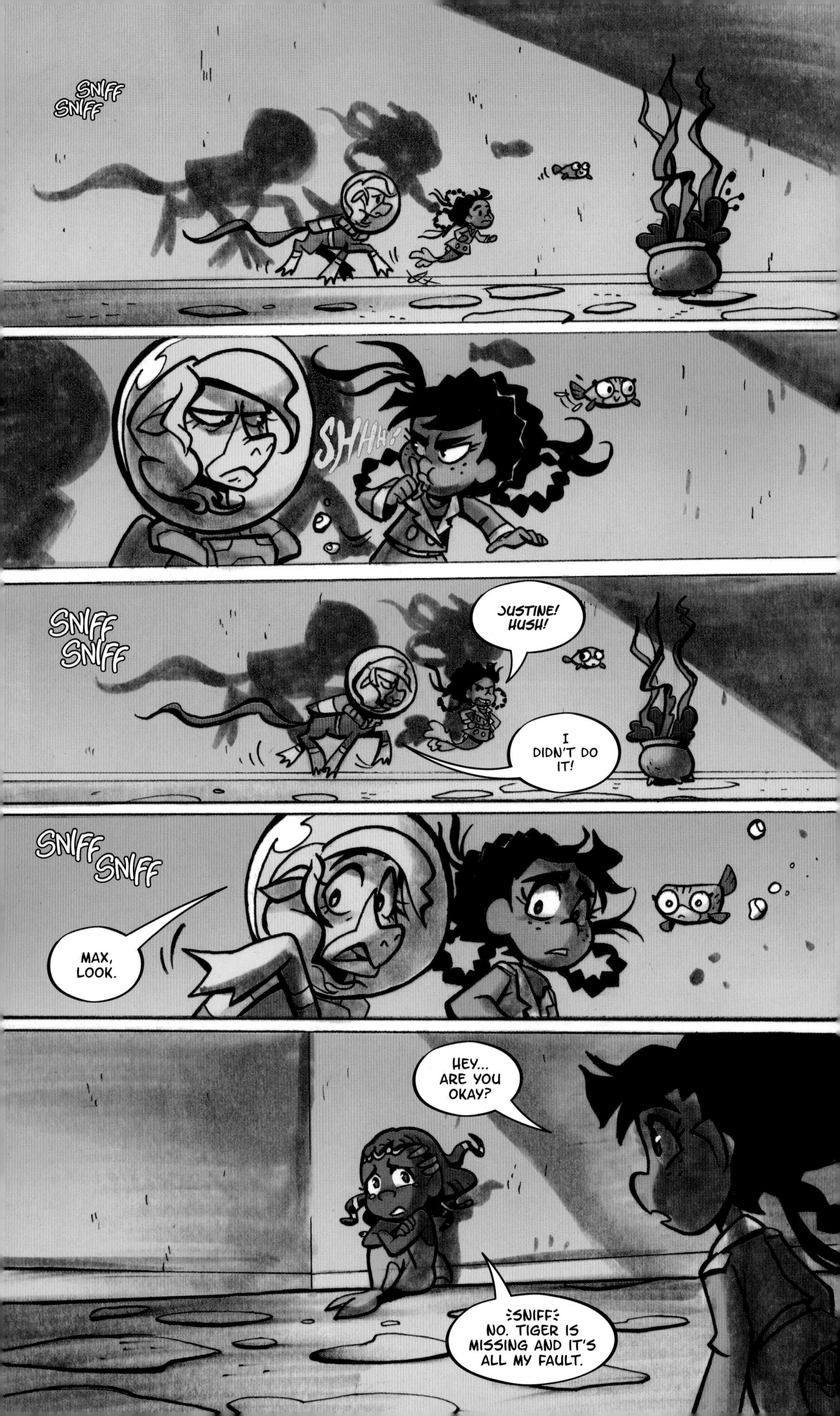

SNIFF SNIFF
SHHH!
SNIFF SNIFF
JUSTINE! HUSH!
I DIDN'T DO IT!
SNIFF SNIFF
MAX, LOOK.
HEY... ARE YOU OKAY?
SNIFF NO. TIGER IS MISSING AND IT'S ALL MY FAULT.

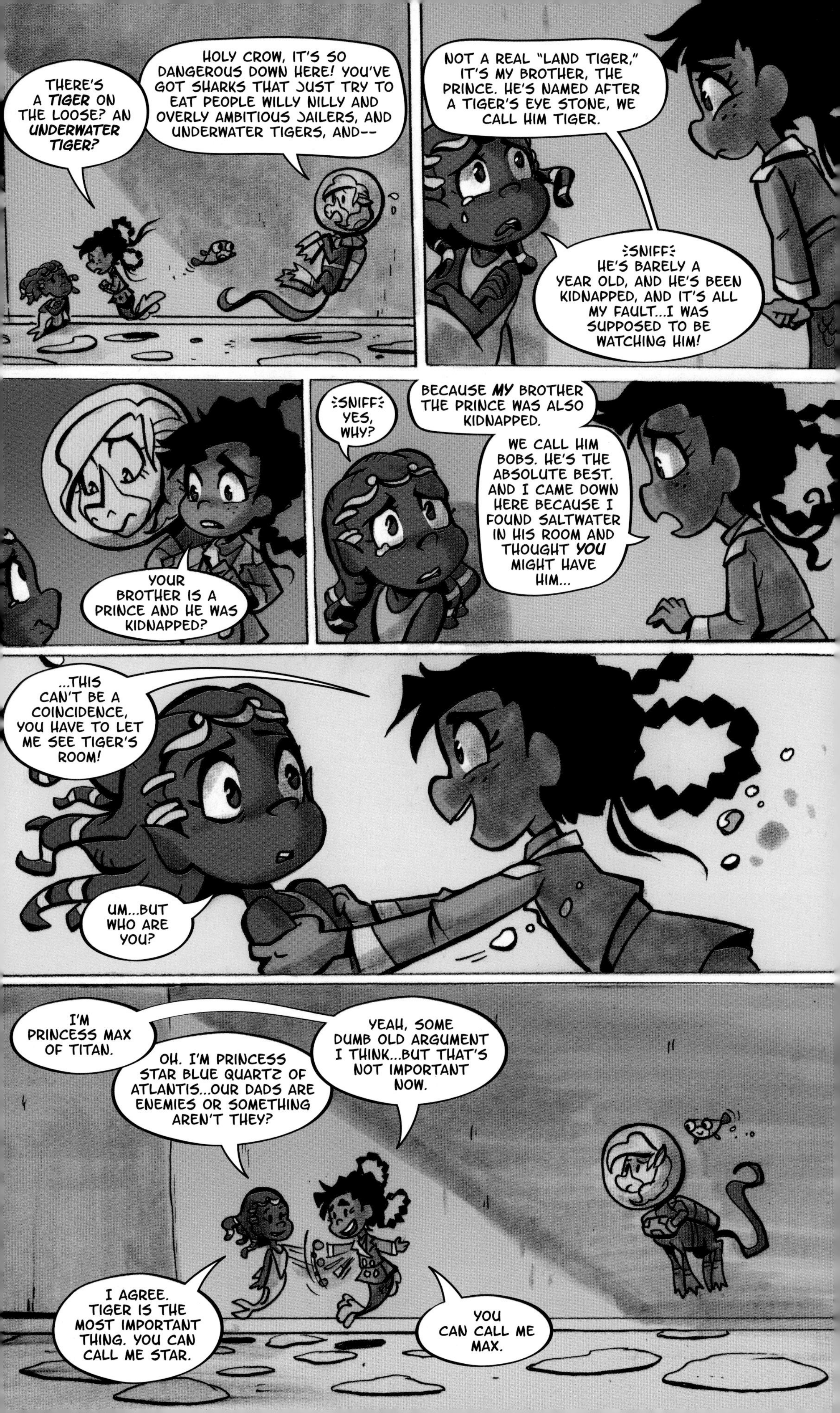
THERE'S A TIGER ON THE LOOSE? AN UNDERWATER TIGER?
HOLY CROW, IT'S SO DANGEROUS DOWN HERE! YOU'VE GOT SHARKS THAT JUST TRY TO EAT PEOPLE WILLY NILLY AND OVERLY AMBITIOUS JAILERS, AND UNDERWATER TIGERS, AND--
NOT A REAL "LAND TIGER," IT'S MY BROTHER, THE PRINCE. HE'S NAMED AFTER A TIGER'S EYE STONE, WE CALL HIM TIGER.
SNIFF HE'S BARELY A YEAR OLD, AND HE'S BEEN KIDNAPPED, AND IT'S ALL MY FAULT...I WAS SUPPOSED TO BE WATCHING HIM!
YOUR BROTHER IS A PRINCE AND HE WAS KIDNAPPED?
SNIFF YES, WHY?
BECAUSE MY BROTHER THE PRINCE WAS ALSO KIDNAPPED.
WE CALL HIM BOBS. HE'S THE ABSOLUTE BEST. AND I CAME DOWN HERE BECAUSE I FOUND SALTWATER IN HIS ROOM AND THOUGHT YOU MIGHT HAVE HIM...
...THIS CAN'T BE A COINCIDENCE, YOU HAVE TO LET ME SEE TIGER'S ROOM!
UM...BUT WHO ARE YOU?
I'M PRINCESS MAX OF TITAN.
OH. I'M PRINCESS STAR BLUE QUARTZ OF ATLANTIS...OUR DADS ARE ENEMIES OR SOMETHING AREN'T THEY?
YEAH, SOME DUMB OLD ARGUMENT I THINK...BUT THAT'S NOT IMPORTANT NOW.
I AGREE. TIGER IS THE MOST IMPORTANT THING. YOU CAN CALL ME STAR.
YOU CAN CALL ME MAX.

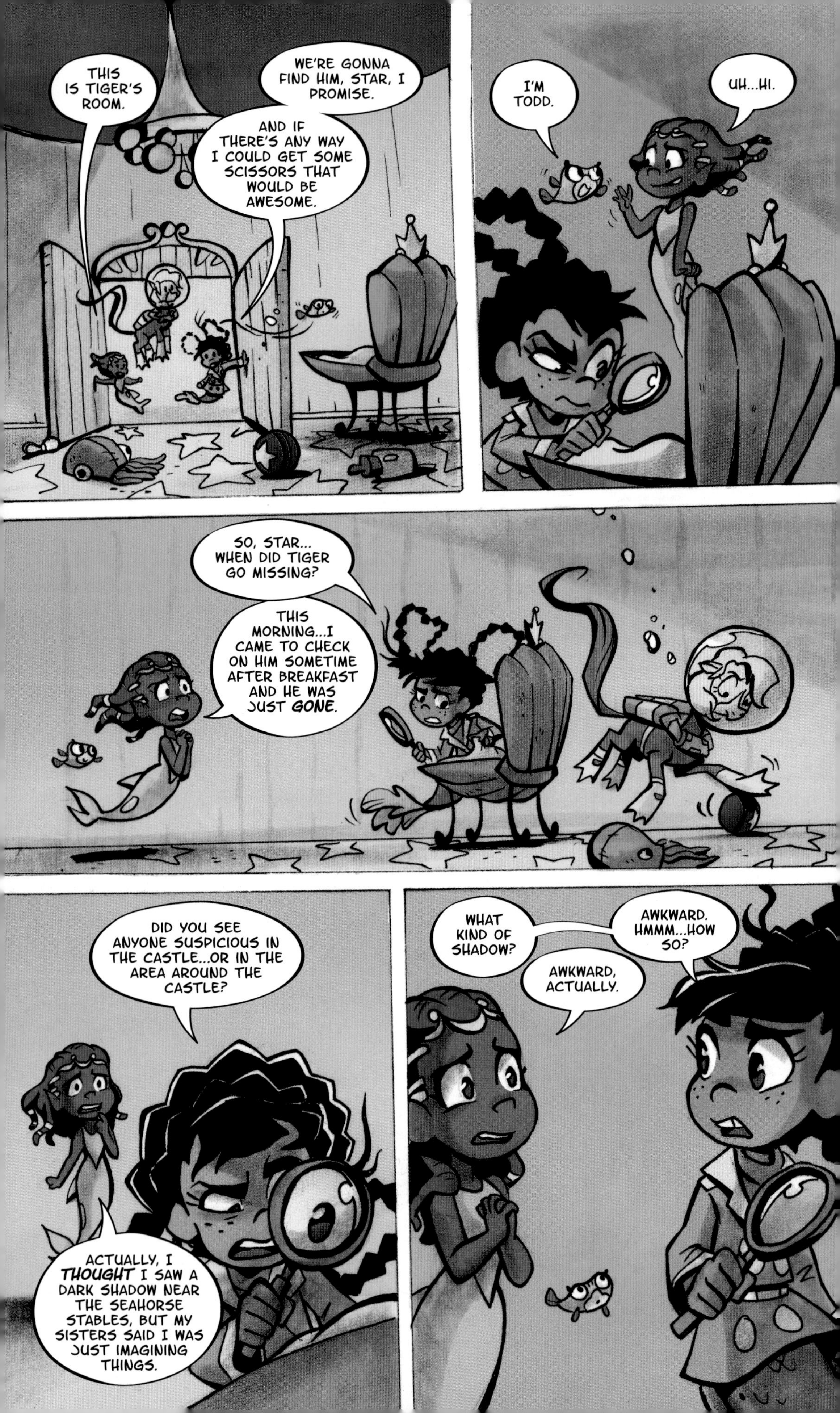
THIS IS TIGER'S ROOM.
WE'RE GONNA FIND HIM, STAR, I PROMISE.
AND IF THERE'S ANY WAY I COULD GET SOME SCISSORS THAT WOULD BE AWESOME.
I'M TODD.
UH...HI.
SO, STAR... WHEN DID TIGER GO MISSING?
THIS MORNING...I CAME TO CHECK ON HIM SOMETIME AFTER BREAKFAST AND HE WAS JUST **GONE**.
DID YOU SEE ANYONE SUSPICIOUS IN THE CASTLE...OR IN THE AREA AROUND THE CASTLE?
ACTUALLY, I ***THOUGHT*** I SAW A DARK SHADOW NEAR THE SEAHORSE STABLES, BUT MY SISTERS SAID I WAS JUST IMAGINING THINGS.
WHAT KIND OF SHADOW?
AWKWARD, ACTUALLY.
AWKWARD. HMMM...HOW SO?

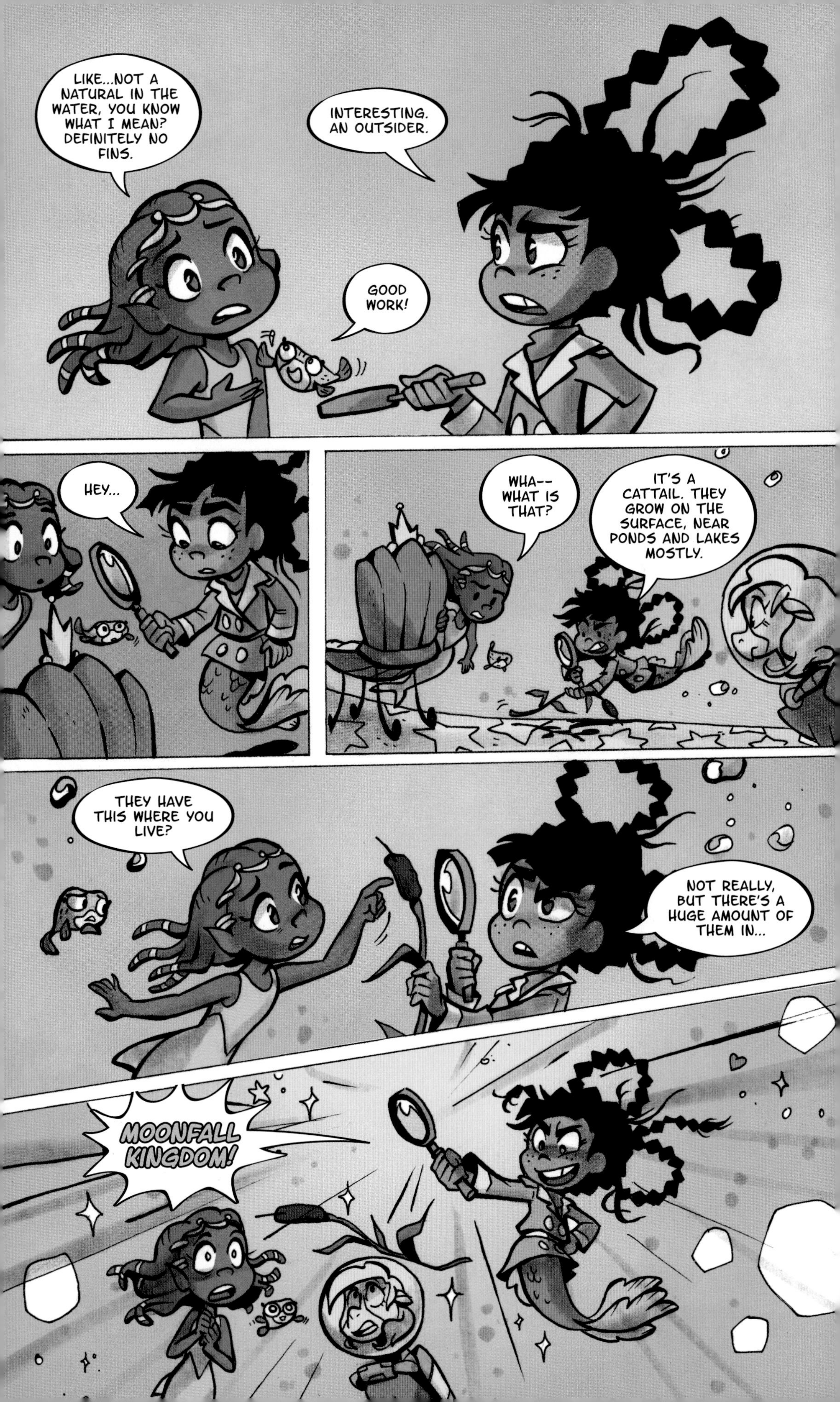

LIKE...NOT A NATURAL IN THE WATER, YOU KNOW WHAT I MEAN? DEFINITELY NO FINS.
INTERESTING. AN OUTSIDER.
GOOD WORK!
HEY...
WHA-- WHAT IS THAT?
IT'S A CATTAIL. THEY GROW ON THE SURFACE, NEAR PONDS AND LAKES MOSTLY.
THEY HAVE THIS WHERE YOU LIVE?
NOT REALLY, BUT THERE'S A HUGE AMOUNT OF THEM IN...
MOONFALL KINGDOM!

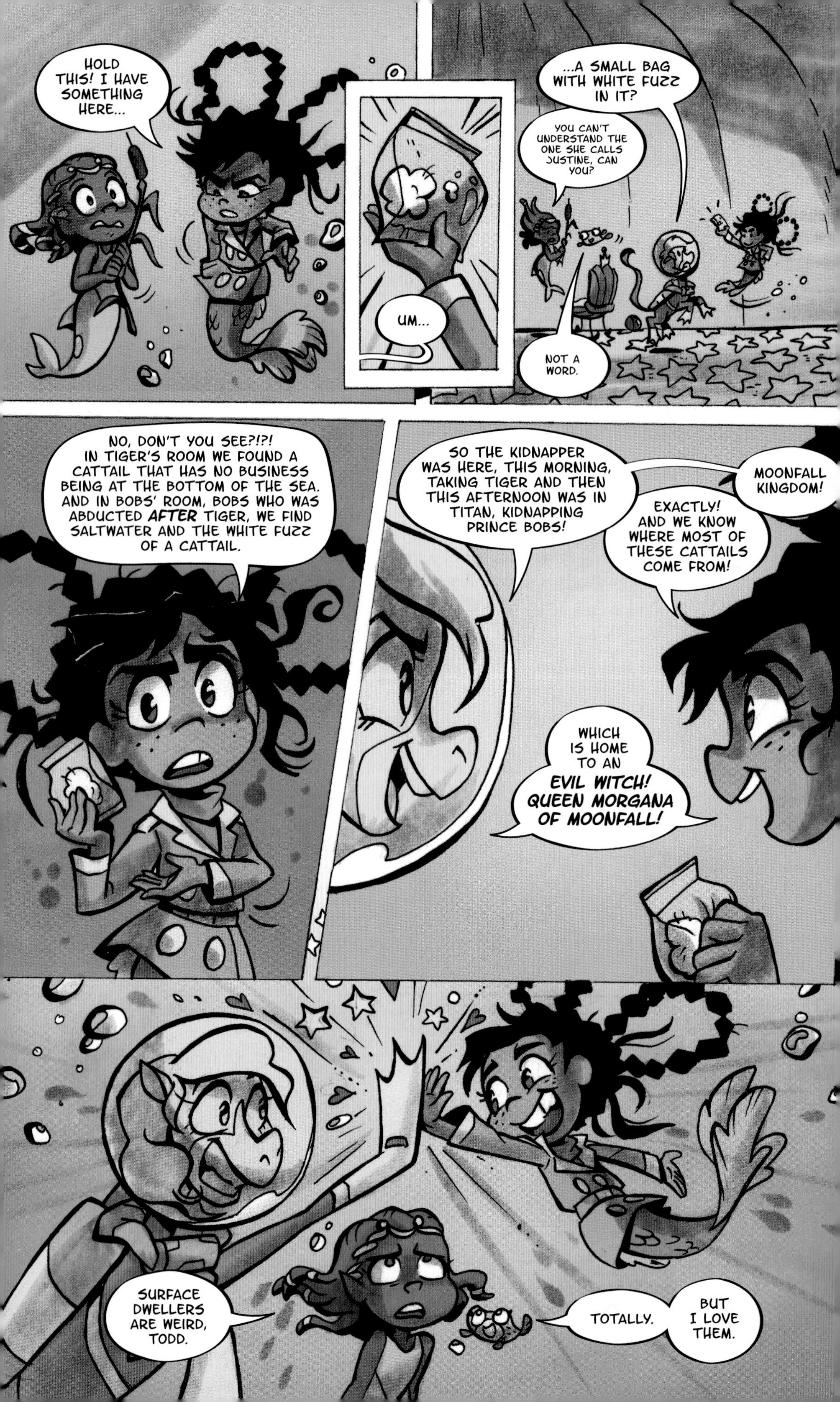
HOLD THIS! I HAVE SOMETHING HERE...
UM...
...A SMALL BAG WITH WHITE FUZZ IN IT?
YOU CAN'T UNDERSTAND THE ONE SHE CALLS JUSTINE, CAN YOU?
NOT A WORD.
NO, DON'T YOU SEE?!?! IN TIGER'S ROOM WE FOUND A CATTAIL THAT HAS NO BUSINESS BEING AT THE BOTTOM OF THE SEA. AND IN BOBS' ROOM, BOBS WHO WAS ABDUCTED AFTER TIGER, WE FIND SALTWATER AND THE WHITE FUZZ OF A CATTAIL.
SO THE KIDNAPPER WAS HERE, THIS MORNING, TAKING TIGER AND THEN THIS AFTERNOON WAS IN TITAN, KIDNAPPING PRINCE BOBS!
MOONFALL KINGDOM!
EXACTLY! AND WE KNOW WHERE MOST OF THESE CATTAILS COME FROM!
WHICH IS HOME TO AN EVIL WITCH! QUEEN MORGANA OF MOONFALL!
SURFACE DWELLERS ARE WEIRD, TODD.
TOTALLY.
BUT I LOVE THEM.

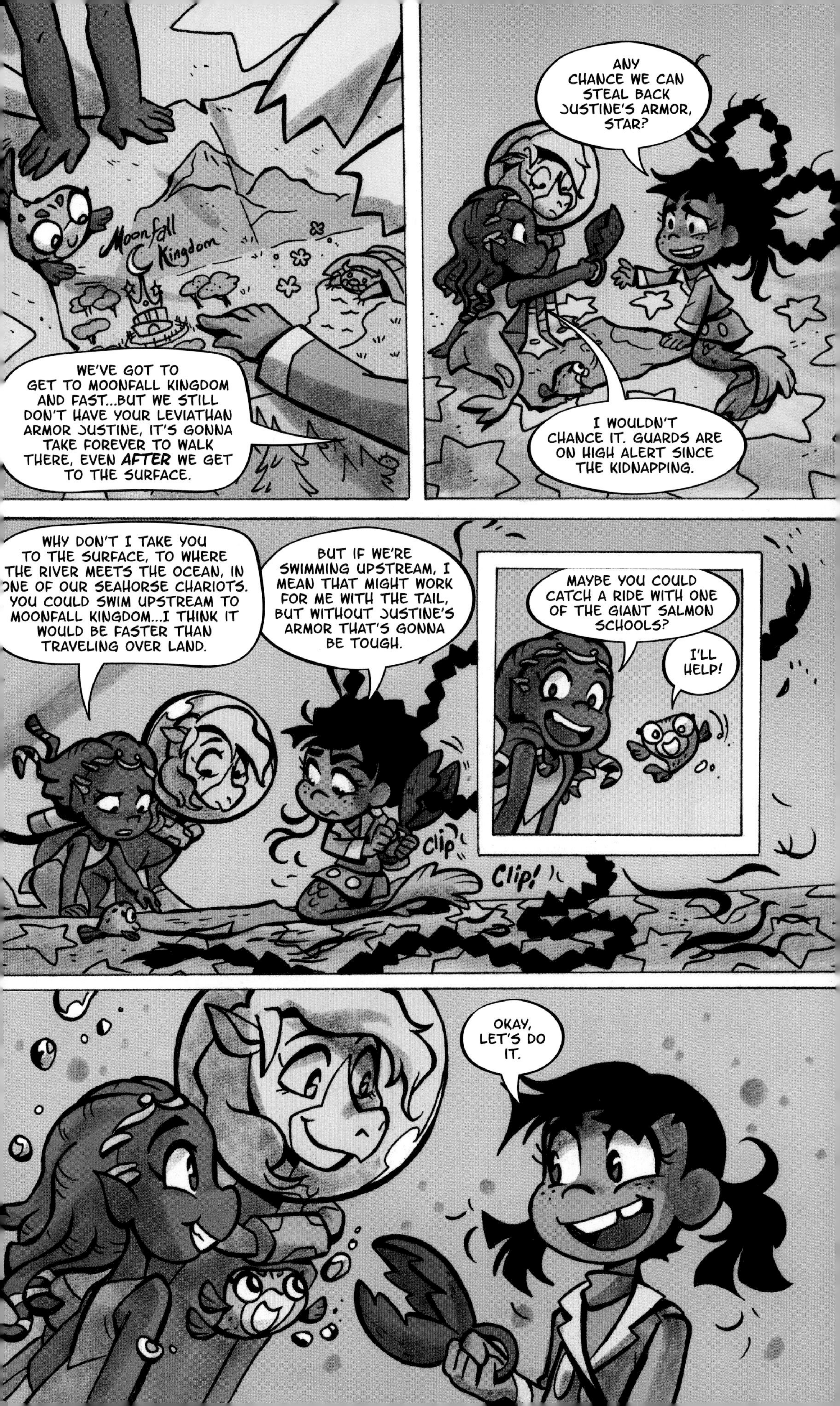
Moonfall Kingdom
WE'VE GOT TO GET TO MOONFALL KINGDOM AND FAST...BUT WE STILL DON'T HAVE YOUR LEVIATHAN ARMOR JUSTINE, IT'S GONNA TAKE FOREVER TO WALK THERE, EVEN **AFTER** WE GET TO THE SURFACE.
ANY CHANCE WE CAN STEAL BACK JUSTINE'S ARMOR, STAR?
I WOULDN'T CHANCE IT. GUARDS ARE ON HIGH ALERT SINCE THE KIDNAPPING.
WHY DON'T I TAKE YOU TO THE SURFACE, TO WHERE THE RIVER MEETS THE OCEAN, IN ONE OF OUR SEAHORSE CHARIOTS. YOU COULD SWIM UPSTREAM TO MOONFALL KINGDOM...I THINK IT WOULD BE FASTER THAN TRAVELING OVER LAND.
BUT IF WE'RE SWIMMING UPSTREAM, I MEAN THAT MIGHT WORK FOR ME WITH THE TAIL, BUT WITHOUT JUSTINE'S ARMOR THAT'S GONNA BE TOUGH.
Clip
Clip!
MAYBE YOU COULD CATCH A RIDE WITH ONE OF THE GIANT SALMON SCHOOLS?
I'LL HELP!
OKAY, LET'S DO IT.

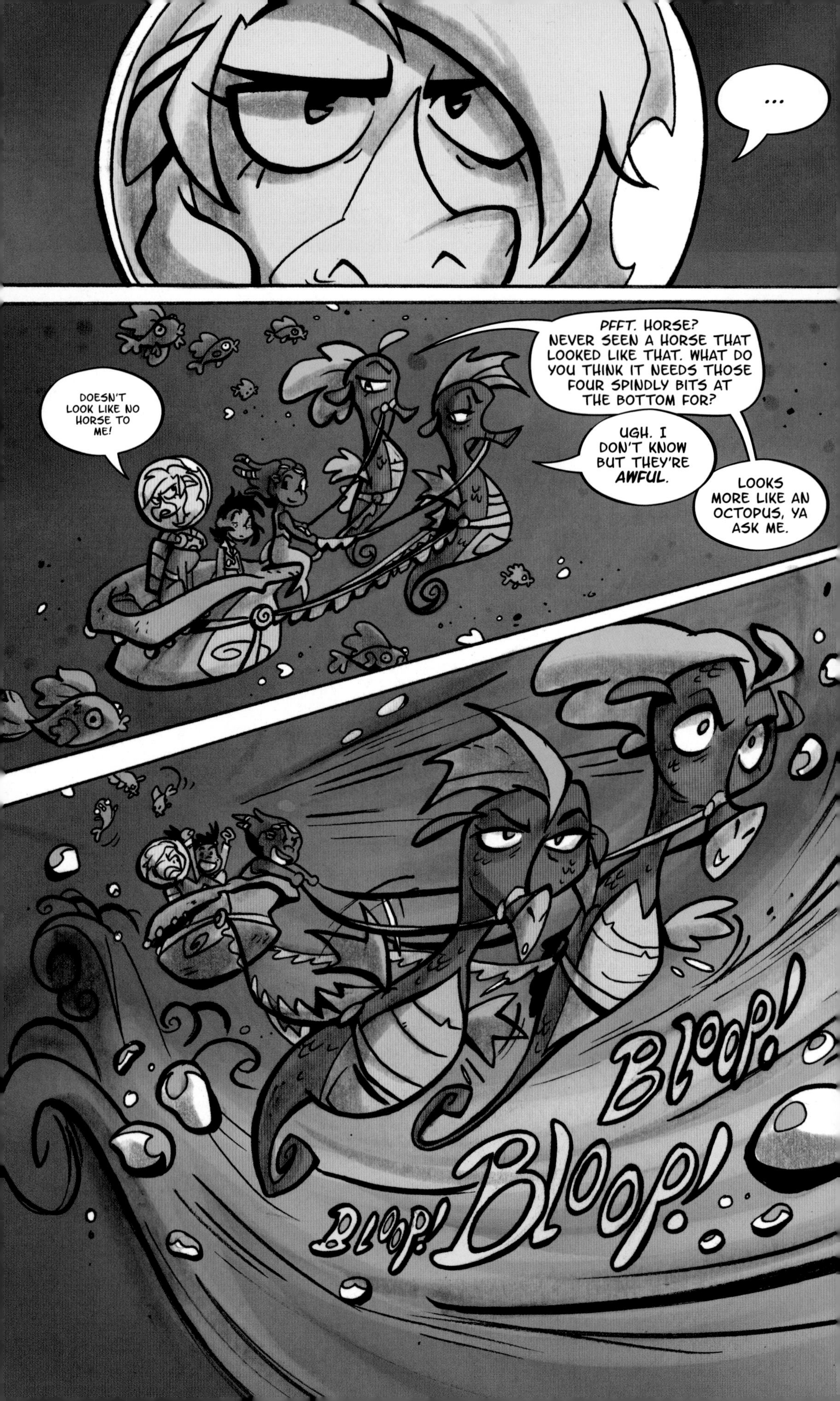
...
DOESN'T LOOK LIKE NO HORSE TO ME!
PFFT. HORSE? NEVER SEEN A HORSE THAT LOOKED LIKE THAT. WHAT DO YOU THINK IT NEEDS THOSE FOUR SPINDLY BITS AT THE BOTTOM FOR?
UGH. I DON'T KNOW BUT THEY'RE AWFUL.
LOOKS MORE LIKE AN OCTOPUS, YA ASK ME.
BLOOP!
BLOOP!
BLOOP!

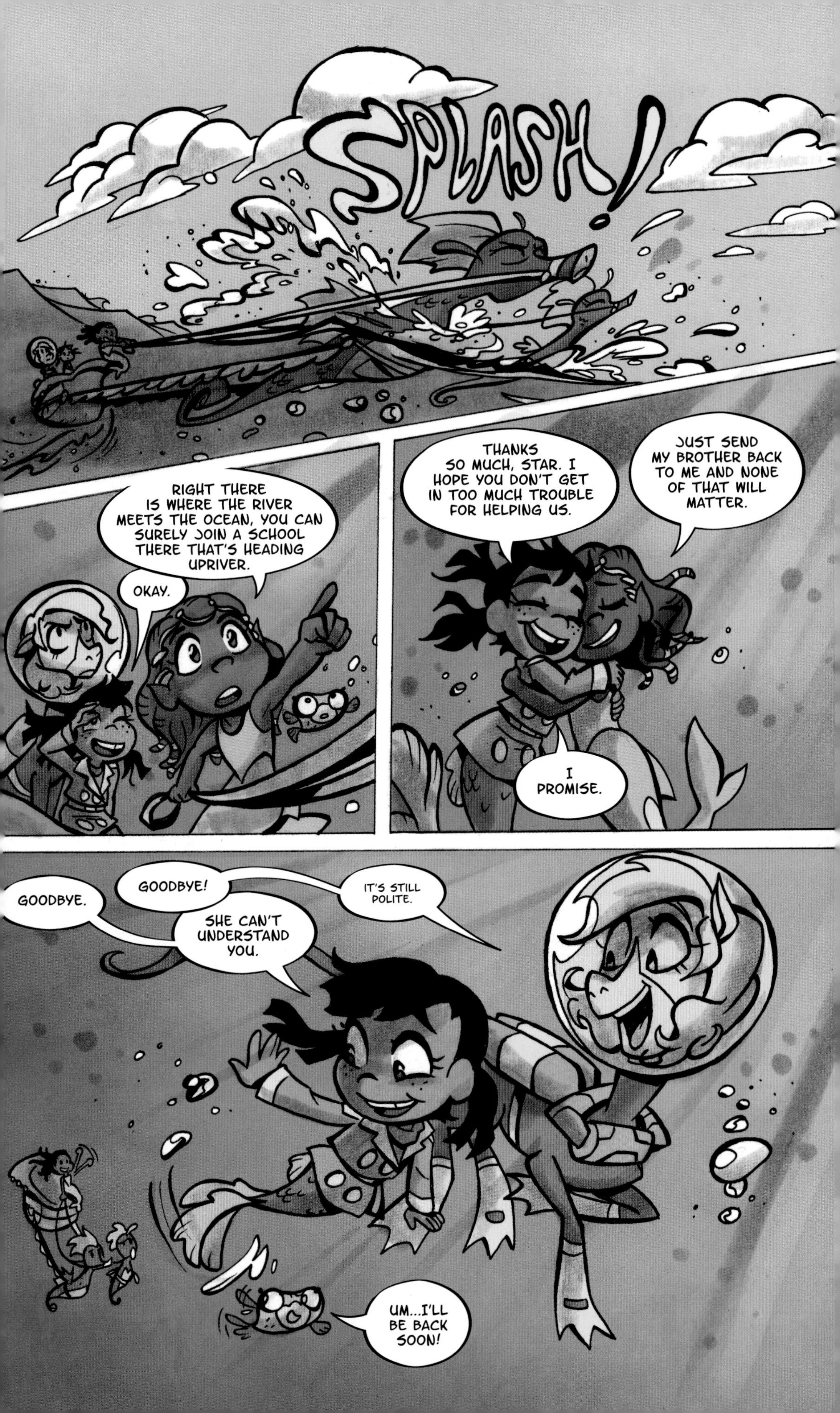
SPLASH!
RIGHT THERE IS WHERE THE RIVER MEETS THE OCEAN, YOU CAN SURELY JOIN A SCHOOL THERE THAT'S HEADING UPRIVER.
OKAY.
THANKS SO MUCH, STAR. I HOPE YOU DON'T GET IN TOO MUCH TROUBLE FOR HELPING US.
JUST SEND MY BROTHER BACK TO ME AND NONE OF THAT WILL MATTER.
I PROMISE.
GOODBYE.
GOODBYE!
SHE CAN'T UNDERSTAND YOU.
IT'S STILL POLITE.
UM...I'LL BE BACK SOON!

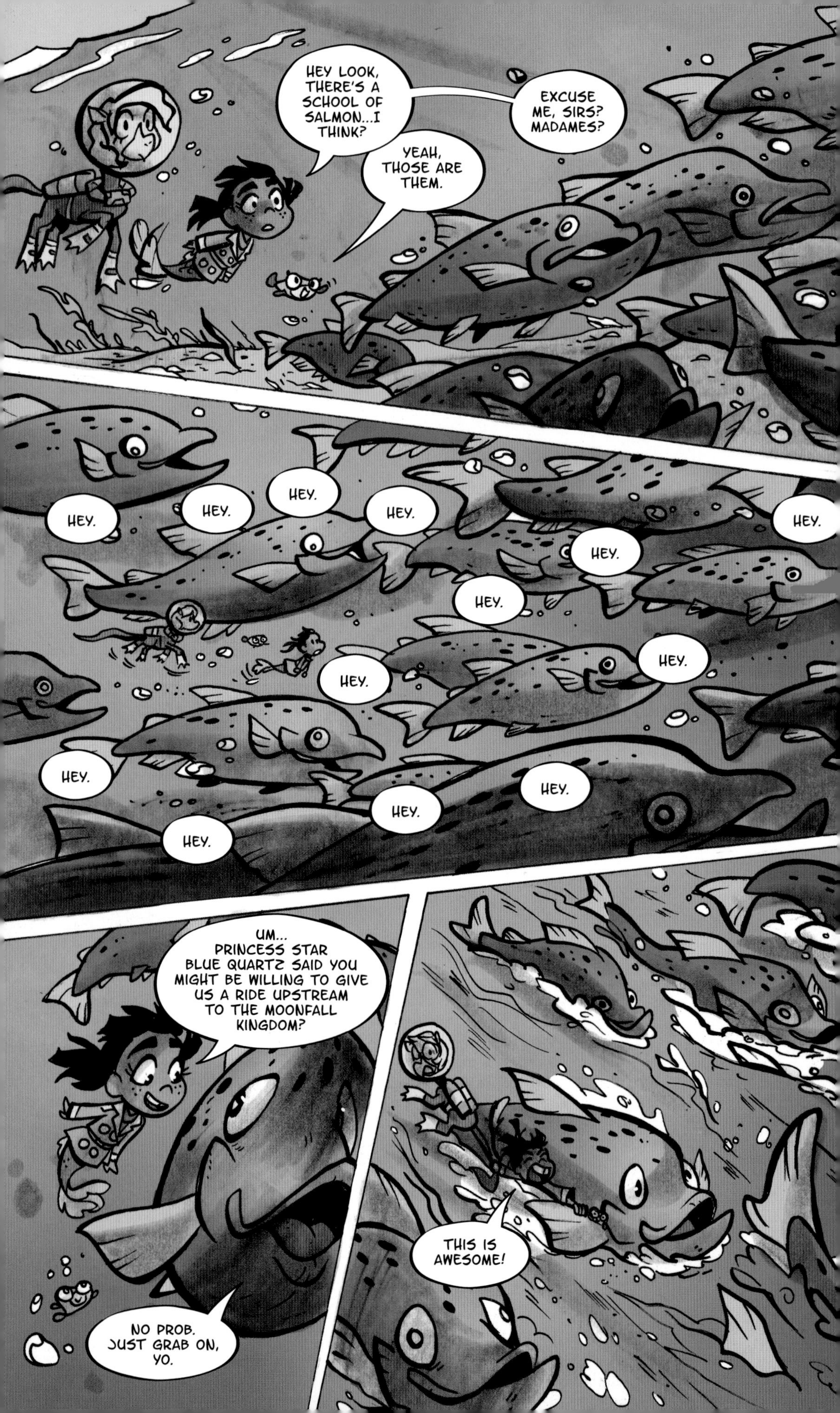
HEY LOOK, THERE'S A SCHOOL OF SALMON...I THINK?
EXCUSE ME, SIRS? MADAMES?
YEAH, THOSE ARE THEM.
HEY.
HEY.
HEY.
HEY.
HEY.
HEY.
HEY.
HEY.
HEY.
HEY.
HEY.
HEY.
HEY.
UM... PRINCESS STAR BLUE QUARTZ SAID YOU MIGHT BE WILLING TO GIVE US A RIDE UPSTREAM TO THE MOONFALL KINGDOM?
NO PROB. JUST GRAB ON, YO.
THIS IS AWESOME!

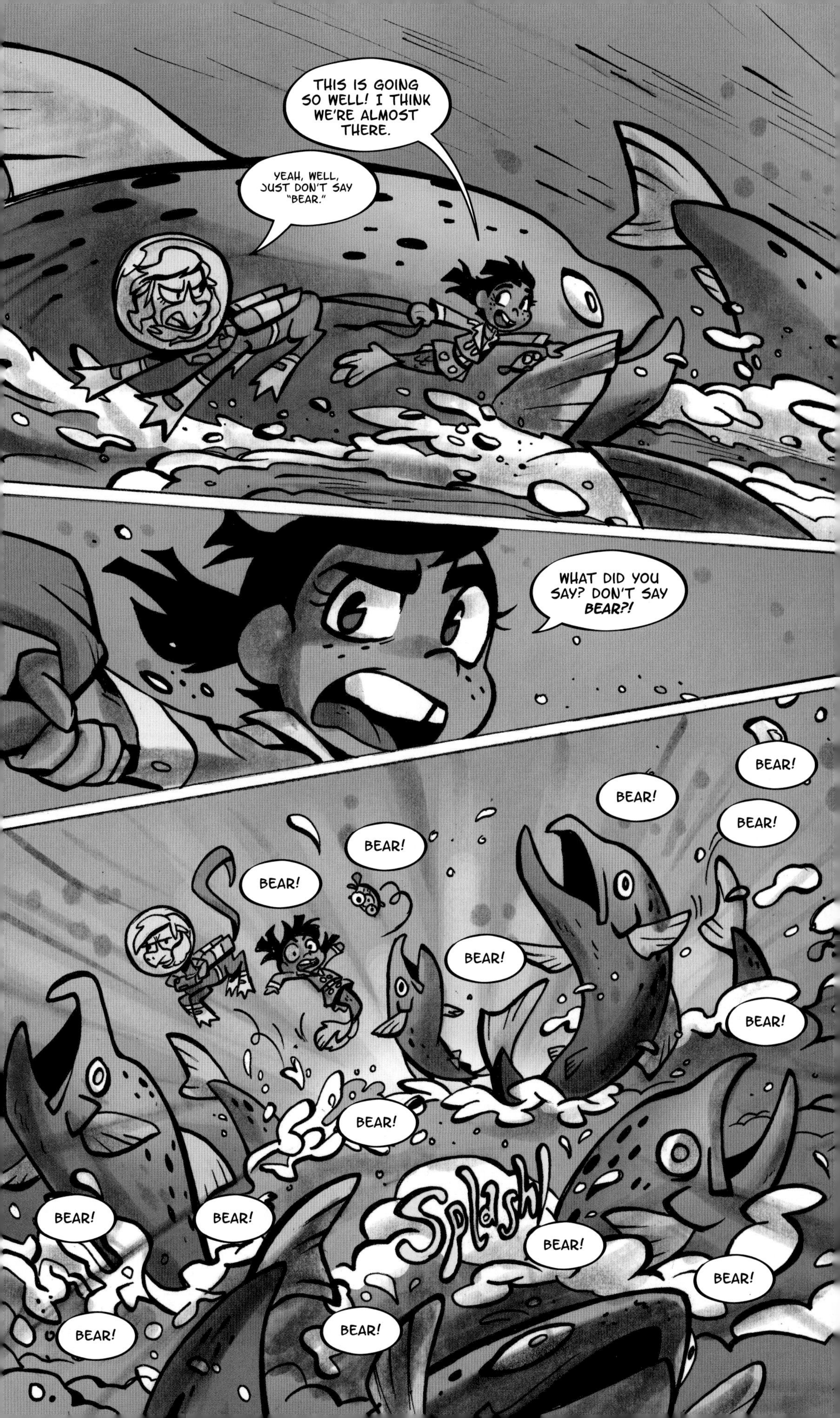
THIS IS GOING SO WELL! I THINK WE'RE ALMOST THERE.
YEAH, WELL, JUST DON'T SAY "BEAR."
WHAT DID YOU SAY? DON'T SAY *BEAR?!*
BEAR!
BEAR!
BEAR!
BEAR!
BEAR!
BEAR!
BEAR!
BEAR!
SPLASH!
BEAR!
BEAR!
BEAR!
BEAR!
BEAR!
BEAR!

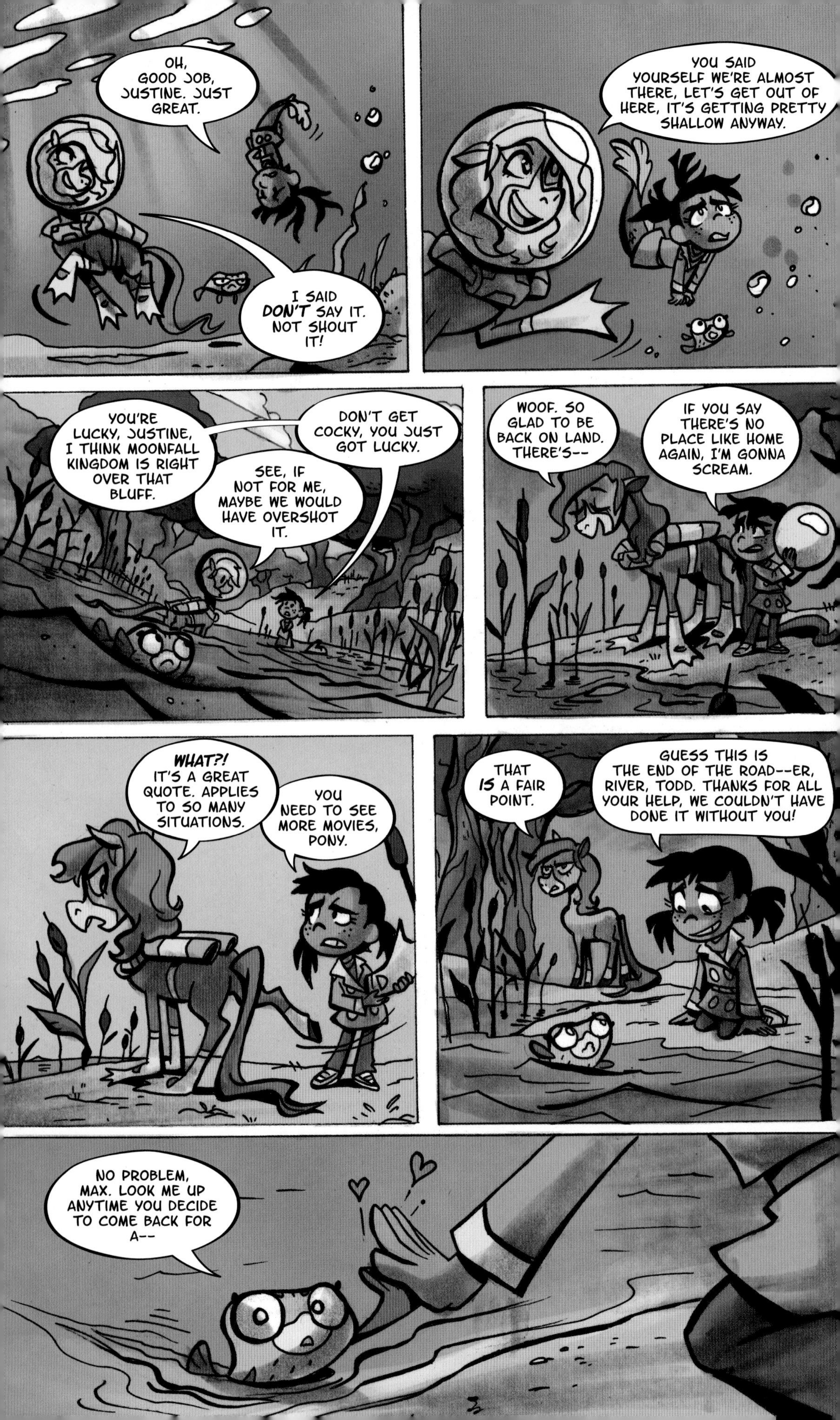
OH, GOOD JOB, JUSTINE. JUST GREAT.
I SAID DON'T SAY IT. NOT SHOUT IT!
YOU SAID YOURSELF WE'RE ALMOST THERE, LET'S GET OUT OF HERE, IT'S GETTING PRETTY SHALLOW ANYWAY.
YOU'RE LUCKY, JUSTINE, I THINK MOONFALL KINGDOM IS RIGHT OVER THAT BLUFF.
DON'T GET COCKY, YOU JUST GOT LUCKY.
SEE, IF NOT FOR ME, MAYBE WE WOULD HAVE OVERSHOT IT.
WOOF. SO GLAD TO BE BACK ON LAND. THERE'S--
IF YOU SAY THERE'S NO PLACE LIKE HOME AGAIN, I'M GONNA SCREAM.
WHAT?! IT'S A GREAT QUOTE. APPLIES TO SO MANY SITUATIONS.
YOU NEED TO SEE MORE MOVIES, PONY.
THAT IS A FAIR POINT.
GUESS THIS IS THE END OF THE ROAD--ER, RIVER, TODD. THANKS FOR ALL YOUR HELP, WE COULDN'T HAVE DONE IT WITHOUT YOU!
NO PROBLEM, MAX. LOOK ME UP ANYTIME YOU DECIDE TO COME BACK FOR A--

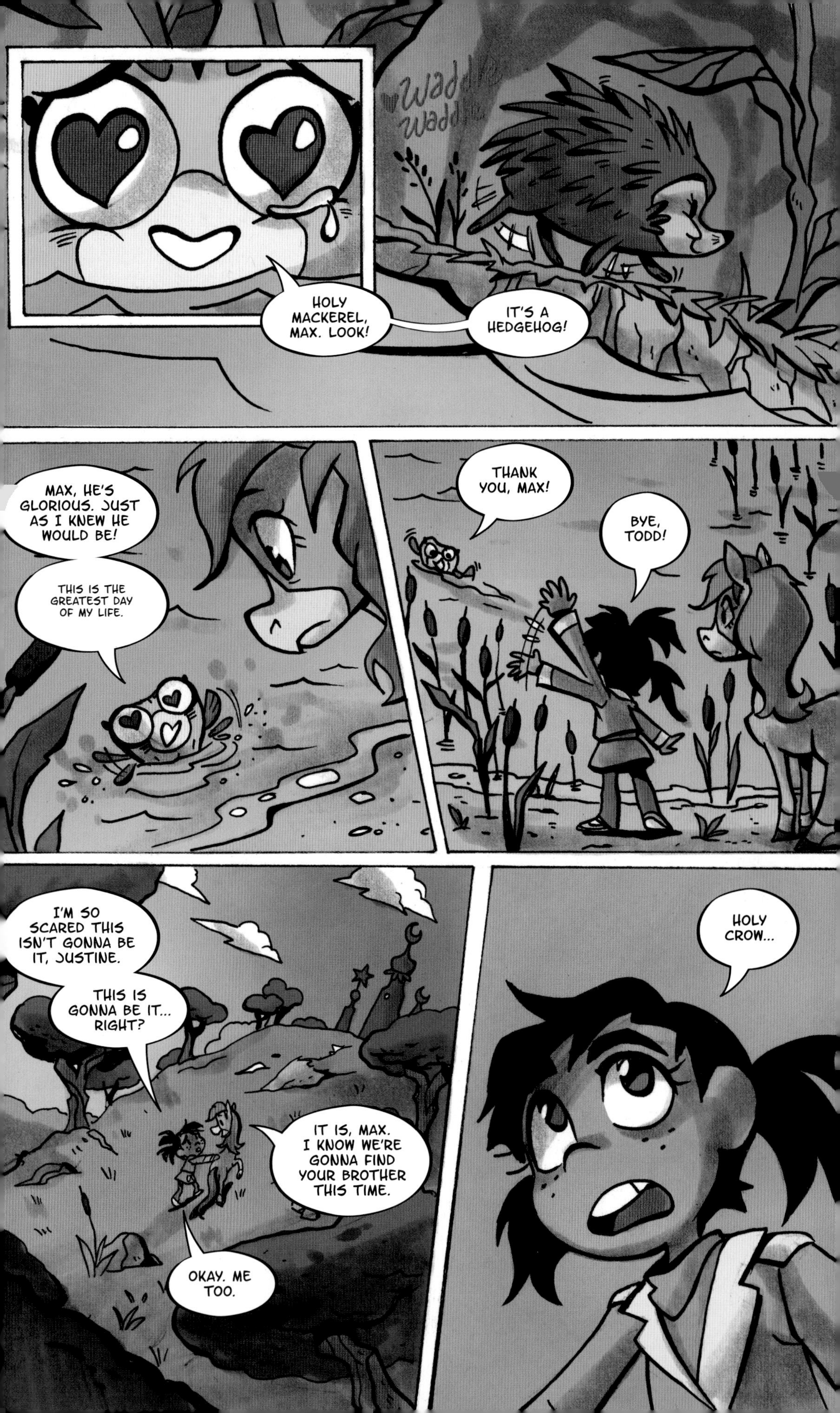

WADDLE WADDLE
HOLY MACKEREL, MAX. LOOK!
IT'S A HEDGEHOG!
MAX, HE'S GLORIOUS. JUST AS I KNEW HE WOULD BE!
THIS IS THE GREATEST DAY OF MY LIFE.
THANK YOU, MAX!
BYE, TODD!
I'M SO SCARED THIS ISN'T GONNA BE IT, JUSTINE.
THIS IS GONNA BE IT... RIGHT?
IT IS, MAX. I KNOW WE'RE GONNA FIND YOUR BROTHER THIS TIME.
OKAY. ME TOO.
HOLY CROW...

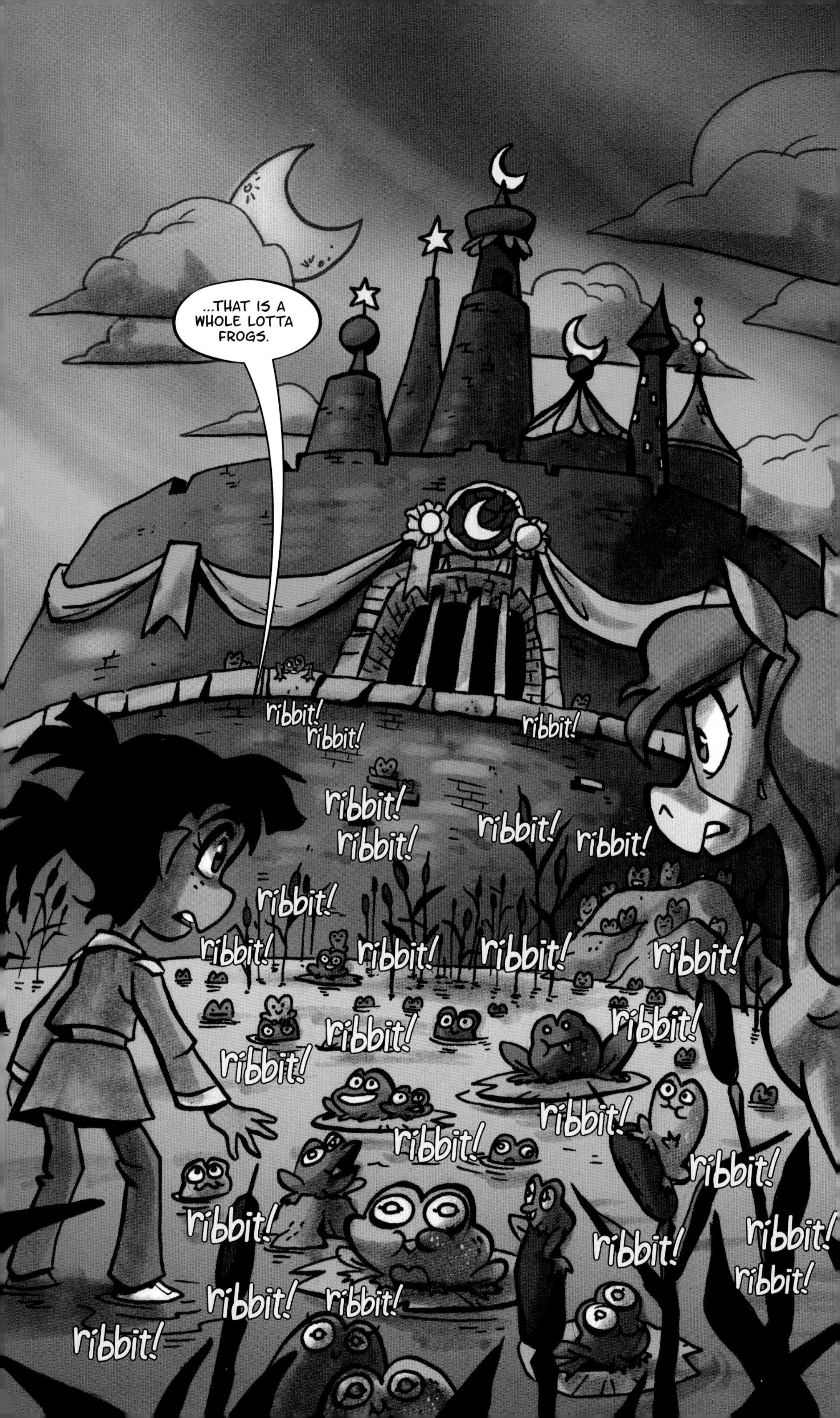
...THAT IS A WHOLE LOTTA FROGS.
ribbit!
ribbit!
ribbit!
ribbit!
ribbit!
ribbit!
ribbit!
ribbit!
ribbit!
ribbit!
ribbit!
ribbit!
ribbit!
ribbit!
ribbit!
ribbit!
ribbit!
ribbit!
ribbit!
ribbit!
ribbit!
ribbit!
ribbit!
ribbit!
ribbit!

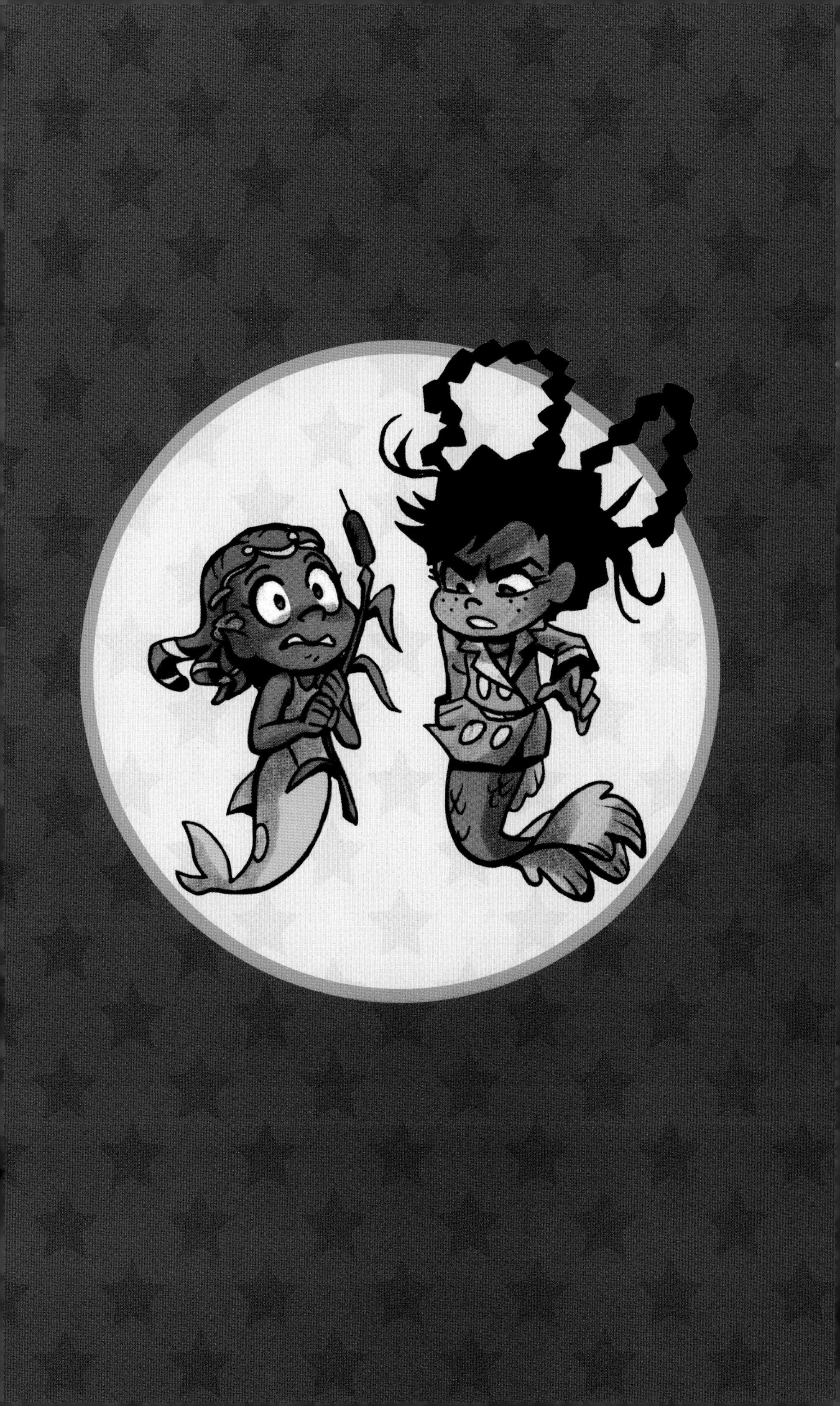

Issue #5 Cover by
SAVANNA GANUCHEAU

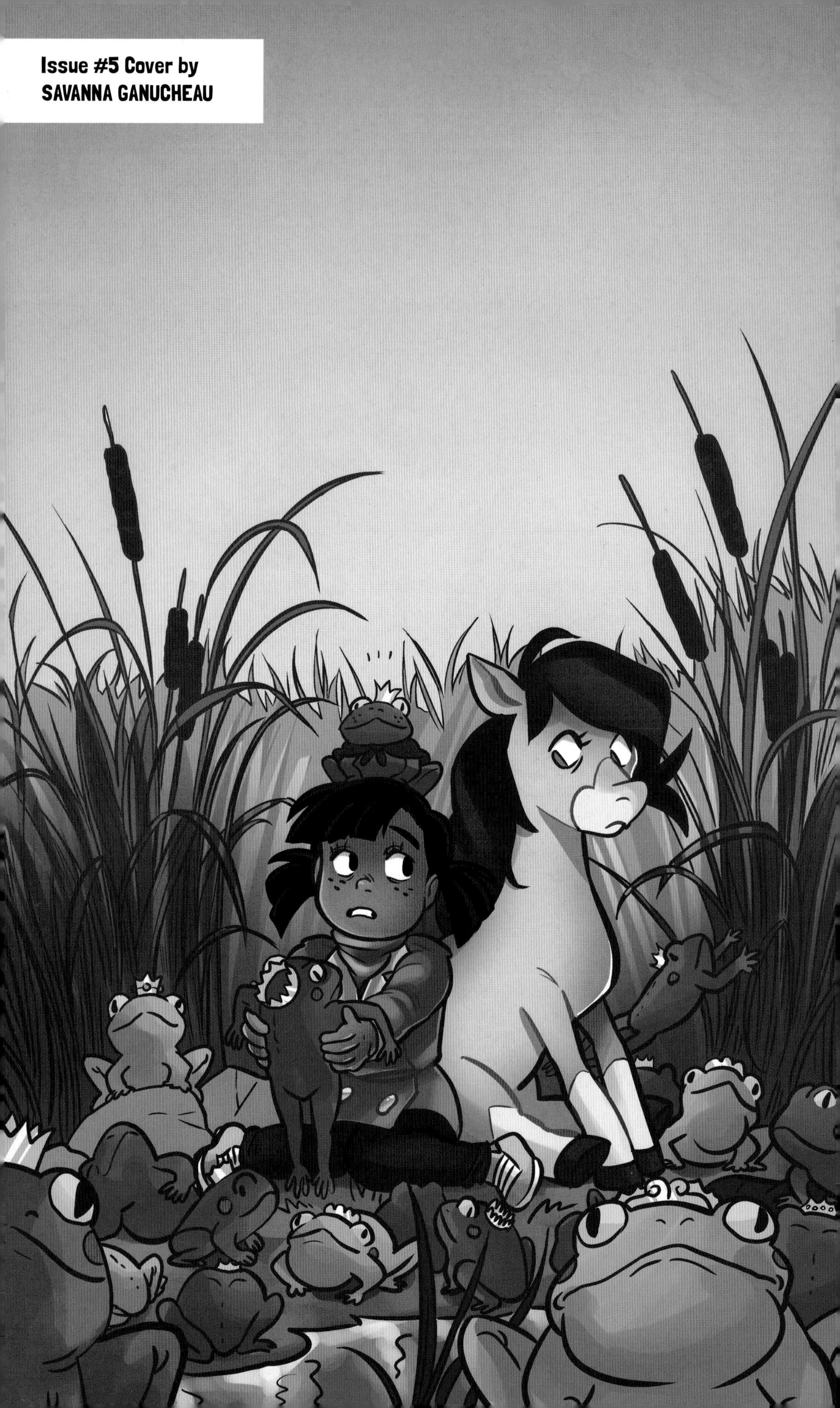

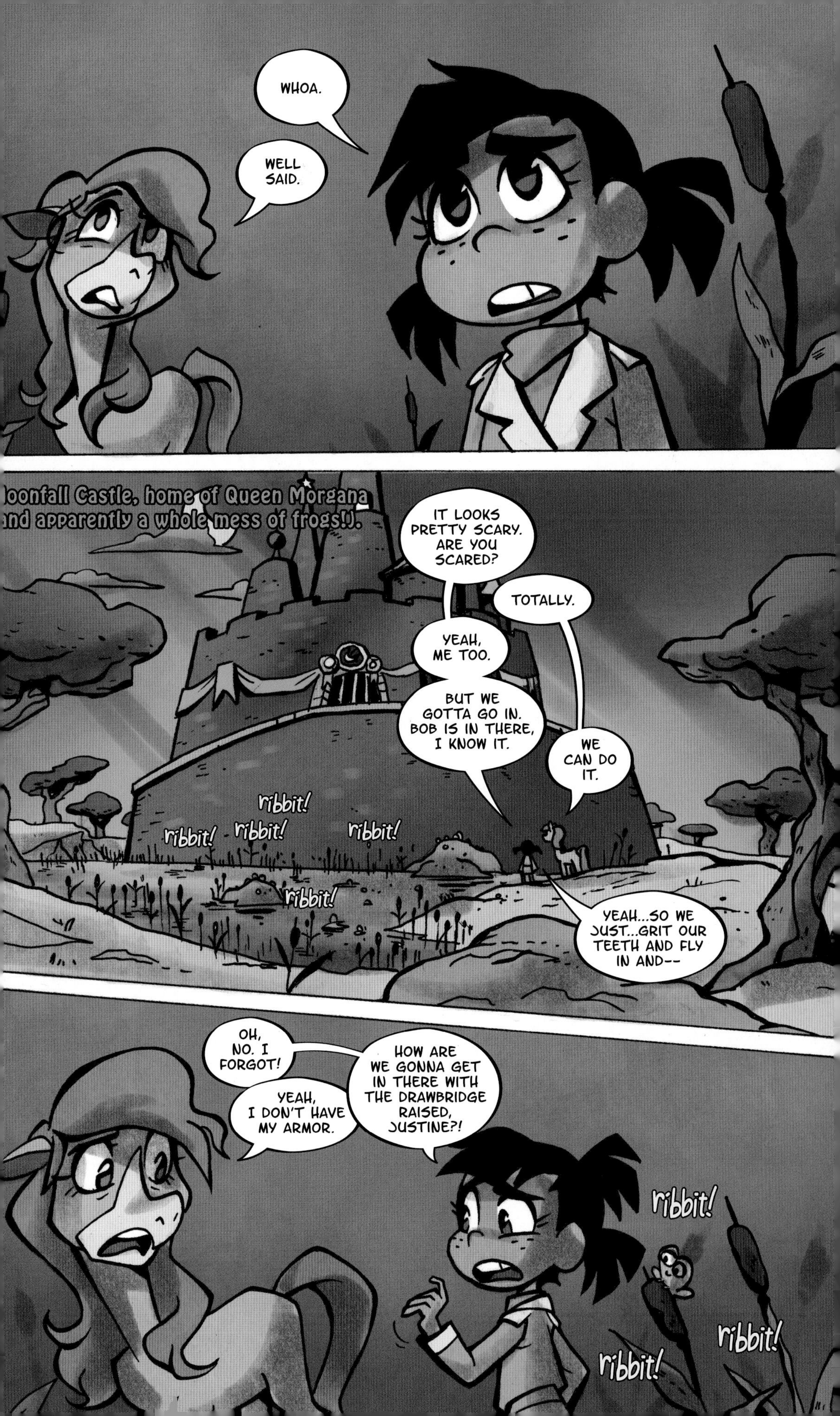
WHOA.
WELL SAID.
oonfall Castle, home of Queen Morgana
and apparently a whole mess of frogs!).
IT LOOKS PRETTY SCARY. ARE YOU SCARED?
TOTALLY.
YEAH, ME TOO.
BUT WE GOTTA GO IN. BOB IS IN THERE, I KNOW IT.
WE CAN DO IT.
ribbit!
ribbit!
ribbit!
ribbit!
ribbit!
YEAH...SO WE JUST...GRIT OUR TEETH AND FLY IN AND--
OH, NO. I FORGOT!
YEAH, I DON'T HAVE MY ARMOR.
HOW ARE WE GONNA GET IN THERE WITH THE DRAWBRIDGE RAISED, JUSTINE?!
ribbit!
ribbit!
ribbit!

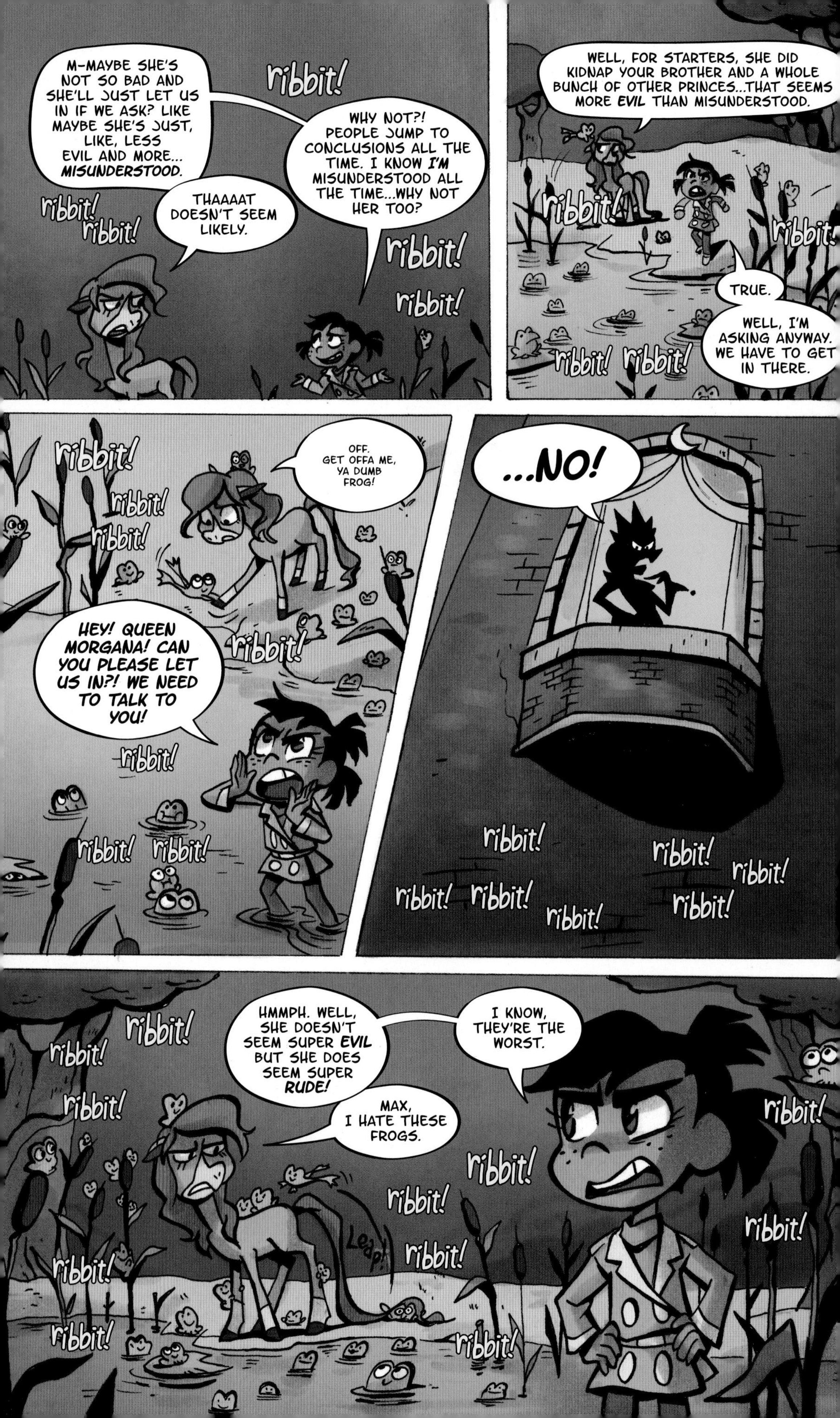
M-MAYBE SHE'S NOT SO BAD AND SHE'LL JUST LET US IN IF WE ASK? LIKE MAYBE SHE'S JUST, LIKE, LESS EVIL AND MORE... MISUNDERSTOOD.
ribbit!
THAAAAT DOESN'T SEEM LIKELY.
ribbit! ribbit!
WHY NOT?! PEOPLE JUMP TO CONCLUSIONS ALL THE TIME. I KNOW I'M MISUNDERSTOOD ALL THE TIME...WHY NOT HER TOO?
ribbit!
ribbit!
WELL, FOR STARTERS, SHE DID KIDNAP YOUR BROTHER AND A WHOLE BUNCH OF OTHER PRINCES...THAT SEEMS MORE EVIL THAN MISUNDERSTOOD.
ribbit!
ribbit!
TRUE.
WELL, I'M ASKING ANYWAY. WE HAVE TO GET IN THERE.
ribbit! ribbit!
ribbit!
ribbit!
ribbit!
OFF. GET OFFA ME, YA DUMB FROG!
HEY! QUEEN MORGANA! CAN YOU PLEASE LET US IN?! WE NEED TO TALK TO YOU!
ribbit!
ribbit!
ribbit! ribbit!
...NO!
ribbit! ribbit! ribbit! ribbit! ribbit! ribbit! ribbit!
ribbit!
ribbit!
HMMPH. WELL, SHE DOESN'T SEEM SUPER EVIL BUT SHE DOES SEEM SUPER RUDE!
I KNOW, THEY'RE THE WORST.
MAX, I HATE THESE FROGS.
ribbit!
ribbit!
ribbit!
ribbit!
Leap!
ribbit!
ribbit!
ribbit!
ribbit!
ribbit!

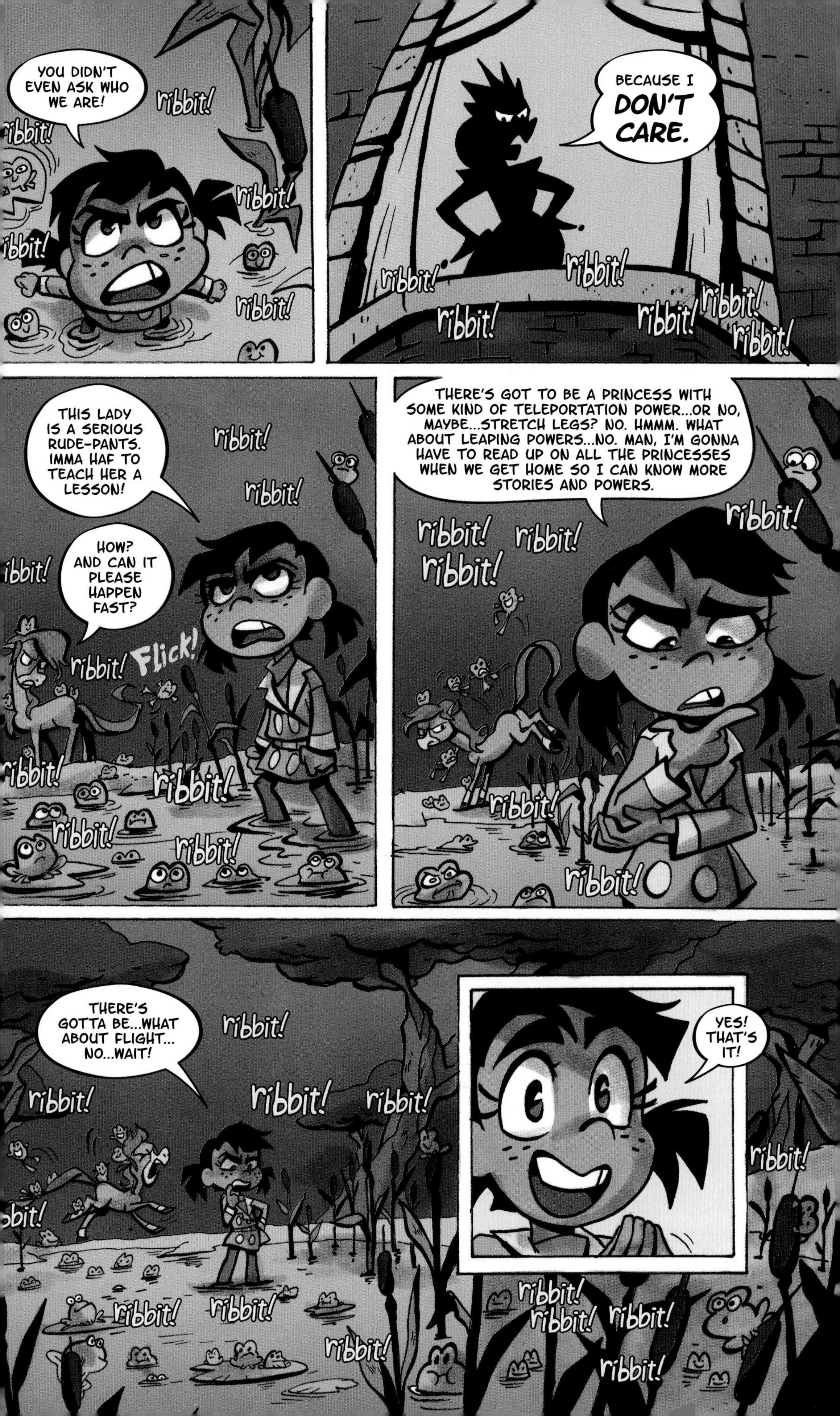
YOU DIDN'T EVEN ASK WHO WE ARE!
ribbit!
ribbit!
ribbit!
ribbit!
ribbit!
BECAUSE I DON'T CARE.
ribbit!
ribbit!
ribbit!
ribbit!
ribbit!
ribbit!
THIS LADY IS A SERIOUS RUDE-PANTS. IMMA HAF TO TEACH HER A LESSON!
HOW? AND CAN IT PLEASE HAPPEN FAST?
ribbit!
ribbit!
ribbit!
FLICK!
ribbit!
ribbit!
ribbit!
ribbit!
THERE'S GOT TO BE A PRINCESS WITH SOME KIND OF TELEPORTATION POWER...OR NO, MAYBE...STRETCH LEGS? NO. HMMM. WHAT ABOUT LEAPING POWERS...NO. MAN, I'M GONNA HAVE TO READ UP ON ALL THE PRINCESSES WHEN WE GET HOME SO I CAN KNOW MORE STORIES AND POWERS.
ribbit!
ribbit!
ribbit!
ribbit!
ribbit!
ribbit!
THERE'S GOTTA BE...WHAT ABOUT FLIGHT... NO...WAIT!
ribbit!
ribbit!
ribbit!
ribbit!
YES! THAT'S IT!
ribbit!
ribbit!
ribbit!
ribbit!
ribbit!
ribbit!
ribbit!
ribbit!

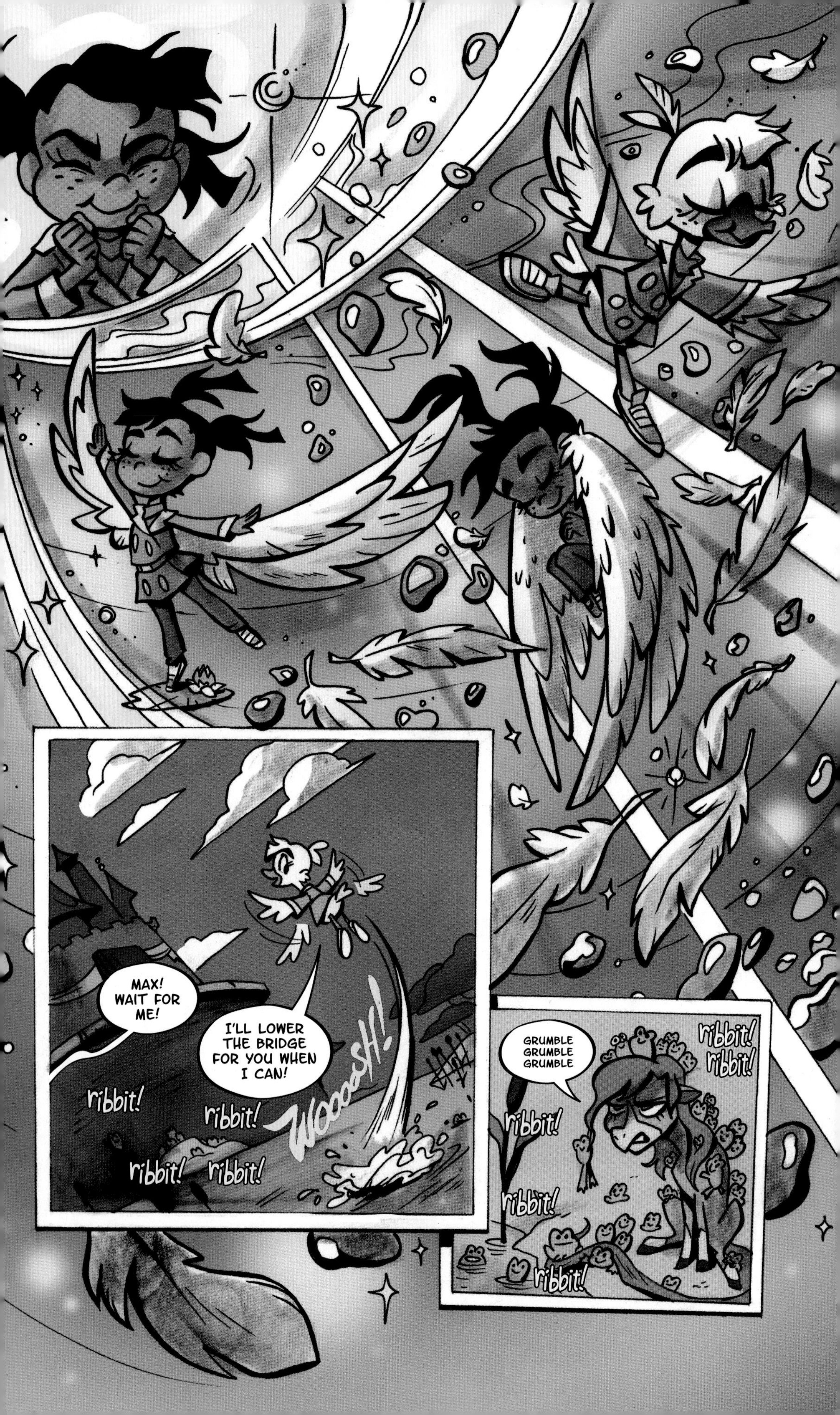
MAX! WAIT FOR ME!
I'LL LOWER THE BRIDGE FOR YOU WHEN I CAN!
WOOOOSH!
ribbit!
ribbit!
ribbit!
ribbit!
GRUMBLE GRUMBLE GRUMBLE
ribbit! ribbit!
ribbit!
ribbit!
ribbit!

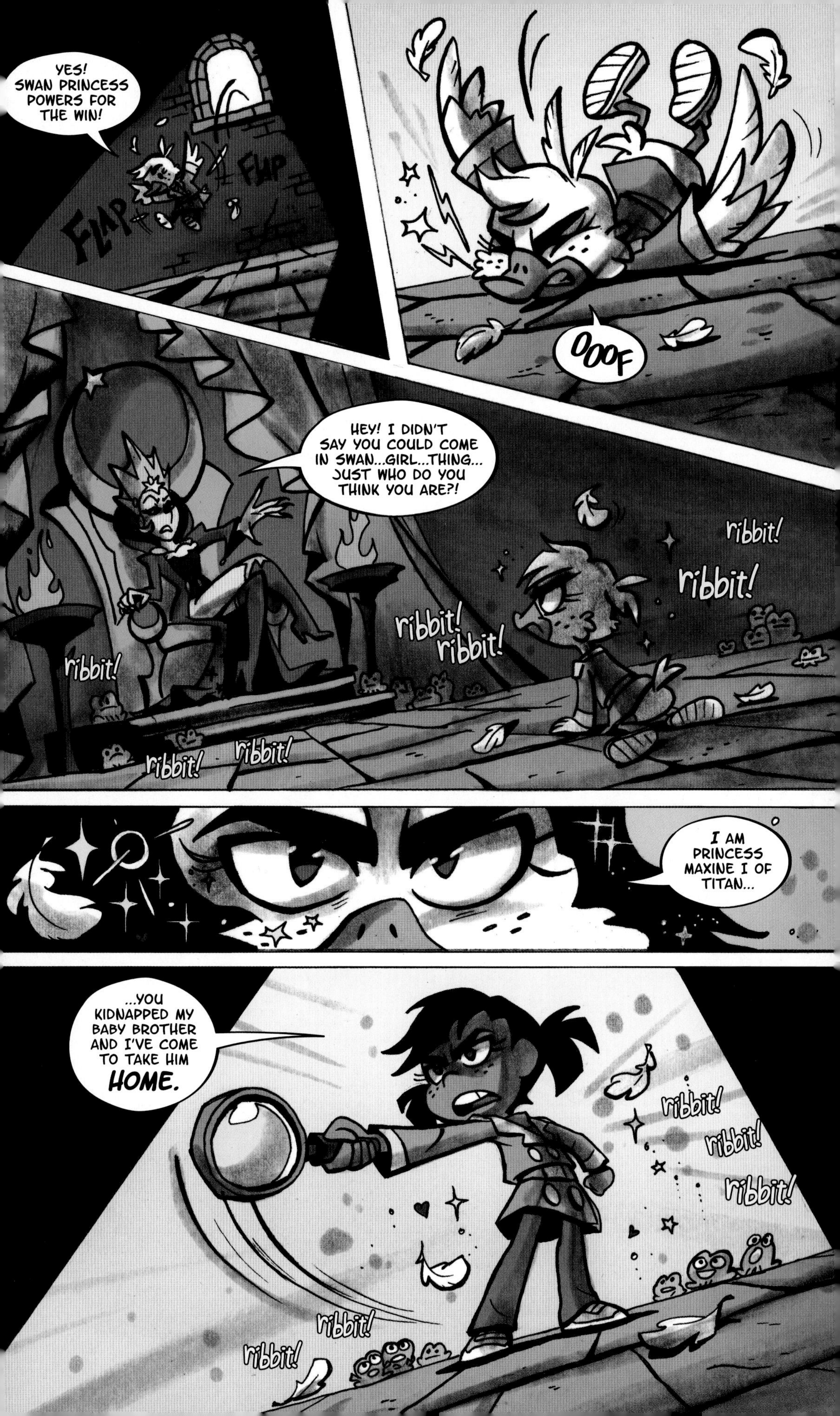
YES! SWAN PRINCESS POWERS FOR THE WIN!
FLAP FLAP
OOOF
HEY! I DIDN'T SAY YOU COULD COME IN SWAN...GIRL...THING... JUST WHO DO YOU THINK YOU ARE?!
ribbit!
ribbit!
ribbit!
ribbit!
ribbit!
ribbit!
ribbit!
I AM PRINCESS MAXINE I OF TITAN...
...YOU KIDNAPPED MY BABY BROTHER AND I'VE COME TO TAKE HIM **HOME.**
ribbit!
ribbit!
ribbit!
ribbit!
ribbit!

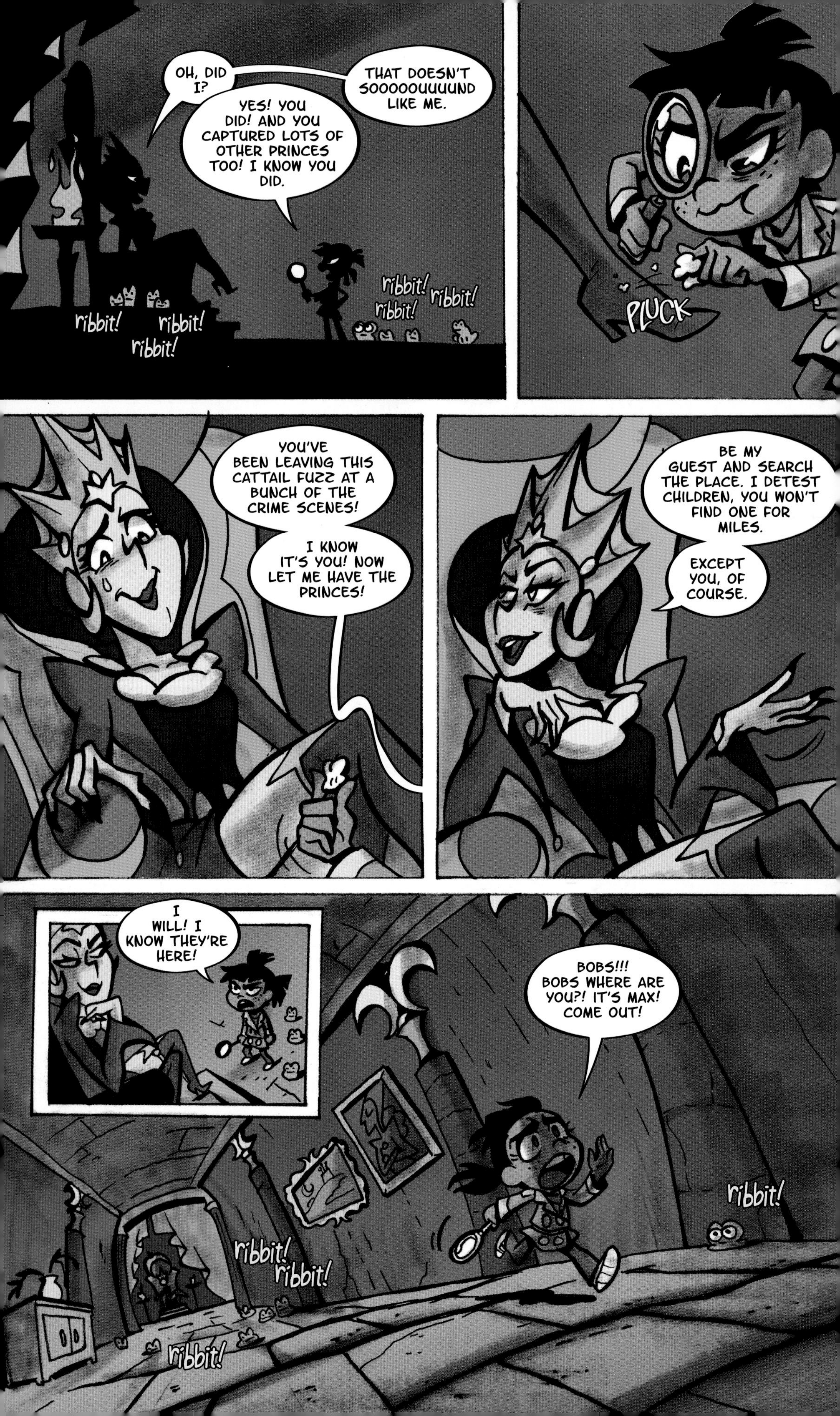

OH, DID I?
YES! YOU DID! AND YOU CAPTURED LOTS OF OTHER PRINCES TOO! I KNOW YOU DID.
THAT DOESN'T SOOOOOUUUUND LIKE ME.
ribbit!
ribbit!
ribbit!
ribbit!
ribbit!
ribbit!
PLUCK
YOU'VE BEEN LEAVING THIS CATTAIL FUZZ AT A BUNCH OF THE CRIME SCENES!
I KNOW IT'S YOU! NOW LET ME HAVE THE PRINCES!
BE MY GUEST AND SEARCH THE PLACE. I DETEST CHILDREN, YOU WON'T FIND ONE FOR MILES.
EXCEPT YOU, OF COURSE.
I WILL! I KNOW THEY'RE HERE!
BOBS!!! BOBS WHERE ARE YOU?! IT'S MAX! COME OUT!
ribbit!
ribbit!
ribbit!
ribbit!

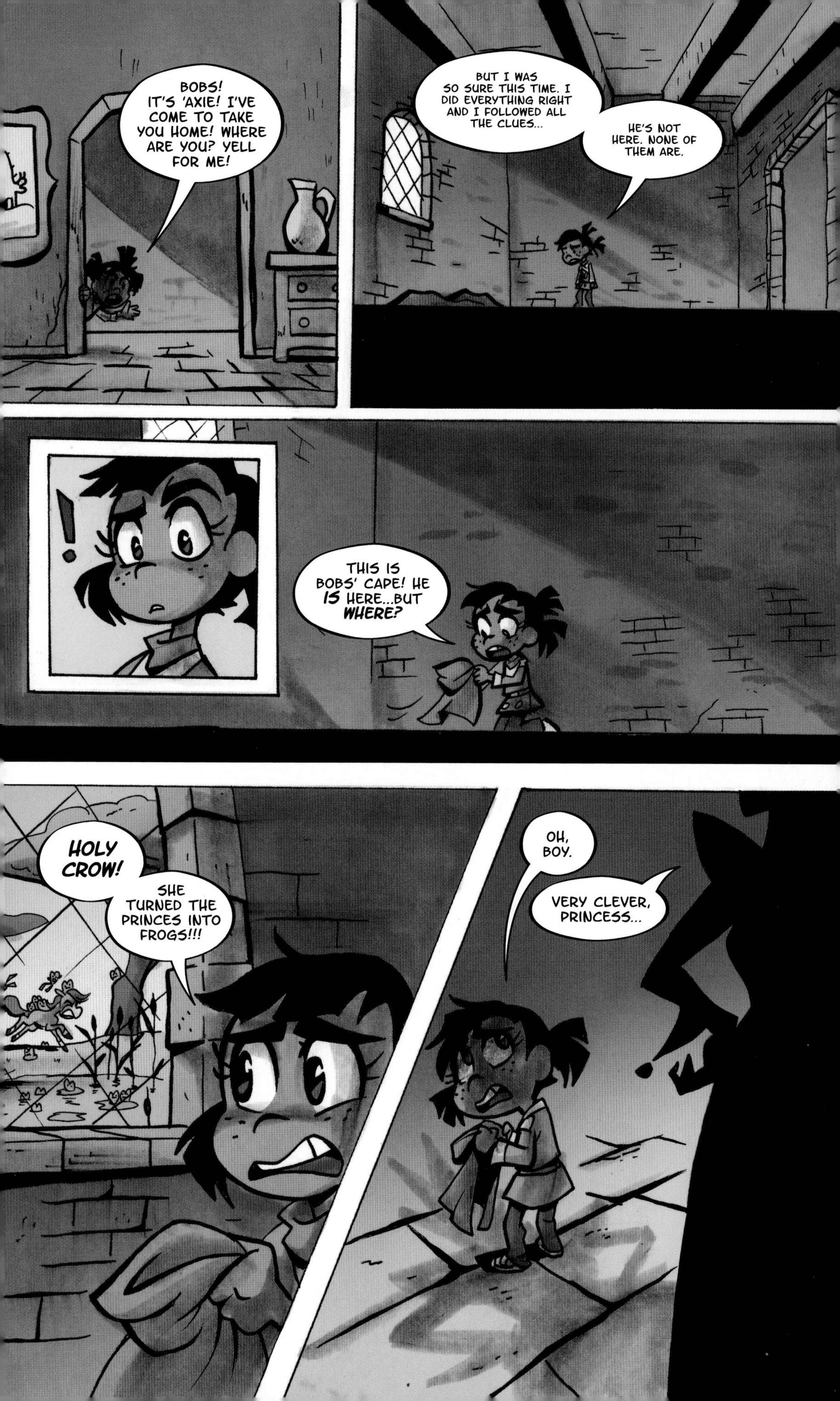
BOBS! IT'S 'AXIE! I'VE COME TO TAKE YOU HOME! WHERE ARE YOU? YELL FOR ME!
BUT I WAS SO SURE THIS TIME. I DID EVERYTHING RIGHT AND I FOLLOWED ALL THE CLUES...
HE'S NOT HERE. NONE OF THEM ARE.
!
THIS IS BOBS' CAPE! HE *IS* HERE...BUT *WHERE?*
HOLY CROW!
SHE TURNED THE PRINCES INTO FROGS!!!
OH, BOY.
VERY CLEVER, PRINCESS...

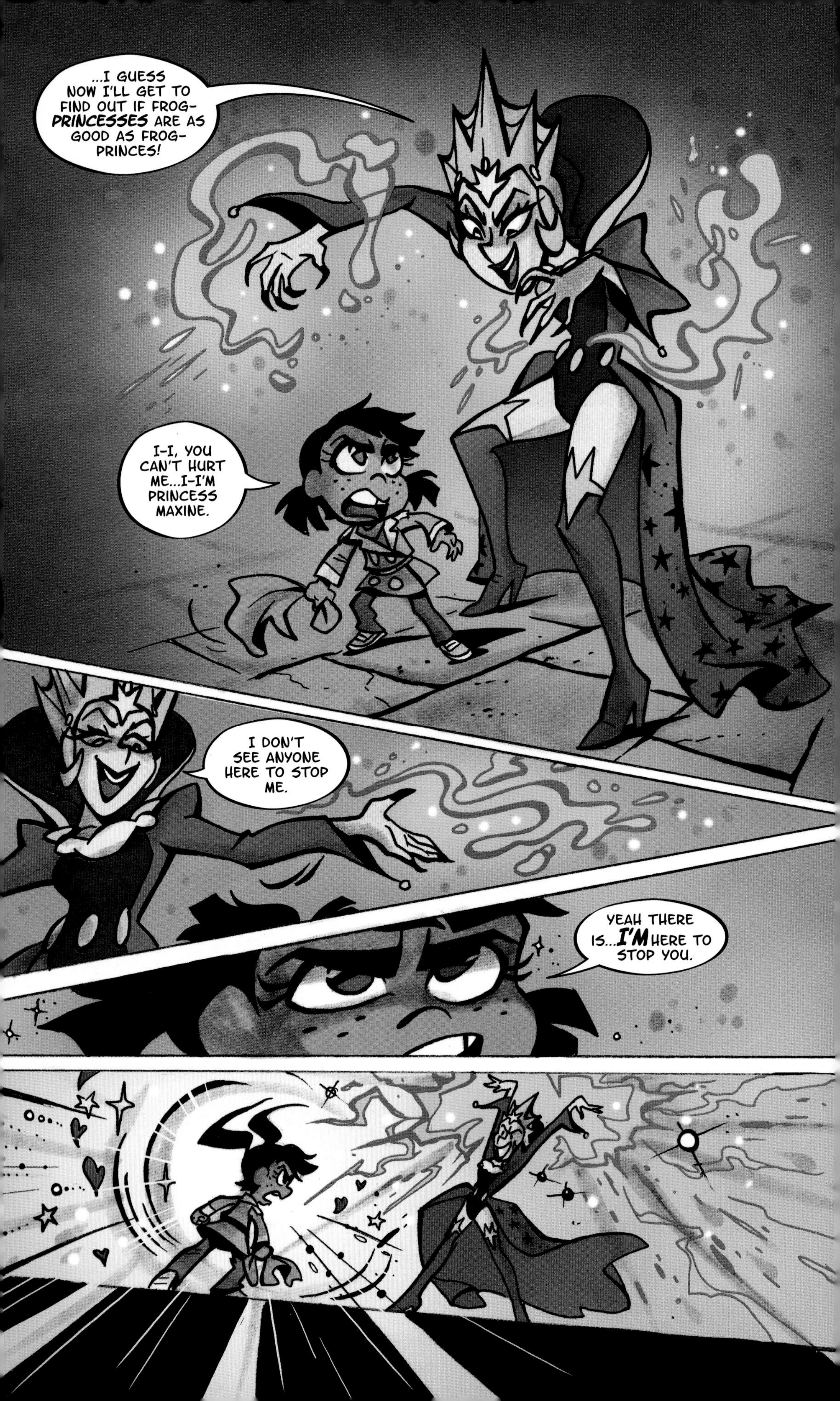
...I GUESS NOW I'LL GET TO FIND OUT IF FROG-PRINCESSES ARE AS GOOD AS FROG-PRINCES!
I-I, YOU CAN'T HURT ME...I-I'M PRINCESS MAXINE.
I DON'T SEE ANYONE HERE TO STOP ME.
YEAH THERE IS...I'M HERE TO STOP YOU.

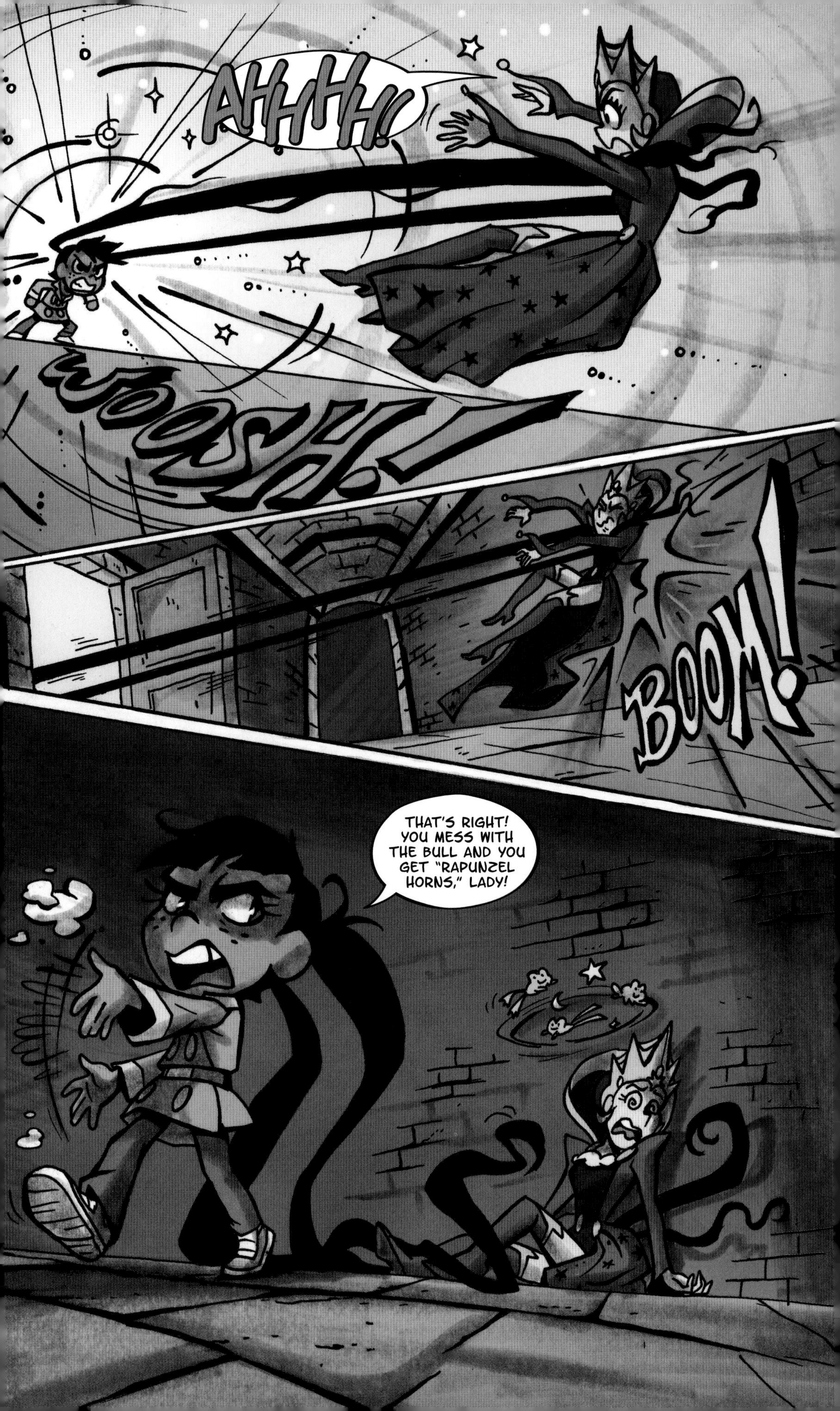
AHHHH!
WOOSH!
BOOM!
THAT'S RIGHT! YOU MESS WITH THE BULL AND YOU GET "RAPUNZEL HORNS," LADY!

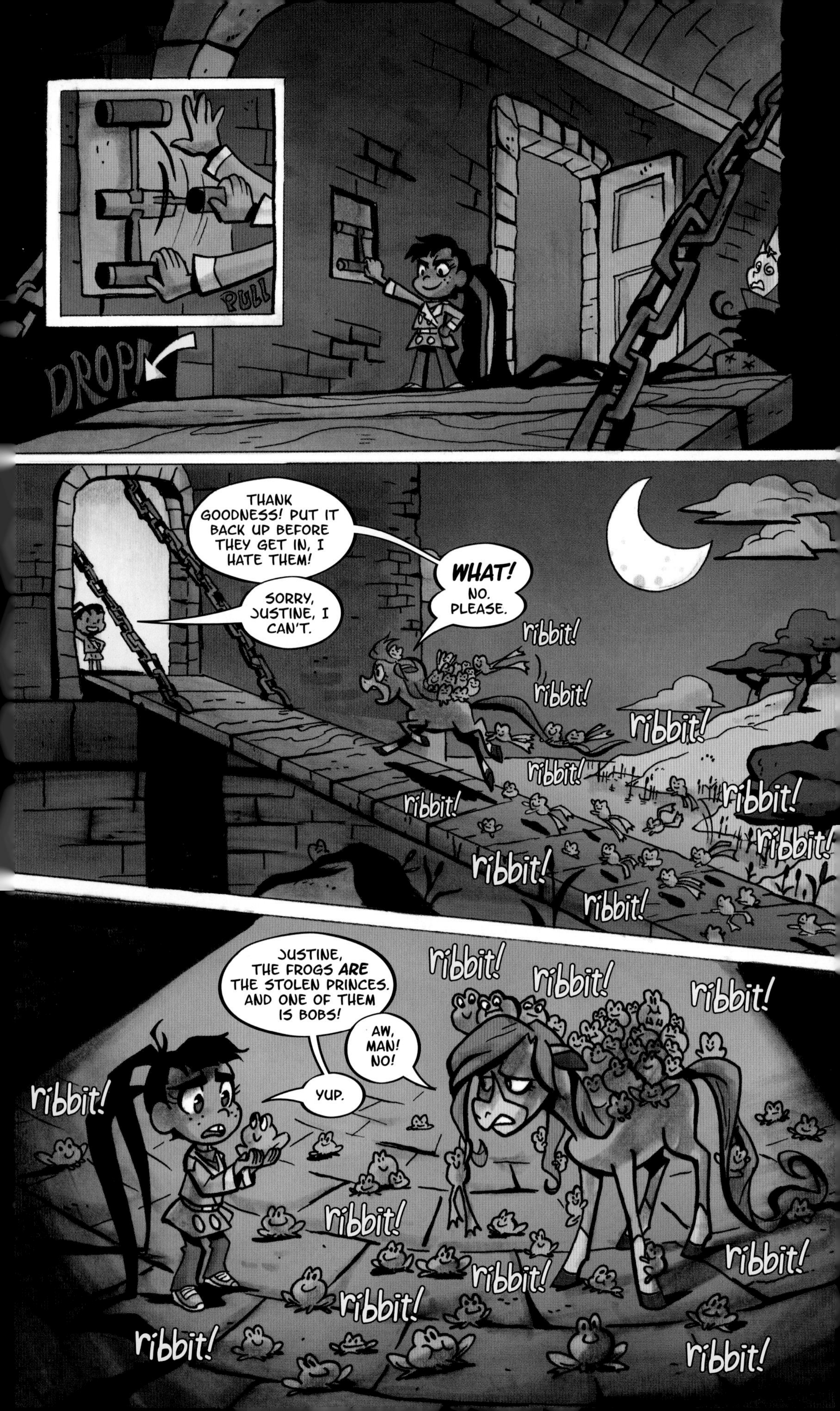
PULL
DROP!
THANK GOODNESS! PUT IT BACK UP BEFORE THEY GET IN, I HATE THEM!
SORRY, JUSTINE, I CAN'T.
WHAT! NO. PLEASE.
ribbit!
ribbit!
ribbit!
ribbit!
ribbit!
ribbit!
ribbit!
ribbit!
ribbit!
JUSTINE, THE FROGS ARE THE STOLEN PRINCES. AND ONE OF THEM IS BOBS!
AW, MAN! NO!
YUP.
ribbit!
ribbit!
ribbit!
ribbit!
ribbit!
ribbit!
ribbit!
ribbit!
ribbit!
ribbit!

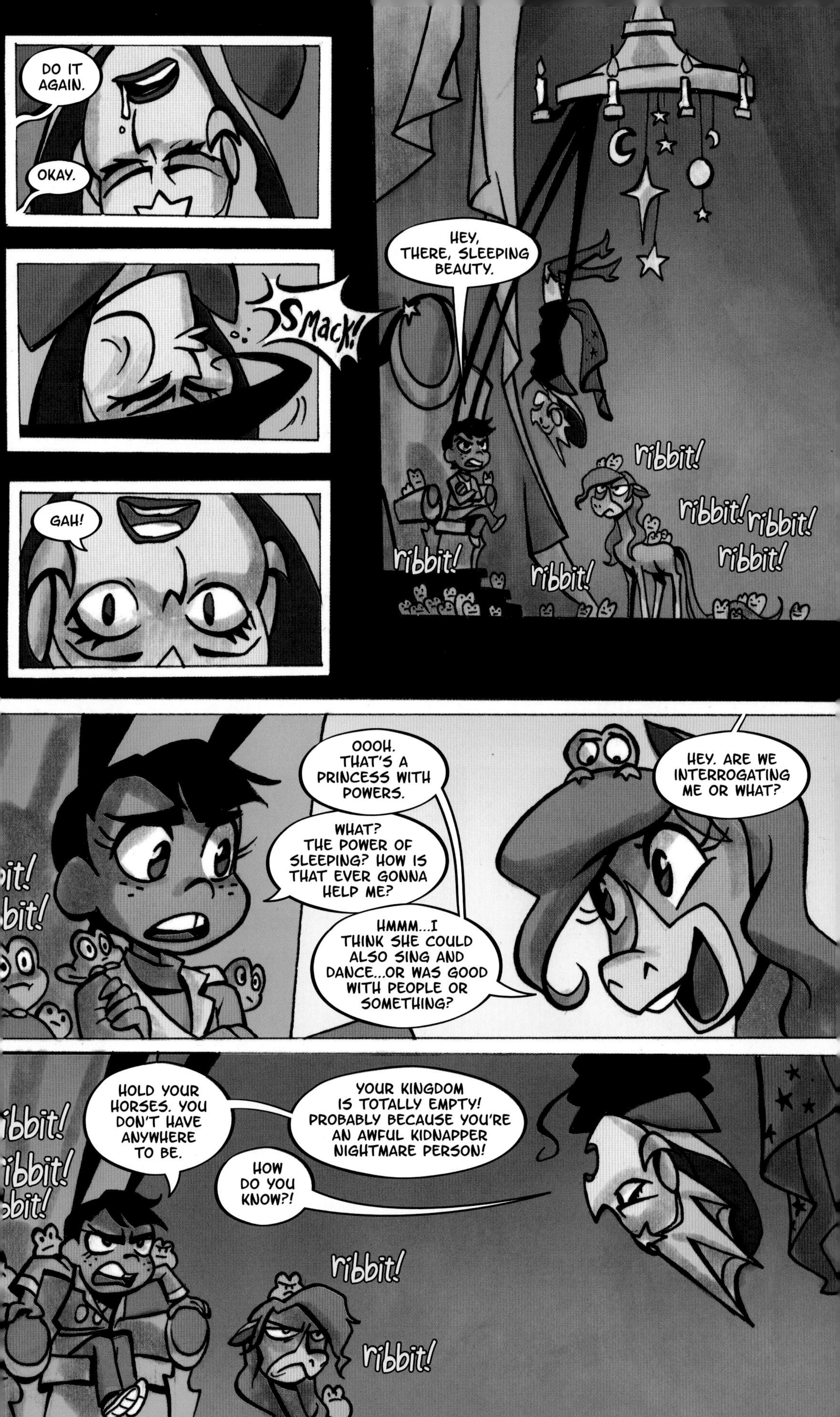
DO IT AGAIN.
OKAY.
HEY, THERE, SLEEPING BEAUTY.
SMACK!
ribbit!
ribbit! ribbit!
ribbit!
ribbit!
ribbit!
GAH!
OOOH. THAT'S A PRINCESS WITH POWERS.
HEY. ARE WE INTERROGATING ME OR WHAT?
WHAT? THE POWER OF SLEEPING? HOW IS THAT EVER GONNA HELP ME?
HMMM...I THINK SHE COULD ALSO SING AND DANCE...OR WAS GOOD WITH PEOPLE OR SOMETHING?
HOLD YOUR HORSES. YOU DON'T HAVE ANYWHERE TO BE.
YOUR KINGDOM IS TOTALLY EMPTY! PROBABLY BECAUSE YOU'RE AN AWFUL KIDNAPPER NIGHTMARE PERSON!
HOW DO YOU KNOW?!
ribbit!
ribbit!

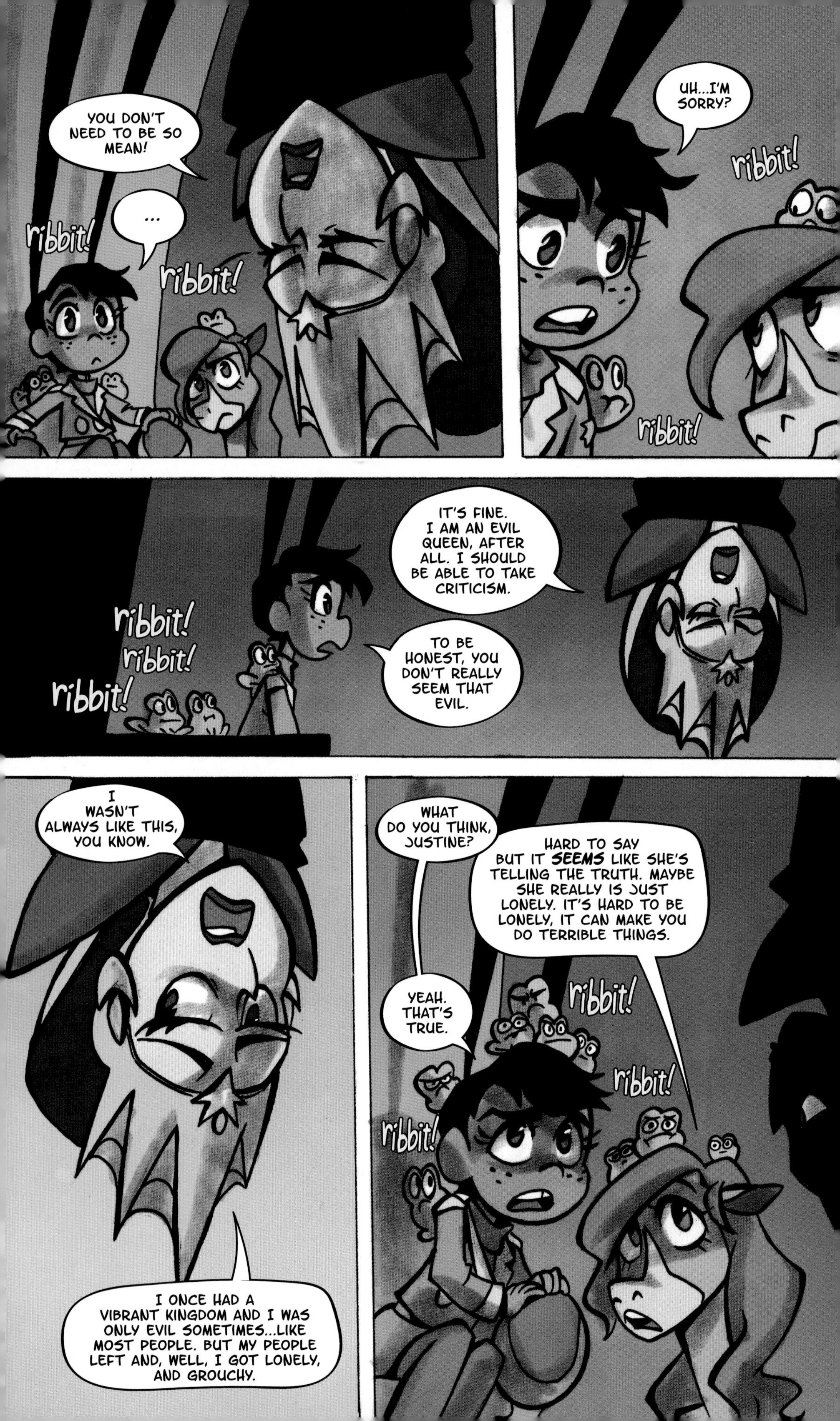
YOU DON'T NEED TO BE SO MEAN!
...
ribbit!
ribbit!
UH...I'M SORRY?
ribbit!
ribbit!
IT'S FINE. I AM AN EVIL QUEEN, AFTER ALL. I SHOULD BE ABLE TO TAKE CRITICISM.
ribbit!
ribbit!
ribbit!
TO BE HONEST, YOU DON'T REALLY SEEM THAT EVIL.
I WASN'T ALWAYS LIKE THIS, YOU KNOW.
I ONCE HAD A VIBRANT KINGDOM AND I WAS ONLY EVIL SOMETIMES...LIKE MOST PEOPLE. BUT MY PEOPLE LEFT AND, WELL, I GOT LONELY, AND GROUCHY.
WHAT DO YOU THINK, JUSTINE?
HARD TO SAY BUT IT **SEEMS** LIKE SHE'S TELLING THE TRUTH. MAYBE SHE REALLY IS JUST LONELY. IT'S HARD TO BE LONELY, IT CAN MAKE YOU DO TERRIBLE THINGS.
YEAH. THAT'S TRUE.
ribbit!
ribbit!
ribbit!

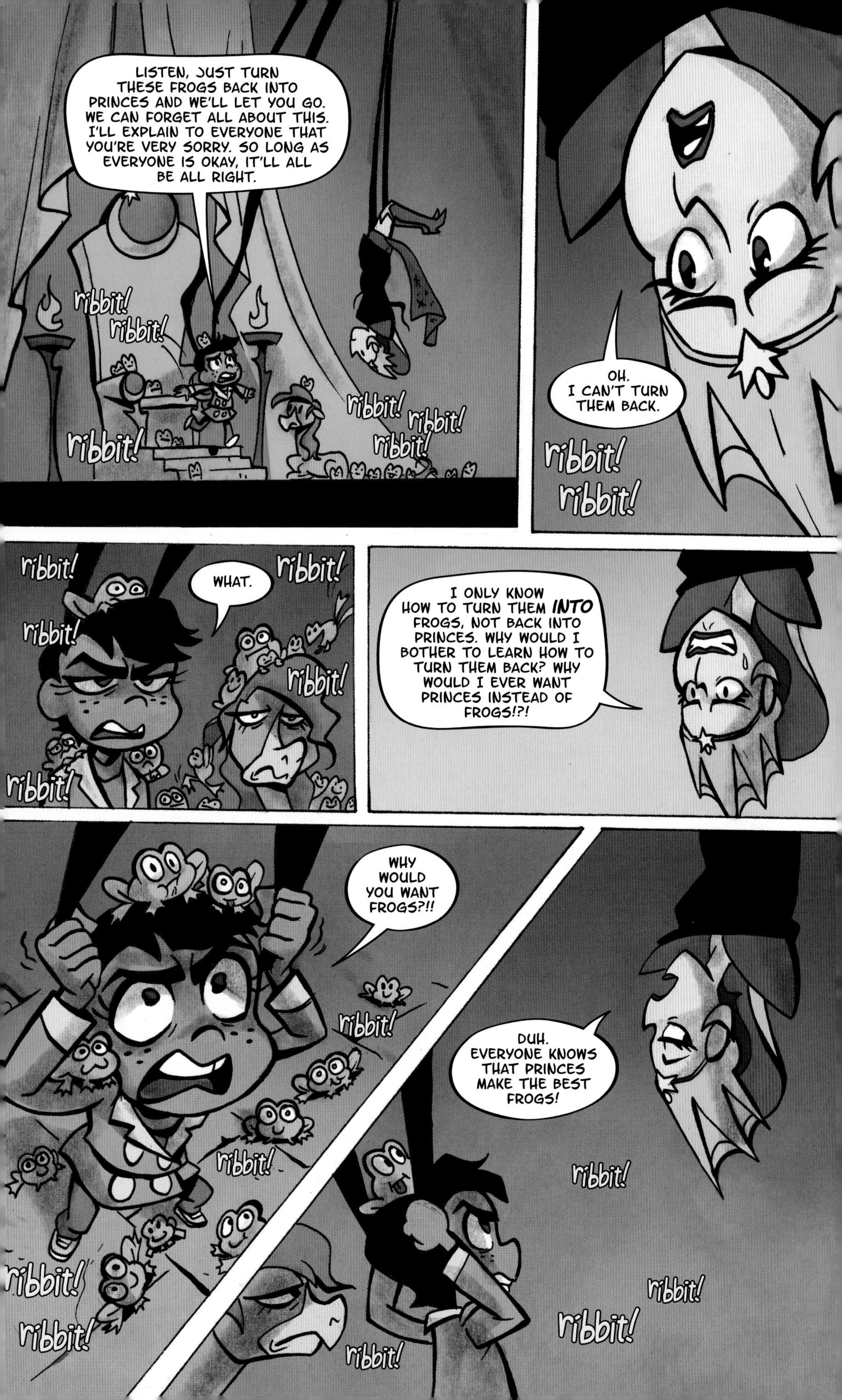
LISTEN, JUST TURN THESE FROGS BACK INTO PRINCES AND WE'LL LET YOU GO. WE CAN FORGET ALL ABOUT THIS. I'LL EXPLAIN TO EVERYONE THAT YOU'RE VERY SORRY. SO LONG AS EVERYONE IS OKAY, IT'LL ALL BE ALL RIGHT.
ribbit!
ribbit!
ribbit!
ribbit!
ribbit!
ribbit!
OH. I CAN'T TURN THEM BACK.
ribbit!
ribbit!
ribbit!
WHAT.
ribbit!
ribbit!
ribbit!
ribbit!
I ONLY KNOW HOW TO TURN THEM INTO FROGS, NOT BACK INTO PRINCES. WHY WOULD I BOTHER TO LEARN HOW TO TURN THEM BACK? WHY WOULD I EVER WANT PRINCES INSTEAD OF FROGS!?!
WHY WOULD YOU WANT FROGS?!!
ribbit!
ribbit!
ribbit!
ribbit!
DUH. EVERYONE KNOWS THAT PRINCES MAKE THE BEST FROGS!
ribbit!
ribbit!
ribbit!
ribbit!

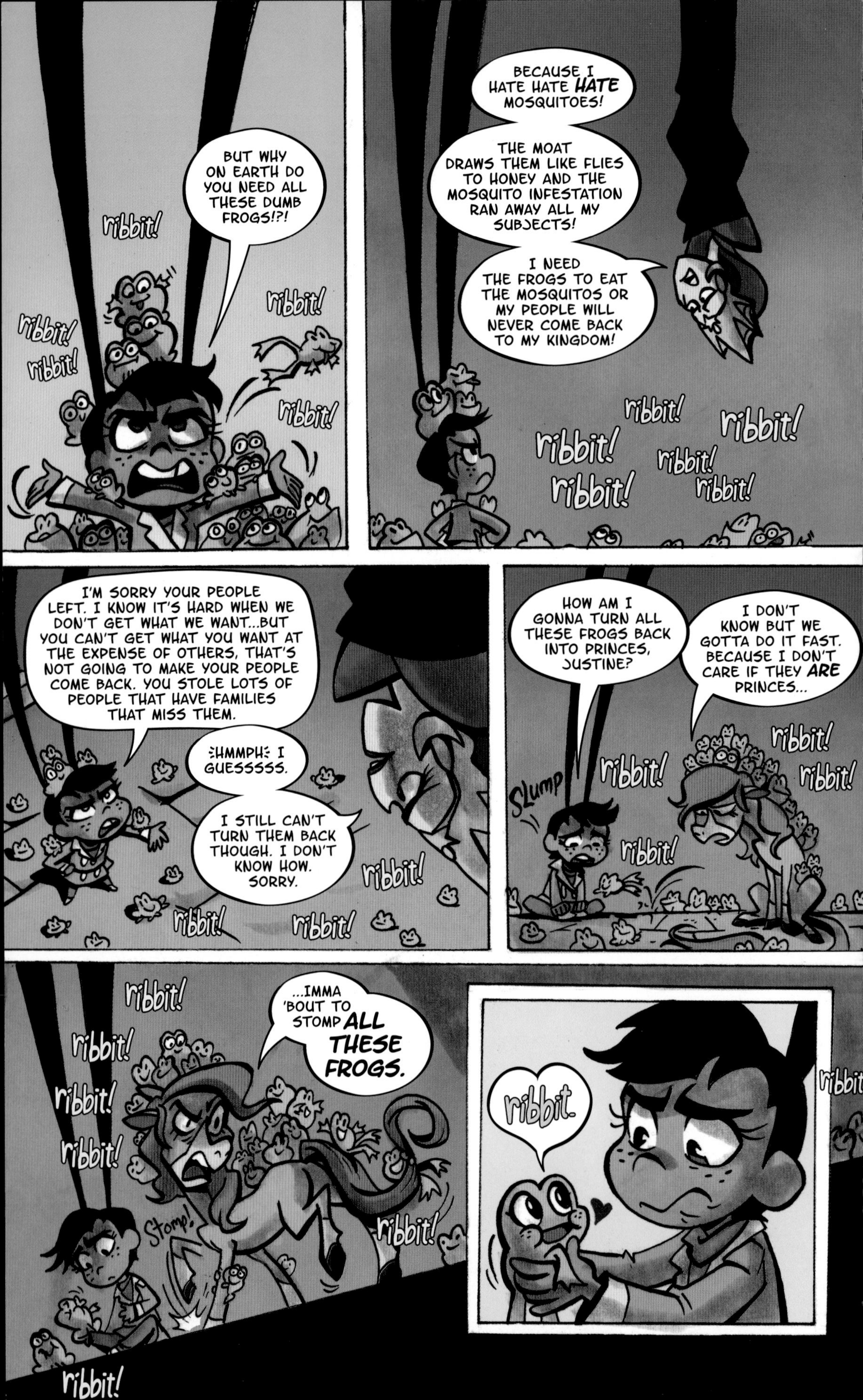
BUT WHY ON EARTH DO YOU NEED ALL THESE DUMB FROGS!?!
ribbit!
ribbit!
ribbit!
ribbit!
ribbit!
BECAUSE I HATE HATE **HATE** MOSQUITOES!
THE MOAT DRAWS THEM LIKE FLIES TO HONEY AND THE MOSQUITO INFESTATION RAN AWAY ALL MY SUBJECTS!
I NEED THE FROGS TO EAT THE MOSQUITOS OR MY PEOPLE WILL NEVER COME BACK TO MY KINGDOM!
ribbit!
ribbit!
ribbit!
ribbit!
ribbit!
ribbit!
I'M SORRY YOUR PEOPLE LEFT. I KNOW IT'S HARD WHEN WE DON'T GET WHAT WE WANT...BUT YOU CAN'T GET WHAT YOU WANT AT THE EXPENSE OF OTHERS, THAT'S NOT GOING TO MAKE YOUR PEOPLE COME BACK. YOU STOLE LOTS OF PEOPLE THAT HAVE FAMILIES THAT MISS THEM.
HMMPH I GUESSSSS.
I STILL CAN'T TURN THEM BACK THOUGH. I DON'T KNOW HOW. SORRY.
ribbit!
ribbit!
ribbit!
HOW AM I GONNA TURN ALL THESE FROGS BACK INTO PRINCES, JUSTINE?
I DON'T KNOW BUT WE GOTTA DO IT FAST. BECAUSE I DON'T CARE IF THEY **ARE** PRINCES...
SLump
ribbit!
ribbit!
ribbit!
ribbit!
...IMMA 'BOUT TO STOMP **ALL THESE FROGS.**
ribbit!
ribbit!
ribbit!
ribbit!
Stomp!
ribbit!
ribbit!
ribbit.

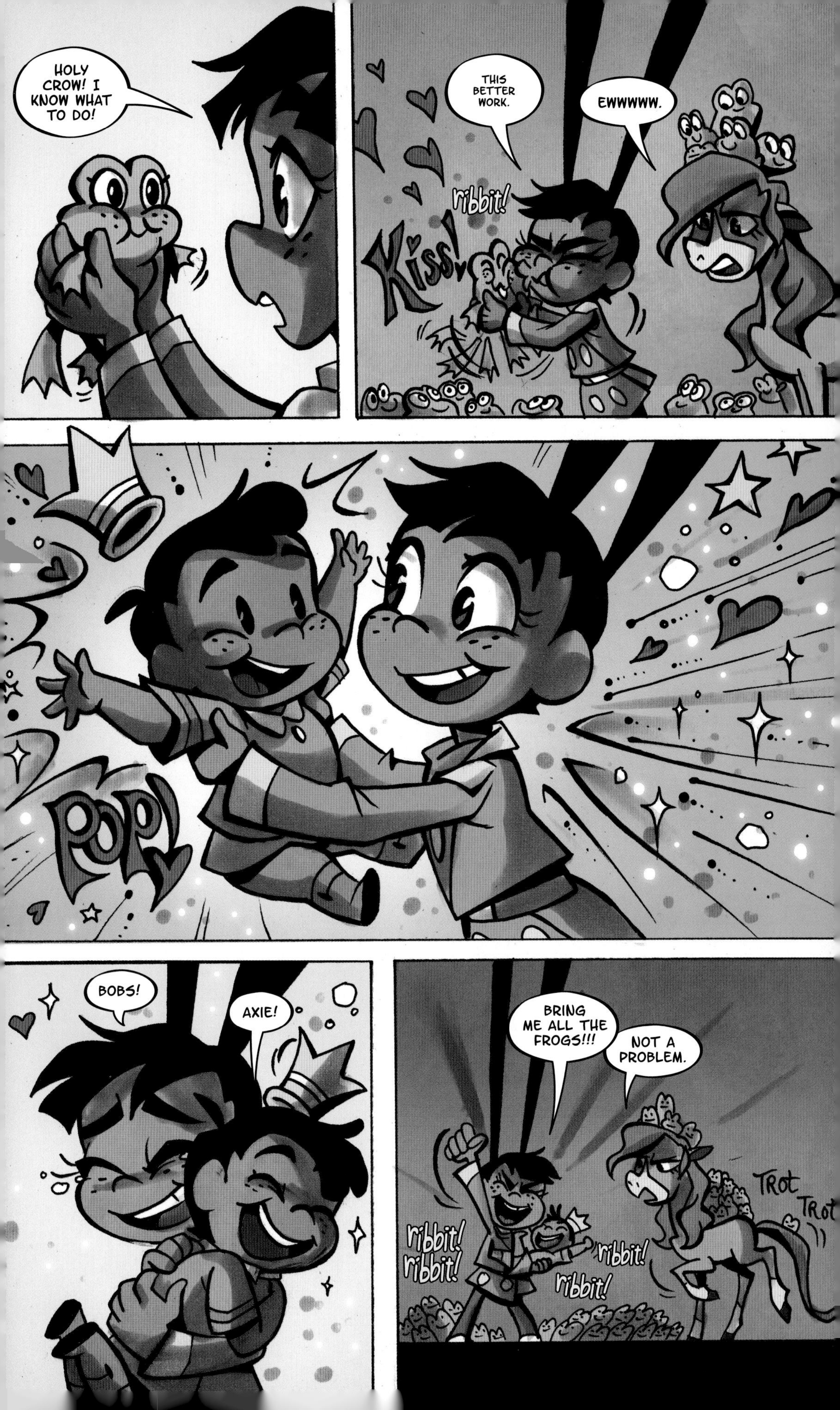
HOLY CROW! I KNOW WHAT TO DO!
THIS BETTER WORK.
EWWWWW.
ribbit!
Kiss!
POP!
BOBS!
AXIE!
BRING ME ALL THE FROGS!!!
NOT A PROBLEM.
TROT
TROT
ribbit! ribbit!
ribbit!
ribbit!

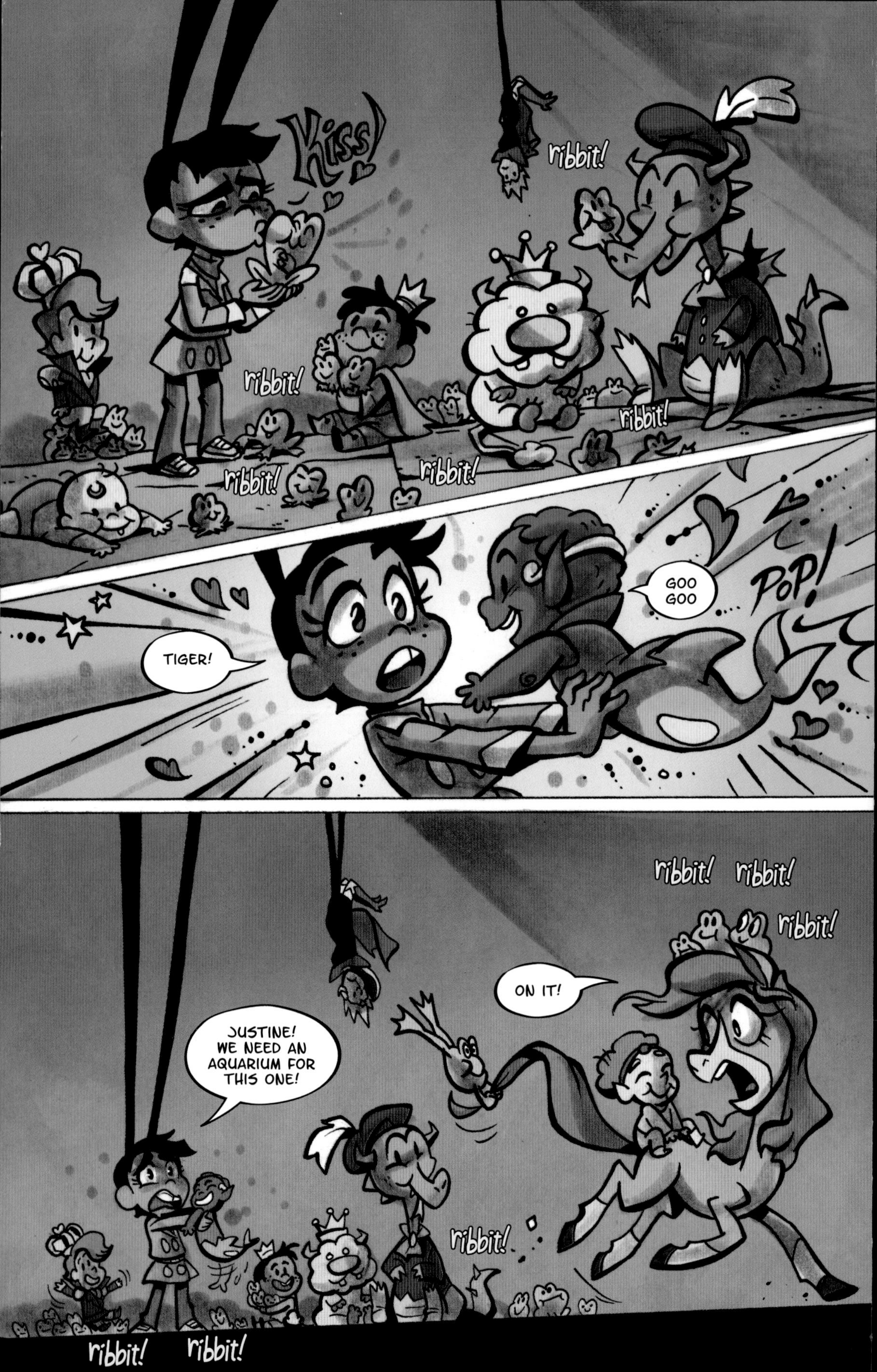
Kiss!
ribbit!
ribbit!
ribbit!
ribbit!
ribbit!
GOO GOO
POP!
TIGER!
ribbit! ribbit!
ribbit!
ON IT!
JUSTINE! WE NEED AN AQUARIUM FOR THIS ONE!
ribbit!
ribbit! ribbit!

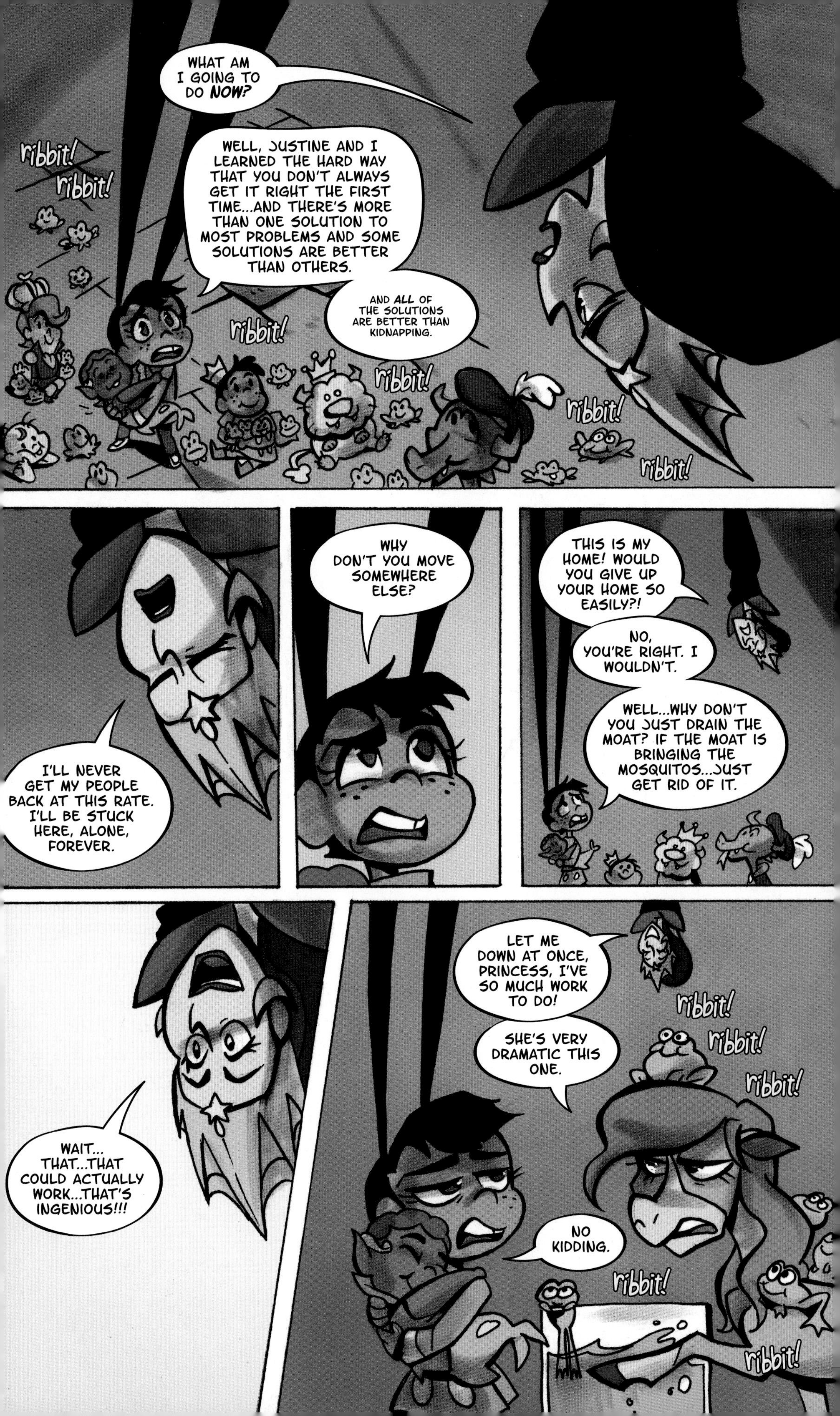
WHAT AM I GOING TO DO **NOW?**
WELL, JUSTINE AND I LEARNED THE HARD WAY THAT YOU DON'T ALWAYS GET IT RIGHT THE FIRST TIME...AND THERE'S MORE THAN ONE SOLUTION TO MOST PROBLEMS AND SOME SOLUTIONS ARE BETTER THAN OTHERS.
AND **ALL** OF THE SOLUTIONS ARE BETTER THAN KIDNAPPING.
ribbit! ribbit!
ribbit!
ribbit!
ribbit!
ribbit!
I'LL NEVER GET MY PEOPLE BACK AT THIS RATE. I'LL BE STUCK HERE, ALONE, FOREVER.
WHY DON'T YOU MOVE SOMEWHERE ELSE?
THIS IS MY HOME! WOULD YOU GIVE UP YOUR HOME SO EASILY?!
NO, YOU'RE RIGHT. I WOULDN'T.
WELL...WHY DON'T YOU JUST DRAIN THE MOAT? IF THE MOAT IS BRINGING THE MOSQUITOS...JUST GET RID OF IT.
WAIT... THAT...THAT COULD ACTUALLY WORK...THAT'S INGENIOUS!!!
LET ME DOWN AT ONCE, PRINCESS, I'VE SO MUCH WORK TO DO!
SHE'S VERY DRAMATIC THIS ONE.
ribbit! ribbit! ribbit!
NO KIDDING.
ribbit!
ribbit!

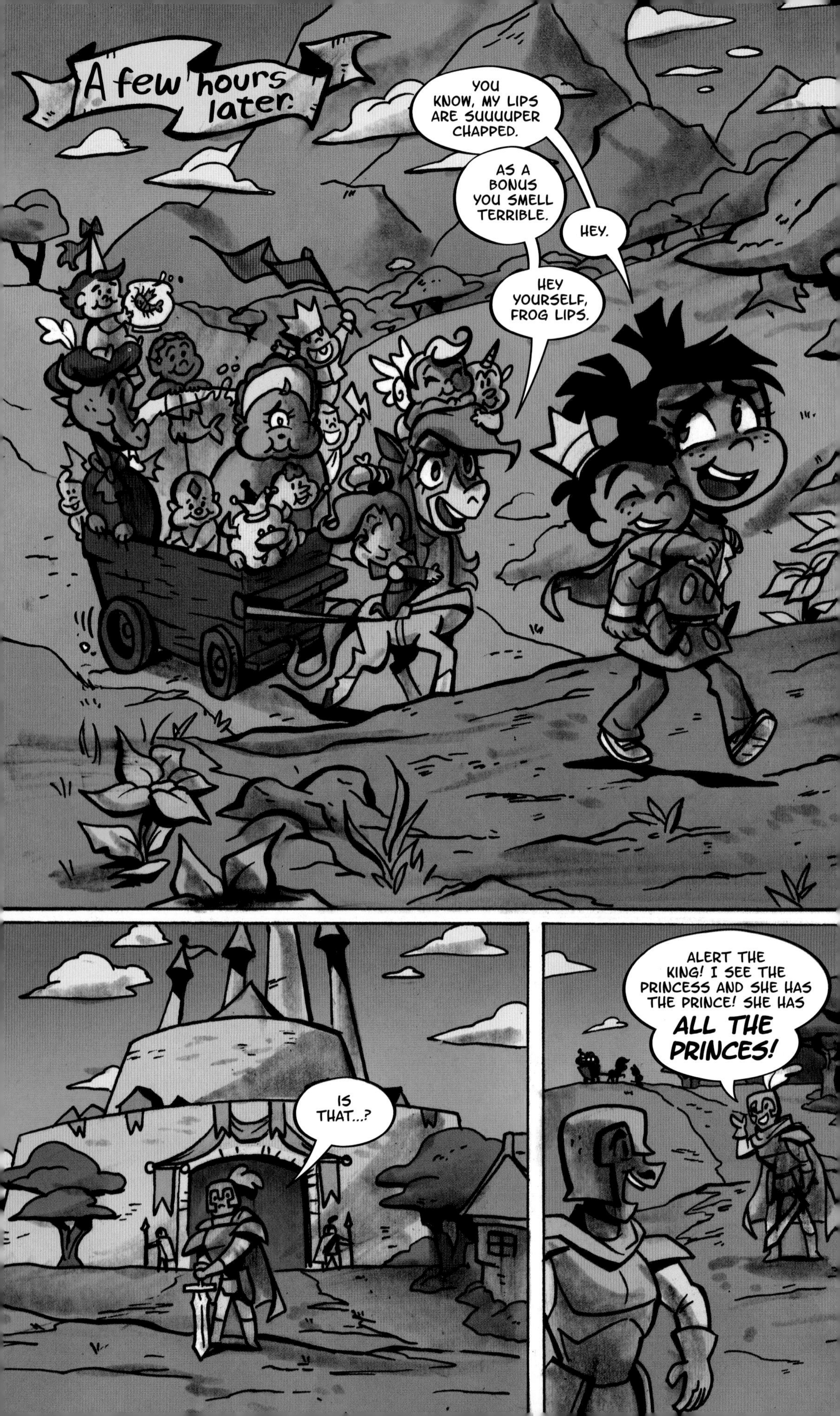
A few hours later.
YOU KNOW, MY LIPS ARE SUUUUPER CHAPPED.
AS A BONUS YOU SMELL TERRIBLE.
HEY.
HEY YOURSELF, FROG LIPS.
IS THAT...?
ALERT THE KING! I SEE THE PRINCESS AND SHE HAS THE PRINCE! SHE HAS ALL THE PRINCES!

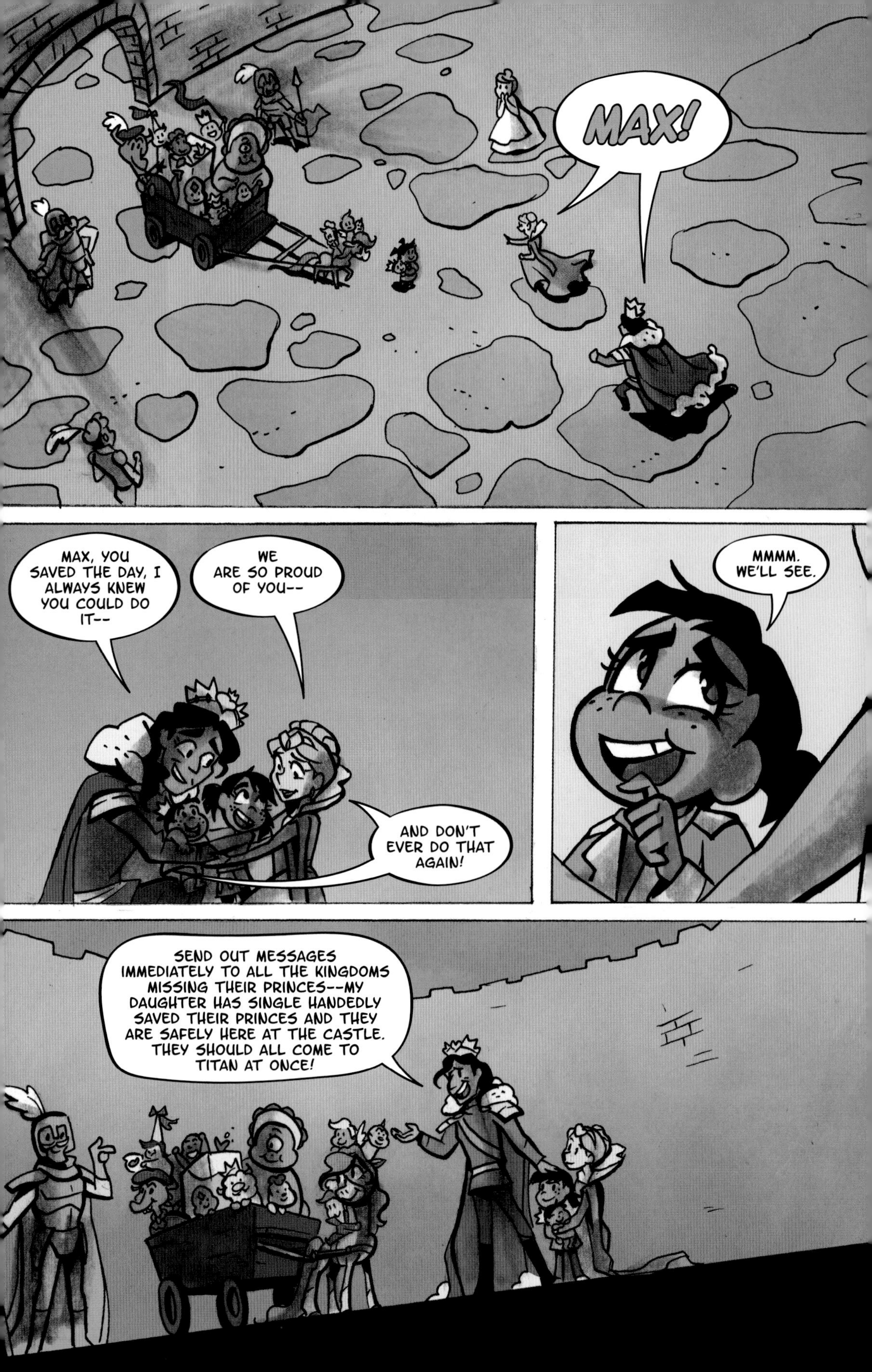
MAX!
MAX, YOU SAVED THE DAY, I ALWAYS KNEW YOU COULD DO IT--
WE ARE SO PROUD OF YOU--
AND DON'T EVER DO THAT AGAIN!
MMMM. WE'LL SEE.
SEND OUT MESSAGES IMMEDIATELY TO ALL THE KINGDOMS MISSING THEIR PRINCES--MY DAUGHTER HAS SINGLE HANDEDLY SAVED THEIR PRINCES AND THEY ARE SAFELY HERE AT THE CASTLE. THEY SHOULD ALL COME TO TITAN AT ONCE!

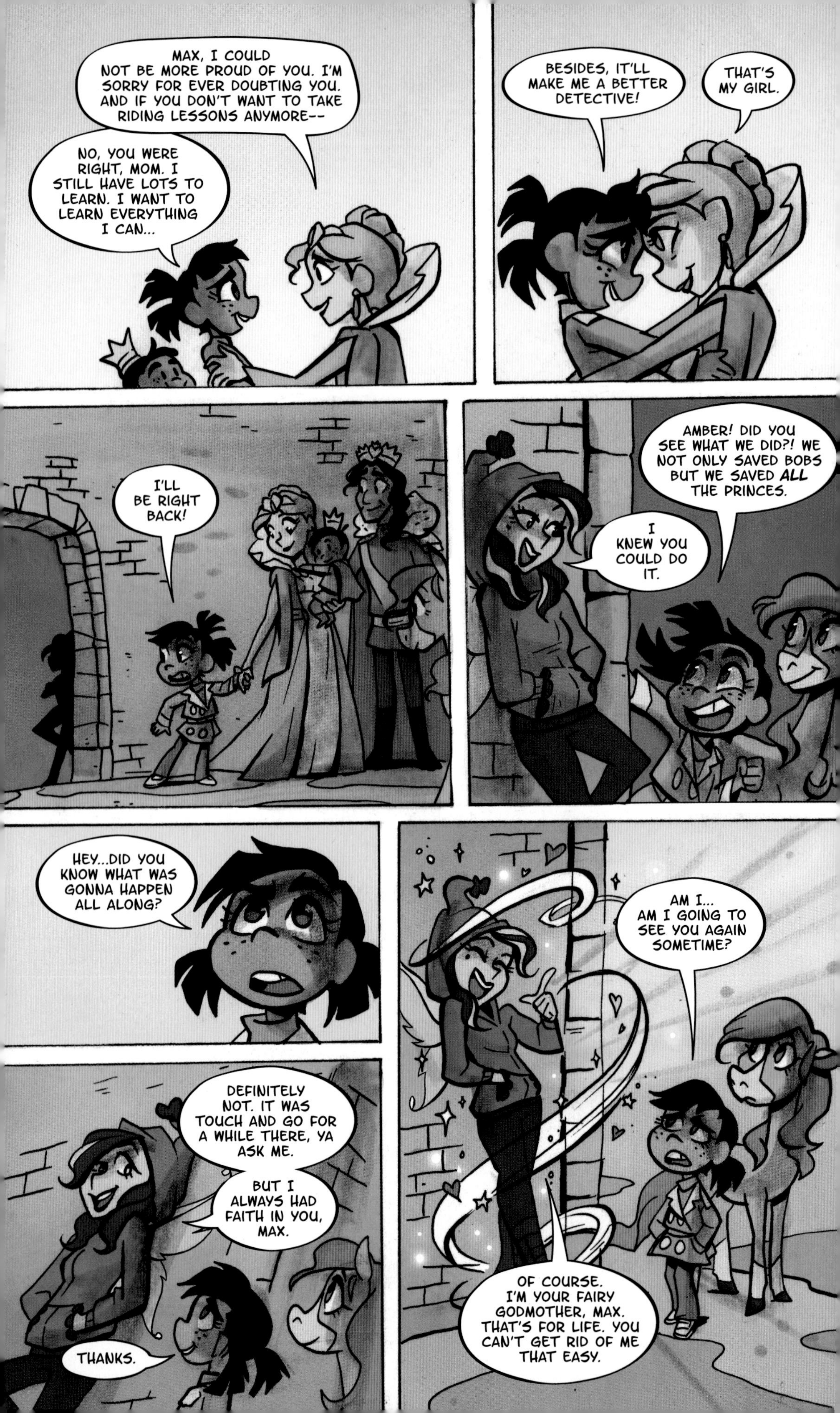

MAX, I COULD NOT BE MORE PROUD OF YOU. I'M SORRY FOR EVER DOUBTING YOU. AND IF YOU DON'T WANT TO TAKE RIDING LESSONS ANYMORE--
NO, YOU WERE RIGHT, MOM. I STILL HAVE LOTS TO LEARN. I WANT TO LEARN EVERYTHING I CAN...
BESIDES, IT'LL MAKE ME A BETTER DETECTIVE!
THAT'S MY GIRL.
I'LL BE RIGHT BACK!
AMBER! DID YOU SEE WHAT WE DID?! WE NOT ONLY SAVED BOBS BUT WE SAVED ALL THE PRINCES.
I KNEW YOU COULD DO IT.
HEY...DID YOU KNOW WHAT WAS GONNA HAPPEN ALL ALONG?
DEFINITELY NOT. IT WAS TOUCH AND GO FOR A WHILE THERE, YA ASK ME.
BUT I ALWAYS HAD FAITH IN YOU, MAX.
THANKS.
AM I... AM I GOING TO SEE YOU AGAIN SOMETIME?
OF COURSE. I'M YOUR FAIRY GODMOTHER, MAX. THAT'S FOR LIFE. YOU CAN'T GET RID OF ME THAT EASY.

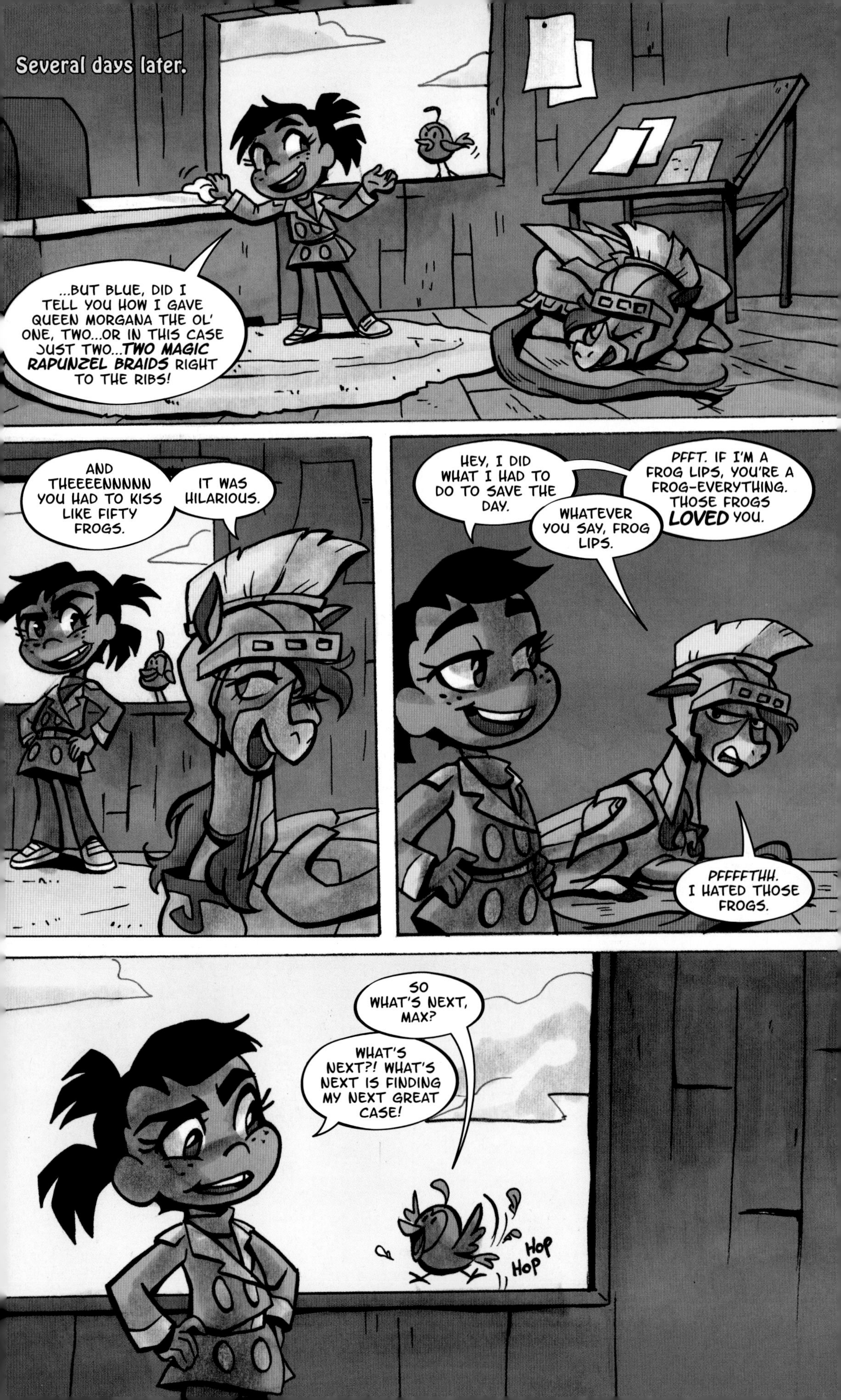
Several days later.
...BUT BLUE, DID I TELL YOU HOW I GAVE QUEEN MORGANA THE OL' ONE, TWO...OR IN THIS CASE JUST TWO...TWO MAGIC RAPUNZEL BRAIDS RIGHT TO THE RIBS!
AND THEEEENNNNN YOU HAD TO KISS LIKE FIFTY FROGS.
IT WAS HILARIOUS.
HEY, I DID WHAT I HAD TO DO TO SAVE THE DAY.
WHATEVER YOU SAY, FROG LIPS.
PFFT. IF I'M A FROG LIPS, YOU'RE A FROG-EVERYTHING. THOSE FROGS LOVED YOU.
PFFFFTHH. I HATED THOSE FROGS.
SO WHAT'S NEXT, MAX?
WHAT'S NEXT?! WHAT'S NEXT IS FINDING MY NEXT GREAT CASE!
HOP
HOP

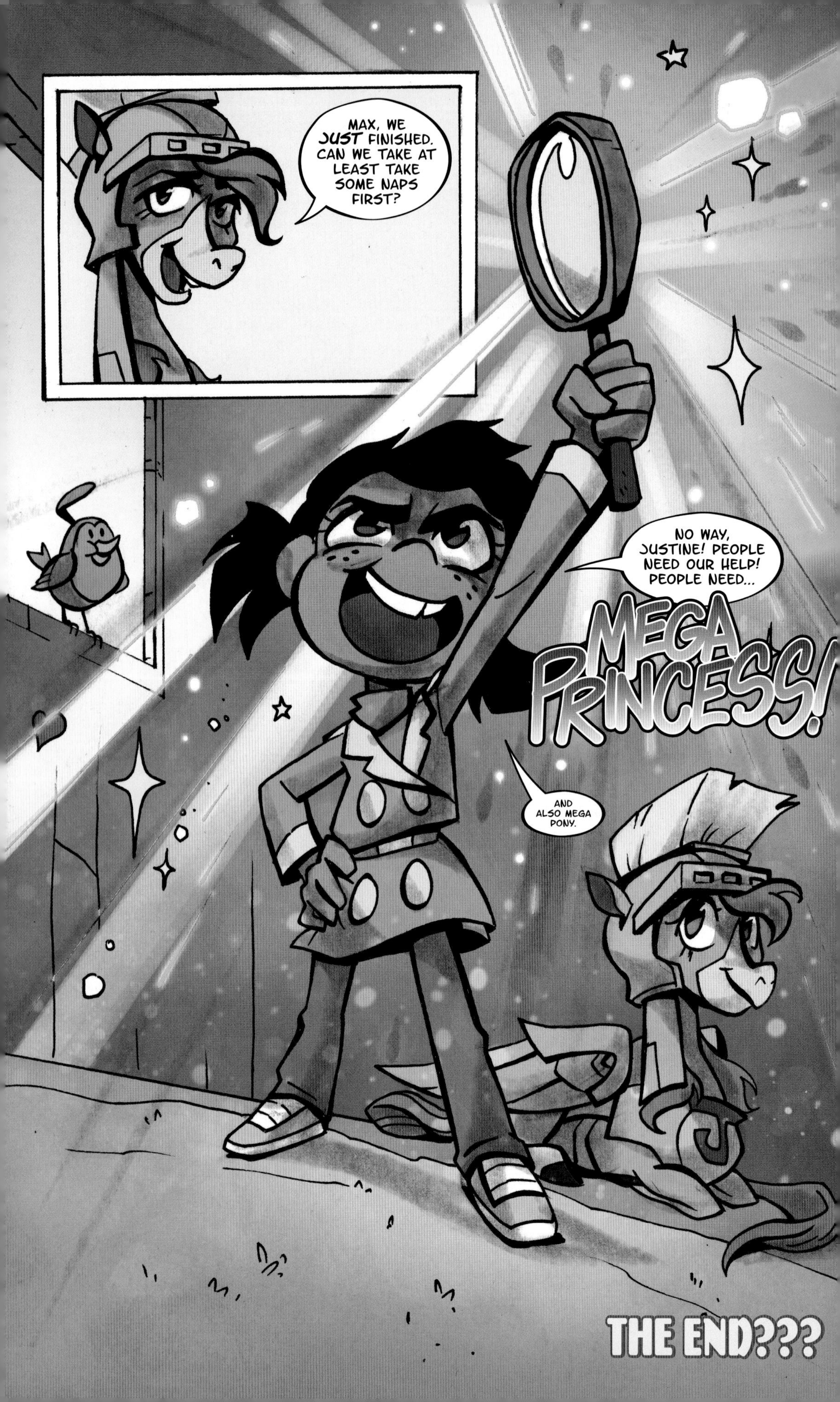
MAX, WE JUST FINISHED. CAN WE TAKE AT LEAST TAKE SOME NAPS FIRST?
NO WAY, JUSTINE! PEOPLE NEED OUR HELP! PEOPLE NEED...
MEGA PRINCESS!
AND ALSO MEGA PONY.
THE END???

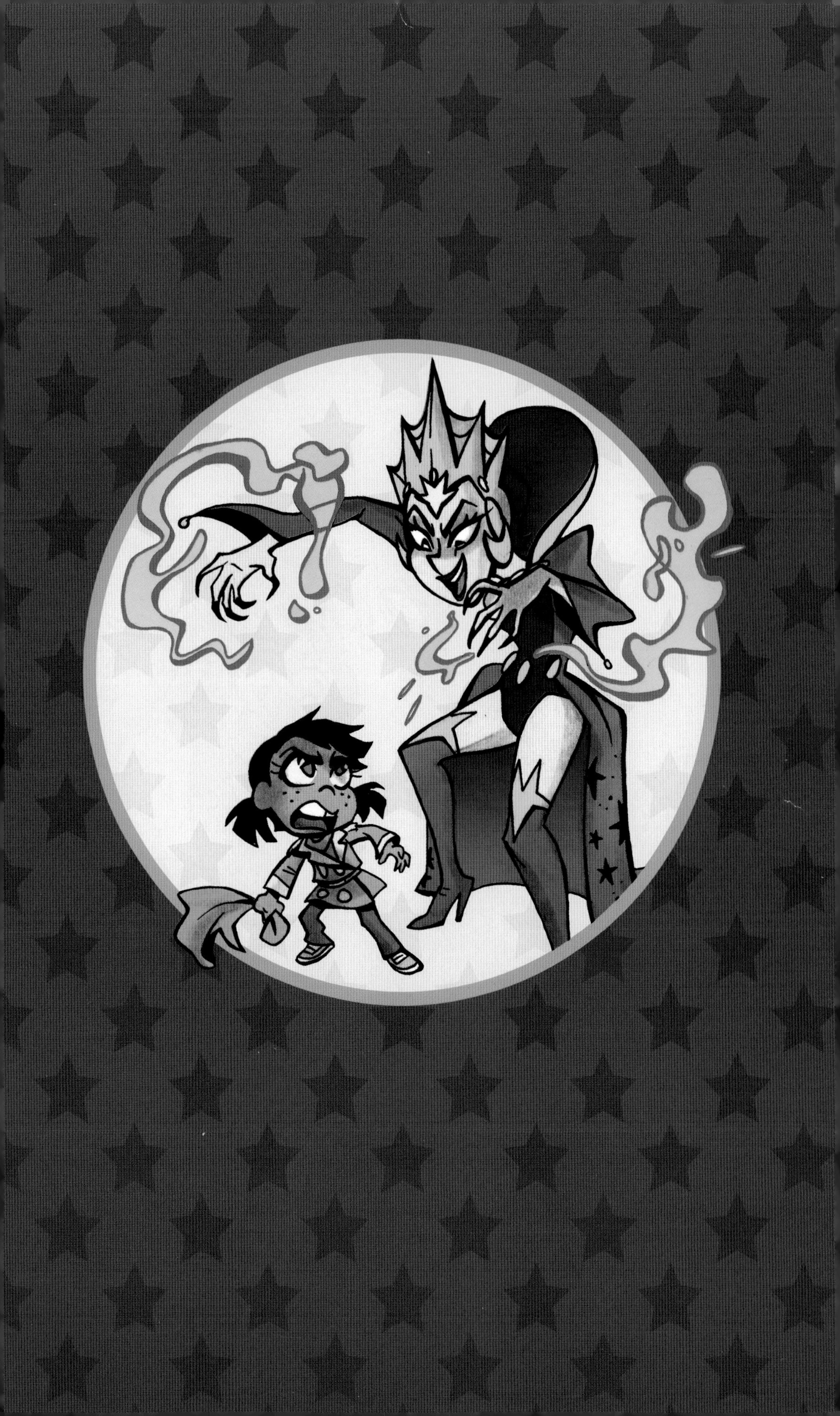

Issue #1 Variant Cover by
KATIE COOK

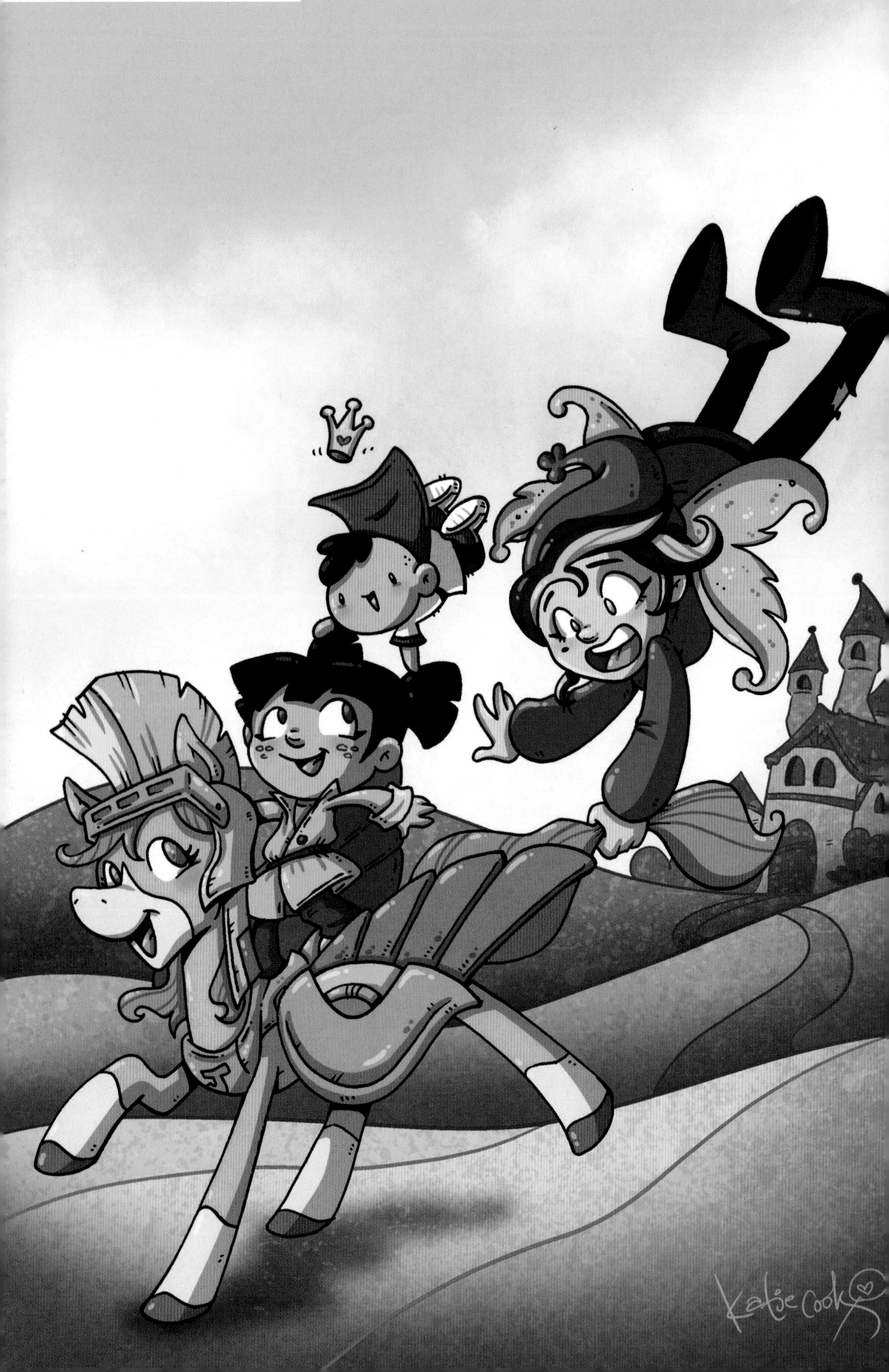
Katie Cook

ABOUT THE AUTHORS

KELLY THOMPSON

Kelly's ambitions are eclipsed only by her desire to exist entirely in pajamas.

Fortunately pajamas and writers go hand in hand (most of the time). Kelly has a fancy degree in Sequential Art from The Savannah College of Art & Design and has published two novels (*The Girl Who Would Be King* and *Storykiller)* as well as a graphic novel with Meredith McClaren (*Heart in a Box)*. She's has written many comics including *Hawkeye, Star Wars, Jem and The Holograms, The Misfits, A-Force,* and *Ghostbusters,* and hopes to write many more. Please buy all her stuff so that she can buy (and wear) more pajamas.

Kelly lives in Portland, Oregon with her boyfriend Adam (who helped create *Mega Princess!)* and they hope to get a sassy kitten very soon.

BRIANNE DROUHARD

Brianne is an artist mainly working in the animation industry. She has contributed character designs and storyboards for Cartoon Network, Marvel, Sony, Disney, WB Animation, and Nickelodeon. She directed, designed, and produced the *Amethyst, Princess of Gemworld* shorts for WB Animation, and is currently storyboarding and directing an unannounced project at Nickelodeon. In her spare time she writes and draws her own webcomic, *Harpy Gee,* along with making an occasional music video for YouTube (*Space Unicorn,* music by Parry Gripp!)

Brianne is based in Los Angeles, California. She misses her cat Skippy, who assisted in holding down the paper while inking most of *Mega Princess!*

M. VICTORIA ROBADO

M. Victoria Robado is an illustrator and comics creator from Argentina. She creates cute worlds full of bright colors and adorable characters. Victoria self-publishes her own comics online and in print, including her latest works *Fragile, Springiette,* and *Never Ever Done.* She also works for several American publishers often drawing covers, generating colors, and letters. You can find her work on *Jem and the Holograms, Mega Princess, Barbie, KISS, Monster Musume,* and more. Besides comics, Victoria dabbles in traditional painting and character design for various merchandise . . . as long as it's cute!

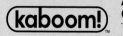